About *The Family Matter*

The Family Matter is a fascinating, well-written read that poignantly describes homelessness while prescribing a powerful, individually based cure that has the potential to profoundly change both the reader and their community.

We are grateful to Dr. Ralph D. Curtin for putting into words not only the plight of the homeless but also the fact that serving the homeless is the path to greater spiritual awakening. Many people see the homeless as a personal sacrifice. This truth is a paradox; the homeless help us much more than we ever help them.

This beautifully written book contains within it revolutionary truths that have the power to illuminate the lives of all readers, as well as those they serve. *The Family Matter* is a concrete story about how service to the poor results in profound enlightenment and a reminder of God's true message to each of us to serve those less fortunate.

LAURA HANSEN, C. E. O.
COALITION TO END HOMELESSNESS
Box 030177
Fort Lauderdale, Florida 33303

the family matter

RALPH D. CURTIN

RESOURCE *Publications* · Eugene, Oregon

Resource Publications
A division of Wipf and Stock Publishers
199 W 8th Ave, Suite 3
Eugene, OR 97401

The Family Matter
By Curtin, Ralph D.
Copyright©2012 by Curtin, Ralph D.
ISBN 13: 978-1-5326-8762-4
Publication date 4/6/2019
Previously published by Oaktara, 2012

* * *

To the faithful few who are called to minister
to the ever-growing community of the homeless
by restoring their dignity and self-worth
and then reintroducing them to a useful place in society.

To my helpmate and friend, Kathy,
who continues to encourage my writing ministry.

1

Laurie pulled out of the NOVA University parking lot onto Oakland Park Boulevard, only to come to a complete stop a mere quarter of a mile later. The incessant road improvements in South Florida once again invaded her schedule. *Why do they have to block off all the main arteries to my home at the same time?* she asked herself. She put the transmission in *Park,* then sighed several times before making a mental note that when she had time she'd send a letter to the Broward County Public Works director and ask him or her if they traveled the same roads they tried so hard to sabotage. If they did, they would have greater consideration for the thousands of frustrated motorists trying to maneuver through the barricades, the long lines of orange cones, the construction equipment, and the work crews that have become an accepted part of the landscape of South Florida. *What if there was an terrorist threat and residents were directed to evacuate? How would the population get off the South Florida peninsula safely?*

It was a full five minutes before the traffic began to move. *Hallelujah!* Moments later she'd connect with I-95 to I-595, where she'd endure the stop-and-go traffic again before reaching her home in Sunrise Park.

She shot a look at the dashboard clock. Her kids were already home from school—alone for fifteen minutes. *Just six more months, then things at home will be different,* she reasoned. *I really hate having the kids come home to an empty house, but we all have to make some sacrifices.*

With three-and-a-half years of college behind her, Laurie felt great satisfaction and fulfillment. Periodically, the complaint from her husband-pastor reared its head: *"You need to wait until the children are older and then you can pursue your goals, but your first desire was to have children and raise them to love the Lord."*

"I can handle it," she said aloud, "I know I can, although it's not easy keeping all the balls in the air at the same time." *Okay, so occasionally I get tired and crabby, but that's to be expected, considering all that's on my plate.*

To be able to meet ministry expectations, wifely and family demands, and still maintain an 3.5 average while pursuing a full-time degree in Human Resource Management was a formidable task for any middle-aged woman. "Yes!" she yelled aloud with glee as she hit the steering wheel. She was going to make it. One more year and she could spend the time with her family they deserved.

The crossover from I-95 to I-595 was heavy today. *Must be an accident. Rats. Now I'll be even later.* Looking west on I-595, the long line of cars meant snail-pace traffic once again.

Twenty-five minutes later, and one-half mile west of Pine Island Drive, the traffic came to a stop. Laurie pulled down the visor and peered in the mirror. Rays of sunlight reflecting off the glass of the open moon-roof backlighted her auburn hair with vibrant vitality. At 38, she showed little evidence of aging. Her facial skin was tight with no signs of wrinkles. Her fellow students remarked that when they saw a photograph of her and her 16-year old daughter, Tiffany, many said they looked like sisters.

The traffic moved, then stopped again. Laurie raised the visor and caught up with the cars in front of her while steering into the right lane. Her exit was coming up.

The traffic stopped at the Pine Island Drive overpass. A disquieting feeling swept over her. She hated to stop at this wretched place! This was where the homeless hung out—in among the Sea Grape trees that lined the expressway. During the day they would don orange tank-tops and hawk newspapers or panhandle with cardboard signs at the signal lights. At night they'd scrounge for morsels of food while hoarding their earnings to buy beer or wine. Some earned enough to buy the hard stuff. When it rained, they scurried like rats up into the overpass trusses and huddle in the concrete nooks and crannies to keep away from the inclement weather. *One of the downsides of living in Florida*, she thought. Many of the homeless from neighboring, northerly states go south during the winter months to congregate on South Florida's streets. *How come they don't enforce vagrancy laws down here?*

A homeless woman walked up behind her on the emergency access road, obviously heading toward the "hang out." The woman stopped next to her SUV and picked up a discarded paper bag from the ground. Reaching inside it, she pulled out a coffee container with a donut shop logo on it.

Laurie's eyes bored into the scene as her heart started racing. The woman's long brown hair was matted and knotted, apparently held in place by grime and residue from the environmental elements to which her body was exposed. Her face bore the effects of years on the streets. Several scabs and numerous blemishes gave testimony of either periodic skirmishes with other homeless persons or inadequate hygiene. Probably both. Laurie estimated the woman's age at about 45 but realized that her poor quality of life undoubtedly added years to her appearance.

Her tattered, soiled clothing gave further evidence of her lowly state. Her red sweater, which might once have been of good quality but was now faded in many places from the intense Florida sunlight, was spotted with what appeared to be food and coffee stains. A large hole under the right arm revealed a discolored tank-top. Typical of the homeless, the woman wore a pair of faded jeans, cut-off above the knees, with several holes that exposed her bare skin. On her feet were overstretched flip-flops.

The woman looked at Laurie, then opened the coffee container and slugged down what was left.

Laurie turned away, revolted by the thought of the woman drinking somebody's discarded coffee. *These people are subhuman and live in a subculture they have created for themselves,* she told herself.

The traffic moved.

Laurie cranked up the CD player volume ,then hit the gas pedal. All the way home, the image of the woman burned into her mind. *What could happen to a person to sink so low? Disgusting! Maybe she has mental disabilities. God, keep her...and them...away from me!*

* * *

Sunrise Park was a gated community in a large subdivision two miles north of I-595 that offered moderately priced homes with built-in swimming pools and one-quarter-acre plots. A common recreation hall/clubhouse for its residents provided suitable accommodations for large parties, if the residents were so inclined. The Bradshaw home was a 2,800 square-foot ranch with a double-car garage and a large Florida room used by the family for entertainment and various projects. Invariably, the extra big room provided an excellent place for storing clutter, the large items designated for the children's bedrooms.

Laurie pulled into the driveway, then pressed the garage opener remote control clipped to her sun visor. As the door climbed to its resting place, Sonny, their aging and oversized Irish Setter, wagged his tail as the official family greeter. "Hi, Sonny boy! It's always good to be home!" she said gleefully as she walked to him and patted his coat. The dog reared up on his hind legs to lean on her with all of his 80 pounds, nearly knocking her backward, then pranced off into the nearby rooms.

"Hi, Mom!" her son, Sean, said as he raced past her with a lacrosse stick in his hand and a face guard on his head.

"Hi!" was all she had time to say before he was out of sight. Seconds later she heard his friends calling out plays from the street as their game began.

"Dinner's working, Mom," Tiffany shouted as she walked into the kitchen. "Now I'm fixing dessert." Tiffany stood next to the stove mixing a bowl of chocolate brownies, then systematically spooned the mix into the baking pan and placed it into the oven before turning the dial on the portable timer. "How was school today?"

Laurie leaned over and kissed her daughter on the forehead. "I'll tell you about my day in school after you tell me about yours."

Tiffany clapped her hands. "Well, first, I received an A in my Bible mid-term. Second, I was asked to go to Leslie's sweet 16 party."

Laurie raised an eyebrow and decided to tackle number two before congratulating her on number one since it did not require a discussion. "By whom, Tiffy?"

Tiffany had many talks with her parents on dating. After countless hours of strenuous debates and policy setting, it was agreed upon by her parents (not by Tiffany herself) that there would be only double dating, and even that would only occur if the designated place was approved by her father. "Andy Madison," she said as she rotated in place. "Dad knows him. He works down at the Pizza Shack after school." To bolster his résumé she added, "His father is one of the trustees at Calvary Baptist, remember?"

"Yes, I recall our discussions." Laurie wasn't crazy about Andy who, though showing great promise as a Christian leader, seemed to lack the backbone needed to get ahead in the world today by looking at his work accomplishments. "And the double?"

Tiffany grinned expansively. "We haven't decided yet. Andy and I will probably talk about it over the phone tonight. We have two possible candidates."

"A word of advice," her mother warned, hoping the candidate they chose would bring strength to her proposal. "Organize your plans before you bring it to your father, or it will not pass muster after dinner."

Tiffany nodded before plugging in the electric coffee pot as her mother picked up the stack of mail on the counter. The commendation on Tiffany's Bible test fell by the wayside and was noted by her as "same as usual" when it came to Biblical agenda. Ironic, since Laurie was a pastor's wife.

"So, how was your day?" Tiffany's gaze narrowed on her mother's face.

Laurie plopped into a kitchen chair and kicked off her shoes as she thumbed through the mail while giving up a giant sigh. "A killer, as usual."

"When do you have to stand before the class and give that oral in Effective Leadership before the class?" Tiffany sprinkled extra seasoning on the baked chicken.

"Oh, that's next week, Tiffy." *Slam!* Laurie crashed the mail down on the table while holding one letter in her hand. "This cable T.V. company is giving me a cramp!" she complained vigorously. "I'm getting sick and tired of them threatening to cut our service when we pay the bill on time." Laurie dropped her head on the back of the chair and closed her eyes for a power nap.

"Dad's home!" Sean's voice, especially when in yelling mode, carried at deafening decibels.

Tiffany's face brightened as she hurried to put the dinner out. "Mom, do you want to freshen up before Dad walks in?"

Laurie opened one eye and forced a smile. "Of course." As she scurried into the bathroom, Sean walked in holding his dad's hand while brandishing his lacrosse stick in the other, with Sonny lagging behind in tow.

Wilson Randolph Bradshaw hugged his daughter as Sean placed his stick in the dining room corner.

Sean sniffed several times, then shot a look at his father. "What's cooking?" they asked in unison.

Tiffany wrinkled her nose. "Your favorite, Dad. Baked chicken." The exchange of looks communicated the strong bond existing between them. He smiled at her and turned as the bathroom door opened.

Laurie yawned as she walked up to him. "Oh, hi, doll!" he said as he embraced her and gave her a kiss. The timer went off, signaling the brownies were done. It was time to eat.

Once seated, Sean extended his hands to his father. "Dad, can I pray tonight?" His father gave him the nod as they all joined hands and closed their eyes while Sean prayed his thanksgiving for God's provision.

"How did school go today?" Randy asked his family.

"I have a game Saturday, Dad," Sean blurted.

"Great. I look forward to seeing you play," his father replied in support. "Maybe we can make it a family affair."

"I got an A in my Bible exam." Tiffany beamed.

Her father clasped her hand. "Terrific!" As he reached for another piece of chicken, he asked Laurie, "How was your day, Babe?"

"Tiring," she said wearily. "So much homework to keep up with along with everything else."

He hesitated, assessed, then responded, "It won't be too much longer and you'll be done. I know how it is."

Laurie scowled at him. "Well, almost."

Randy winced at the inference but decided to let it pass. Previous discussions about Laurie's desire to get her college degree while the family was dependent on her staying at home only resulted in an argument. Whenever Randy pointed to negative statistics showing factors that contribute to the demise of the family, of which two career households was one, Laurie retaliated by bringing to his attention that she had worked a full-time job to put him through Bible college to get *his* education. Now it was *her* turn; the family would survive.

"Uh, how are things going down at the church, Dad?" Tiffany asked, discerning the rising tension.

Randy caught Laurie's eye before giving his daughter a thumb's-up. "Things are going fine, Tiffy, going fine." Making a general broadcast to the table, he added, "The deacons and I met this morning to thank the Lord for blessing the ministry. We are experiencing an unprecedented period of numerical growth, while at the same time, the Lord is providing our financial needs and even wants. We noted that, with these favors, the Lord is bringing the congregation to the place where they are striving for a greater degree of holiness and commitment."

Sean gave a garbled whistle. "Sounds like we're on the right track with God."

"Yes, it does," Randy replied. "Nevertheless, I believe the Lord is blessing us while at the same time saying that we need to get 'our ducks in a row' because He is going to use the church for something big real soon."

Historical precedence in Randy's life dictated that, after a season of blessings, the Lord brought a mighty challenge into his life. Ever-fresh in his memory were the blessings and soon-to-follow period of testing when he was in Bible college. During his first year at Trinity College he was randomly selected out of a group of 15 students by his homiletics professor to preach a sermon at chapel one morning. It became apparent after only five minutes of preaching that he possessed the spiritual gift of oratory, powered by the Holy Spirit. The faculty, along with his fellow students, were impressed by his skill to reduce deep theological truths to simple principles and deliver them with such authority and conviction that the audience was moved to tears. This was followed by many more appointments to preach at Trinity. But that all changed after he went home on Christmas vacation when his pastor asked him to deliver the sermon for Sunday worship. It turned out to be a humbling experience.

Riding on his spiritual high and confidence from college, he believed he could simply "wing it" by pulling one sermon from his archives delivered at school. He spent only 15 minutes reviewing the homily on the Power of Pentecost, then boldly went before the congregation to proclaim it.

God apparently didn't approve of Randy's heart condition, because he blanked out five minutes into his delivery. The pastor had to step in and preach an impromptu to cover for him. Several weeks of reflection on his relationship with the Lord followed. It always reminded him of Jesus' coming into his ministry. Right after he was anointed by the Holy Spirit at his baptism, he was cast out into the wilderness to be tempted by Satan for 40 days. He learned an important lesson: Don't presume on the Lord; if you remain humble before your God, He will lift you up.

"Well, whatever that 'big thing' is," Laurie said with feeling as she demonstrated with her hands, "I hope God doesn't drag our family into it. I have enough on my plate just to get through school."

Both Tiffy and Sean stopped chewing and shot looks at their dad.

"God's abundant grace will enable us to bear up to whatever test He may choose to draw us closer to Himself," Randy said in a wounded tone. "I, for one, want to be part of God's 'big thing'—heaven forbid we'd be left out as a family."

Laurie squinted at her husband, then pursed her lips as she calculated her response. In her mind, the blessing-testing equation worked well in the church but not in the family. She had no problem separating the two. If God wanted to test her husband and his ministry, so be it. She'd support him in prayer, but to test his family to bring the same results seemed unreasonable. Why should they suffer when it was his church that would benefit? *No argument tonight.* "May it be so," she said with a broad smile.

Tiffany seized the moment. "I made your favorite dessert, Dad. Nice warm brownies with walnuts. And we have chocolate-chip ice cream."

Randy pushed his plate away. "Sounds good." He reached over and patted Tiffany's arm. Her flowing red hair and radiant smile were two of her best features. "You're one beautiful young lady," he added with admiration.

Tiffany brought the brownies as Laurie poured Randy's coffee. "Tiffy, tell your father about your plans," Laurie said with cloying sweetness.

"I was going to, Mom, but not right now," Tiffany protested.

"Now's as good a time as any," her mother replied tonelessly. "Tell him."

Tiffany laid the platter of dessert in front of her father, then sat next to him. "Andy Madison asked me to a birthday party next week and, knowing how you feel, we'll probably ask Richie Vale to double with us. I promise to be home on time. Say yes, Dad, please."

Randy knew the Madison boy and his family. Solid Christians. As for the Vale boy, he knew nothing but trusted his daughter to make good choices within family guidelines. "No problem."

Tiffany shot her fist up in triumph as she winked at her mother. "Yes!"
Randy exchanged looks with Laurie, who simply shrugged.

* * *

The 25-minute drive to Plantation Gate Christian Church allowed Randy ample time to plan out his day. It also provided him with transitional time to set aside his family cares and prepare for the increasing needs of his congregation. Many times the two merged so inextricably that he carried both throughout the day. *If one can't take the heat...*

"Yes, Lord, I know," he said out loud. "If I can't manage both, I should get out of the kitchen."

My grace is sufficient, remember?

"Yes, Lord, I remember."

The early morning commuter traffic came to a stop. Randy stuck his head out the driver's window to see a Broward Sheriff's officer directing the flow of cars. The traffic light at Nob Hill Road and Broward Boulevard was out once again. Randy paused in his ruminations to survey the community. The one-time affluent area that formerly boasted of prime-class housing and elegant shopping malls appeared to be changing. Now, strip malls offering specialized food, clothing, and services to meet the growing demands of the changing neighborhood lined the streets. Ethnic houses of worship were popping up to reflect the cultural influx South Florida was experiencing. Immigrants from the Caribbean and South America were rapidly settling in the area, while Middle-Eastern families were becoming more conspicuous as well. The thought of how to minister to this cultural mix was becoming more time-consuming. *How can we effectively meet the needs of this cultural influx in this changing society? How can we embrace them with the love of Jesus in this culturally diverse community?* Historically, crime rates skyrocketed soon after the neighborhoods changed, driving many long-time residents out. If this trend continued to encroach on his church, it could pose a potential threat by forcing many of his members to move out as well. It was a problem several of his fellow pastors had already had to deal with...and, too often, unsuccessfully. *Lord, I can't worry about this*, he thought. *This church is your ministry. Today is Wednesday; think on your Bible study.*

So thoughts of his lesson in Romans filled his mind.

* * *

8

The 750-seat sanctuary of the independent Plantation Gate Christian Church was built in 1974 on five acres of land. Auxiliary buildings included a 24-room educational building and a 300-seat fellowship hall. The sanctuary boasted an impressive brass spire, stained glass windows, and a fieldstone facade, set apart by a sprawling lawn augmented with prolific shrubbery. Inside, the church possessed traditional furnishings including cushioned oak pews, a wall-to-wall balcony, and 40 modern light fixtures hanging from a 35-foot ceiling. Behind the altar area were the administrative offices, bathrooms, and storage areas. The pastor's office was unusually large, affording Pastor Randy ample room for his prized bookcases and a corner sporting two stuffed chairs for his counseling quarters. Set apart on the diagonal was his oversized mahogany desk and computer console. Soon after his calling to Plantation Gate five years ago, Pastor Randy hung up his pictures on the wall and placed above the doorway a plaque that read, *My Second Home.*

It was a mere five minutes after he set his attaché case and lunch box next to his desk that the church doorbell rang, giving an early-morning wake-up call.

Less than a minute later, his secretary/assistant, Yvonne, stuck her head into his office doorway. "Pastor Randy, a woman is here looking for assistance. Deacon Lester won't be here for another hour. Can you speak with her?"

Randy stood. "Sure, tell her I'll be right with her."

The number of people looking for daily assistance had quadrupled since he took over the pastorate. Plantation Gate was one of the few churches in the community that still operated a food pantry. Other pastors confided in him and said their congregants lost heart in the projects because they failed to see any fruit from that kind of ministry. Rarely did any of the needy return and visit the church. They cited an ungrateful community of needy people and thought it prudent to invest the Lord's money in other areas of evangelism that would yield higher spiritual dividends. Randy often thought that those church members neglected or conveniently overlooked Christ's teaching in the parable of the Sheep and Goats, where he proclaimed that indeed it was He who was hungry and you gave me something to eat, it was I who was thirsty and you gave me something to drink. I was the stranger and you invited me in, I needed clothes and you clothed me, I was sick and you looked after me.

Carrying his Bible, Randy walked outside the rear entrance of the church offices to find the woman sitting demurely on the bench outside the fellowship hall, holding a handkerchief to her nose. She looked up with pleading eyes. "Can you help me?"

Trying to overlook her disheveled appearance and unpleasant odor, Randy sat next to her and replied cautiously, "If we can."

"I don't have any money or food, or even a place to live," she said just above a whisper.

"We can help you," Randy promised. "But our church policy prohibits us from giving you any money." He clasped her hand. "However, we can help you in other ways."

She nodded. Glancing down at their clasped hands, she cracked a smile. "Whatever help you can give me would be greatly appreciated." With that she gazed out the window some imaginary spot on the horizon.

Years of experience in counseling homeless people qualified Randy to assess the woman. She appeared to possess the faculties, both in speech and awareness, of an educated person. He surmised by the way she presented herself that, at one time, she may have been a woman of substance, now on the streets of Plantation, living from hand to mouth. *Lord, what could have happened to this poor woman?* Randy grew thoughtful. "What is your name?"

"Stephanie." She maintained her fixed stare.

Randy guessed the woman's age to be in the 40s, but the streets rapidly aged people beyond their years. "Well, Stephanie, I'll get you some food from our food storage room, and then I'll be right back." He opened his Bible, pulled out a tract, and handed it to her. "In the meantime, please read this."

She regarded him with a tearful eye as she took the pamphlet.

Five minutes later he returned with two plastic shopping bags filled with a variety of cans and boxes. He also handed her a small booklet. "Here are some meal vouchers for Piccadilly cafeteria. This should help you get by for a while." There was no provision in the church budget to give nonmembers any financial assistance, even if intended for housing. "Unfortunately," he added ruefully, "we can't help you with accommodations. I wish it weren't so."

Her eyes flicked to his, then away. Sadness swept over her face, yet he detected no bitterness. *Rare.* She nodded with apparent understanding while reflecting on his remarks. She put the vouchers in her rear pocket, then pointed to the tract and then to his Bible. "Pastor, you seem like a nice, kind man, concerned with helping people. Answer me this: where in God's counsel does it explain why someone has to pay for their mistakes by losing everything they own, including their family, while others who commit more heinous crimes seem to walk off into the sunset and have a great life?"

Randy set the bags down and stared at the woman. His discernment proved true. Stephanie was no ordinary woman. "Whoa," he said with surprise. "That's a heavy question. One that requires a study in the sovereignty of God." He paused. *Go ahead, ask her*, came a voice from within. "Stephanie, I'd like to invite you to our Wednesday night Bible study tonight." He jerked his thumb over his shoulder. "We meet in this fellowship hall at seven o'clock. I believe the rest of the study group would also like to hear God's teaching on your question."

Stephanie stuffed the tract in the same pocket with the vouchers, then grabbed the plastic handles on the bags. Slowly she looked skyward and then into Randy's face. "I'll think about it."

With her shoulders drooping from the weight of the bags, Stephanie walked off the church property and back into the streets.

In all his years of ministry, Randy was never moved in his heart as much as he was by this brief encounter with Stephanie. It was very strange.

Randy had no idea that God had sent this woman to be the very vessel He would use to bring His church to the next level.

2

The hostess of Plantation Gate Christian Church possessed a unique gift for calculating the amount of food necessary to accommodate those congregants coming to the fellowship supper each Wednesday night. Consistently, more than half the church membership turned out for her cafeteria-style dinner for the opportunity of attending the Bible study that followed, as well as catching up on all the church community news.

Pat, the hostess, brought a new theme to the dinner table each week: Israeli, Italian, Greek, Brazilian, Irish, English, Chinese, Caribbean, never excluding any other foreign dish she could think of from other places on the planet. Tonight, the theme was Italian—Pastor Randy's favorite.

"Well done, Pat," Randy said as he saluted her from the food line. Pat glowed, accepting the compliment with humility. Randy turned to Laurie standing in line behind him and signaled her to acknowledge the hostess's efforts. *Why should I have to remind her to be civil? She's the pastor's wife and should be cordial.*

Laurie gave Pat a torpid glance before she forced a smile. "Nice."

"Good turnout tonight, Pastor," Randy heard from behind. He turned to see his deacon, Lester Rogers, holding his tray with his wife, Gatha, standing next to him. Together they served the Lord by supporting Randy and the church in every way possible, despite their advancing years.

"Double portion tonight, Pastor Randy?" one of the women servers asked.

Randy patted his stomach. "Mercy, no!" His acid-reflux condition would never tolerate the Italian food unless he was willing to take antacid tablets every hour for the rest of the evening. "Once around is enough for me."

Judy Edelson, the wife of one of Plantation Gate's deacons, walked up to Laurie as she was being served. "Laurie, who's on babysitting tonight?"

Laurie blinked, then turned to Randy with inquiring eyes.

Randy hesitated. "I believe it's Sharon and Betty tonight."

Judy's eyes flicked to Laurie's, then nodded as she walked to the back of the line.

"I suppose I should have known that," Laurie whispered in Randy's ear as she moved along the line. Overseeing the scheduling of the babysitting list each month was one of the duties Laurie volunteered for as part of her ministry service. There were many times when she strangely found it hard to invest time and effort in her husband's church, thinking it were only *his* and not *their* ministry,

Discomfort niggled in the pit of Randy's stomach. *Let it pass.* "That's all right. The schedule changes so frequently, it's hard to remember everybody's name."

Laurie made a mental note to pay more attention to the names on the list next time. She didn't want to be looked upon as a pastor's absentee wife.

Randy felt a tap on his shoulder as he walked away from the serving line. Tiffany stood next to him with a her finger pointing toward the rear entrance of the fellowship hall. "Dad, uh, there's a woman asking for you over by the door." Tiffany then clapped her hand over her mouth and, with a muted voice, added with slight disdain, "She looks hungry."

Seconds later, a distinct hush came over the room as the congregation's attention turned toward the visitor.

Randy turned to see the woman, Stephanie, giving the fellowship hall a visual inspection, then narrowing her gaze to the food tables. "Oh, that's Stephanie, a homeless woman who came to the church this afternoon," he replied as he set his tray down on a nearby table. *Wow, she came!*

Laurie rotated in place and locked her eyes on the red sweater spotted with food stains.

Randy was walking toward Stephanie when suddenly he was pulled from behind.

"That woman was walking along I-595 when I was coming home from school yesterday," Laurie whispered in his ear. "Did you see her up close? She's disgusting!"

A frosty silence. Then, after several seconds of contemplation, Randy murmured back, "And what would you have me do, throw her out?" *Lord, what is the message you're trying to tell our church?*

Laurie drilled her eyes into Randy's and said in a reasonably controlled voice, "Wilson Randolph Bradshaw, don't you dare invite her to sit down with the congregation!"

Randy whirled on her, then discreetly shuffled her to the nearest corner as several sets of eyes followed them. "Laurie, what's the matter with you?" he asked with heightening alarm. "This woman is in need, and it's our job to minister to her!"

Laurie squeezed his arm and through clenched teeth replied, "I won't be able to eat with her here. Give her some food and coupons to the cafeteria and send her on her way."

"Dad, that homeless lady over there is asking for you," Sean announced as he walked up to his parents huddled in the corner.

Randy camouflaged his disappointment in his wife as best he could and tried to regain his composure. "Tell her I'll be right over," he advised his son. Sean marched off as Randy mechanically removed his wife's grasp. "We will discuss this in private, Laurie, but for now, I have every intention of making that woman feel comfortable in this church." With that he walked to the door.

Lester and Gatha jumped up from their table to join Randy and Stephanie at the door, their ministry gifts of mercy and compassion overruling church protocol. "Pastor, may we help?" Lester asked.

"Get her some food?" Gatha said.

Randy noticed Stephanie had managed to wash her face and comb her hair but apparently was unable to shower or change her clothes. Her body odor slowly permeated the area. "Stephanie, this is Lester, one of our deacons, and his wife, Gatha," he said with a broad smile. "They will escort you through the food line." Randy thought on Laurie's remark and added as he pointed to Lester's table, "When you get through the line, you can sit with them, and I'll catch up with you later."

"How did she find out about the church dinner?" Laurie asked the moment Randy returned to their table.

"I invited her to the Bible study, and she probably read the weekly program on the outside bulletin board this afternoon. It mentions the dinner," Randy surmised.

"I can't believe you'd invite someone like that and expose our congregation to her sort," Laurie fumed.

"When she came looking for food assistance, I simply invited her to our Bible study. That's all."

Laurie gave Randy the cold shoulder, finishing her meal in silence. Sensing the widening chasm, Randy solicited her favor. "May I get you a cup of coffee?" Laurie nodded without emotion.

Deacon Ronnie Edelson met Randy at the coffee urn and scratched his head as he peered back at Stephanie at Lester's table, then over to Laurie. "Pastor, is everything all right with Laurie? She looks really perturbed over the visitor."

Randy opened the spout on the coffee urn and filled two cups. "School is taking its toll on her. She's tired and irritable tonight." *Great. Does she have to be so obvious?*

Ronnie had his own thoughts on Laurie's attitudes and what the role of the pastor's wife should be in the pastorate, but this was not the time to discuss their different philosophies of ministry. He'd wait for a more convenient time to counter the excuses. Ae said as he walked off, "Let me know if I can help."

Once Randy delivered Laurie her cup of coffee, he did a deliberate 180-degree turn and walked over to sit next to Stephanie. Most of the eyes in the room focused on their table. "I'm so glad to see you again, Stephanie," he said cordially. He looked down at her food tray to note that it appeared as if she had licked it clean.

She scanned the room with piercing eyes, then asked bluntly, "What about the rest of the congregation, Pastor Randy? Are they equally as glad?"

Randy was embarrassed for their rudeness. "Never mind the rest of the congregation. You are welcome in our church." Compassion surged over him as if the Holy Spirit were guiding him into a new ministry: that of reaching the homeless. "We have plenty of room for you," he added warmly.

We'll see about that, Stephanie didn't say.

"It's time to get our Bible study started," Randy announced to the table as he glanced at his wristwatch. He stood said to Lester and Gatha, "Please see that Miss Stephanie is escorted to our Bible study room."

They nodded as he walked away.

* * *

Teaching the Bible was Randy's thing. In seminary he excelled in both teaching and preaching; but, in due process, after teaching at Trinity College and Moody Bible Institute for over seven years, he recognized his strength was in his desire to teach doctrine and have that affect behavior and be blessed by seeing lives change. It was a gift few expositors possessed. Teaching doctrine is often thought of as being boring or complicated, to be confined to the academic arena. But Randy made it interesting, and at times simple, so that the deep things of God could be grasped by the everyday man in the pew.

Time for praise and prayer. Three women from the congregation stood in front of the Bible study group: one took the praises and prayer requests; the other led the singing; the third played the piano. Together they lifted the hearts of the study group to renewed heights in preparation for the Word of God to be delivered by Pastor Randy.

After 25 minutes of praise and petition, Randy got the nod from the pianist. As he walked up to the lectern, his eyes selected out of the group both Laurie and Stephanie, seated rows apart. *What a dichotomy these two women present to the church.*

He signaled a helper to distribute chapter outlines, then wrote out on the whiteboard the chapter highlights. "Tonight we continue in our study of Romans," he began, "picking up where we left off, in chapter eight.

"Paul introduces this classic chapter on somewhat of a lighter note where he encourages the Christian to live life through the Spirit. From there he progresses to warn of the battle of the carnal mind verses the spiritual mind, reminding us that we can have victory over the flesh through the Spirit of God. Shortly afterwards, Paul embarks on his treatise of predestination, election, and eternal security."

Randy looked up from his notes to gauge his audience. They were all attentive. *So far so good.* "In this monumental passage, Paul attempts to explain that God has a divine purpose for each and every believer who comes to the Lord through Christ. From the time of the creation of the universe, even before the foundation of the world was laid, He had selected out of the mass of humanity who would be saved and how they could bring glory to God through their lives. This is predestination. Later, in chapter nine, Paul illustrates this truth though the example of chosen instruments, citing Jacob over Esau, Israel over the Gentile nations, and then explaining that God's purposes are inscrutable by using the metaphors of the potter and the clay as an example of His divine will. In other words, God has the sovereign right to choose who will be saved and who will not, all to bring about His purpose of the greater good.

"Paul's explanation of God's prerogative of election, is admittedly, a difficult doctrine to grasp. We could say that Christ's atonement on the cross of Calvary rendered the world savable, and from that unique experience, redeemed those who were chosen by the Father to inherit eternal life in heaven. This also includes God's sovereign choice of those who would be destined to damnation." He turned the pages in his Bible to Ephesians. "Paul helps us understand this deep truth where he adds in chapter 1, verse 11: *"In him we were also chosen, having been predestined according to the plan of him who works out everything in conformity with the purpose of his will."* He scanned the group's faces, knowing this teaching would elicit a response.

A hand shot up in the air. It was Laurie's. "The study of this doctrine always gives me a headache," she lamented. "I have a problem understanding it. Can you explain it further?"

Several heads turned and studied her quizzically.

Randy thought it inappropriate for his wife to ask such a controversial question at a Bible study from the perspective of her own discovery. It would be the kind of question a nonbeliever would ask in a public forum. *Don't you already know this?* "Yes, we can explore this now."

He recalled some of the teaching notes he'd memorized, then explained what he believed was a question about election. "That some in time are given faith in God and that others are not given faith proceeds from His eternal decree. Election is then defined as the unchangeable purpose of God whereby, before the foundation of the world, out of the whole human race, which had fallen by its own fault out of its original integrity into sin and ruin. He has, according to the most free good pleasure of His will, out of mere grace, chosen in Christ to salvation a certain number of specific men, neither better nor more worthy than others, but with them involved in a common misery."

He allowed the group to digest this truth. "Furthermore, this doctrine dictates that God, out of His most free, most just, blameless, and unchangeable good pleasure has decreed to leave in the common misery into which they have by their own fault plunged themselves, and not to give them saving faith and the grace of conversion, and finally to condemn and punish them eternally for all their sins.

"But so that we don't view this as a negative, let me say that election involves rescue from sin and guilt and receiving the gracious gifts of salvation that includes His fellowship through His word and Spirit." With a broad smile, he concluded, "To us, that means salvation brings personal privilege, blessing, security, and comfort for the elect." Glancing at Laurie, he noted that she simply nodded at his answer.

"Pastor, what does it mean," an elderly widow by the name of Mary asked, "when the text says, *'Who shall separate us from the love of Christ?'*"

"Good question. This too is connected to the doctrine of election, only this broadens it to include the fact that once saved, always saved. It refers to eternal security. In other words, it's God's insurance policy for the elect. If we have truly been regenerated in the Spirit according to Titus 3:5, we cannot lose our salvation, we cannot be separated from God, and there is nothing in the universe that can rob us of that, regardless of what happens in life. Plain and simple."

Laurie seesawed her head while the rest of the group showed a sign of relief, not because Randy's discourse appeared to be over, but that their salvation was secure in Christ. And they knew it.

A hand from the back of the room was raised. Randy immediately recognized the red sweater and braced himself accordingly. "Pastor Randy, I have a question relative to your discussion on predestination."

Randy scanned the group. They appeared to be shocked that this homeless woman would have the gumption to ask such a question from her lowly station in life. Laurie appeared repulsed. "Yes, I remember you had a question when we first met," he said as a muscle jerked in his left cheek.

Every eye in the room was riveted on Stephanie as she sheepishly stood. "For the past three years, I have been searching for an answer to this question that I suspect is related to what you call predestination. Why would God punish one person for a lifestyle that dishonored Him, while not punishing another for the same thing?" She focused on the ceiling as if to recall something, then said with a blink, "Doesn't it say in Job that God does not show partiality to princes and does not favor the rich over the poor, for they are all the work of his hands?" She slowly sat down as every head turned toward Randy for the response.

He couldn't believe this woman was reciting Scripture—and making application to her own situation. It was rare, even in and among his own people. Yes, many non-Christians read the Bible and knew salient verses, but this sounded different coming from a homeless person. However, he'd try to explain this truth to Stephanie's satisfaction. Although he couldn't remember that verse in Job, he knew Christ capsulized that principle in the Sermon on the Mount: *"He causes his sun to rise on the evil and the good, and sends rain on the righteous and the unrighteous."*

"An important question that troubles many," he began. "In defending the providence of God, I believe the Bible makes it clear that He has a perfect plan in place. And in this perfect plan, God often uses apparent reverses in a person's life to either draw that person to Himself, or, if they so chose, to harden their hearts so they drift further away from Him. Mistakes, as you point out, are often part of that process.

"By way of example, a Christian will suffer an ethical failure at work and then, when the Holy Spirit convicts him or her, they confess to their employer, who in turn shows no mercy and fires them. On the other hand, a non-Christian can commit the same or worse violation, never thinking of confessing, and get away with it. In the past, we've seen this type of injustice in the political arena.

"We know, however, that God does keep a series of books and that they will be opened at the Great White Throne Judgment. These books record every act performed by man, and in addition to being judged by the Law, man will receive punishment based on these deeds. In other words, the day is coming when the playing field will be leveled and scores left imbalanced for eons of time will be settled." He smirked. "Many times we hope God would mete out divine retribution here and now to those who flout their sin in God's face, then get it in the hereafter as well, but God is very gracious and merciful, not wanting any to perish, but that all would come to repentance. The adage, 'we expect mercy for ourselves and judgment for others' is equally noteworthy for consideration."

Deacon Edeleson stood and opened his Bible. "Pastor, just to reinforce your position, there's a verse in Deuteronomy—32: 4—that supports this view. It says, *"He is the Rock, his works are perfect, and all his ways are just. A faithful God who does no wrong, upright and just is he."* Edeleson smiled at Stephanie as he sat down.

Randy acknowledged Ronnie's edification, then summarized his own viewpoint. "One could say 'what goes around, comes around,' but often that doesn't cut it when attempting to understand God's dealing with those who do wrong and appear to get away with it. I think it's better to look at this theodicy from God's perspective if we can. The events in a person's life can either be used to exercise them to righteousness, which is salvation and sanctification, or to bitterness, which ends in separation or rebellion. It will always be God's best that, when a trial is presented, we are exercised to righteousness.

"It has been my personal experience, and that of many testimonies, that whenever God takes something away from his children, he replaces it with kingdom gifts that have much greater value." He shot a look at Stephanie, who nodded in assent. Closing his Bible, he asked, "Does anybody have any other questions?"

It seemed like a sigh of relief came over the study group, as if they were theologically exhausted and needed a breather. No hands were raised. Randy then called upon Lester to close the study with a word of prayer.

When Randy caught a glimpse of Laurie, her hands were crossed over her chest while tapping her foot on the floor.

* * *

The ride home was anything but peaceful. "She's disruptive!" Laurie argued. "Can't you see that if this woman comes back to our church, people will leave?"

Randy glanced at Tiffany and Sean in the backseat. He would not argue in front of his children. "Laurie, I'm not sure where you're coming from, but we need to look at the possibility that the Lord is in this," he began calmly. "Besides, what's wrong with trying to help this woman? After all, isn't that what ministry is about—helping people?" *Why this antagonism? Surely she has done you no harm.*

"We're helping our own people," she replied tersely. "Remember, charity begins at home. Besides, I don't think our church will respond well to this caliber of people. Obviously they want something for free."

"Well, the Gospel is free," he replied impulsively. "Besides, we *have* been meeting the needs of our people, but I believe it's time to expand our borders to reach others in the community."

The feeling was mounting. Later, he'd come to realize that it was really more than just a feeling; it was a leading. A leading he believed would end in a calling and then to a conviction to help those needy people.

"Does it have to be the *homeless?* Can't we have an outreach to those who are working, who are an asset to society, instead of those who have a welfare mentality, always looking for a handout?"

Randy scratched his head. *This dark side of my wife is emerging more frequently. She's undergoing change. What other views might be changing? Her views toward hard, controversial issues such as abortion, homosexuality, and divorce?*

"Laurie," he said, turning on his soothing voice, the undertaker's voice, "why are you getting yourself all upset over this one woman? We've fed many homeless individuals and families through our food pantry over the years, so why are you so adamant about this *one* woman?"

Laurie's eyes penetrated his. "Don't you see that this woman is different from all the rest? All those *homeless* people you helped before never came back to visit our church to attend a worship service or Bible study, despite your invitations. They just took the handouts and moved on. She's the only one who did come back." She raised her voice two octaves. "You heard the questions she asked at the Bible study. She's smart and cunning. I wouldn't be surprised if she has some plan to fake a slip-and-fall incident on church property, then get a sharp lawyer and sue the pews right out of the sanctuary."

Randy regarded her with bewilderment. "That's ridiculous! Now how could you know that?" *Why would your mind go there? Have you no compassion for the less fortunate?*

"Call it woman's intuition, if you will. I don't trust her. Plain and simple."

Why is it so hard to appeal to her in the Spirit? He threw one hand up in the air while keeping the other on the steering wheel. *Is that your real reason?* "We will leave this with God," he said with finality.

A deafening silence accompanied the rest of the drive home.

* * *

The telephone was ringing as they walked in the door. Laurie waved it off and motioned to Randy to pick it up. It was Deacon Ronnie Edeleson. "Pastor, Judy and I have been in prayer for the past half hour about the Bible study and the way things went down."

Randy took the wireless phone into his study as Laurie and the children headed to their respective bedrooms. "The way *what* went down?" Randy replied, knowing full well where he was going with the conversation.

"Well," Ronnie ventured, "is everything all right with Laurie?"

"I'm sure," Randy said, attempting to circumvent any discussion, "why?"

"Pastor, forgive me for saying this, but as we listened to that woman, Stephanie, ask you her question, everybody noticed the expression on Laurie's face that told of some kind of pain."

"I wouldn't call it pain," Randy proffered. "Let's say she had a very tiring day and leave it at that."

Ronnie was known in the congregation for always supporting the pastor. They were tight. They had the same purpose in ministry: to exalt the Savior by lifting up the Word of God while proclaiming the Gospel. They ministered to the congregation, prayed regularly, played golf, and their families went on excursions together. Ronnie was always on the side of the pastor, yet not succumbing to the syndrome of becoming a "yes" man to act as a rubber stamp for his approval. When he thought the pastor was wrong, he appealed to him in the Spirit until unity was achieved, thus bringing honor to the Lord by maintaining a level of accountability. But when it came to his wife, Ronnie knew he was trespassing. "If you say things are okay, we'll leave it there."

Randy ended the call and replaced the phone, but Ronnie's concerns troubled him. *Lord, were Laurie's feelings toward this woman so transparent? Help me to be open to Your leading without sacrificing family harmony.*

* * *

Laurie stole away to her bedroom bathroom, closed the door and studied her reflection in the mirror. She began to knead her temples. Her head hurt. Perhaps it was from stress, or school, or just life. She didn't know which, but seconds later, fragments of distorted memories drifted into her mind. Distasteful and troublesome vestiges from long ago of a dirty old man wearing a red sweatshirt with food stains. She grimaced in renewed pain as she felt a wave of nausea come over her.

3

Blackening alto-cumulus clouds were forming over the ocean to the east. *Not a good sign,* Randy thought as he peeked out his church office window. Many thunderhead clouds invariably meant torrential rains in Florida, especially in late September. Foul weather was something he could do without today. *A reflection of my mood as a "hangover" from last night's argument?* he asked himself. He rubbed his forehead in an attempt to assuage the oncoming cluster headache brought on by the stress of the bedroom dispute that followed Laurie's private call-to-arms. Her flare-up of such extreme anger was very disturbing.

His undertaking to bridge the gap in his marriage brought on by a homeless woman seeking help resulted in a crash-and-burn failure. Laurie refused all attempts at reason, often speaking to the bedroom wall as if to enlist its support for her cause. Then came the frigid stares, followed by a period of frosty silence. In her own inimical way, she culminated the evening by emotionally severing the relationship by seeking sanctuary in a book, then turning off the bedroom light with a melodramatic flare.

The saga continued at breakfast with Laurie holding fast to her conviction, then looking to the children to champion her as they gulped down their PopTarts and orange juice. But their refusal to ally themselves with her only brought further concerted signs of disapproval. Surprisingly, and this Randy attributed to her newly acquired mood swings, the disruption in the household did not seem to bother her as she left for school. *Lord, why am I so troubled in spirit? Time to put aside your worries,* he commanded himself with strengthening resolve.

He spent some time in prayer, asking for an extra measure of grace, then swallowed a pill he kept in is pocket for his headaches. *A sermon to encourage the people to continue to trust the Lord would be in order,* he thought. He turned to 1 Samuel 30 in his Bible to review the account of David destroying the Amalekites after they raided and plundered his campsite, taking all the woman and children captive. *Sweet passage,* he reminded himself. One that he often turned to during periods of discouragement. The part where David turned to God and *"found strength and encouragement in the Lord"* after his troops blamed him and threatened to slay him for the raid was especially meaningful. The outcome where David believed God and recovered everything always brought a renewed spirit to go on.

The phone rang, then seconds later his secretary, Yvonne, stuck her head into his office doorway. "Telephone call, Pastor Randy. It's a Mrs. Lambert from your son's school."

Randy sighed at being interrupted during sermon preparation, but in the early years of his ministry he'd promised the Lord that he would be flexible to the needs of others. Naturally his family was a priority.

"Hello, Mrs. Lambert. This is Pastor Randy. How can I help you?"

"Mr. Bradshaw, I wanted to talk to one of Sean's parents about his work," she said with reservation. "I was going to call Mrs. Bradshaw at home, but your son has repeatedly said his mother is at school."

"Is everything okay with Sean?"

Silence.

"Not exactly," she replied after what seemed to be an interminable period. "Usually I'd send a note home asking for a parent-teacher conference, but in your son's case the problem is not too serious, so I thought I would make a telephone call instead. But, then again, I believe Sean's behavior could be the sign of a deeper problem."

Randy could feel the hairs on his neck stand on end. He switched the phone from speaker to handset then walked to close the door. "What about his behavior and what kind of a problem?"

"Sean is a bright student," she affirmed, "but lately he seems to be very distracted in his class work, causing his grades to drop. My reason for this call is to ask, without prying, if there is anything wrong at home that I should be made aware of?"

Randy squeezed his eyes shut. "There's nothing wrong at home that I'm aware of, Mrs. Lambert. The family is doing fine," he replied in defense, hoping for more information.

"I'm glad to hear that," she said, but her tone conveyed disbelief. "However, if you don't mind me saying so, I've seen this kind of behavior pattern in students before. I've been teaching for over 20 years, and Sean's conduct is often linked to inattentiveness on the part of the parents."

He sat on the edge of his desk, staring at the wall map of Israel as the wave of incredulity mixed with guilt swept over him. "Inattentiveness? Not likely...why, we're a very close family...I'll have a talk with him," Randy stammered.

"I'm sure your son will respond favorably," Mrs. Lambert said in conclusion. "He's a fine boy."

Randy thanked Mrs. Lambert for her concern and assured her that he would take every step to remedy the situation. He hung up the phone, then ran his fingers through his hair. Renewed pangs of guilt pricked his heart as he mentally reviewed Mrs. Lambert's call. He was deeply disturbed.

Seconds later he put his head down on his desk to take a power nap. *Just let me rest for a moment and process this information....*

A sharp knock at his door shattered his meditation. He bolted upright. "Yes, come in!"

The door opened and Yvonne appeared with deacons Lester and Ronnie trailing behind. "Pastor Randy, your deacons asked to speak with you," she proclaimed in dismay.

"Pastor," Lester began apologetically, "this is sort of unannounced, but we were hoping to speak with you privately."

"Of course," Randy replied while waving Yvonne off.

Yvonne exited the room, leaving Randy alone with his deacons.

Lester and Ronnie each grabbed a stuffed chair and moved it closer to Randy's desk, then sat down and exchanged looks.

"Pastor, we are concerned about Laurie," the aging deacon said. His hands shook slightly as they dangled on the edge of the armrests. "We noticed her behavior at the Wednesday night fellowship dinner and Bible study and frankly"—he glanced at Ronnie as if to get confirmation—"we were surprised to see her reaction to that homeless woman. We were wondering how Laurie feels about reaching out to such people as the homeless, and if there may be a potential problem?"

"What Lester is saying, Pastor," Ronnie interrupted with a tinge of impatience, "is that we've noticed a shift in Laurie's demeanor and attitude over the past several months. It appears she's become very indifferent toward this ministry. Her unfriendly response to Stephanie is a case in point. Lester and I have discussed it and prayed over whether to come to you, but we believe something is wrong."

Randy's eyes darted back and forth between his two deacons, shifting his weight in his chair as he braced himself for what appeared to be a dumping session. "It sounds like you're both building files," he said as he sat back with his arms crossed. "What other observations have you made?"

"No, we're not building files, Pastor," Ronnie replied humbly. "It is because of our love for the Lord, our church, and both you and Laurie, that we feel obliged to tell you when we suspect a problem is developing that could affect the overall ministry, that's all." He bowed his head. "We've noticed that since Laurie went back to school this year to finish up her degree program, she has become mentally and emotionally detached from the congregation. What we are asking is, is there a problem we should know about? One we can all pray about? How can we help?"

Randy slowly exhaled as he considered their grievance. *Lord, what do I tell these two faithful men?*

Ronnie, a handsome, olive-skinned Jewish believer who received Jesus Christ as his Messiah 15 years before, came to serve as his deacon at Plantation Gate after spending five years in a Hebrew-Christian fellowship where he learned in-depth Jewish evangelism from a converted rabbi. Subsequently, his knowledge of the Hebrew Old Testament enabled him to masterfully argue apologetically with any Jewish person about the validity of Christ's claims to be the Jewish Messiah. Together with his wife, Judy, who had become a completed Jew at age 18, they were a formidable twosome who loved the Lord and their ministry at Plantation Gate. Yes, both had their difficult sides. Ronnie was overly dogmatic and intolerant of ministry abuses, often bordering on the offensive, while Judy was very critical at times, but, in truth, her critical nature often proved to be an accurate assessment. *At times I needed that.* Besides, because they were really involved, they had become Randy's chief advisors when he asked for a discerning pulse on the congregation.

In Lester Rogers, Randy saw a revered father figure in the church. Randy respected the man as a spiritual leader who, despite his lack of education and business aptitude, saw beyond the failings of men and tirelessly worked to promote unity among the brethren. He was a passive man who turned his advanced age into a vital asset by allowing the Holy Spirit to empower his body to overcome the laws of nature. He would not give in to the maladies of the flesh but would endeavor to assist the pastor in whatever way he could— this being his 25th year of membership at Plantation Gate.

Inwardly, Randy knew neither had a mean bone in his body. Further, if they had to come to their pastor about his wife, he knew they did so out of love. Then there was the issue of their need to take steps to protect the congregation. Again, he agreed with their reasoning. *But did they have to come to me right after the call from Sean's teacher? Do I need a double whammy today?*

Randy swallowed hard as he thought on the implications with Laurie, then said dolefully, "I believe you both want God's best for the ministry here at Plantation Gate. And I believe you know my heart is to serve the Lord and to give Him *my* best. But as for Laurie, I will not try to justify her behavior, only to say that she has not been herself, and I believe this is due to the pressure of her schoolwork together with the responsibilities of her wifely and motherly duties. Nevertheless, I will talk to her about your concerns. So for now, leave it with me." *Do I bring out a bad spirit in her, Lord? Am I neglectful and thereby causing Laurie to be bitter?*

Ronnie responded with a smile at Randy that conveyed confidence. He then nodded to Lester, who clucked approvingly and said, "Pastor, you know that we're in your corner."

Moments later Randy was left alone with his thoughts.

* * *

Outside the pastor's office, Ronnie realized that, in Randy's explanation, he never once mentioned Laurie's role in ministry.

* * *

Prokofiev's violin *Concerto No. 1 in D major, Op. 19* echoed loudly throughout Randy's car as he sat in the driveway contemplating his next move. *David's guitar soothed Saul's hostile and unsettled spirit*, he reminded himself. Unlike Saul, who simply found quietude, classical music had a profound, transporting affect on Randy; he was conveyed to the heavenly places where his spirit found rest and tranquility despite his tumultuous surroundings.

"Lord, I ask for direction. Should I discuss the phone call from Sean's teacher and the visit from the deacons about Laurie, or should I leave it to a more suitable time?" he prayed aloud. Seconds passed, then he pressed the *eject* button on the CD player.

Quiet.

More meditation.

By the time he reached his destination, his spirit testified with God what he should do.

* * *

Bright sunshine broke through the clearing skies striking the sanctuary at Plantation Gate's multicolored stained-glass windows, casting resplendent rainbows on the church pews as the congregation meandered in for Sunday worship. Deacons Lester and Ronnie attended to ushering while Judy, at the front door, handed out the schedules as the people approached. Gatha Rogers slowly walked up and down the aisles working the congregation with her love

26

and goodwill, greeting each person with a smile and a handshake and often a hug to select individuals who looked like they needed one.

Laurie sat in the front row with Tiffany and Sean, checking the time on her wristwatch, wondering when Randy would emerge from his "sequester," as she called it. In this brief 10-minute period before the service began, he remained in solitude, beseeching the Lord for His anointing.

It was now 10:59 a.m. with the service beginning in one minute. The congregation was seated, the choir was in place, Michael, the music minister was ready, but Randy was still not visible.

Laurie drilled her eyes into Tiffany to signal a warning after she waved hello to one of her friends sitting in a back row. *Where is he?* she asked herself. *He knows I like the service to start on time.* She turned to Sean as he thumped his leg up and down and squeezed his kneecap in protest. "Stop it!" she snapped. Tiffany and Sean rolled their eyes. *God, why am I so impatient lately? Why do my kids get on my nerves?*

She glanced toward Tiffany again. *I can't stay annoyed at her, even though I see much of myself in her.* A beautiful young lady with flowing red hair neatly gracing her shoulders. Sculptured facial features set off with deep blue eyes that screamed out with the desire to grow up rapidly and dimples that cried out to remain a child. Tall, very tall. Almost five-foot-nine and only 16 years old. *Wow.* A real knockout. *We're going to have our hands full keeping the boys away from her.*

A hug and smile for Sean. Natural athlete. Smart. Rising to challenges with the eye of the tiger as his target. His star on the rise. *Watch out, world!*

The door adjacent to the altar or stage opened abruptly. Randy walked in with Stephanie and some other man who also looked homeless.

"Oh, brother," Laurie muttered, tracking their every movements.

"What is it, Mom?" Tiffany asked, slightly alarmed.

"Your father has guests," she whispered with a tinge of sarcasm.

Tiffany assessed the scene but said nothing.

Randy gestured for Lester to come forward and escort Stephanie and her companion to a pew to the right of the altar, then walked up to the pulpit to give the invocation to begin the service. He began by praying for America, its president and leaders, then asked the Lord for a special blessing for the nation of Israel, then added an admonition for those in the churches who had fallen into apathy. He concluded with his usual request for the Holy Spirit to use the Word of God to speak through him to challenge the Christian and to meet the needs of his congregation. As he was about to give the pulpit over to his music minister, Michael, he added a postscript to his opening prayer as he nodded toward Stephanie and her companion. "Lord, bless the unfortunate among us, and enable us to do thy will in ministering to them." He walked off the altar platform and sat next to Tiffany as the choir began to sing *Majesty.*

Michael called the congregation to stand as they sang, giving Randy an opportunity to glance over at Laurie. She was grinding her teeth as her eyes followed the words of "Majesty" on the overhead screen. He reached behind Tiffany for Laurie's hand, but she pulled away, then raked his face with a lethal gaze. He recognized her rebuff immediately and silently prayed for her, even though he felt like scolding her for her need to hang onto a fight.

Five hymns and 15 minutes later, Michael signaled Randy to ascend the altar to give his sermon. His text was from Philippians 4:7 and Roman 5:1. It was a powerful homily on acquiring the peace *of* God by surrendering over their authority to Christ after experiencing peace *with* God at the point of salvation. Sensing the Spirit of God to be moving, he felt compelled to make an altar call. The response was overwhelming.

More than 20 people, including Stephanie and her companion, walked down the aisle toward him. Randy motioned for Lester and Ronnie to assist, then pointedly held out his arms for the two homeless guests to come to him. Feeling on fire for the Lord and filled with the power of Pentecost, he embraced them both. He placed his wireless lapel microphone on *mute* and asked them both, "How should I pray for you?"

"Pastor Randy," Stephanie said as she nodded to her companion, "this is Marty, and he wants to get right with God. He asked me to take him to you."

Randy smiled at Marty, then turned to Stephanie and said, "And what about you? Do you want to get right with God?"

Stephanie pulled back. "I'm not ready," she said discordantly.

Randy discerned that the Holy Spirit was moving in her heart, yet it was not God's timing for her to come to salvation. He turned to Marty, whose tears streamed down his face. "Pastor, my life is a wreck," Marty whispered. "I need Jesus to save me"—he wiped tears on his dirty shirt sleeve—"to forgive my sins; then I can try to have a normal life once again."

Randy flipped his microphone off mute, then put his arm around Marty while holding Stephanie's hand and turned to the congregation. "This brother has asked for Jesus to forgive him of his sins. He is ready to repent and turn his life over to Christ. Let us all join in prayer and ask our Heavenly Father in Christ to wash him in the blood of Christ so that his sins may be forgiven!"

"Amen!" cried out several voices.

A sudden hush came over the church as they prayed for Marty. Moments later Randy turned the microphone off and prayed with Marty to receive

Christ as his Lord and Savior. At last he said aloud, "All the angels in heaven now rejoice over Marty's decision to be saved." He hugged Marty, then faced him toward the congregation. "Now, for the first time, it gives me great pleasure to present to you for fellowship, *Brother Marty."* Several "amens" were heard once more. Randy's face beamed.

Overwhelmed by the emotional electricity, Laurie choked up, proud of her husband and his ability to preach, his ability to discern the needs of men. He was a spiritual man, dedicated to God's purpose. But then she shifted her focus to the two people standing next to him.

Stephanie wore the same soiled outfit from Wednesday, only now she had a red barrette in her unkempt hair. *Nice touch.* Marty had the components of the street plastered all over him. His left eye was swollen as if he were punched and beaten in a brawl with some street hoods the night before. His peppered beard was cropped and caked with residue from past meals. Spots of blacktop tar from the streets and food stains speckled his T-shirt. *And what was that protrusion in his abdomen? I've seen it before. It looks like a herniated stomach muscle right at the belly button. Yes, I'm sure that's what it is.* It was grotesque. A lump the size of a large lemon stuck out from underneath his T-shirt, accentuated by a paunch that hung over his pants. Laurie swiveled away in disgust.

After the benediction many well-wishers approached Marty to shake his hand as Randy and Laurie walked to the front door to say their good-byes to the departing congregation as they filed out the door. Randy motioned for Lester to close the building and winked at Laurie. "What do you say we have Ronnie take the kids home, and you and I go out to lunch?"

"Yes, I'd like that." Her voice was highly spirited, but her eyes told of undercurrents. "We should talk."

* * *

Danny's '70s-theme diner was a favorite pit stop for the Bradshaw family. Each of the items on the diner menu were named after a famed rock-and-roll star of their high school era. It brought back favorable memories and acted as a common denominator to begin conversations. When the waitress arrived, she wore an outfit to commemorate the period and a name tag celebrating a female vocalist. Her tag read Carol King.

"I'll take a Bobby Hatfield (from the Righteous Brothers) hamburger," Randy said with a broad smile. "And a small Everly Brothers coleslaw on the side, with a Neil Diamond cola."

"I'll have the CCR (Credence Clearwater Revival) salad with extra chicken," Laurie ordered, "and a Blood, Sweat, & Tears malted."

When the waitress left, Randy exuberantly reached for Laurie's hand. "God's Spirit was really moving this morning. Marty coming forward to receive the Lord reminded me of the proverb, *'One man pretends to be rich, yet has nothing; another pretends to be poor, yet has great wealth.'* Here is a man who has nothing of the physical world but now has everything of the spiritual world. I'm excited to see what God is going to do in his life." *Yes, this was the payoff,* Randy thought. *When our church ministers to the homeless, believing it to be the fertile field God has called us to, we will see fruit.*

"I see you're trying to reach out to these homeless people," Laurie replied, squeezing his hand, "but I'm not sure I'm ready for it. What's more, are *you* ready for it? I mean, they're extremely needy and demanding. This could really impact our family, not to mention the congregation. Do you believe the congregation is prepared to take on such a responsibility?"

Randy saw a weakening of her defenses, yet suspected her questions were rooted in her disdain for the unaccomplished. "I believe the Lord is testing our reaction to these two homeless people, waiting to see how we treat them. If we treat them in a godly way, the Lord will enable us and bless us accordingly."

She swallowed hard. "You mean by sending us more homeless people?"

"Perhaps."

She smirked cynically. "We both know how the Lord operates in matters such as this."

Randy grabbed her other hand. "Yes, I know the Lord has a great sense of humor and will probably send us hundreds of homeless people."

A chill ran up and down Laurie's spine. She sighed deeply and threw her hands up. "Who was it that said," she recollected, *"'for if their purpose or activity is of human origin, it will fail. But if it is from God, you will not be able to stop these men; you will only find yourself fighting against God?'"*

"It was Gamaliel, the Pharisee. He said that about the Apostles in the Book of Acts." Amazed at his wife's insightful application, he wondered if it some kind of prophetic utterance. *Lord, does she really mean this?*

Their orders arrived.

* * *

"We need to stop at Winn-Dixie to get some vegetables and eggs for the morning," Laurie reminded Randy on the way home.

The mood between them was congenial, even carefree. He knew he couldn't wait any longer to bring up the issues bothering him. Moments later, he pulled into the shopping center on Nob Hill Road, located a parking space, and shut off the engine. As she opened the door, he said, "There's something I've been meaning to tell you. Something you should know."

"Oh?" She closed the door and scanned his face. "What?"

He tapped the steering wheel with his index finger. "I received a phone call three days ago from Sean's teacher. She called to advise me that his work is suffering, and his grades are dropping."

"Are you serious?" Her voice rose.

"Very. She quizzed me about our home life. She wanted to know if everything was okay because he fit the profile of a student that was not getting the proper attention from his family."

"And what did you tell her?" she snapped.

"I told her that our son is a fine boy, that there were no problems at home, and that I would talk to him. But I wanted to talk to you first."

Laurie sat mute. When her eyes darted to his finger tapping on the wheel, Randy recognized the killer look and abruptly stopped.

The whole thing was eating up his insides. *I can't hold it in. You know how I am.* He reached into the glove compartment for a antacid tablet, popped it in his mouth, and gave it four chews before swallowing the chalky mass. *I have to get it all out.* "Then, before the phone was cold, Lester and Ronnie showed up at my doorstep."

Laurie stiffened. At times the deacons could act like pallbearers at a funeral. "Oh, great. What did they want?"

Randy knuckled the steering wheel with both hands. "They came to counsel me."

"Yeah, right." She rolled her eyes. "It was about me, wasn't it?"

"Well, yes."

With rising anger, she said, "Okay, Wilson Randolph Bradshaw, let's have it. What was their beef?"

"Hold on, Laurie. Don't unravel on me," he placated. "Lester and Ronnie are godly men with the ministry, their pastor, and his wife's interest at heart."

"Don't give me their résumé!" she demanded. "What did they say?!"

Knowing her temper had a short fuse and that provoking it only meant a protracted argument, he attempted to minimize the confrontation. "Calm down, Laurie. Just calm down, and we can discuss this."

That was the wrong thing to say, like throwing gasoline on a fire. "I'm *waiting*, Randy!"

"They asked if there were some kind of problem at home. They claim that over the past several months you have become distant, even detached toward the ministry. Some of the exact words they used were *indifferent* and a *change in attitude*. They cited your reaction to that homeless woman as an example of the outworking of that state of mind."

She shook her head in disgust. "When they drop a complaint, they use a bomb, don't they?"

"They mean well."

"And what did you say to them?"

"I said you were under a lot of pressure with your schoolwork and your family responsibilities."

A grimace appeared. "I don't need this stuff, Randy. At this time of my life, I need freedom from the demands of the children and *your* ministry if I am to finish school. Remember, I have a life too."

"*Our* ministry," he corrected but decided not to pursue and debate her logic. She didn't have the presence of mind right now to hear what he wanted her to hear. Nor, for that matter, what God wanted her to hear—that her heart was growing cold toward Him.

"Fine. "Our ministry." After several minutes of contemplation, she reached for the handle and opened the door.

"Hold it!" Randy said with controlled alarm. "Is that it? No discussion? No resolution? Just a grand exit?"

She closed the door slowly and faced him squarely. "I'm sick of the whole 'church thing.' I need a break from those people, your deacons, the homeless, and the ministry at Plantation Gate. Until I finish school, *I need to be ministered unto!* I can't act in the capacity of a pastor's wife and minister to others right now. I don't have the strength or the ability to keep all these plates balanced and spinning in the air. Can you understand that?"

Randy shot up a prayer, asking for the wisdom to counsel his own wife, an elusive gift few possess. "Yes, I can understand where you're coming from." He sighed. "We'll just have to trust the Lord to get us through, that's all."

"As far as Sean is concerned," she said with a voice vibrating with emotion, "I'll spend more time with him, do more things with him, and bring him back around again. "I'll make it up to him."

Randy's breath caught in his throat at this watershed discussion in their relationship. "Praise the Lord," he said with a tear in his eye.

Laurie stepped out of the car to attend to her shopping.

4

The long line of illuminated taillights in the Nob Hill Road Elementary School zone only meant one thing to Randy: Delay. The white-and-black-lettered sign with the yellow flashing light on busy streets in South Florida always galled him. *Up North they do it differently*, he thought. Up there they strategically placed schools in areas *away* from the main roads. *Suck it up, Randy. Remember, it gives you time to think.*

The line inched along until it came to a complete stop at the traffic light at Cleary Boulevard, where the sign that made him happy appeared: *End school zone.*

Yes! He gazed off down the road waiting for the light to turn green.

"Paper mister?" an aging street merchant asked as he flashed the *Florida Sentinel* in front of his face.

"No thank you, pal." *That's what I get for keeping my windows open.* He pressed the buttons to raise all his windows.

As the traffic stood still, two other men wearing red T-shirts holding plastic containers and a newsletter vigorously walked up and down the median. One stopped in front of Randy's window and held up his container in one hand and the newsletter in the other. His image flashed in Randy's mind, but he couldn't place the face. They were distributing *The Homeless Outreach Gazette* while asking for donations. Randy reached above his sun visor and pulled out a five-dollar bill; this was his weekly offering to the homeless. He lowered the window, dropped it in the container, and waved off the offer of the free paper.

"Pastor Randy?" the man said.

Randy took a double-take. It was Marty. "Well, hello, brother!" he blurted. "I didn't recognize you at first." He was clean shaven with his hair washed and neatly combed. His stomach protrusion was slightly camouflaged by his new, loose-fitting T-shirt that bore the name of the outreach group.

Two horn blasts from behind.

Randy glanced into the rearview mirror and saw a motorist's obscene gesture. "Come to the church today, and I'll treat you to lunch."

"You got it, Pastor." Marty winked and backed off as Randy stepped on the gas pedal and sped away.

* * *

Lester handed Yvonne the tithes and offerings count from the Sunday worship service. "We made budget," he proclaimed with a grin. Lester was in charge of assigning select members of the congregation to the counting committee, an offshoot of the finance committee that oversaw the church's annual budget.

"Praise the Lord, once again," Yvonne said with her usual cheery face, even when they didn't make budget. Moments later the outside office door abruptly opened with Marty holding a stack of the newsletters under his arm. "Can we help you?" she asked with slight consternation as she scanned him up and down, her cheery face vanishing.

"Is Pastor Randy in?" he asked sheepishly as he stepped gingerly into the office.

Yvonne had little experience in dealing with the unfortunate. "And *who* shall I say is asking for him?"

"I'm a friend of…," he started to say.

"Well, hello, Marty!" Pastor Randy popped his head out his office door. "I thought I heard a familiar voice." He turned to Yvonne. "Please show my friend in."

Yvonne stroked the side of her face in an attempt to conceal the reddening. Randy made himself a mental note to speak to her regarding her apparent attitude toward the homeless. After escorting Marty to the pastor's office, she closed the door behind him.

Randy pointed to a vacant chair. "How is Stephanie?"

Marty sighed as he sat down. "She wasn't feeling so good this morning. I think she was heading for the homeless shelter to try and get some medical attention."

"Is it anything serious?" Randy probed.

With shoulders hunched he said, "Could be. We homeless people have a multitude of medical problems. In some cases, we die quickly, while in others, there are infected limbs or poor circulation or wounds that won't heal because of an untreated diabetic condition, so we just die a slow death."

The hairs on Randy's neck stood on end. His compassion for the homeless was growing with every passing encounter. "Tell me what happens when a sick homeless person goes to a hospital for help."

Marty's lips pursed in a soundless whistle. "You don't want to know, Pastor. It's rough out there if you're a homeless nobody."

"Tell me, Marty. I want to know," Randy pressed.

"If a homeless person goes to a hospital," he began somberly, "and it's an emergency...you know, if one of us was hit by a car by some careless driver while standing in the streets hawking papers or asking for donations for the Homeless Outreach, then we'd probably not be turned out. But if it's something like this..." He stopped suddenly, lifted his shirt, ad pointed to the hernia. "Then we're given a pat on the head with a cold handshake and released to the streets to tough it out until the condition becomes life-threatening."

"Unbelievable." Randy reached for one of the Homeless Outreach newsletters. "What are these people able to do for you?"

"This organization gives us dignity and hope. Before I connected with them, I was what some called 'a powerful environmentalist.' I roamed the community around I-595 with a shopping cart scrounging aluminum cans and bringing them to a recycling plant for pennies so I could eat. I maintained my sanity and independence by cleaning up the streets from people who throw their empty beer and soda cans out their car windows. Before that I just sponged off society at a busy intersection with a tricky cardboard sign that said, *Will work for food.* But now that I've joined up with HO, they give me a place to eat, and I earn enough to go to a diner once in a while."

"Sounds like a worthy league of people eager to help the homeless." Randy decided to look into the organization to see how his church could assist them to meet the needs of the abandoned. There were just too many encounters with the homeless for him to ignore God's leading.

"It's a shame the HO doesn't get any consideration from public officials," Marty lamented.

"Oh? How so?"

"Well, the mayor of Sunrise Park arbitrarily decided to invoke an old law on the books that says a person cannot go on to the paved portion of the street to solicit donations. It seems that the city has never enforced this law on the regular newspaper vendors or the firemen who stand on the corners waving a boot in the air looking for donations. But this mayor decided that we should go. He doesn't want the homeless coming up to cars and asking for anything. So we have to stay on the medians to sell *The Homeless Outreach Gazette.* This severely limits our ability to raise money. Of course, if we were collecting money for any other cause, be it AIDS or for some high school fundraiser, it wouldn't be a problem. But for the homeless, it is."

"What about door-to-door?"

Marty shook his head. "The director feels it's too intrusive. People don't want the homeless traipsing around their neighborhoods asking for charity.

Even though it's protected under a Supreme Court ruling upholding a First Amendment right, homeowners feel intimidated when a stranger knocks on their door seeking donations. "Besides, our people suffer enough in life. They don't need annoyed residents making rude and demeaning comments like, 'Go get a job, you lazy bum,' then slamming a door in their face. No, something has to be done to make it easier for us."

Randy's heart broke for him and his cause. If he had a solution for this, he'd rival Solomon. "Sounds pretty grim, Marty."

"It does. But for me, things are different now. I have a renewed hope."

Randy quickly connected the dots. "You mean now that you're right with God by receiving Christ yesterday?"

Marty gave him a thumbs'-up. "Amen."

"How about a cup of coffee before we go to lunch, Marty?"

Marty's face radiated a smile, reveling in the conversation. "Sure."

Amazing how some people's lives are so quickly changed by a touch of the Master and a helping hand from one of His servants. Randy walked across the room and opened the door. "Yvonne, can you fix us up two cups of coffee? Cream and sugar." He stopped short and added, "And how about some of that chocolate biscotti and those little sticky buns?"

Seeing tears in Marty's eyes, Randy pulled his chair closer. "Would you mind telling me how you came to be like this? I mean, what's your story?"

Marty's eyes flicked to his face, then away. Seconds later he gazed intently at Randy. "I can trust you, right?"

Randy made two quotation mark gestures with his hands. "Pastor's confidentiality."

Marty mentally traveled back to recall the events that led up to his homelessness. He squirmed in the chair while extracting painful memories. "It was about six years ago when it all happened. I was working as a stockbroker for a major brokerage firm in New York, providing a comfortable life for my family—my wife, Jill, and our two teenage boys. I had been with this company for over 20 years when I decided to go back to school and get my graduate degree. It wasn't easy for me to take on 12 credits per semester— "full-time" school—while still performing my full-time duties with my company. Of course, I still had my family responsibilities. Then, in my last year of school, I guess the course load got to me and my judgment became clouded; I had an ethical failure at work. I confessed to our corporate home office, but despite my appeals for mercy in consideration for my faithful years of service, they fired me. I managed to finish school and get my graduate degree, but I couldn't get another job in the brokerage business because my former employer filed a misconduct report with the State. So I had a record. I had a graduate degree, but no job.

"My wife tried to keep us afloat, but her job didn't pay enough. In time we cashed in our insurance policies and withdrew all our savings just to live on. Nevertheless, within a year our home was foreclosed on. I was so humiliated. My relatives disowned me. My friends bailed. After another year of searching for a different line of work, my wife met someone else." His eyes misted as he rubbed an imaginary ring on his finger. "I even had to sell my wedding ring and all my jewelry. After a while, there was nothing left to sell."

"The children?" Pastor Randy asked.

"Our two boys went with their mother." He pulled a plastic sandwich bag with several photos from his pocket and thumbed through them. "They're safe now," he said painfully. "Their mother married a wealthy entrepreneur who can take care of all of them." He rubbed his eyes. "I didn't have the strength or faith to overcome the pain, so I hit the streets. My life revolved around a bottle of bourbon and any other medicinal remedy to ease my hurting heart. In time the pain gave way to anger and I started to steal to live, I guess to try and get back at the 'establishment.' But, fortunately, that was short lived. When I began to sober up, I realized I had no one to blame but myself. But by then, three years had passed." He shook his head and looked heavenward. "Thank God I never did hard drugs.

"I have no money, no home, or apartment. No household goods or clothes except those on my back. But I do have my memories as I hold out the cup to those who pass me on the street." He shrugged in a self-deprecating way then stuffed his treasured sandwich bag into his pocket.

Randy rose to his feet and put his hand on Marty's shoulder. "You now have more than many do. You have Jesus as your Savior."

Marty looked up at him. "I wonder what God is going to do with my life."

Yvonne knocked on the door. "Pastor, your coffee and goodies."

Randy opened his office door and took the tray. "Ah, the nectar and food of the gods!" He closed the door again. "Marty, I believe the Lord will use your experiences as a platform for ministry, if you allow Him. "If you are of the mind to turn your life over to Him, He will totally change it so that it becomes a sweet offering unto Himself. This is God's way."

"It's a cinch my life needs to be under new management," Marty agreed.

Over the next hour, Randy laid out a plan of discipleship and commitment for Marty to grow in the grace and knowledge of Christ. He was excited to get started. As they left for lunch, Randy hummed the hymn, "Redeemed."

* * *

Randy swallowed an antacid pill to help combat his acid-reflux condition as he walked into the church office area. The chicken caesar salad he'd had for lunch didn't agree with him. He nodded to Yvonne, who sat busily working on the church's computer terminal. "Got a minute?"

The hackles on Yvonne's neck rose. She knew Pastor Randy long enough to know when he was grieved in his spirit and needed to talk it out. She saved the budget data on her computer, then slid off her chair. "Coming."

Randy escorted her to the chair in front of his desk, then pulled up another chair and sat next to her. "I'm not sure what the mind of the Lord is regarding the future outreach ministry here at Plantation Gate, but one thing is for sure: we need to be of one mind in order for the Lord to bless us. That means, starting from the administrative staff on down to the man in the pew, that we have the proper attitude toward the people God sends us."

Yvonne nervously shifted her weight in the chair. Her keen discernment alerted her to the problem. "I know I didn't react to that man like a Christian should have," she admitted. "I've already gone before the Lord and asked him to cleanse my heart."

Randy recognized repentance when he saw it. "Good. Praise the Lord. Now let's move on. I'd like you to contact the director of the Homeless Outreach newsletter organization and make me an appointment to meet with him. I believe the Lord's Spirit is moving in our midst and He has a message for us, and I don't want to miss the call."

"I want to be a part of that blessing too." Yvonne smiled broadly and exited the room.

Five minutes later she announced that a cordial meeting with Sam Knowles, the director of Homeless Outreach, had been made. He would come to Pastor Randy's office tomorrow at one o' clock.

* * *

Arriving home one hour before Laurie or Tiffany allowed Randy ample time to be alone with his son. He checked his watch and ticked off the minutes before Sean would get off the school bus. In the meantime he rehearsed what he would say: *Be objective*, he commanded himself, *get to the heart of the matter. No finger-pointing or blame-shifting. Resolve quickly.* He fixed himself a cup of coffee and waited.

Five minutes later, the front door swung open and Sean scaled the stairs to his room. Then the bathroom door slammed, but seconds later opened with gusto, hitting the doorstop with a thud.

"Sean, I'd like to talk to you," his father called. "I'm coming up."

"That's cool, Dad," Sean called back.

Randy stumbled over his son's lacrosse stick propped up on the hallway wall. He walked into Sean's room, sat on his bed, and looked around to remind himself of the diversity in his son's interests. Here was a boy who apparently loved the Lord, who maintained a good Christian witness among his friends, was a real "jock," and loved the natural sciences.

By the window stood a 5-inch Schmidt-Cassegrain reflector telescope on a tripod. Adorning his walls were a series of celestial photographs that attested to his interest in astronomy. The photographs were prints from the Hubble telescope featuring the interior planets as well as deep-sky pictures. In addition to a chart showing the Right Ascension and Declination of the planets and the constellations in the Northern hemisphere were large prints of the Horsehead and Cone nebulae. Filling another wall were poster-size photos of the nebulae in southern Orion and a rich star field in Cygnus. Randy marveled at the photographs. *How manifold are thy works, Oh Lord!*

"So, what's up, Dad?" Sean stood in the doorway, swaying back and forth.

Randy nodded toward the bed. "Sit down a minute." Turning on his soothing voice, his everything-will-be-all right voice, he added, "We need to talk."

Sean's worried eyes were riveted on his father's. He walked to the bed and sat next to his father. "Is everything okay?"

Putting his arm around his son, Randy asked, "You would tell me if there was anything bothering you, right?"

"Sure, Dad." he said, biting on his pinky finger.

"I'm troubled over your schoolwork. I have a feeling there's something bothering you, and I'd like to talk to you about it."

"Did Mrs. Lambert call you?" he asked as a wounded look surfaced.

"Yes, and we had a nice conversation about you. It seems that she's concerned about your ability to focus on your work and suspects there's a problem at home." He pulled his son closer. "Is that so? Is there a problem at home that we should talk about? You can tell me, Sean. I'm your dad, and I love you and care about your life."

Sean fidgeted for several seconds. "Um."

"Whatever it is, you can tell me," Randy ventured.

"There's nothing wrong." Sean's elusive eyes roamed the room.

Randy remembered a verse out of Proverbs: *The purpose of a man's heart are deep waters, but a man of understanding draws them out.* He had to probe his son gently. "Okay, let's say you were unhappy about something that was going on at home, but you were afraid to ask Mom or Dad any questions. So what effect would that have on you? Well, it could make a difference in many things. For example: the way you perform at school as well as the way you interact with your friends. It might even spill over into your lacrosse. Then, of course, it might change the way you act at home. While we haven't noticed much of a difference at home, there must be something bothering you; otherwise Mrs. Lambert wouldn't have called me. So, how about it? Tell me what it is. No matter how serious, you won't get into trouble."

Sean shrugged twice, then stared downward. A tear fell on the floor. "It's Mom," he said finally. "I can't talk to her anymore. When she comes home from school, she always acts like she's far away, and I don't want to bother her about my problems. When she's working on her papers at her desk, I know that's a bad time too. So I just keep to myself." He shook his head. "I know I can talk to you, but sometimes I like to talk to Mom about some things."

Randy felt a sad pang in his heart. "Mom's almost finished with school," he consoled, "so that will lighten up her schedule. Then she'll be able to spend a lot more time with the family."

"Dad, let's be honest," Sean said with a wry expression. "Mom's probably planning on getting a job after she graduates, and things will only get worse."

Mythical philosophies that taught otherwise were burned away with the fire of discovery. Randy marveled at his son's instinctive powers. Nevertheless, he had to dispel any faulty reasoning that could only polarize his relationship with his mother. "Not necessarily." He waved dismissively. "Your mother loves you very much and her family is a priority. That means that once school is over, and our lives return to normal, our family will get her full attention." *Isn't that right, Lord?* he asked himself.

A deep sigh, then, "I guess so." He looked his dad in the eyes and smiled.

"I don't want you to worry about it, Sean. You'll see—everything has a way of working itself out." He stood and extended his hand for a high-five. "Are we in agreement?"

Sean returned the high-five. "Can we pray about it, Dad?"

Randy stuck his tongue into his cheek. *Hmm, shouldn't I have asked that?* "Of course."

* * *

It was Tuesday night. The night designated early in their marriage as a special evening for Randy and Laurie. The night when controversial or argumentative issues were avoided in order to promote the alchemy and commonality between them. Often filled with reminiscing and reverie, it was a night set aside for romance and fun that augmented any spontaneity that may arise during the rest of the week. A night they both looked forward to.

As Laurie walked in the house from school she quickly noticed two candles burning amidst two place settings on the dining room table. Complete with cloth napkins and the good silverware. Two glasses of sparkling water adorned the table as well. *Looks good.*

"Dinner will be ready in ten minutes," she heard Randy shout from the kitchen. "Go make yourself comfortable." He walked to the stereo component system and turned on the CD player. Seconds later Rachmaninov's *Piano Concerto No. 2, Op. 18* flowed softly throughout the rooms.

"Sounds terrific," she replied while walking to the bathroom. She stopped short. No noise from the children. "Where are the kids?"

"I dropped them off at the bowling alley. We're good for a few hours."

"Nice." *This guy turns my toes up; he thinks of everything.*

The dinner was especially planned for Laurie. Poached salmon along with a hollandaise sauce with couscous, water chestnuts, and steamed asparagus. A bakery-bought cheesecake served as the dessert along with French roast coffee.

Minutes later Laurie walked out from their bedroom wearing her robe over a black negligee. She took one look at the dining room table, focused on the poached salmon delicately placed on a platter and adorned with several parsley sprigs, then up at Randy and said with a whistle, "You really know how to show a girl a good time, don't you?"

Randy scanned her up and down with an amorous gleam. "Just for you, baby, just for you." He escorted her to her seat.

"Oh, so gallant!" He brushed the hair on her neck aside and kissed her. "A portend of that which is to come?"

"Setting the night up," he replied with a boyish grin.

The dinner went well, with Randy directing the "breezy tour," as he called it. The kind of conversation that purposely avoids any theme that could lead to conflict.

With the dessert served, Randy embarked on perilous waters. "I spoke to Sean today about the call from his teacher."

Laurie slowly placed her coffee cup on its saucer as her glowing countenance faded. She looked intently at him. "And?"

He returned the stare. "It went very well."

"Tell me what he said."

Fully cognizant of her unwitting favoritism toward Sean, he had to mollify the charge for the benefit of both of them. "He said that he loves you and misses your little talks, that's all."

She held his gaze, then said, "Oh, that's it?" Definitely relieved.

"That was it. From there I simply advised him that once school was over, you would have a lot more time to spend with him. He was fine with all of it."

She nodded in appreciation. "That's right. Thanks for smoothing things over."

The rest of the evening went exactly as he had planned.

* * *

"Ah, yes, *Things To Come*." Randy scanned his library shelves for reference for his Wednesday night Bible study. "The consummate text on End Times by Pentecost." He opened the book to the section on the Pre-tribulation Rapture position to refresh his memory, then walked to his computer console where his Bible lay open to the book of Revelation. Tonight he would be teaching on Bible prophecy in conjunction with Dispensationalism.

A knock at his door...

"Pastor Randy, a Mr. Sam Knowles is here to see you."

Randy looked at his wristwatch. Exactly one o'clock. He walked into the office lobby to see a well-dressed man carefully examining the Bible land photographs lining the walls. "Hello, Mr. Knowles," Randy greeted cheerfully, "I'm Pastor Randy."

As Sam Knowles pointed to the signature on the matte of the photograph of the Temple Mount from the Mount of Olives, he asked with wonder, "Did you take this?"

"Ah, yes." Randy motioned to the entire wall of photos. "These are large prints made from 35 mm chromes I took when I hosted my last tour to the Holy Land."

"Isn't that the Wailing Wall?" Sam gestured to a 18x24-inch Cibachrome taken at night with only the security lights reflecting off the ancient monument.

"Yes," Randy said, glowing.

Sam then stepped closer to see the fine detail where prayer requests from the faithful were written on small pieces of paper, then wedged between the massive stones that made up the Wall.

Randy then moved to another large print. "And this is the ancient synagogue at Capernaum on the shore of Lake Galilee." Stepping to another of the Garden Tomb, he said, "And this is Christ's tomb." He grinned. "Of course He's not there, thank God."

"Yes, thank God," Sam agreed as he scanned the beautiful array of photographs. "Really excellent photography," he marveled. "Someday I'd like to go there."

"May it be so," Randy replied as they walked into his office. Randy closed the door behind them and escorted Sam to one of the stuffed chairs. "Tell me about your ministry, Sam. I'm really very interested in it."

"We had a humble, yet unusual beginning. Back in 1996, I was standing on the corner of Commercial Boulevard and I-95 holding up a cardboard sign that read: *Help The Homeless* when a man pulled up in a luxury car, rolled down his window, and asked to speak to me. Warily, I put down the sign and walked to his car, where he invited me in. I had second thoughts, but then I compared the clothes I was wearing—a ragged pair of jeans and flip-flops with a Marlins sweatshirt—to the three-piece suit he was wearing and figured, *What have I got to lose?*

Once I got in his car he motioned to his driver, who in turn pulled around to a gas station across the street. His driver went in to the convenience store and brought out two cups of coffee and cream-filled donuts for us both. I couldn't believe what was happening! This man quizzed me for at least half an hour, then picked up his cell phone and made several inquiries about me while I sat in his car. Next, the man, whom I later found out was a partner of one of Broward County's largest real-estate developers, offered to finance a homeless person's shelter if I would run it. What he saw in me I'll never know. Flabbergasted, I agreed. From there we set up several meetings and then, within three months, I was off the streets, behind a desk, and wearing all new clothes."

Pastor Randy was stunned. Sitting with him was a squat, bald, and homely man, chosen by a humanitarian philanthropist who was directed by divine providence to select a man off the streets to run an organization that would meet the need of hundreds of vagabonds and misfits. The impact this kind of program would have on society seemed unprecedented. *Isn't that just like God! To choose from among the common and turn it into precious gold. To rebuild a broken vessel and turn it out to do wonders on the earth. Oh, how marvelous!* And this unpretentious man, who remembered from whence he came, fully aware of his background of homelessness, now determined to use that resource as a platform to help others. *Unbelievable!*

"That's a fantastic testimonial. You see, Sam, I have a burden from God to help the homeless, and as a pastor, I am thinking of asking our congregation to support your work. But I'd like to know a little more about those you've helped before I proceed. Can you help me with that?"

"Of course." Sam blinked several times as if to recall detailed information. "I distinctly remember one case where a young lady of 24 came to our rescue home one day about a year ago. She sat with me for over an hour and unloaded her story. Quite unbelievable, yet common among the homeless. She puffed heavily on her cigarette as she explained that she couldn't pinpoint how she got where she was, but her mind wandered back to a time when, nine months earlier, she'd learned she was pregnant. When she came home from the doctor's office, she was bubbling with excitement at the thought of telling her boyfriend. When he came home from work to their apartment, she told him that he was going to be a father. His countenance changed, and he said he needed to lie down. He was asleep when the young lady went to bed hours later. Sometime during the night she was violently awakened to her boyfriend punching her repeatedly. When he finally stopped, she went into the bathroom, where she knew she lost the baby. That was the last time she saw her boyfriend.

"After her hospital stay, she moved into a hotel about an hour away. She had not talked to her parents in years and when she called them, they immediately hung up. She knew the little money she had would not last, but she couldn't bring herself to get a job, let alone get out of bed. She had dreams of her girlhood days with her family. Of the Christmas they spent in London, where elegant men and women drank champagne and dined luxuriously. Dreams of when she was 17 and a group of her friends had rented a cabin in the Catskill mountains where they frolicked in the snow and drank cocktails in the hot tub. Dreams of when, at 22 she and her boyfriend pulled the levers at the casinos in Las Vegas and spent the rest of the evening in their hotel room, celebrating each other.

"Then dreams of her unborn baby interrupted all of those other dreams. They would be playing dress-up, going to the zoo, getting ready for the prom. All those dreams ended when something terrible happened to the child. During her waking hours, she would watch the television and start crying hysterically whenever she saw a pregnant woman. After six months, she was kicked out of the hotel for nonpayment of her rent. She spent six weeks on the streets dodging the police until she was picked up sleeping under a bridge on I-595. They took her to our shelter, where she began to regain her health and reasoning powers.

"We asked her if she had any work skills, and she said she had worked in a nursing home as a cook for a couple of years. The next day we called day-labor and they sent her to the local hospital as a dishwasher. The little money she made went to her uniform and her stay at our shelter. The work was tiring and repetitive, but it was better than lying under a bridge. She often said she was discouraged at being homeless, but she had a good spirit and didn't blame others for her misfortune.

"Then one day, as she headed for the hospital kitchen, one of the nurses stopped her and asked her to follow her upstairs instead. Unbeknown to her, the nurse had spoken to the kitchen staff and had her transferred to the upstairs nursery. Once she heard those words, her heart jumped for joy. Her first duty was to hold a little baby girl whose mother had neglected her. She was unrespondent and would need a lot of love, nurturing, and a special touch to survive..." Overcome with tears, Sam dabbed at his eyes.

"This young lady spent the entire day holding this child," he added through muffled tones. "She rocked the infant back and forth, sang her lullabies, and softly cooed in her ear. When the day was over, she reluctantly went home. It had been the best day of her life. Better than London. Better than the Catskills. Better than Las Vegas. When she went to bed that night with five other girls in the room, she thanked God for this little infant who gave her a day of joy. She fell asleep smiling. That night all her dreams had happy endings."

"That's an incredible story!" Randy shook his head in wonder. "It really lifts you spirits to know how God is working in and among the people so often ignored by society."

"Yes, that young lady is now one of our captains who oversees some of the newer entrants who come in off the streets. Of course, not all our stories have happy endings like this one," Sam noted. "We have a man in our shelter who has two Master's degrees, but in his late 40s came down with mental illness. He has no family and no insurance. He had several jobs in the past, but was fired. Occasionally he works odd jobs but can't earn enough to get a home or even an apartment. Besides, he needs someone to look after him. Sometimes he finds folks to share a place with, but that doesn't work out for long periods."

Sam's chin firmed in determination. "Approximately 22 percent of the single homeless population suffer from some form of severe and persistent mental illness, while only 5-7 percent of homeless persons with mental illness require institutionalization; most can live in the community with the appropriate supportive housing options. Many of the homeless are working; at least 20 percent of the urban homeless are employed." His eyes glimmered with frustration. "A recent study of 27 U. S. cities found that there are infants and children on the streets. You know why? Because 52 percent of the emergency shelter requests by needy families were denied." Tears threatened again. "These are my people, and they need help."

Randy was speechless. He knew he had to help, somehow. His relationship with God dictated that he couldn't say no, and he believed God was engineering a plan. "How can we as a church help you?"

"First, we need help with area churches to fight against the politicians seeking to rid the towns of the homeless. Second, we need spiritual and financial support for my people."

Randy suddenly saw Sam as a type of deliverer—a Moses who would lead *his* people, as he put it, out of the wilderness of the abandoned, into the Promise Land of integrity and productivity. For the next hour, they discussed strategy, visions, and resolutions. They parted as friends with a purpose.

Reveling in promise and fulfillment, Randy called Laurie on her cell phone to share with her his wonderful experiences with Sam Knowles.

But when she heard the account, she hung up on him.

5

The view of the sanctuary pews from the pulpit on Wednesday afternoon differed dramatically from the view on Sunday morning. There were no people, no deacons, no organist, no pianist. No members of his family. Just oak pews and walls spattered with multi-colored light coming in from the floor-to-ceiling stained glass windows. Of course the blue and gray carpet added to the hues and tones, creating a warming atmosphere, but the sanctuary remained cavernous without the people that made up the church. *It's not the building, but the people who make up the church*, Randy reminded himself.

He stood in the pulpit scanning the pews, remembering where the members of his congregation sat on Sunday. *People are so predictable.* Each member, each week, systematically entered the sanctuary, then mechanically, as if preordained by some divine decree of predestination, sat in the same general area, if not the same pew, week after week. *Territoriality fanatics unite!* Despite his encouraging pleas and tactics to bring his people to mix with guests and fellow congregants, man in his perpetual resistance to change, invariably returned to his designated nesting spot.

Looking at his wristwatch: *In an hour Laurie will be here for Bible study night. I need to decide how to react to the hanging-up tactic.* Scanning the pews once again: *Lord, why is she this way? Why the hardness to these homeless people; even the things of ministry? A conundrum—that's what it is. A mystery wrapped up in an enigma, that's what I'm dealing with.*

"Pastor Randy?" he heard from the side aisle.

He turned to see Yvonne walking into the sanctuary from the narthex. "Yes?"

Yvonne walked face down toward the pulpit with the wireless phone in her hand. "Pastor Randy, can we talk a moment? I just received a disturbing phone call from my sister in New Jersey."

"Of course." The need for counseling often coming at unusual times, he escorted her to the nearest pew and sat down. "What's the problem?"

A few tears appeared in the corner of her eyes as she fiddled with her hands. "Well, you remember my younger sister, Julie, who has been living with a man for the past eight years, right?"

He nodded. "Yes, you've talked about her often."

"Well, he just walked out on her and their little boy, and she's crumbling fast."

"Ugh." In quick reflection, he remembered reading about the alarming statistics regarding households headed by unmarried partners recently and the impact it has had on society. Households with couples living out of wedlock grew by almost 72 percent during the past decade while other studies uncovered the sad fact that cohabitation increased by close to 1,000 percent from 1960 to 1998. *Yes, Lord, it seems the institution of the family is unraveling at a rapid pace.* The old taboos against divorce and cohabitation are going the way of the dodo bird: into extinction, with society abandoning its commitment to lifelong marriage.

"I think my sister can make it, but I'm worried about Matthew," she lamented.

"Matthew?

"That's Julie's son by Steve, the turkey who bailed out on her."

Randy shook his head and quoted, "Oh, what evil webs we weave." *Another episode in society that leads to the future life of the homeless.* The tragedy of an increasing number of children within the homeless population coming in part from the disintegration of the family. The breakdown of traditional family structures and values, along with divorce, desertion, and separation making the home as unstable as the Mideast peace talks. "Tell me what happened."

Yvonne dried her tears. "She found out he had been molesting Matthew for the past year...from when he turned seven. She told him she was going to report him to the police and that she hoped they locked him up and threw away the key. So he took off. How could she be so lacking in discernment? Now her child has been scarred for life because of her poor choices."

Shaking his head again, sarcastically: "Nice guy." *Another disaster to add to the rising statistic that supported the claim that living together doesn't work for society. What was the percentage of sexual abuse of children by a household member?* He couldn't remember, but it was a dreadful figure. He only knew that as a society we are at great risk in a culture where anything goes and children are being born without the stability of marriage. "This is serious stuff, Yvonne. Tell me something about her relationship with God. Perhaps we can start there."

"She claimed to have had a salvation experience when she was in high school, at a camp meeting, but frankly, I've never seen any fruit from her so-called experience." She sighed. "I really don't think she's saved."

"That's a good starting point right there: her relationship with God. She needs to be assured of God's never-failing love for her. In her affliction, let's pray she seeks the Lord. Perhaps now would be a good time to share the gospel with her. Yvonne, she and her son are going to need good Christian counseling. I can recommend someone if she's interested."

She looked aside so as to envision her sister's suffering. "I know she's a wreck right now…wondering where to go, who to turn to."

"Don't you think you should go to her? Try to minister to her?"

After reflection: "I want to go, but we'll see what happens after a few days. For now, I'll call and try to convince her to seek out a nearby pastor."

"You don't think there's any cause for alarm, do you? I mean, there's no possibility of her committing suicide, do you?" Rightfully, as a counselor, the law required that if there is any mention of suicide by a counselee, the counselor must notify law enforcement authorities.

"No, of that I'm sure."

"Good. Let's pray together and ask the Lord to intervene on her behalf so that His Spirit may meet her needs, beginning with her salvation and then on to this situation."

Yvonne nodded, and they prayed, believing.

* * *

Redeemed, how I love to proclaim it…Randy's cell phone chimed with his favorite custom Christian hymn that he'd downloaded off the Internet. "I stopped off at home and picked up the kids. I'll be there in 30 minutes so we can talk," Laurie declared in an irritated tone. *Click.*

Looks like I'm in for a fight. Predictable. Almost without fail, Satan and his cohorts were out and about, harassing, inciting chaos and spreading seeds of discord on a night designated for spiritual nourishment. Bringing malevolence and discontent into the lives of the Christian church, invariably stoking the fires of unbelief just before the Wednesday night Bible study was what they did best. All with the purpose of discouraging the Christian. *Well, he's not going to get the victory tonight,* Randy pledged.

* * *

"How deep do you want to get involved with *these* people?!" Laurie snapped the moment she stormed into Randy's office, with Tiffany and Sean trailing behind.

Randy refused to argue or discuss controversial ministry subjects in front of his children. He smiled as he pointed his index finger and said, "Tiffy, Sean, we'll meet you in the fellowship hall for dinner." They shrugged, did an abrupt about-face, and walked out. Once out of sight, Randy closed his office door. "Laurie, sit down and cool off!" he ordered.

Her eyes drilled into his as she put on her battle dress. "I will not!" She circled the room twice and then mounted her war horse. "Just what is going on with you? Why are you flying off on this tangent to bring in homeless people?" She jammed her hand on her hip. "Is this some crazy whim of yours to cause the congregation to do penance over some sin?"

"It's nothing like that. I believe the Lord is bringing the homeless into the church's path to both minister to them in their needs while blessing us along the way. That's it."

"While you *entertained* those characters Stephanie and Marty, I let it go, thinking this was simply a passing fancy. But now that you're making arrangements with the head of Homeless Outreach to ratchet up this relationship, I must object."

Turned the other way? Ha! You complained from the minute the homeless came through our doors. Oh, how we can delude ourselves. "Object all you want," he argued, "but if this is of the Lord, your objections will not be able to stop what God is doing. You will not be able to fight against God."

"You're starting to have a shelf-life problem," she said in mock solemnity. "You're unwittingly quoting from the Pharisee Gamaliel, and it doesn't work here."

"Tell me then, what does work with you?! Unless an issue has something to do with your schooling and your career, it doesn't work. Is that it?" He could feel his anger mounting. *Don't retaliate! Don't win the battle and lose the war. Cool your jets.* He reigned in his emotions and approached her.

She held her hand up. The conversation was over.

"Do we have to fight about this? Especially right before Bible study?" he entreated. "I know you may not agree with my philosophy of ministry right now, but can't you be patient so we can see what the Lord is doing here?"

Suddenly, in her mind's eye, the flashback of a dimly lit room in the rear of her home church came into view. It was the athletic equipment storage room for the youth group. She was running an errand for the youth pastor when she turned to close the door, only to see the man with the red sweatshirt watching her from behind. Laurie squeezed her eyes shut to rid herself of the memory. *Go on!* she demanded of herself. *Forget!* she commanded. Seconds later she took a deep breath.

"Are you all right?" Randy asked, wondering why her demeanor changed.

Resolute: "Okay, okay, fine. We'll call a truce for now." Amazingly, her attitude changed as if she had zoned out momentarily. It was as if she just turned a switch in her mind and wiped away the quarrel. She smiled at Randy as she recounted her day at school. Then they went to dinner with Randy making a mental note of the disturbing change in her behavior.

* * *

As Randy and Laurie walked up to the door of the Bible study room, they heard what sounded like the human *buzz* of heated debates. They exchanged glances, then Randy opened the door. "What's all the commotion about?"

Ronnie Edeleson walked up to him and handed him an e-mail from a well-known evangelical research group. He scanned his congregation and realized they were all busy reading and discussing copies of it. The title was "Unbelieving born-agains."

"Unbelievable," Ronnie said as he walked away.

Laurie gave the back of Ronnie's head a dirty look, then pulled the e-mail out of Randy's hand, read the highlights, then handed it back to him. "Where does this guy get all these numbers from?" she said sourly.

"Let me see that." Randy knew the notable survey group was very reliable and not given to exaggeration. He read the paragraph headings as he walked to his chair. There were random survey results along with various high-profile Christian leader quotes ranging from disbelief to outrage. *Christians are not all that interested in converting the heathen. Christians now embrace the modern orthodoxy of tolerance and inclusion over the traditional teachings of their faith. Twenty-six percent of born-agains believe all religions are essentially the same and that 50 percent believe a life of good works will enable a person to get to heaven. More than 35 percent of born-again Christians do not believe that Jesus rose physically from the dead. Over half of the born-again Christians do not believe that the Holy Spirit is a living entity. Ten percent believe in reincarnation while 29 percent believe it is possible to communicate with the dead.*

He snapped the edge of the paper and flared his nose. *This stuff really sets my teeth on edge!* He turned to Laurie. "This is a well-documented source, so I guess we'll have to give this a serious look tonight." Folding up his prepared Bible study and setting aside the outlines, he made his mind up. He would change the topic of the Bible study. "Now, before everybody goes out of fellowship over this article, let's have a word of prayer and then dig into the

Bible to see what God has to tell us tonight." His calming voice brought a hush over the room as everybody bowed their heads.

The door opened while they prayed, and Stephanie and Marty quietly slipped past him on into the rear of the room, where they sat down. Randy peeked through his fingers to see Laurie rolling her eyes at the new arrivals.

Randy acknowledged the new arrivals with a nod, making a mental note of Stephanie's haggard condition, then said, "We're going to change the topic of our study tonight to *regeneration*. We'll cover the subject of discipleship another time." He opened his Bible to Titus. "The time has come for us to clarify an important truth: many so-called believers have never been regenerated in the Spirit, and therefore remain in unbelief. I know this flies in the face of contemporary thinking and theology, but the Scripture is our standard of truth and it says, *'Not by works of righteousness which we have done, but according to his mercy he saved us, by the washing of regeneration, and renewing of the Holy Ghost.'*" He closed his Bible and placed his right hand on top of it, Swallowing hard, he held up the e-mail. "I've been your pastor for over five years now, and I will tell you before God that, although this letter is disturbing, I'm not surprised at the findings.

"Before I came to his church, I made a pact with God that I would never take anybody's salvation for granted. In other words, just because someone claims they believe in God and comes to this Christian church and reads the Bible, that does not make them a believer in the truest sense of the word." He jerked the e-mail letter into the air. "This survey is strong evidence of how American Christianity is quickly conforming to the dominant secular culture, making it extremely difficult to distinguish between the two."

He took a visual survey of the room. "I know many of you in a real personal way. I know your places of employment, your homes, your children, your aspirations, and even your weaknesses. But I cannot see into your hearts. I cannot see your souls; therefore, I cannot pass judgment on whether or not you belong to Christ. Yes, many of you have demonstrated Christian virtues and good works, but that does not constitute a relationship with Christ brought about through the process of regeneration. That, praise God, can only be accomplished through the operation of the Holy Spirit.

"In truth, I'll tell you it has been my observation that it was easier to recognize a born-again Christian 20 years ago than it is today, and I believe it's because many churches are undergoing an unprecedented period of compromise. This compromise wears camouflaged clothing, duping unaware men and women into thinking they're saved when indeed they are not. There is no fruit of their salvation experience, and they are Christians in name only."

Stephanie's hand shot up. "Pastor Randy, can you explain what you mean by fruit?" Several heads turned toward her, while Laurie steeled herself.

"Sure. I believe there is more to salvation than the fruit of the Spirit that Paul explains in Galatians 5. For that matter, many can exhibit love, joy, peace, patience, etc., and still not be regenerated in the Spirit. However, when the Spirit of God comes into a person, there are three major changes that come over a sinner." He turned to the whiteboard and delineated the three changes, then explained as he pointed to each one. "The first is a genuine sorrow over one's sin. This is exhibited in true repentance. We become acutely aware that our own personal sin nailed Christ to the cross. Second, we look at our lives and see that we need to drop out those things that dishonor the Lord. We stop those habits and practices typical of nonbelievers. Naturally, those things don't happen overnight, but evidence of one's salvation experience becomes clear when we begin to systematically rid our lives of the cravings, indulgences, and downright wrong behavior we've been involved in before we met Christ. This is referred to as the process of sanctification. And finally, there is a burden for the lost. We are really concerned for the salvation of unbelievers, especially those in our purview: our spouses, our parents, our children, our fellow employees, and friends.

"If a so-called convert doesn't exhibit these things in time, and I'm not talking years, but a much shorter duration, then I seriously doubt the person was regenerated." He stopped talking and tapped the whiteboard several times to renew their attention. "Just imagine a man walking down a street and suddenly hearing a woman cry out for help. He turns and sees a house on fire with this woman hanging out the window, nearly overcome with smoke while flames are all around her. What would you think of this man if he acted cooly by putting on airs and, with a degree of nonchalance, just walked on by? Totally ignoring this woman's cry for help when it was within his power to rescue her. Of course, it is unthinkable!

"And so, too, is it to think that a real Christian would not witness for his Savior, knowing that mankind is doomed to hell without receiving Christ. It, too, is unthinkable! Every Christian should have a God-given desire to share his faith with the unregenerate. And this is only one of the evidences of salvation. The other two are equally substantive." Holding up the e-mail once more he concluded, "When you start claiming that your faith and Biblical principles are more than just a mental state that gives you a warm, fuzzy feeling, asserting instead what you believe is objectively real and valid for everybody, then you become an intolerant menace to society and must be silenced. This is one of the reasons why there are so many 'closet Christians' who are under no conviction to share their faith with the world. Either they don't know the first thing about evangelism or they are afraid to offend people. In either case, it is unscriptural. By contrast, radical Islam and Jehovah's Witnesses along with other cults, have no qualms about broadcasting their beliefs before the world. Thus, we see that from the Church on down to the Christian parent, to the individual, we are unable to influence society as we should. We lack the power of the Holy Spirit to bring about change from the present apathetic state of the Church. Accordingly, we can expect to see greater compromise in the Church in the future."

Ronnie Edeleson stood up. "Pastor, can I share something out of this book?" He held up Samuel Chadwick's *The Way of Pentecost.*

Randy groaned in his spirit, hoping the deacon would amplify his position. "Okay, sure." His eyes flicked to Laurie, only to see her give a long theatrical sigh. *She built a case against him; that's her problem.*

He nodded and read, "'Stage-lights have found their way into the Church. The red glare dazzles, but it does not burn. Fireworks are brilliant, but they end with the hour. No ideals are kindled, no ministry impelled, no sacrifice inspired. The pretense of spirituality is the worst profanity.'" He sat down.

Now that was in the Spirit! "That was a good word, Ronnie, and that sums up many of the churches today. All bells, whistles, and programs, but no power of Pentecost."

A hand next to Stephanie's went up. It was Marty's. "Pastor, you speak about a Christian bearing 'fruit.' But what about those who are what I call 'pseudo-believers' who claim to be a born-again Christian but certainly don't exhibit it in their lives?"

"He means somebody like Bill Clinton, et. al.," Stephanie blurted out. She nudged Marty and added cynically, "You know, professing to be a Christian while living a colossal lie before the nation."

Randy waved her off and said in dismay, "Whoa, Stephanie! We're not here to judge anybody. That's God's business. As far as former President Clinton is concerned, he'll have plenty to answer for before God."

She nodded with a devilish guffaw then gave Marty a high-five. "Yeah, but I'd like to see a little justice in this world, here and now!"

Marty looked up at Randy. "The wheels of divine justice turn very slowly and grind very finely." Several people turned toward him and applauded.

Take control, Randy's spirit demanded. He would not take any questions tonight but would insist they go home and digest his teaching. "Okay, you've heard my teaching on this subject. Now I would like you to go home and meditate on this subject. Examine yourself before God and ask yourself if the

Spirit attests to your salvation, then act accordingly." He paused. "Now let's move the agenda. Lester has some announcements."

Lester rose and walked slowly to the lectern. "Pastor asked me to pass along the following information for you to mark you calendars. Number one: We are going to have a local representative of the Homeless Outreach come to speak to us next week to explain his ministry. Number two: Pastor has contacted Moishe Rosen from the *Jews For Jesus* outreach ministry who will be conducting a seminar of Jewish Evangelism here in November. Please pray about these events and plan to give them all your support. We will be announcing committees for the November seminar shortly." He sat down.

Randy scanned the room to get a feel for the reaction to Lester's announcement. Two controversial issues that are extremely low rungs on the nominal church calendar ladder were presented: an outreach to the homeless and the Jew. Now it was up to the congregation to show their spiritual backbone and obedience to the Bible's teaching on the poor and God's covenant people, Israel.

Chatter. Lots of chatter.

"Let's quiet down," Randy urged. "With these announcements it should be apparent to you that our church is taking a different direction than in the past. While we were concentrating on ministering to each other, with a limited degree of localized evangelism, we must begin to broaden our vision to include both the homeless and the Jewish population around us. In this way we shall fulfill what I believe is the true message of the Great Commission."

The chatter resumed as Randy called Ronnie to close the meeting with prayer. *Lord, we have work to do here in this church,* Randy said to God.

No sooner were the last praises to God out of Ronnie's mouth when Laurie deliberately approached Randy. "What's this all about? Now we're building a platform onto our ministry out of the homeless *and* to the Jew?"

He softly held her arm and walked with her to the nearest corner as Stephanie signaled her need to talk to him. He gestured an acknowledgment, the told Laurie quietly but firmly, "This plan to reach the homeless and the Jewish people is really just an extension of our outreach program. So why do you have such a problem with it?"

Tapping her fingers sequentially against the wall: "I just do, that's why. I can't fathom your reasons for abandoning our mission here. We're doing fine the way things are, so why change them? Now you have to climb up on your white horse and lead a crazy crusade to save the rest of the world."

"No, just the homeless and the Jewish people," he retorted with a warning frown. *Lord, help!*

"And since when did you suddenly feel an urge to reach out to the Jewish population?" she asked with stinging sarcasm.

"Since I came under conviction several days ago that we are too complacent here in this church and that we need to be more obedient to the Scriptures. This act of obedience includes the nation of Israel." He retaliated with a snort: "Does Romans 1:16 ring a bell?"

"Don't you get sanctimonious with me Wilson Randolph Bradshaw!" she barked.

Stephanie harrumphed. They simultaneously turned toward her, slightly embarrassed. "Pastor Randy, can I speak to you?"

Laurie gave him a venomous look. "We'll continue this at home." She peered at her wrist watch and ordered, "You take care of the kids." She turned on her heel and stalked out of the room. Nearing the door, she brushed past Ronnie and Lester, making sure to give them an icy expression of disapproval. Moments later she drove out of the parking lot.

Randy swallowed hard, trying desperately to put the latest altercation out of his mind. He blinked, then asked himself the question he couldn't voice: *What do I do with Laurie now?* He gazed at Stephanie, her expression enigmatic. "Are you all right?"

"I should be asking you that question," she said, jerking her thumb over her shoulder toward the door.

Randy kneaded his temples in pursuit of relief. "You heard?"

"No, but the fierce physiognomy said it all."

The study of facial expression. Oh, I see. "We have a slight disagreement over ministry philosophy. Nothing serious," he countered in meek defense.

Fancy lady no like the homeless, she didn't say. "Too bad. Listen, Pastor, can we talk?"

Randy leaned back against the wall. "Sure, but we need to sit down." He led her to the nearby row of chairs, glancing at the doorway as Marty peeked his head in. Stephanie spotted him and gave him a dismissive wave. Seconds later, Tiffany and Sean walked into the room. Their AWANA and teen class were over, and they were searching for their mother.

"Just give me a few minutes," Randy said, "and I'll drive you home."

They shrugged and retreated out of the room into the hallway.

"I was hoping to talk to you, but I can see this isn't a good time." Stephanie coughed several times, then fished a cough drop out of her pocket and popped it into her mouth.

Randy noticed her pallor. "Marty said you were sick several days ago. Have you seen a doctor?"

"Nasty cold," she said wearily. "I was planning to go to the shelter for a voucher to a doctor, but then it got better. So I just let it go."

"You should have that cough looked at."

"If it gets worse I will," she pledged. She cracked a smile. "Thanks for caring. Now for my situation." She wiggled in her chair as if to settle in, then shot a look at the doorway. "I enjoy coming to this church, but there are some things I need to talk to you about before I dig in. Things like what I was like before..." Her eyes brimmed with tears. "....before...." She sniffled as several tears dropped on her sweater, then pointed to her soiled clothes. "...before I hit the streets."

Randy's heart jumped. "Don't be so hard on yourself, Stephanie. Remember, you're very important to God, and he has a special plan for your life. So don't give up."

"I wish I could be more positive, but life is *hard*, especially for the homeless." She rubbed her eyes on her sleeve. "I didn't mean to slobber all over the place," she confessed, "but I guess I just need someone to talk to."

The way of the transgressor is hard, he couldn't say, reminding himself of the truth that life without Christ is *hard*. "Now, now," he consoled in a soothing voice. "Remember you have friends here who care for you, and that should make you feel better."

She nodded in strained composure. "I hope so."

"You do."

There was a rustling at the doorway—Tiffany, attempting to be unobtrusive.

They reflexively turned toward the disturbance. Randy frowned at Tiffany, then told Stephanie, "Let's plan to meet tomorrow so we can talk further, okay?"

"Sure."

He prayed for her.

* * *

"She looked really beat, Dad," Tiffany observed.

"Like she could use a shower and good meal," Sean put in.

The ride home promised to be interesting, Randy noted to himself, with his children old enough to form opinions based on their visual inspections. "Yes, I'm sure she has looked better," he replied in Stephanie's defense.

"Did she tell you how she became homeless?" Tiffany inquired with compassion.

He turned to read her expression. "No, not really. But I think she plans to. She's coming to the office tomorrow. Perhaps she'll tell me then."

Tiffany gazed out the window and said woefully, "You don't think she sleeps under the bridge on I-595, do you? That would be really terrible."

"No, she said she goes to sleep at the Homeless Outreach shelter."

"Is our church going to do something to help her? I mean, we just can't let her stay on the streets or live in a homeless shelter for the rest of her life."

A peculiar silence. Then: "Tiff, you sound like you've taken an interest in her."

With a shake of her head Tiffany replied, "I just feel so bad for her."

A strange anomaly in the world of Plantation Gate Christian Church, he thought. *Here is my daughter, with a heart awakened by the Spirit to reach out in mercy to the unfortunate while her mother is repulsed at the very notion of being in the same room with them.* "Maybe the Lord is speaking to you about ministering to her."

"Maybe."

"Does this mean we have to ask her over for dinner, Dad?" Sean's curious voice from the back seat asked.

Randy just looked into the rearview mirror and raised his eyebrows.

* * *

The moment Randy pulled the car into the driveway, apprehension filled his heart. The message the house seemed to signal was loud and clear: *Stay away.* The front door outside light was out, and the rooms facing the street were in darkness. As soon as he placed the transmission in *park* and turned off the ignition, the car doors flew open, and Tiffany and Sean raced into the house. *Always in a hurry.* He paused to gaze into the obscurity of the blackened windows. *No movement.*

A slow, dispassionate pace characterized his walk from the driveway through the rear patio and into the playroom that connected to the rest of the house. A brief perusal of the immediate rooms revealed a potentially militant atmosphere. No lights, no TV, no music, no wife or children. Only an illuminated room deodorizer that cast an eerie shadow into the adjoining kitchen and dining room, which were also darkened.

He tiptoed down the main hallway toward the bedrooms, then stopped midway to listen. Silence. Laurie and the children must already be in bed, he reasoned. *Noise!* Behind him he heard the rustling of papers. He turned toward the guest bedroom, where a light from under the door shown brightly.

He took a deep breath and opened the door.

Laurie sat on the bed with her laptop computer to one side and a textbook on the other. In her hands she held what looked like lecture handouts. "Studying for an exam?" he asked, wanting to mollify her.

No answer, just a lethal glance. His stomach flipped as he stepped in the room and slowly closed the door behind him. Within seconds he could almost feel her intensity filling the room with a charge of electricity. He sighed in desperation. He'd rather stick needles in his eyes than argue with Laurie. *Lord, I can't handle another disagreement about ministry tonight. Give me strength!*

Finally, after what seemed like an interminable period, she said, "A quiz."

He pulled up the vanity chair and sat next to the bed. "Can we talk a moment?"

A muscle jerked in her left cheek, but no answer. Initially intent on intractableness, then at last, "What is it?"

"Laurie, we can't go on like this. Whatever your problem is with our ministry, we need to talk about it before the congregation realizes we're fighting over policy decisions."

"Did I hear you right?" she snapped. "Did you say *our* ministry? *Policy decisions?* When all the time you take steps to exclude me from *your* church."

"*Our church*," he corrected.

"No," she countered, "*your* church. You and *your* deacons made a decision to bring in the homeless and the Jewish community without as much as mentioning it to me. Correct?"

"Let's be honest. It's become increasingly obvious that your interest lies in your schoolwork and your own agenda. So when it came to these issues, I didn't think you were interested. So I conferred with Lester and Ronnie on the matter, and we all agreed to move forward with it."

Another reason to cut those Pharisees out of my life. "Convenient."

"Please don't seek sanctuary in one- or two-word answers," he rejoined hotly. Then with a sharp invective, "The truth is, you've turned your back on the church. Focusing on the homeless and now the Jewish thing are only excuses to justify your behavior."

"Watch it, Randy!" she warned with a killer look.

He fell silent momentarily. Then, after deep contemplation, "Laurie, the truth is that you're having a problem with Jesus. You're not satisfied with him."

He stood and walked out.

6

Thursday's drive to the office proved to be an unpleasant experience. The pain radiating from Randy's right temporal zone to directly over his right eye where the unremitting pressure caused the eyelid to droop only aggravated his spirit. With nose and eye watering accompanying the pain, it was obvious another cluster headache was upon him. *As if the pain of dealing with Laurie isn't bad enough.*

He mentally checked off any of his diet violations from the day before, suddenly recognizing the culprit: chocolate. *That's what I get for indulging.* He rubbed his temples in an attempt to soothe the pain, promising to strictly adhere to his neurologist's orders once again. *No chocolate, no peanuts, no cold cuts, no bacon, no Swiss cheese, no donuts, no canned soups, etc.! How's a man to live?* he asked himself. But then again, obeying the doctor's migraine diet was far superior to staying up all night with a pounding headache, or for that matter, relying on a Midrin to ease the suffering.

He checked his watch and calculated the average duration of his headache to be slightly over three hours. It was 9:10 a.m. Just a little over a half hour of agony remained before it would begin to lift. *Okay Lord, no more chocolate,* he pledged. Again.

When he arrived at the church there were two unfamiliar cars in the parking lot next to Yvonne's. *Hmm, strange for a Thursday morning.*

"Pastor Randy," Yvonne greeted cordially, "Nancy and Sharon are waiting to see you in the library."

"Did they say what they wanted?" he asked, curiously surprised to have an unexpected visit from two of his Sunday school teachers.

"No, only that they wanted to see you."

Randy walked to the library to greet the ladies, then escorted them to his office, where he directed each of them to sit in a stuffed chair. "What a pleasant surprise to see you this morning," he began with a broad smile. He retrieved a folding chair from his closet for himself. "So, what brings you girls out this early in the morning?" Nancy was a middle-aged mom with two teens in the youth group. Her husband sang in the choir. Sharon, a longstanding member at Plantation Gate was a divorced woman who served as the assistant church hostess.

Nancy nervously massaged her hands in her lap for several seconds before turning pleading eyes to Sharon. "Well," she began hesitantly, "Sharon and I were talking after your Bible study last night and..."

"Nancy's not sure she's saved, bottomline!" Sharon interrupted with finality.

"Oh?" Randy replied, slightly overwhelmed. Nancy and her husband had come to Plantation Gate three years ago from another church with an official letter of transfer. Naturally, it was assumed that a genuine profession of faith had already been made and attested to—a matter that Randy would later investigate in order to amend future church policy.

"On my way home from last night's Bible study," Nancy explained with her voice vibrating with feeling, "I meditated on what you said and realized that I've never exhibited those things you described that follow regeneration by the Holy Spirit. I had made a so-called 'profession of faith' when I was a teenager at a youth rally, being afterward swept up in church polity and all the fun and games that accompanied my old church. But I can honestly say that, last night, for the first time, I truly understood where you were coming from. Last night, I really heard what you said."

The very thing I was praying for. Oh, how I love you Lord! "Well, what did you do about it?" Randy queried.

She dabbed her eyes as an expansive smile broke out. "I wouldn't dare say anything to my husband about this, but early this morning I went into the bathroom, closed the door, dropped to my knees, and cried out to God to save me. I confessed my sins to Christ and took Him at his word. It made all the difference in the world."

"You see, Pastor," Sharon explained with raised eyebrows, "all these years she thought she was saved, but she never really examined herself in light of the Holy Spirit. She needed to be challenged."

A verse shot into Randy's mind: *"Examine yourselves to see whether you are in the faith; test yourselves."* "Yes," he agreed, "we all need to be regularly challenged in the spirit as the Lord deems necessary." Randy rejoiced with them, then turned to Nancy. "Now go home and tell your husband the good news."

Moments later he was reveling in the joy of the Lord.

* * *

"Good news?" Yvonne asked Randy as he walked into her office after Nancy and Sharon departed.

"Yes, very good news," he replied. "Nancy Kline got saved last night."

"You mean she wasn't saved, and she was a Sunday school teacher?"

Randy flinched at the question. "It happens." He pulled up a chair next to her at the computer console. "This is the outworking of a church ministry that neglects to teach doctrine regularly. My observation over the years is that there are scores of church members who don't know what they believe. Sure, they know the basics about the patriarchs and Christ dying on the cross, but when it comes to important issues such as regeneration, eternal security, predestination, and the differences between Reformed and Dispensational theology, unfortunately, most Christians don't have a clue."

Yvonne looked heavenward. "Lord, let me not be guilty of spiritual lethargy. Cause me to know what it is that I believe."

Randy knew his secretary had a solid relationship with Christ and marveled at her tenacious love for His Word, and an unabashed zeal to witness for the Lord. His only concern for her was in the area of her pride when it came to ministering to the homeless or other unfortunates. But he knew she was working on it. "Amen," he affirmed. "What's the update on your sister, Julie?"

Her face brightened. "A wonderful turn of events. Last night I called her and, although there's no word on the guy she was living with, thank God, she told me that she visited with a nearby pastor of a Bible-believing church who really helped her. Ironically, he's the pastor of a church just around the corner of her house, but she never bothered to go there because she believed they were, as she put it, 'Bible stompers.' But once she sat with him, her fears and misconceptions evaporated.

"She said he uses a counseling method called"—she searched for the right word—"*nu-thet-ic,* or something like that, and that she has some homework assignments that include keeping records of excuses and sinful behavior patterns that are harmful to her. Then he wants her to get into a church, hopefully his."

Randy nodded. "That type of counseling is called *nouthetic,* a Bible-based form of confrontational counseling pioneered by Dr. Jay Adams, designed to bring the person to the realization that oftentimes their sin and sinful ways cause problems in their lives as well as others. It's very effective when they face them and resolve to live a life that honors the Lord."

"Well, I'm delighted she's going in the right direction."

"What about Matthew?"

"He's coming along," she said with relief. "This pastor had his youth pastor stop by their home and talk to him. Then he invited him to a youth

Bible study and he seems to like it. The kids in the youth group welcomed him. I'm praying both he and my sister will turn their lives over to Christ."

"May it be so."

The phone rang. Yvonne noted the number on the caller-ID and turned to Randy. "It's your wife."

Randy inwardly braced himself for a fight. "I'll take it in my office." In the distance of 30 feet, from Yvonne's desk to his, he shot three prayers up to the Lord to intervene in his private crisis.

"Can we smoke the peace pipe?" Laurie asked as her opening remark.

"I don't smoke," he replied jokingly as his heart did a flip. Seriously: "Of course."

"Randy," Laurie said apologetically, "I've been a real jerk. I don't know what comes over me at times, but I called to ask your forgiveness so that we can renew our relationship."

"Done," he replied. *"Not seven times, but seventy-seven times," right Lord?*

"Can I buy you lunch at Hops?" she offered.

The way to a man's heart is through his stomach. "Sure, say when."

"I'll meet you at 11:30. Love you, mean it,bye."

The phone call ended, but Randy was disturbed with lingering thoughts over their deteriorating relationship. Nevertheless, he bowed his head in prayer and thanked the Lord that Laurie had taken the initiative to call him.

* * *

"I'll have a bowl of the potato soup and a large chicken caesar salad," Randy told the waitress. "And a diet Coke, no ice," he added as an afterthought.

"I'll have the same, only hold the soup," Laurie said.

The waitress wrote down the order and walked away.

"I'm glad we put our little spat behind us," Laurie began with a luminous smile.

"I believe Satan gets the advantage over us when we argue. Especially when it has to do with either our intimate relationship or the working of the ministry."

Laurie nodded in agreement with his interpretation of Pauline doctrine. For an instant she stared at an imaginary spot in the air and murmured, "Sometimes I don't know what comes over me."

Randy perceived a breakthrough. "You mean with controlling your angry spirit?"

She took a deep breath. "Yes, among other things."

Randy squeezed her hand. "Don't be so hard on yourself. We all have our moments." *Oops! I just violated an important aspect of Biblical counseling: no minimizing.* "On the other hand, I believe we all need to be teachable by the Spirit. Self-examination is a powerful godly attribute that leads to spiritual maturity." *Careful, Randy*, he reminded himself, *not so didactic.*

The waitress brought the drinks.

"But Randy," she temporized as she withdrew her hand, "don't you think *we should agree* on the proper philosophy of ministry for our church before you start bringing in the homeless and reaching out to the Jews?"

Whoa! Where did that come from? Surprised at her dogged tenacity, he took a slug of his soda. *Now I see more clearly. You're sorry about starting a fight, but there's still no reform in your thinking.* "Once again," he replied firmly, "I, along with Lester and Ronnie, believe this is the proper direction for our church. And besides, the congregation is rallying behind us."

"Lester and Ronnie seem to have quite a bit of clout in our church nowadays," she said with sarcasm.

"You're just mad because they came to me about your attitude."

"Well, I can see you're not letting me get away with anything," she allowed with a snort.

We've been down this road before. Whenever I yield to your self-aggrandizing nature, the monster from your ID invariably demands more. In turn, you get worse. "We need to put the Lord first, Laurie. Ask ourselves, what would Jesus have me do? This reasoning will keep us from straying into areas that cause conflict in our lives and the lives of others. As far as Lester and Ronnie are concerned, they are spiritual men, dedicated to our church and their pastor. They meant no harm by coming to me about you."

There would be no victories for Laurie today. She stared at him impassively for a moment, then said, "Fine." She turned to look for the waitress, then added, almost as a footnote, "So, in other words, you don't think the homeless will make our church look bad? That the church will not suffer if we reach out to the homeless and now the Jews?"

She just won't let it go. "No, I don't," he said with strengthened resolve. "And if you're worried about sophisticated, classy people being scared off, let me remind you that, in Jesus' day, they were the ones who gave him most of his troubles. And as far as Jewish people are concerned, you don't have a problem with Ronnie and Judy, do you?"

She conceded, reluctantly. "Fine." As the waitress brought the lunches, Laurie switched the conversation to revolve around her schoolwork.

* * *

"Hello, Pastor Randy," Stephanie said wearily as he walked into the church office.

"Well, hello yourself!" Randy replied cheerfully. The angst and strain of the lunch encounter with Laurie now faded into oblivion.

"Did you remember I was coming in to talk to you?"

His morning had begun with the shocker of his Sunday school teacher getting saved. Lunch with Laurie was another eye-opener with unsettled conflict, and who knows what the afternoon would bring.

"Sure, I remembered," he said, motioning her into his office, making sure his door was left open. "You're looking considerably better."

"Feeling better, too. Thank you. I'm trying to take better care of myself," she pledged with a nod.

Randy's eyes connected with hers. Her demeanor was significantly improved, but her soiled clothing lacked any semblance of improvement. "So where did we leave off last night?"

Stephanie momentarily fiddled with her fingers. "I've been coming here for about a month now, on and off, and only now do I feel comfortable enough to talk to you."

"I'm delighted to hear that," he replied, recognizing the forthcoming catharsis.

"I'd like to tell you a story," she began, "and I'm hoping you will apply your counseling experience to what I will ask when I'm done."

"I'll do my best," Randy promised.

She dropped back into the chair and closed her eyes as if to retrieve from her archival memory a hallmark episode. "Where do I begin? Oh, yes. It was a broiling hot summer day in the streets of Fort Lauderdale nearly three years ago, and the wretched humidity was on the rise. Shoppers were busy window shopping, with people rushing back and forth, looking for that one-time big sale. Some were fanning themselves as they sat down at the outside tables at nearby restaurants sipping their refreshing drinks.

"As I stood on the corner of Los Olas Boulevard and A1A, I saw her. She was a middle-aged lady, with dark hair matted in the back with strands of gray beginning to appear. Her face was weather-beaten. I guess you could say it was bronzed from the sun, with several wrinkles straining to emerge. Beads of sweat dripped down her forehead, only to be restrained by the yellow bandanna she wore around her head. As I looked at her, I noticed that her clothes seemed to hang on her like an oversized house dress with all those big flowers on them.

"She was pushing a shopping cart from a nearby grocery store, and it looked like she was collecting junk off the streets. I became curious as to what the cart might contain so I walked closer. I couldn't tell whether she was pushing the cart or if the cart was dragging her. Inside the cart were paper shopping bags full of clothes—some clean, some dirty. There were paper cups, plastic forks, and spoons sticking out of one of the bags, along with some plastic plates. A foul-looking box of donuts and what appeared to be a bag of fast-food hamburger and french fries perched on top. On the back of the cart was a neatly folded quilt with a pair of dirty sneakers hanging on one side and a plastic bottle of water hanging on the other.

"When I tried to pass her, I saw her face up close. Her eyes were withered with sadness while it appeared she had a lot of spunk left in her. It was my impression that, at one point in her life, she had been very pretty. Right then she passed a storefront and looked at her reflection in the glass. She paused and stared at her image. It appeared as if she was about to cry when suddenly someone came up behind her and called her a loser and a drug addict. She looked down at the sidewalk and slowly moved on. Saddened, I wondered, *How did this lady get to where she is now? What mistakes did she make? What grievous sins did she commit that she's sentenced to this kind of punishment? Does she not have a family to worry about her? Did they turn their backs on her for any particular reason? Or is she plain stupid?*

"I asked myself how God could permit this kind of thing to happen. Where was her faith? Or did she stop praying all together? Where were her hopes and dreams now? Were they all assembled in the shopping cart? Where had she been? Who was she?

"As she came upon a corner trash receptacle, she rummaged through it, then pulled out a jagged piece of a mirror. She spit on it, rubbed it several times on her shirt sleeve, and peered closely at herself. That's when one of my questions was answered. That bag lady was me."

"Oh, my!" Randy spoke in a hoarse whisper, astounded at the self-deprecating narrative.

"Now you know a little bit about me, Pastor Randy." Stephanie appeared relieved, yet apprehensive about follow-up questions.

And yes, there were a multitude of questions he wanted to ask her. Questions left unanswered in her story: How did you get to that place in life where you decided to hit the streets? What calamity precipitated it? And, of course, the question she raised, "What sins did she commit?"

Did sinful living automatically mean disaster? What about those who live upstanding, moral, ethical lives and still experience catastrophes? What about those who flaunt and flout their abominable sin in God's face and walk off into the sunset of life and never experience any kind of remorse or retribution for their wrongdoing? What about the Jobs of this world who do nothing to deserve divine wrath, yet are plagued with misfortune, yet persevere with honor to the end? No, this was not the time to ask these deep questions, for the Spirit constrained him, saying, *"There will be another time, another place. Let it go."*

"You mentioned earlier that you would have a question for me."

"Yes." Her eyes watered.

Randy reached over to his desk and handed her a tissue.

"Is it possible we can be really forgiven of our sins, and know it for sure?"

Randy was delighted her question did not focus on another theodicy on how to explain God's dealings with his creation. Why there is evil. Why there are times when evil seems to triumph. Why some divine decree designates one woman to be homeless and another to live a life of ease and comfort. Although he believed she exhibited significant academic insight in their Bible study Q&A period, today's question seemed to be pointed more at her spiritual and emotional acumen.

He smiled. "The short answer is a resounding *yes.* We can know for sure because we have God's promise, and we have it in writing!" He quoted from memory a verse out of Psalms that promised God has removed our transgressions from us as far as the east is from the west, and then how Micah had told of God hurling our sins into the depths of the sea. From there he explained Christ's statement in Mark 2 where he said to the paralytic, *"Your sins are forgiven,"* defining the one and only, God in Christ Jesus, who is able to forgive sin.

But her heart was not ready to receive this truth yet.

He prayed with her to seek God's answer for her life, then escorted her out of his office, leaving the business of conviction and the time of conversion up to God's Holy Spirit.

* * *

Where did the week go? Randy thought as he looked at his iPhone calendar. The jolt that it was Wednesday took him totally by surprise. *Ah, yes, succumbing once again to the tyranny of the urgent. 4:00 p.m. item: Meet with Sam Knowles. Hopefully, he'll be on time so I can get more background information on his ministry before he makes his presentation to our Bible study group.*

Sam was on time. Actually, he came ten minutes early so he could explore Pastor Randy's Holy Land photographs once again. As he surveyed the pictures, he comported himself with dignity and professionalism so as to be a striking example of a man determined to succeed in life. Randy would soon learn that his external composure was only a manifestation of his internal values.

"Good to see you again, Mr. Knowles." Randy greeted the man with a handshake.

"If we're to be friends, you must call me Sam," he corrected humbly.

"Sam it is." Randy ushered him into his office.

"I thought I'd give you an update on Marty Fitzgerald," Sam said.

"I'd very much like to hear about him. We're growing fond of him around here."

"Well, he was operated on two days ago for a herniated stomach muscle, and I'm happy to report that he's doing fine. He should make a full recovery."

Randy reached for a notepad. "Where is he?"

"Northwest Regional Medical Center. Room 208."

Randy nodded. "I'll make it a point to visit him tomorrow." He set the notepad down and then crossed his legs. "Tell me what's new down at Homeless Outreach."

Sam's face illuminated. "We've embarked on a new program called Operation Rescue that will help us locate homeless people who have no place to sleep for the night. We've coordinated the program with the local police who will notify us when they locate such a person so we can pick them up and deliver them to our shelter. This rescue team will respond to a homeless person 24/7. It's our way of extending our outreach in the community. We also are keeping watch on the John Doe cases in area hospitals. We recently had a case where a young gentleman was hit by a car and the police had no luck trying to identify him. The hospital called our OR team, and in turn his picture was broadcast on the local TV stations. Within an hour, an assisted-living facility in Hallandale called to say he was one of their clients.

"Two days after this incident, the OR team was called out to help the police with a homeless victim living under the I-595 overpass at Flamingo Road. When the team got there, the odor of urine and rotting garbage from a nearby dumpster radiated outward to where they were nearly overcome with the stench. The elderly man appeared to be sleeping in a fetal position with a flap from a large cardboard box covering most of his body. Next to him was a large dog, who seemed to be guarding him. As the team approached him, the dog attacked and the police had to put him down. Naturally the man woke up, startled and totally disoriented. The team identified themselves and moved closer. They noticed he had a plastic Christmas wreath hanging above his head, fastened to one of the overpass trusses with Velcro and duct tape. A length of garland was strung between the abutment bolts and hanging on the garland were two candy canes."

"But Christmas is still three months away!" Randy exclaimed.

"They came to find out he's been there since last Christmas. It seems this man was suffering from acute amnesia, selling flowers that he would steal from the backyard of a nearby nursery and buying food with the money. Fortunately, the police found him and now he's being treated at Broward General."

"It seems that Homeless Outreach is doing so much for the community," Randy remarked, "yet your organization receives so little media attention."

"Because the media and the public see us as a nuisance, not as an outreach to help the unfortunate. If the politicians have their way, we'll be forced to close shop."

"You mean there are lawmakers who want to get rid of you?"

Sam sighed. "One man come to us for help because he was ordered to stop feeding the homeless at the Fort Lauderdale beach. You'd think the authorities would allow the starving to be fed, but no, we had to go to court in order to feed people who would otherwise go hungry." He lamented, "It's a shame. Really a shame."

"What you need is a foundation to administrate and oversee the operation of Homeless Outreach who in turn could raise charitable donations to fund your programs."

"You're right. One that would also organize a hotel and food pantry much larger than our little quarters to accommodate the rising homeless in this county."

Randy sighed. "Such a formidable undertaking, yet one the Lord can help you to accomplish." *Speaking of the Lord...*

Randy knew it was the right time to probe into Sam's life. Enough "ministry" language had been bantered about, but no direct questions were asked. He had an inner prompting to explore his association with God. "By the way, Sam, where do you stand with Jesus Christ? Do you have a personal relationship with Him?"

Sam appeared to take an internal assessment then said, "I belong to a nominal Christian church here in Fort Lauderdale, and yes, I believe I have a good standing with God. As far as my relationship with Christ is concerned, well...I guess you could say I've been a Christian since I was born, and yes, I have a relationship with Christ through my family heritage and my church."

Sam's answer opened the door for Randy to introduce his salvation argument. Consistent with nominal Christians in their defense was that they were "saved" by being "born a Christian" or connected somehow to a Christian church, thus they believed they were a bona-fide Christian. But, Biblically speaking, that did not constitute a salvation experience where one's sins were forgiven and then you received eternal life with Christ in glory. "Okay. But did you ever pray to receive Christ as your personal Savior? Confession and all?"

Sam looked perplexed. "No, not really." Then came the justification argument. "But I'm sure God sees my work down at Homeless Outreach and my faithful service at my church. That should count for something."

"Yes, it does." *Good works don't count toward salvation but do indeed work toward spiritual discipleship and heavenly rewards after one confesses Christ.* "But critical to God is one's decision to receive his Son, Jesus Christ, as Savior. That's done by simply confessing that He died on the cross for your sins and inviting Him to come into your life."

"When you put it that way, it seems rather simple," Sam reasoned.

"It's so simple that most people miss it. Mankind is so inclined to complicate the salvation issue through theological and cultist exercises that once the truth of receiving Christ is made known, they don't believe it. They believe it should be Jesus 'and' something else. Or in other words, Jesus 'plus' good works, or Jesus 'plus' my religious heritage, or Jesus 'plus' obeying the Mosaic Law or a host of other obligations. But it's just not so."

Sam nodded in intellectual assent. "Something to think about."

Randy retreated into silence to see if God's Spirit was drawing Sam into further discussion and possible decision, but it was not meant to be. Not now anyway. Sam glanced at his watch and squirmed slightly. The discussion on the issue of salvation was over. "Sam, how do *you* define homelessness and what are some of the reasons homeless people give for their homelessness?" Randy asked to break the tension. Yes, the question had already been addressed in his mind, but he needed to hear it from a man who experienced it and lived to rise above it.

"The answer to the definition question," he replied after sitting upright, "is namely an individual who lacks a fixed, regular, and adequate nighttime residence, or an individual who has a primary nighttime residence that is"— he clicked them off on his fingers—"a supervised publicly or privately operated shelter designed to provide temporary living accommodations or a public or private place that provides a temporary residence for individuals intended to be institutionalized or a public or private place not designed for, or ordinarily used as, regular sleeping accommodations for human beings. That includes clients staying in an emergency shelter or a hotel or motel paid for by a shelter voucher, or a client living in an abandoned building, a place of business, a car or other vehicle, or anywhere outside. A national survey placed the homeless into four categories: Literally homeless, those sleeping in an emergency shelter; hidden homeless, those individuals sleeping in vehicles or abandoned buildings; precariously housed, those people in transitional shelters or voucher lodging; and finally, the at-risk-of-becoming homeless, those living in a conventional dwelling unit, but having been without a permanent home in the past.

"When our clients here in Florida were polled, they told us their reasons for homelessness. I guess you could say this is a random sampling of the national dilemma. They said they couldn't pay the rent, or lost their job, or were doing drugs, or the landlord made them leave, and of course, violence in their family. They are the dominant reasons." He sighed. "But the long answer is more complicated and often involves other factors."

"Go on, I'm interested in the reasons," Randy said.

"A case study in Massachusetts that I believe is also a representative slice of our nation revealed there are 22,000 homeless individuals statewide, with over 6,200 homeless adults in Boston alone who have no place to call home. One-half of the homeless work full-time jobs but are unable to obtain affordable housing. Approximately 40 percent of the homeless are Veterans and about 37 percent are drug or alcohol abusers. Another alarming stat is that 25 percent of the homeless in emergency shelters are reported to have AIDS or are HIV positive. Mental illness, limited education, catastrophic physical illness, severe childhood or midlife trauma, gambling and unplanned pregnancy were also cited as reasons."

Randy's evaluation of this man sitting next to him in his office was soaring. This man had all the facts and figures of his ministry at his disposal. Amazing. A walking testimony to a modern-day deliverer who knew academically, statistically, and most importantly, historically from experience, where his people had been and where he should lead them. "Sam," he began after deciding to take action, "suppose I contact area associational churches and discuss with my fellow pastors the plight of the homeless and solicit their support. To engage other churches to form a coalition to help fight the war against homelessness would be a worthwhile ministry outreach for the churches here in South Florida. In addition, I hope to convince them to assemble a forum to discuss political reform toward the homeless as well. After all, if the Christian church can't help those in our own backyard, how can we in clear conscience, peddle our Gospel to other nations?"

"Good point," Sam agreed with heightening enthusiasm.

"I will also put together a task force to look into a public trust foundation that will oversee the operation and in turn help finance your mission."

Sam looked troubled at the thought of a public trust. Bringing the public into the decision-making process of Homeless Outreach could spell trouble if outside supporters who were only concerned about how to turn a profit on their investment became intricately involved. "We'll take the public foundation for support under advisement. But as far as the churches are concerned, we are in total agreement."

"Good," Randy said. "I'll keep you informed as to the progress of our task force." The issue of public support would be tabled for now, pending further discussion.

"Oh, by the way. Stephanie seems to be doing better," Sam added. "She said to tell you she would see you on Sunday with some of her 'associates,' as she put it." His eyes brightened. "She's doing so well, in fact, that we're thinking of asking her to take on some responsibilities down at the shelter. Maybe even a captain. We'll see."

Randy was delighted. "She was in to see me a few days ago, and I believe she's going to be a great help to you in the future and even to our church."

Sam smiled expansively at the confirmation that one of his people was beginning that process of graduating back into society. "Thank God. Fruit of our labors!" He stood up, stretched and yawned, then departed, leaving Randy to his afternoon while he ran some errands before returning for the evening service to make his presentation to the congregation.

* * *

The meeting where Sam explained his outreach to the Bible study group was overwhelmingly received by the congregation. "God must be in this!" Randy exclaimed to Sam amidst much good-natured back-pounding and bravado. They wanted to be in the place of blessing. If God were moving Plantation Gate in the direction of ministering to the homeless, they wanted to be where God was working.

Laurie raised her brow in challenge to Randy, but this time he was impervious to her attitude.

7

The nice feeling of wearing a long-sleeved shirt reminded Randy that fall had finally, once again, come to Florida. *It was a long, hot summer.* Autumn in Florida did not bring colorful changes in the foliage of the trees like up North, but it did bring temporary relief from the tropical heat and the solace that hurricane season was nearly over.

The refreshing change in the weather also meant that one could drive the roads of South Florida with the car windows down and not be concerned about one's deodorant failing or having a sizzling hot dashboard on the way to work. But, for Randy, his work was not work in the truest sense of the word. His work was a joy, not contingent on pleasurable events, but the kind of joy that comes from God's Spirit that enables one to rise above unhappy events by keeping their eyes on their Savior.

For Pastor Randy, working for the Lord in ministry brought purpose and spiritual fulfillment to life. For him, being separated from secular employment to a full-time ministry was a unique calling that only a select few enjoy.

He arrived at Northwest Regional Medical Center, parked in one of the designated clergy spaces, then walked to the security desk for a pass. He announced his intention to visit Marty Fitzgerald, then took the elevator to the ICU ward. Privileged as a pastor to visit patients at any time, he took this liberty to stop off and see those who may need some spiritual uplifting. *Hospitals can be very dreary places for the aged, the terminally ill, or those about to undergo or recovering from serious surgery. I'm sure they can use a visit.*

Marty was in room 208, a double-occupancy room facing south that overlooked the city of Sunrise, two miles north of Plantation Gate. The room was painted a sterile gray with a withdrawn white curtain separating the two beds. Marty lay asleep with several tubes protruding out of his body, a heart monitor with a digital readout that appeared to be fluctuating in the normal range, and an IV. A bed tray with untouched hospital food stood off to one side. His stomach seemed to be bulging under the bedcovers, no doubt from the swelling of the surgery and bandages around his abdomen. His face, however, did not reflect pain, but his newly acquired relationship with Christ; one of peace and contentment.

In the other bed, an elderly man with black hair and encroaching white roots sat up on his bed watching a rerun of *Murder She Wrote* on TV. Randy gave him a wave and silently mouthed a *hello*. The man returned the greeting with a feeble nod. As Randy sat on the chair next to Marty's bed he recognized a copy of *World* magazine next to a Bible on top of Marty's night table. *Good magazine with conservative Biblical views.* He leafed through the magazine, stopping to read the editorials responding to the latest tripe from the liberal pundits who continue to trade character for cash. Cries from the Left and their special interest groups espousing the rights of homosexuals and the ACLU's fight to rid the land of any vestige of God, from the removal of the Ten Commandments right up to the removal of "In God we trust" from American currency appeared to fill the pages of the monthly publication.

Randy looked up from the pages and gazed out the window. *Lord, how long will You look on? How long will You allow them to distort the truth under the guise of "rights"? I know the day is coming when You will be vindicated. So until then You must want the Christian Church to press on toward that victory by standing firm on the Word of God and legally opposing the assiduous attack by the Left who attempt to dismantle the divine restraints You put in place to control the practice of depravity: the conscience, civil government, the family, and the church.*

A nurse walked in to check Marty's vital signs. She took his pulse, then proceeded to evaluate his monitors. Seconds later she smiled at Randy as she pulled the privacy curtain around Marty's bed. From there she stepped to the adjacent bed to give Marty's neighbor the same treatment, then walked out of the room.

"Hi, Pastor," Marty croaked out, shattering Randy's reverie. "It's so good to see you."

Randy set the magazine down on the table and gave Marty a luminous smile. "How are you doing?"

"I'm a little sore," he said with a raspy voice as he ran his hand over his stomach region. He attempted to lift his head but gave out with a groan and dropped his head back into the pillow. "I'm really looking forward to getting out of here as soon as the doc says it's okay."

"Can't wait to get to church, eh?" Randy joked.

"You said it, Pastor." Marty beckoned Randy to his mouth and whispered as he pointed at the next bed, "This guy next door, Freddy is his name, is not a believer, so let's start up some dialog to kindle his interest."

Randy got the message and grinned. "Okay," he whispered with a wink.

Marty pushed himself up in the bed a few inches. "So tell me, Pastor

Randy," he said as loud as his lungs would allow, "what is your sermon on this week?"

Randy played along. "The love of God."

"Ah, yes, 'the love of God,'" Marty repeated with a twinkle in his eye. "The very thing that brought Jesus to the cross and freed me from the chains of sin."

They both paused and nodded to each other as the volume on the TV suddenly dropped.

"That's right. If it weren't for the love of God, Jesus would have had no reason to die for sinners." Randy turned his head toward the other bed and recited, *"But God so loved the world that he gave his only son that whosoever would believe on him would not die, but have everlasting life.'"*

Marty nodded then jerked his thumb toward the other bed. "And it's so easy to get on the right side of God, isn't it, Pastor? I mean, we don't have to jump through hoops or perform any special works in order to get to heaven. Am I right?"

Amazing, Randy thought, how Marty, an emerging Christian, knew how to ask the right questions that would hopefully elicit the proper response that could provoke the average listener to pursue the truth. "It's so easy, Marty, that most people miss it. Man invents his own path to God through acts of good works or through counterfeit mediators while all one needs to do is to acknowledge Jesus as Savior and confess their sins and they can be saved."

Randy walked outside the curtain and peeked over at Freddy. His eyes were closed, and he was clutching the TV remote. He looked like he was sleeping. Randy shrugged and walked back to Marty's bed. He bent over and whispered in his ear, "He fell asleep."

"Too bad," Marty breathed. "Oh, well, there will be another time."

"So tell me, has the Lord spoken to you through all this?" Randy asked, deliberately engaging him to lift his spirits. "I mean, has he given you any direction as to what you'll be doing when you get out of here?"

Silence. Then, "Yes, he has. I believe he wants me to help my own people, you know, the homeless like myself. Now that I have purpose, I want to be productive and have my life count for something to make it easier for others who are following me down the same road I have traveled. Since the Lord has given me a new lease on life, I want to give something back to those people who helped me along the way. Something that will last for eternity."

Randy knew exactly what he meant. Sharing his new salvation in Christ with others would be his new mission. He patted Marty's shoulder. "A noble task that will bring great rewards!"

A prolonged cough from Freddy interrupted them, followed by his impotent voice: "Say, Marty, what's all this stuff about God anyway?"

Marty turned his head toward the bed behind the curtain and, with a hoarse voice said, "We thought you were sleeping." Turning to Randy, he said, "Hopefully he heard us."

"I heard you," Freddy said.

Randy and Marty exchanged looks; waiting. Seconds later Marty muttered, "Freddy must have ears like a bat."

"Pastor, could I speak to you?" Freddy said in a raspy voice.

"Of course." Randy walked over to his bed.

"I don't know if the nurse said anything to you, Pastor," Freddy said as tears streamed down his face, "but I have a terminal condition and I'd like to know more about what you were talking to Marty about just a while ago."

"Oh, I didn't know!"

"Of course you didn't," Freddy said as he managed a smile. "It's lung cancer, and I don't have much time left."

Randy scanned the area around his bed and noticed two clear plastic bags dangling from his bed with colored tubes draining into them as a mute testimony to his failing health. "Is there something you'd like to talk about?"

"I want to get things right with God," he mumbled in a raspy whisper. His hands shook and his chest heaved. "Before it's too late," he whimpered.

Randy realized that Freddy was deeply troubled. The kind of trouble that stains the soul and cannot be washed away by mere time, activity, or determined suppression. He grasped one of Freddy's hands. "The Lord is a forgiving God to all who come to Him. Do you want me to pray with you now?"

Freddy nodded, then squeezed his eyes shut while tightening his grip on Randy's hand.

Randy shot a look over to Marty and signaled to him that he too should join them in prayer. In less than two minutes, Freddy was reciting a prayer to God that Christ would wash him of his sin and place his name in the Lamb's Book of Life.

As Randy drove out of the hospital parking lot, he thought, *I have the best job in the world!*

* * *

The ride back to the church was euphoric. To think that the God who assembled and maintains the universe would use a mere speck of dust, a mortal man, to bring the whole counsel of the Bible's plan of salvation to a lost soul while he lay dying in his bed was nothing short of spectacular, and humbling. He had to share the exhilaration. He pulled out his cell phone and pressed and held the number 3 key. Seconds later his number appeared on Laurie's phone as it beeped. "Hello there, big guy! What's up?"

"You're certainly in a good mood," he replied, somewhat surprised.

"Just pulled an A in my American Literature course!" she exulted. "Of course, I had to study like crazy for it, but it was worth it." She paused. "Is everything all right?"

"Yes. In fact, fantastic. I just experienced the joy of leading a man to Christ!"

"That's wonderful, Randy. Was it somebody that came to the church for counseling?"

"No, actually, it was a man in the hospital bed next to Marty."

"Marty, the homeless man who came to the church?"

"Eh, yes, Marty the *homeless* man." *Oh, how that title would hurt him now that he's found new life in Christ.* "The man who had that stomach problem, the herniated muscle. He had it operated on."

"Oh, I didn't know that he was in the hospital. Why didn't you tell me?"

A deafening silence.

Randy swallowed hard. "Humph, I thought I did."

"No, you didn't," she insisted. "See, this is what I mean about including me in things like this so that I don't look like a 'turkey' to the congregation."

Uh-oh. Must be a mental block, he didn't say. *Are you really interested?* "No matter. The important thing is that the man made his peace with God. As far as Marty is concerned, he's doing better."

"That's good. What's the rest of your afternoon look like? Do you want to meet for lunch?"

"Not today. I need to make a series of phone calls this afternoon to recruit some associational pastors to help with the plight of the homeless. I'm determined to build a consensus in the denomination to form a coalition to work for some political reform to aid the neglected element in our society."

The homeless thing again. Mushrooming into a major project that will totally consume him. "I see." A pause. Something was triggered. Several fragments from the past drifted into her consciousness. She suddenly saw herself back in the athletic equipment room facing the man with the red sweatshirt. He was leering at her and rubbing his hands together. *"Hi, ya, honey,"* he said.... She snapped out of it. "Well, have a great afternoon and I'll see you tonight."

Randy could sense her disappointment over the phone. Whenever Laurie disapproved of something, she'd unwittingly verbalize it with the profound *I see*, ordinarily followed by a parenthetical pause that always exaggerated her negativity. "Are you all right?"

"Sure, I'm fine," she replied with finality. "See ya."

Click.

Randy's heart was grieved. *What would it take to win her over to the church's mission?* Leaving it with God was his only option.

* * *

With the Atlantic Association church roster and a cup of coffee on his desk, Randy sought to choose those fellow pastors he'd ask to join in the coalition of the homeless. Of the 165 churches in Broward and Miami-Dade counties, only 17 fell within the a 20-mile radius of Plantation Gate Church. Those were the candidates he selected to call.

"Where are you going to start?" Yvonne asked as she brought him a carob bar as a lame substitute for a chocolate-covered Oreo that he preferred to accompany his coffee.

"With the pastors I'm the friendliest with," he replied wryly as he eyed the sweet offering.

Yvonne smiled and walked out of his office.

"Redemption Baptist Church, good afternoon," the receptionist answered gingerly.

"This is Pastor Randy over at Plantation Gate church. Can I speak to Pastor David please?"

"Just a minute please." He heard a click as he was put on hold.

"Hello, Randy! How's the Lord treating you?"

"Always with grace. Always with grace," Randy replied.

"Amen," David agreed. "So are you staying out of trouble?" he asked coyly.

"Trying to, but failing miserably." They both exchanged a hearty laugh.

"So, how can I help you, brother?" David asked.

After dispensing with the amenities, Randy turned to a more serious tone. "Dave, the Lord has impressed upon me the great need here in South Florida to minister to the homeless. This need has been brought to my attention by several homeless people who have come to our church over the past two months, together with my meeting with the director of the Homeless Outreach, a man by the name of Sam Knowles."

"The Homeless Outreach?" David said with rising enthusiasm. "Aren't they the gang that wear the colored T-shirts and ask for donations at the traffic lights?"

"Yes, that's them."

"Man, there's an army of them. They seem to be stationed at every intersection. Tenacious little buggers."

Randy's sensors went on alert. "There are over 200 in Broward County alone. Do you think this is something you and your church would be interested in getting involved in?"

"We might be," David said with diminishing fervor. "You realize, of course, that I would have to clear any extension of our ministry through our deacon board, and then see how the congregation felt about it."

"Yes, I suppose I understand that, but David, can you see yourself being a part of an outreach that can bring the Gospel to the discards of America? The people who are despised and rejected even as our Savior was?"

"Not everybody has the same vision as you, Randy," David reminded him. "But I will certainly pray about it and consider it."

Randy suddenly realized he was getting too pedantic. He had to lighten up and allow the Holy Spirit to move in the hearts of the area pastors so they would catch the vision too. "No, you're right. Not every pastor has my vision. But do what you can, David and get back to me."

"Will do."

Randy hung up the phone and took David's answer to be a definite *no*. If the pastor did not have the heart to support a project, then what could be expected of the deacon board? The congregation? *It would have to be a God thing.* Sure, his heart could change in time, but if this project were of the Spirit, then the Spirit would give testimony immediately.

He paused before making the next call to pray and ask the Lord to prepare his heart for rejections and excuses, reminding himself that if this project was a God-thing, nobody would be able to stop it. Minutes later, with strengthened resolve, he picked up the phone and punched in the number for Pastor George Melford at First Alliance Baptist Church.

Pastor George answered the phone. "First Alliance, can I help you?"

"Hello, George!"

"Hello, Randy! Is it time for our luncheon already?"

George and Randy met for lunch with several other pastors once every eight weeks.

"No, not yet."

"Family okay?"

"Yes, we're all fine."

"How's Plantation Gate doing?"

"The ministry's doing well. Yours?"

"We're in the beginning stages of a bond issue to build a new sanctuary. We've outgrown the old one…you know how it is," George declared gleefully.

Randy had not experienced that aspect of church growth, so he didn't know how it was but looked forward to it in the future. "In view of that, this might not be a good time to ask you about joining in a neighborhood improvement project, but if you can see your way clear, I'm working on a project that needs a lot of help."

"No problem, buddy," George replied. "Just name it. I can always make time for you."

"Well, I need area churches' support to form a coalition to meet the needs of the homeless here in Broward and Dade counties."

"To the homeless?" he asked, almost incredulously.

"Yes, my heart has been leaning toward an outreach to them. We have our congregation's backing, but one church is not enough to reach the homeless community here in South Florida."

"Go on."

"What we're looking to do is form an *alliance* among area churches to meet the growing need of the homeless community. This coalition of churches would act like the Red Cross to the homeless people. When there's a disaster, they come in and provide shelter, food, medical, and other restorative acts to bring the calamity victims back to some degree of normalcy. I believe the Christian church can also rise to meet the challenge of the homeless in a similar way. While the Red Cross is financed mainly through contributions and other fund-raising programs, the coalition too would be financed through church giving, along with their own fund-raising programs."

"So then you would place them in *mission* status?" George asked.

"Yes, you could say that," Randy replied with a degree of suspicion.

"Um, well, I don't think it would work for us then, Randy, because we have an extensive foreign mission program. Our church supports three missionaries—one in Chile, South America, another in the Sudan, and another in northern France."

"Which is terrific," Randy countered with rising concern, "but what about a *mission* to those unfortunate people right here in South Florida that need to hear the gospel? What about them? Shouldn't we try to evangelize those within our own community as well?" He raised his voice an octave. "The people who are labeled by society as misfits need our help too. The people who are wandering around on the highways begging for a handout to keep from starving are every bit as needy as those in a remote village outside of Paris who are well clothed but reject the truth of the gospel!"

"Okay, okay." George expelled a sigh. "I see your point."

The tension wilted as Randy summarized his call. "Go to your members and ask them to help."

"I will, Randy, I will. God bless."

Randy replaced the phone on the cradle and stared at it as his thoughts carried him off to his college days when he'd attempted to work part time at telemarketing to help pay his tuition. *Oh, how I hated when people said no.* Somehow he always took the *no* as a personal rejection. *They weren't rejecting me, they were rejecting the product I was selling,* he reminded himself. *Yeah, it shouldn't be, but somehow my calls to fellow pastors are turning out to be the same thing.*

He paused in his "telemarketing" for a cup of coffee and a biscotti. Fifteen minutes later he resumed his efforts, but the response was somewhat the same. The three pastors he called were either downright disinterested, resistant, apathetic, or had misaligned priorities that prohibited them from getting involved. He stopped and prayed again, then scanned the Atlantic Association directory of churches once again. When his eyes fell on a Messianic synagogue, his heart fluttered and he reached for the phone.

"You've reached Beth Yeshua. This is Avi Bekker," the voice said.

At first Randy thought it was a recording. "Avi? This is Randy Bradshaw from Plantation Gate church."

"Well, hello, brother," the friendly voice replied. "I'm sorry I haven't been to the association meetings for the past two months but I've been very busy here with my congregation."

"Whoa, Avi. That's not why I'm calling," Randy replied apologetically. "I'm calling to see if you would be interested in joining a coalition of area churches to help the homeless."

A slight pause, then Avi said, "Yes, I would be."

Randy was speechless. Yet, it was the kind of response to be expected when the issue was one of God's Spirit. "But I didn't really explain."

Avi cut him off. "No need, brother, no need," Avi said with definite resolve. "You see, Jewish folk around the world can sympathize with oppressed and neglected people. We can relate to those who are wandering around aimlessly with no home. We can empathize with those who the world at large rejects as being different. It would be an honor to be involved, and you can count on my people as well."

"You're the best!" Randy exclaimed exuberantly.

Avi cleared his throat then asked, almost suspiciously, "How have you made out with the other pastors in the association?"

"Uh…"

Conveying skepticism based on Randy's reaction: "Not too well, I gather."

"Well, you know, the idea has to be cleared through channels, and congregation approval is needed," Randy said cynically.

"Let's face it, brother, if a pastor really wants a program, for the most part, they get it. It's a question of getting behind it and believing it is best for the kingdom of God. Then they can sell it to their congregations with no problem. The real dilemma is whether or not the area churches see the homeless as a viable mission field and whether their congregations would be willing to meet the needs of the less fortunate by moving out of their comfort zone. It's sort of the way they look upon reaching out to Jewish folk with the Gospel. In their hearts they know what God says about embracing the Jewish people but choose the path of least resistance, believing their congregation would object. They have that anti-Semitic sneer, but they refuse to admit they are anti-Semitic. I see that same sentiment toward the homeless.

"Unfortunately, many of the churches are being swept up in the ABCs of the new holy trinity: Attendance, Building, Cash, and it's difficult to gain their attention to return to the Great Commission that commands a dynamic 'GO,' rather than the newly adopted reversal of the Great Commission, which is being interpreted as 'COME.' The trend is to draw the unchurched into the sanctuary with programs that seem to violate the Great Commission that calls us to *go out* and bring the truth to the unchurched. In a way it gives Christians an excuse not to learn how to evangelize the unsaved. It's really sad."

"You're right." Randy marveled at the rabbi's spiritual insight.

"Count me in. And what's more, I'll make some phone calls to some of my fellow constituents who I know believe the way I do. I'll call you later with their names." He hung up the phone.

Unbelievable. Who would have thought I'd get that kind of cooperation from a Jewish-Christian pastor? And the way he put it: "You see, Jewish folk around the world can sympathize with oppressed and neglected people"really rang true.

Three hours later Avi Bekker called back with the names of four other pastors from the association who were a definite yes. That gave Randy the five churches he needed to begin the coalition. He couldn't help but wonder what kind of persuasive methods Avi used to convince them.

* * *

A pleasant scene awaited Randy as he pulled into his driveway. Tiffany frolicked on the front lawn exhibiting her newly learned gymnastics moves while Sean tossed his lacrosse ball to Jason, his neighborhood friend. Laurie sat on the front stoop with a cup of tea cradled between her hands, watching her children act their age.

Randy sat beside her. Sonny ran to greet him, slobbering Randy's face with his cold nose. "Nice evening," he began as he scanned the early October sky. "Not too hot. Not too humid. Just right." He turned toward her. "A great evening for a walk."

She took one more swig of the tea, then set the cup down on the stoop. "Sounds good."

Randy smiled at her and reached for her hand as he stood. She glanced at him, then held her hand out. In one swoop he pulled her gently toward him and gave her a kiss. "You're my girl, right?"

Laurie started to push away, but Tiffany and Sean saw the maneuver and paused to watch their parents embrace. They exchanged glowing smiles. Laurie caught their look and returned the kiss, then gave them raised eyebrows. "Pretty slick, Mr. Bradshaw," she whispered in his ear.

Randy tugged her arm to get her started on their walk. "You're my girl, right?" he repeated.

Laurie knew she could not win in this discussion following the afternoon skirmish with her husband. There were certain stimuli clauses and actions that simply melted her heart and caused her to recall the wonderful times they had together. Whatever conflict they would experience in life, they still had their pleasant memories to fall back on that acted like a wonder salve to bring about healing. The "you're my girl" phrase, together with the invitation to take an evening walk, easily eclipsed the afternoon tussle. "Yes, I'm your girl."

Within minutes they were walking side by side down the street.

"So, tell me about Marty," Laurie said as she bent over to pick up a piece of litter, stuffing it in her pant pocket.

Delighted at her interest, he replied, "He's doing well. They operated on his stomach hernia, and he should be up and around within ten days or so."

"What ever became of that woman, Stephanie?"

Randy was surprised that she asked about Stephanie, but held off on any judgments that could possibly skew the mood. "I haven't seen her in about 10 days, but I hear she's doing fine. In fact, Sam Knowles from Homeless Outreach said she would be coming to church tomorrow for the Bible study."

With some of her friends, he didn't add.

No reaction, just a, "Oooo-kay."

Randy stopped his forward movement and looked her in the eyes. "You're all right with that?"

"What can you do, right?" She threw her hands up in the air. "You can't fight 'city hall.'"

"You'll see, Laurie, God is going to do great things at Plantation Gate." Adding to his regained optimism: "In fact, I received a favorable response today in my first attempt to rally some neighboring churches to form a coalition to meet the growing needs of the homeless community."

"Really?"

"Really! Strangely enough, the breakthrough came when I called Avi Bekker of the Beth Yeshua messianic fellowship. As a Jewish believer, he immediately identified with the homeless dilemma and promised his support. A few hours later he called to tell me four other fellow Pastors wanted in as well. So we now have the makings of a task force."

"'*If God be for us, who can be against us*,' right?" she quoted halfheartedly as she turned around.

Randy turned with her. "Exactly."

Within minutes they were back at the house.

"I'll go in and start dinner," Laurie announced once they set foot on their property. Tiffany ran to join her mother as Randy sat on the front stoop to enjoy his son's lacrosse practice drills.

"Is Mom coming back out, Dad?" Sean yelled from the street.

"No. Your mother is making dinner."

Sean waved good-bye to his friend and walked up to his father. "Dad, can I talk to you for a minute?"

"Of course," he replied as he scooted over two feet. "Have a seat."

Sean carefully laid his lacrosse stick on the grass. "Remember our talk last month...you know, about Mom?"

"Naturally, I remember."

Sean nervously kicked at a stubborn weed that sprang up in the crack between the sidewalk slabs. "Well, Mom hasn't been able to help me with my homework at all, and I was wondering if you talked to her."

Randy's heart sank. His involvement with the homeless had distracted him from attending to his own family's needs—a troublesome syndrome often accompanying the pastorate and disrupting the home life of many clergymen. He exhaled. "Yes, I did, and I was hoping your mom would have gotten with you by now, but obviously she has other things on her mind."

"I figured as much, Dad, but..." Sean's eyes misted. "I miss talking to her."

"I know," Randy soothed as he stood to put his arm around his son.

"Is it"—he choked up—"her schoolwork?" Sean lowered his head.

Randy lifted his son's chin. "I'm sure it is. And it won't be too much longer and Mom will be done. Then things will be different."

"Yeah, but can I hold on until then? That's the question, Dad. I need her now." He picked up his lacrosse stick and held it at arm's length. "Sports can only fill up your life so much. Then you need the Lord and your family to fill in the holes."

A dart pierced Randy's heart as his son uttered a profound cry for help. Sure, the Lord must be first—he knew that. But from an 11-year old boy's perspective, sports often took first place for a season. "Sean, I'll always be here to talk to you. Wherever I can, I'll try to make up for your mom's absence."

He nodded. "Okay, Dad."

"That's my boy!" Randy said as they walked together into the house.

* * *

The broiled filet of tuna smothered in Teriyaki-sesame sauce was Randy's favorite fish dish. Salmon came in second, with swordfish a close third. Laurie preferred shellfish while the kids opted for macaroni and cheese. Everybody was happy with their dinner, that is, until Tiffany asked innocently, "Dad, how is Stephanie doing?"

Randy shot a look at Laurie. She appeared to ignore the question. "Last I heard she was doing well. Sam Knowles said something about her bringing some friends to the Wednesday night Bible study."

"Now *that* will be interesting," Laurie blurted out.

All heads turned toward her. A tense silence followed.

Tiffany stared at her mother. "What's the matter? Don't you like the homeless?"

No answer from Laurie, just a drilling of her eyes into an imaginary mark on the distant wall as she calculated her response. Finally, "I have my own view of those people, and I don't feel comfortable discussing it in this kind of a forum."

Tiffany shrugged and continued to eat her dinner.

"They're the same as any other person, only they don't have a job or a home and they don't have Jesus," Sean added publicly in meek defense.

"Not really," Laurie snapped as she pushed her plate away. "And since everybody is ganging up on me, let me say that I believe a ministry to the homeless will be the demise of our church." She wiped her mouth with a napkin and raised her voice an octave. "If that's what you people want for our church, then count me out! I believe God wants more from our church than to be a homeless shelter."

A muscle jerked in Randy's left cheek. "Nobody's 'ganging' up on you. We're simply having a friendly discussion on the subject, and I think the children should be included in it."

"Okay, fine," she replied, placing both hands squarely on the table as if preparing for a fight. "Then tell me why it isn't the responsibility of the churches of other religions like the Catholics, the Methodists, the Lutherans, the Episcopalians, and let's throw in the Mormons and the Jehovah's Witnesses to provide for the homeless. Why our church? What makes our church so special that we have to divert our resources and manpower to a thankless bunch of people who are too lazy to get jobs and who are too irresponsible to handle their problems correctly. Why our church? Answer me that, Pastor Randy!" That was her first salvo.

Randy swallowed hard. Tough questions from a tough woman who had helped him steer the course of the church in the past, now looking to derail God's purpose. "Because I've come to understand that no other church wants them. So he has raised us up to meet their needs and be obedient to God."

Laurie blinked several times, as if she didn't expect that kind of an answer. She began to cry.

Tiffany stood and put her arm around her mother as Sean reached over and grabbed her hand. "Mom, don't cry," they said in unison.

"Laurie, please," Randy begged. "Try to understand."

She abruptly stood, shaking loose her children's hands. "Pray for me," she addressed the table. Then she pivoted on her heel and walked out of the kitchen. That was her second salvo.

"What are we going to do, Daddy?" Sean asked through a moan.

His father shook his head. "I don't know, Sean. I don't know."

Sonny ambled into the kitchen and placed himself at Sean's feet in his own inimitable way of attempting to relieve the dispute, but he went unnoticed.

8

Surveying the parking lot from his office window and counting the rows of cars often had sway over the degree of enthusiasm by which Randy preached his sermons. If the lot were at least two-thirds full, his zeal for God and his energy level was at its zenith. If the count fell below one-half, generating the necessary vim and vigor needed to keep the church family's interest fell dramatically in concert with his decline of spiritual motivation. Randy used what he called the "lot scale" to gauge his congregation's commitment to the church, be it a good or bad method, God would tell, yet, it was his way of evaluating their allegiance to both God and his ministry.

More than two-thirds tonight, Randy thought as he peeked out behind his window curtain. "Cool beans. We'll have a good Wednesday night Bible study."

Moments later a white paneled van pulled into the lot with the lettering *Homeless Outreach* in bold italics inscribed on each side below the windows. When the side door opened, Stephanie stepped out, followed by two men and two women. Then the driver emerged, falling in line behind the group as Stephanie and her associates made their way into the fellowship hall.

Randy gulped. "This is going to be interesting," he said to himself and proceeded to join them.

Stephanie took point and led the group to the fellowship hall and then directly to the food line where Pat, the hostess, simply nodded in bewilderment, then excused herself and quickly walked to the kitchen to bring out more dinners. Ronnie and Judy Edelson immediately stopped eating and walked to the group to extend a hearty welcome. A flurry of chatter broke out, signaling the congregation's awareness of the homeless contingent.

"That's what we get for opening the door," Laurie said in a huff to Tiffany and Sean as she nodded toward Stephanie and her friends.

"What do you mean, Mom?" Sean asked innocently between swallows.

Tiffany raised her eyebrows defensively. "What's wrong with them? They're not hurting anybody."

Without an ally to support her complaint, Laurie simply replied, "Oh, nothing I guess," and kept eating as she monitored their every move through the line.

Two male members of the contingent in ragged T-shirts and shorts passed through the line, then eyed the dessert table and hurriedly walked to it, helping themselves to two portions of the chocolate cream pie and one portion of the fruit salad, each. A few members turned their heads in dismay as the homeless men scanned the assembly searching for an open seat.

"Oh, God, not here," Laurie grumbled as she placed her handbag on the vacant seat next to her. With her foot she dragged the open chair next to it and placed her Bible on it. "For your father," she said to the children.

They both looked at her and shook their heads.

"Hello, Mrs. Bradshaw," Laurie heard from behind. She stiffened upon hearing a strange voice, suspicious of its origin. She slowly turned and saw Stephanie holding her dinner plate while poised to be invited to sit in the chair between Tiffany and Sean.

Laurie noted she wore a different outfit that was clean, yet probably used, and her hair was cut shorter and stylish. *Oh, God, not here. Help!* she prayed. "Nice to see you again," she replied cordially.

"Sit here, Stephanie!" Tiffany said gleefully as she stood and pulled out the chair next to her.

Stephanie nodded and shot a look at Laurie for approval. Laurie took a breath, then slowly returned the nod. *Lord, why are you doing this to me?* Laurie prayed again.

Stephanie sat and began to eat her dinner.

Sean asked, "Stephanie, do you have any family?"

Stephanie sheepishly glanced at Laurie, then back at Sean. "I did at one time, but no longer."

"Oh, what happened?" Tiffany asked curiously.

A red wave of embarrassment swept over Stephanie as she set her plastic fork on the table. Laurie kicked Tiffany under the table for asking the question as Stephanie prepared to answer. "Well, let's just say that I made a series of bad choices that led to my losing the only thing that was really important in my life." She picked up the fork and added, "Let's leave it there for now."

With her tongue in her cheek, Laurie pondered Stephanie's remark. Seconds later she handed Sean her cup and said, "Honey, would you mind getting me another cup of coffee?"

Sean took the cup and walked away as his father came in the door. Randy walked over to the table and sat next to Laurie. He smiled. "I see you two are getting to know one another. How nice."

Stephanie and Laurie exchanged looks. Laurie consciously suppressed her revulsion and replied, *"Very* nice."

Turning to Randy, Stephanie pointed to her associates. "See, Pastor Randy, I brought more people to your church."

With that, Laurie carried her plate to the garbage can as Sean handed Stephanie the cup of coffee. He signaled his friends, then took off for the playground as Laurie began visiting the other tables, leaving Randy and Tiffany alone with Stephanie.

"Yes, I see." Randy scanned the fellowship hall, noticing Stephanie's friends while following Laurie's travels. "I hope they feel welcome."

Tiffany steepled her fingers on the table and asked Stephanie, "How are things going for you down at the center?"

A smile emerged, as if Stephanie was surprised a young teen would move out of their comfort zone and ask such a question. "They are going well, especially since I've been placed on the vocational training staff to help eligible candidates become more employable and also self-sufficient productive members in our community. We are graduating over 20 clients from the program to self-sufficiency each month."

"Interesting," Randy said with a nod. "Mr. Knowles mentioned he wanted to use you in the organization."

Tiffany gave Stephanie a strange look, taken aback with her vocabulary. She moved her chair closer. Her mother gave her the evil eye, but Tiffany didn't register the complaint in her mind. "I was wondering what happens to a homeless person when they come to the shelter? Are they required to work?"

Stephanie swallowed her last bit of food, then wiped her mouth with a napkin. "Most of them are. There are three different job assignments for the client. One is to be a newspaper vendor; two is to work around the shelter in the kitchen or do housekeeping. Three is to have an outside job. Some, however, just hang around because they can't work. Naturally, there are extenuating circumstances that go beyond these, like when a homeless mother with kids comes in. They can't work at all.

"While the public only sees the vendors or collectors on the street, there are others who are unable to vend because of sickness or an accident they had that got them fired and are too weak to do anything. For those unfortunates, the vendors share their money. But in a case like mine, Mr. Knowles is letting me fill in a staff member's position because she's out on maternity leave."

Randy joined in the conversation. "Where do you see yourself down the line? You know, when you're able to move away from the shelter."

A sparkle appeared in her eye. "I hope to be a counselor in a homeless shelter so I can help others in their journey toward self-respect and worth in the community."

"A noble goal," Randy said. "And with God all things are possible."

They all nodded in agreement.

Tiffany tapped her fingers sequentially on the table for several seconds. "Dad, can I keep Stephanie company at the adult Bible study tonight?"

"I don't know of any reason why you can't," he answered.

Tiffany smiled at her father then motioned to Stephanie to follow her. As Stephanie walked out of the fellowship hall, her associates trailed behind her. Randy grinned. Stephanie resembled the fabled Pied Piper.

The moment Tiffany, Stephanie, and her entourage cleared the fellowship hall doorway, Laurie walked back to the table. "What was all that about?" she asked with her hand on her hip.

"That, my dear, is our ministry bearing fruit," he replied crisply.

Laurie could feel her blood getting hot. *Why do these people bring out such a bad spirit in me? Why am I so repulsed over them?* she asked herself. She unwittingly sat next to Randy and said nothing as she scanned the rest of the tables, noting the congregation's mood and pondering her reaction. *They apparently were not bothered by them. They evidently have accepted them. They are enjoying themselves in good conversation while I sit here stewing in my own broth. Am I blind to what's happening, or am I the only one looking to protect the ministry and my husband from failure? Is this outreach bit to the homeless a God-thing?*

"If our other members were as conscious of inviting their 'associates' as Stephanie was, our church would exceedingly meet the spiritual needs of this community," Randy said, breaking into her deliberation.

Laurie slowly digested Randy's remark. "Maybe you're right." Seconds later she stood and walked out.

* * *

This Wednesday night Bible study was, by Randy's standards, light fare. He didn't feel the need to go deep into theology, so he expounded on selected parables of Christ in the New Testament, finalizing the study with the parable of the Creditors and Debtors out of Luke chapter seven. As was his custom during his Bible studies, he asked for questions. One of the homeless women sitting in the back of the room who wore a red baseball cap and appeared to be middle-aged raised her hand. "Pa'tor Randy," she said in broken English. "I have a que'tion."

"Of course," Randy replied. "By the way, what is your name?"

"Viola," the woman answered as she removed her hat. Once the hat was removed, it became obvious that patches of her hair was missing. "Your explain'ng of this story 'bout Jesus forgiving that sinful woman was talking 'bout me."

"Oh?" Randy said as a host of heads turned to look at her. "Do you want to share something with the class?"

"Oh, brother, here it comes," Laurie muttered. *Why does he allow these people to do this?*

"Yeah, okay." She exchanged a glance with Stephanie, who gave her the nod. "But I ain't looking to hurt nobody since I really don't know anybody here, but let's face it, we all have our little secrets, right?"

"I guess," Randy said as he scanned the crowd and braced himself for some shameless soul-bearing.

"Yeah, I'm like that sinful woman, all right. Ya see this?" Viola said as she tilted her head forward, pointing to a six-inch scar on the top of her skull. "I got this little souvenir seven years ago when the guy I was wit' hit me with a board when I wouldn't give him some of the crack I was hiding for myself. Three days in the hospital."

"Nasty," Randy commented as he looked on in amazement.

"And ya see this?" she went on as she rolled up her soiled shirt sleeve, revealing a crude tattoo on her forearm of a cross with a crown above it made from a ballpoint pen. "I made this when I was in jail for trying to sell my kid."

At least three woman from the congregation covered their mouths with their hands as the shock of Viola's unfolding confession echoed off the walls.

"Ugh," Laurie whispered under her breath. *You see what I mean. These people are low-lifes.*

"Yeah, I was in jail, people," she said, almost apologetically. "I spent five years in the 'slammer' at Okeechobee for trying to sell my cute little three-year old girl to buy a stash of OxyContin—ya know, the painkiller that gets you high—but I got busted by an undercover cop. And the judge was mean. Really mean. He didn't want to hear no story. No excuses. He said I was not fit to have a child, so I had to sign custody of my little Amy over to her grandmother before they took me away. After I got out, I didn't have the guts to face either one of them, so I hit the streets and have been on them ever since."

She began to tear. "It's the guilt of my little Amy that gets me. It's the gift that keeps on giving, ya know what I mean? I can't get rid of it. It's always ripping and tearing at me and won't let me go. At night I see her face in the shadows and wonder how she looks now. Sometimes I think I will call her, but I'm too 'shamed, too 'shamed." Her companion stood next to her and put her arm around her. She started to sob. "I'm like that sinful woman in that story." She paused to wipe her tears, then blurted out, "Can Jesus ever forgive me?"

Three members of the congregation rose and surrounded her and her companion, each putting a hand on her shoulder as they closed their eyes in silent prayer.

"Of that you can be sure, Viola," Randy replied, himself filled with emotion. "He is ready and able to forgive all those who reach out to him." He signaled Ronnie and Judy Edeleson, who also stood and made their way toward Viola. "Brother Ronnie and his wife will share with you the wonderful forgiveness in Christ we receive when we ask him into our lives." With that, they escorted Viola into the adjoining room where they counseled her in the ways of the Christian, then prayed with her to invite Christ into her heart and experience his overflowing forgiveness.

Randy waited several moments to see if God's Spirit was stirring the hearts of others as well. No other responses. *There will be another time, Randy,* the Spirit prompted. He hesitated another moment, then called upon Lester to close the meeting with prayer.

"Now that was something you don't see everyday," Laurie quipped to Randy as the class emptied out.

Randy leaned back against a wall in exhausted triumph. "No, but I believe we are going to see a lot more of it as time goes on."

Laurie stood at the classroom doorway then peered back into the room to see Tiffany in a huddle with Stephanie and her other companion. *Now what's going on? Does it never end?*

Randy surmised what was happening and lured Laurie out of the room and toward his office. "Looks like some heavy counseling going on back there; praise the Lord!" he said as he jerked his thumb over his shoulder.

"I don't want Tiffany involved in that kind of messy stuff," Laurie protested. "She's an impressionable young teenager."

"That's true, but if God is going to use her like a youthful Daniel to be set apart to minister to others, who are we to interfere? Besides, whatever they could talk about, I'm sure she's already heard it in school. We can only protect her innocence for so long, Laurie. I'd rather she learned about the hardness of life here in a secure church setting than on the street, where most of today's youth hear it. That way we can give her spiritual support. It's time we allowed God's Spirit to shield her from the temptations and evil doings of the world. It's time she applied all the Christian principles we've tried so hard to impart to her."

The realization of the truth of his words swept over Laurie. *He's right. I have to let her go.* "I'm scared, Randy," she said, grabbing his arm.

Randy said gently, "You'll see. God will honor her caring for others. Just wait and you'll see."

* * *

The ride home proved to be a joyful occasion for the Bradshaw family. Laurie set aside her bias toward the homeless and listened to her daughter's radiance emerge like a wildfire. "It was unbelievable, Mom!" Tiffany gushed. "This lady with Stephanie by the name of Alexis was ready to give her life to Christ. I just sensed it and asked her if she wanted to pray with me to receive Christ as her personal Savior and..."

"...and?" Sean asked with bated breath.

"...and she said, 'yes.' I couldn't believe it! Mom, you should have seen her face after we prayed." Tiffany's voice was choked with emotion. "It was unbelievable—to see how she truly believed and received God's forgiveness. Her whole face lit up after we prayed as if the Holy Spirit confirmed it in her heart right there and then!"

Laurie swiveled to watch her daughter's face as she related the story. She might not have believed the conversion experience, but she had to believe her daughter. It was unmistakably a genuine testimony of God's saving power. "I'm curious about the details. How long has she been homeless?"

"She said about two years."

"Wow, that's something," Sean piped in.

"Did she say anything about her past?" Laurie queried.

"Um, well, yes," Tiffany replied.

Laurie's radar antennae shot up. "Oh, like what?"

Tiffany gulped. "She has AIDS."

Laurie's outrage skyrocketed and she slammed the side of Randy's seat. "You see what happens when you let them in!"

"Mom, she's being treated, and she's no longer using drugs," Tiffany argued.

"Tell me everything!" Laurie demanded.

Tiffany sat in the back seat to relate the details to her mother. "Back in Jacksonville, she was studying to be a massage therapist and went to a bar one night and met this guy, Benny, who worked at a sporting goods store. There was an immediate attraction, and the two started to date. Before long they moved into Alexis' apartment and made plans to get married.

"Alexis had a long history of drug use but had been clean for two years before she started seeing Benny. When she started to feel sick, Benny insisted that she see a doctor, but she ignored his pleas and wrote the illness off as the flu. After a month her condition worsened so she decided to break down and go to a medical clinic. She was not prepared for the results. She had contracted AIDS from a dirty needle some time earlier in her drug abuse past.

"Devastated by the news, Alexis decided that she couldn't live with the guilt of having given the AIDS virus to Benny, so she decided to take her own life. She waited until he left for work then swallowed a bottle of aspirins. But God had other plans. Benny forgot his cell phone and came home 20 minutes later only to find her sprawled out on the bed, nearly unconscious. He immediately called 9-1-1, and within 20 minutes they were pumping her stomach. She survived the attempted suicide and sought treatment for the AIDS.

"Benny came down with AIDS shortly afterwards and took off, leaving her alone. She received a note from him six months later. He said he'd been with many other women since her, and she believes he probably infected them all before he finally died. Heartsick, she burned the note, then took his picture and some belongings and left her apartment. She didn't talk to any of her loved ones and didn't return to work. Instead, she slept on the streets the first night, and the night after, and the night after. She lost over thirty pounds trying to starve herself, occasionally giving in to her growling stomach betraying her plan to die.

"She thumbed all the way down to South Florida and through a series of events found herself at Homeless Outreach where she befriended Stephanie. Within three weeks of their meeting, Stephanie invited her to come along to our Bible study."

"Remarkable story. *'Oh, the depths of the riches of the wisdom and knowledge of God! How unsearchable are his judgments and his paths beyond tracing out!'*" he quoted in astonishment. "Just think of the glory to God— three homeless persons have come to Christ in the past three months." He ticked them off on his fingers. "There's Marty, there's Viola, and now Alexis." There was also Freddy in the hospital, but he wasn't a homeless person.

"Seems like the Lord is really blessing our church, Dad," Sean observed.

"Nice story, but what do we do about her carrying AIDS, Randy?" Laurie persisted without emotion. "She could infect the whole congregation."

"We needn't worry about that, Laurie. To date, AIDS can only be passed on to others through sexual intercourse, needles, and the like."

"I heard that mosquitoes can carry AIDS, Dad," Sean added uninvitingly.

"That hasn't been proven, and I'll thank you for not butting in," his father reproved.

Laurie folded her arms across her chest. "I still don't like it. It makes for bad business when you invite this element of society into the church."

Randy gave her a stare, then slapped the steering wheel. "Since when is ministry a *business* or a money-making enterprise? I was of the persuasion that we are running a church and that our mission is to help people, not make money, regardless of their race, social, financial, or *medical condition*."

Laurie returned the stare. "We can help *normal* people. *Normal* people, Randy, get it?!" She turned her body toward the window for the rest of the way home.

Randy prayed for understanding so he could communicate with his wife on ministry matters without her protests. *I thought she might have had a change of heart after our little walk and dinner conversation around the table, but I guess not.*

* * *

Things always look better in the morning, Randy thought as he awoke to the melody of a songbird. He lifted his head off his pillow and glanced out the bedroom window at his Royal Poinciana tree where a mockingbird chirped his tune to welcome the sunrise. He blinked several times before realizing he was alone in bed. *Where's Laurie?* He was always the first one up in the morning to put Sonny out in the backyard to do his business and to start the coffee. He glanced at the alarm clock: 5:45 a.m., 30 minutes earlier than regular reveille for a school day. *Something's up. Maybe a divine opportunity? May it be so!*

He sat up in bed and turned his head to align his senses. First he heard a rustling of the frying pans; then he smelled coffee brewing. He jumped out of bed, quickly washed his face, then walked into the kitchen.

"Good morning, Babe. You're up early. Couldn't sleep? Was it our conversation last night?" He sat at the table and reached for the coffee pot, pouring himself a full cup.

"I guess you could say that." She turned toward him. "More accurately, I couldn't sleep because of the blight that has hit our home. I'm troubled about the divergent attitude and approach to church ministry that has come between us. I've come to believe that this homeless person's situation has taken on the form of a *blight* that has been amplified by our personal disagreements, the overall impact it has had on our children, and on my schoolwork as well. The whole thing has me in a quandary." She took a deep breath as if it summon courage. "I decided not to return to church for a while until this whole thing blows over. You can take the children when you go, and I'll stay home and have my own private time of worship and Bible study."

Randy saw red. He slowly lowered his coffee cup and set it on the table. Unwittingly, he gripped the edge of the table and dug his fingernails into the underside as he mentally counted to 10. "You will not!" he replied with finality. "What you need to do, Laurie, is to repent before the Lord of your attitude and behavior toward God's people, and make up your mind to accept them as part of our congregation."

"They will overrun the church, Randy!" she breathed. "Can't you see this crusade of yours will bring ruin to the church? Are you so blind that you can't see they are using the church as a crutch and as a place for a handout? That they will scare *normal* people away?"

Randy immediately recalled her use of the word *normal* from the night before. He wondered if Jesus thought the blind, the lame, the woman caught in adultery, and the homeless of his day were normal or abnormal. By Laurie's reckoning, the Romans, the Temple leaders—the Sanhedrin, the Pharisees, and the Sadducees—along with the Jewish aristocracy were normal. But it was those "normal" people who crucified Him while the "abnormal" people believed in Him. So, what is normal?

"As long as I am the head of this household, we will operate as a Christian family. And as long as I am pastor of Plantation Gate Christian Church, you will comport yourself in such a way as to complement the position that God has placed me in." He aimed a finger in her face. "Are we clear?"

Laurie was not prepared for an all-out war that could seriously jeopardize their marriage and severely injure the children. There would be other ways of control that would avail themselves in the future; she was sure of that. But for now, capitulation was in order to keep the family peace. "You win, Randy. You don't win fairly, but you win."

"And while we're clearing the air," he added, "would you mind telling me why you can't find time to spend with your son? We've talked about your meeting with him and helping him with his homework and taking more of an interest in him, but you totally forgot about it. Can you explain that?"

If I didn't have to spend so much time thinking about that Stephanie, I'd have more time to spend with our son, she didn't say. "All right, all right. Guilty." She raised her hands in mock surrender. "What do you want me to say? You want an excuse, or do you want to take me out into the back of the house and shoot me?"

Lord, help! What is wrong with this woman? "Laurie, you need to make the children a priority in your life. Plain and simple."

"Oh, here it comes," she said with controlled anger, "my schooling, right? It's the school you're talking about that is getting in the way, right?"

"Laurie," he reasoned calmly, "your schooling has consumed you. Your pursuit for a degree has eclipsed everything else around here. Your ministry, your family, and our marriage. And I believe it's because of some strange guilt deep in your soul that you are so against our outreach to homeless people. Specifically, you're focusing on Stephanie as some kind of scapegoat, and God will not honor that attitude in your life."

A long sigh, then: "I'm taking the day off from school today so I can spend some time alone," she said contritely. "I think I'll go to Butterfly World for the morning so I can get some peace of mind. You know, be surrounded by nature for a few hours to clear my head. Is that okay with you?"

"That's a great idea," he said. *Hopefully God's Spirit will communicate with you through the beauty of His natural world, because I sure am not able to get through to you,* he thought of adding but didn't. He extended his hand to her and said in a conciliatory tone, "You're my girl, right?"

There would be no more arguing today. "Right."

* * *

Butterfly World in Coconut Creek is a park-like aviary with numerous paths that meander through tropical plants and flowering shrubs that attract various butterflies. Benches, fountains, and soft classical music provide a restful atmosphere where man can connect with the natural world if only for several hours out of the busy day.

In addition to the 3,000 or so solar-flyers that flit from plant to flower and occasionally land on the nature lover at any given time, there are observations labs where the scientific- minded can watch the caterpillar spin its chrysalis that hosts the soon-to-emerge butterfly. A suspension bridge spans a man-made lake that connects to an island featuring a walk-thru hummingbird and lorikeet aviary. Outside the aviary there are more paths with benches that link numerous plant and flower research stations for ongoing study to preserve the life of the butterfly along with a museum and insectarium for the entomology enthusiast.

Laurie arrived at the welcome center and opted for a guide book that gave a history of the facility along with a description of the multitude of butterflies that one could locate on the self-tour. Once inside, she realized it might not have been a good choice to visit the aviary on a weekday. Besides the regular traffic of tourists and photographers, there were at least six groups of school children of varying grades receiving first-hand instruction by group guides. *So much for the solitude, Laurie. Tough it out, girl.*

She walked through the entry gate where she was greeted by a host of free-flying members of both the Nymphalidae and Pieridae family. Several winged wonders soared past her head as she walked toward a bench. Once she sat down, two Heliconius Melpomene butterflies landed on her shoulder. She looked at them as they went into a pairing session. *How come they can get along so well, and we can't?* she asked herself.

Walking further, she came upon a Passiflora vine that serves as the caterpillar food source for the Heliconius butterfly. Hovering around the vine were two uninvited wasps, known enemies of the beautiful butterfly. Alongside the vine was a info-sign listing several adversarial predators that prey on the butterfly, namely wasps, spiders, ants, frogs and lizards. She studied the wasps as they zoned in on a butterfly egg attached to the underside of a leaf on the vine. *Parasites! God, why did you create parasites?* She pondered her situation. *Parasites? God allows them because they are an important element in the circle of animal, insect, and plant life. They clean up the excesses and keep nature in balance. But do we need them in the human arena? In the church? No,* she thought. *They only bring death.*

She gazed off into the distance and saw a vacant bench situated next to the indoor waterfall that emptied into a goldfish pond. *Ah, another refuge,* she thought, *this time away from the crowd.* Adeptly, she strolled past the array of curious bug-watchers and plant lovers as she called them until she arrived at her desired location. Once there, she realized why the bench was vacant. An intermittent misting system that irrigated the butterfly-attracting plants was in operation, spraying a fine mist over the area where the vacant bench stood. *Figures.* She moseyed down another path that featured several species of exotic moths clinging to tree branches. Next to a nest of the giant Atlas moths was a info-sign that informed the inquiring mind that butterflies principally fly in the daytime, while moths primarily fly at night. *Hmm. Foraging at night. More parasites,* she reasoned. *Only these guys are night feeders.*

Several steps later she stopped in her tour to once again sit on a bench. *Laurie, do you see the corollary here?* she asked herself. *Yes, parasitic "night feeders" are sucking the very "nectar" out of our church. That's what I see.* "But I don't think Randy sees it," she whispered aloud, "and if I don't do something about it, the parasites will suck the very life out of our ministry."

She strengthened her resolve and determined in her heart to look for an opportunity to fix the problem.

9

The morning argument with Laurie echoed in his ears despite the Christian classical music coming from his office CD player. *I won the battle, but I'm losing the war.* Randy believed it was a victory of a sort, but the term didn't ring true when dealing with his wife, notably the wife of a pastor. Victory in military terms meant winning or conquering, and he knew that, in a spousal dispute, there were no winners or conquerors. Victory in spiritual warfare meant satanic or demonic forces were defeated through Christ's blood on the cross. That is true victory since calling upon His blood for defense meant certain triumph for the Christian. But victory in this sense when dealing with a marital disagreement between a married couple was more like a detente because a real victory on either side would probably lead to a divorce. So the best he could hope for was a cease-fire until things changed, or until she changed.

A thought occurred to him. *Change? She seems to be undergoing frequent emotional changes.* He walked from his desk to his computer and went online and located WebMD through a search engine. He keyed in *bipolar disorder* and within seconds was reading the description: "mood swings back and forth between depression and mania." The report added, "...surveys indicate that people commonly view depression as a sign of personal weakness, but psychiatrists and psychologists view it as real illness. Women are two to three times more likely than men to suffer from depression. Experts disagree on the reason for this difference. Some cite differences in hormones, and others point to the stress caused by society's expectations of women." He reread the description. *This is not describing Laurie, even though she displays mood changes ,because she is not given to depression, nor does she show any personal weakness. It must be something else. Could she be going through the change of life? But she's too young.* He dismissed the bipolar or depression thing out of hand. He also dismissed PMS since her spurts in behavioral change frequently erupted long after her period had concluded. No, it had to be something else.

He shut the computer down, went to his bookshelves, and pulled out one of his counseling reference books. Within moments he was reading extracts that dealt with depression and how the author believed there were those who genuinely suffer from mental illness or clinical depression and that this kind of behavior required treatment from a physician, but there were also documented cases where the depression was attributed to unconfessed sin. "'Sin leads to guilt and depression, sinful handling of sin further complicates matters leading to greater guilt and deeper depression, ad infinitum,'" he read aloud. *Hmm. Could it be that she's on the cusp of depression from some sinful condition?* he asked himself. "Those depressed clients who do not exhibit a medical condition should be counseled on the basis that their behavior is rooted in unconfessed sin," he whispered to himself. Although Laurie did not manifest signs of acute depression, she did to a degree, fit the profile of a person who was deeply troubled in spirit. *Something to think about.*

"Pastor Randy, a call for you," Yvonne said softly as she stuck her head into the doorway of his office. "It's Avi Bekker from Beth Yeshua."

He replaced the book. *Hopefully, Laurie's soul-searching episode at Butterfly World helped her.* "Hello, Avi," he said into the phone. "How is the Lord treating you?"

"Always with grace. Always with grace," he replied joyfully. "Say, listen, Randy, I called to ask you how things are going with that Homeless Outreach project. It's been a few weeks since we talked. What's going on?"

"Well, people are getting saved. That's the good news. Three souls came to Christ from the homeless group since we began our outreach. The bad news is that I've been busy over here putting out several small domestic fires, and I haven't had the time to devote to this project."

"Can I help you with it?"

"That would be a good idea, Avi. Let's have lunch tomorrow. My treat. This way we can assemble a plan and get moving on it."

"Sounds good." They agreed on a convenient location to meet. "Okay, brother, I'll see you tomorrow."

A thought occurred to Randy. "Oh, before you go," he said with phone in hand, "our church has invited Moishe Rosen to speak here in November and I'd like to extend the invitation to you. Mark November 15 on the calendar. I'll send you more info as we progress toward that date."

"'I will bless them that bless thee,'" Avi quoted mechanically from memory.

"I know, I know. See you tomorrow." *Click.*

Randy turned on his iPhone to enter in his luncheon appointment with Avi Bekker and spotted a "note" icon flashing. He touched the screen with his finger and the note popped up: *Wedding Anniversary in ten days, buy Laurie a gift.* He listed his lunch appointment then turned off his iPhone. *I need to shop for her gift today. Don't wait until the last day,* he warned himself. He looked at his watch and realized it was time to move his daily agenda to the next step. "Yvonne," he called out, "we need to talk."

"Coming," she replied. Seconds later, note pad in hand, she entered his office.

He handed her his sermon outline to be inserted into the Sunday bulletin and answered one letter to a prison inmate requesting a Bible, then reviewed his music minister's budget for the month. After scanning the expense ledger he said, "Remind me to talk to Mike about his music ministry budget when we meet next Monday. He went over this month." Yvonne nodded and made the notation. "Send a letter to Moishe Rosen that we need the title and theme of his presentation that he plans on delivering next month," he added as he mentally worked his daily checklist. He assigned several mundane tasks, then remembered the faces from Wednesday's night's Bible study that were missing. "Give John Mills and George Dimakos a call to see if they are all right. They were not out to the Bible study last night." He raised a finger and nodded. "That's it for now."

Yvonne started to leave. "Oh, by the way, whatever became of your sister, Julie, and Matthew?" he asked.

She sat back down again. "I heard from her yesterday. She just finished her fourth week of counseling with the pastor of the church near her home. He really helped her with the transition from the awful live-in relationship with that guy who fathered Matthew to a relationship with the only One who will never leave her or forsake her."

"You mean she received Christ as her personal Savior?"

"I wish it were so. No, not yet, but she's progressing toward that decision. She's reading her Bible and going to Bible studies there at the church. She mentioned that she wants to join the church and be a part of the congregation." She stopped and made a victory sign. "I just know that the Lord is going to save her and her son."

"Now you're talking!" he replied jubilantly. "How *is* Matthew doing?"

"He's undergoing a healing. The youth pastor has taken him under his wing and a meaningful bonding between them has taken place. He really made him feel comfortable in the church."

Randy paraphrased a verse out of Joel to fit the occasion. "The Lord will restore to your sister everything the locusts have eaten. You'll see. He will bring her to salvation and restore them as a family, then use their experience to give something back to the kingdom. Such is the way of the Lord."

Yvonne smiled. "It sounds like you just uttered a divine oracle."

Randy returned the smile. "Let's say we pray that my 'oracle' goes from my lips to God's ears."

"Amen."

The office door opened and closed.

Yvonne turned toward the door as Randy walked to his doorway to see Marty walking to them with a manila envelope under his arm. "Well, hello brother!" Randy said.

Marty said with a boyish grin, "Do you remember that fellow in the hospital bed next to me that you led to the Lord? A guy by the name of Freddy?"

"Of course," Randy replied.

"Well, after I was discharged from the hospital I called his family and they told me that, when he came home from the hospital, he was a changed man. He had a peace about him that caused his family to wonder whether or not he had an emotional breakdown while in the hospital. But when they questioned him further about his newfound peace, he told them he had prayed with a pastor to receive Christ and was now ready to meet God, if He so chose that for him."

"That's a wonderful testimony to the Lord," Randy added in amazement.

"It gets better. It so happens that the Lord did take him two weeks later, and after his funeral, his wife and children started going to a Christian church."

Randy was overcome with Marty's account. *Even in death, the Lord will be lifted up and fruit will emerge from the gospel seeds planted,* he thought. "You'll see how the Lord will use that family in a mighty way."

"It was just another confirmation to me that the Lord is guiding me into his service," Marty observed.

"May it be so," Randy agreed. He looked Marty over. "How's the stomach?"

Marty pulled his shirt out of his pants to reveal the incision. The stitch line was still red and swollen, but the protrusion was gone. He slapped his stomach in a macho way and said, "Looking good."

"My, my, you sure *are* looking good." Randy scanned him one more time. His newly gained appearance reflected his walk with God. He was clean-shaven and his hair neatly cropped; his fingernails clean. He wore a sport shirt with a pressed pair of pants and nice brown loafer shoes. He even had on a belt. It was obvious he was regaining his self-esteem while God was rebuilding him. Randy nodded in approval then motioned for him to sit down. "Tell me, Marty, have you defined your ministry yet?"

Marty nodded and opened the manila envelope. "Yes, I have," he replied as he pulled out several loose-leaf pages of paper and placed them on Randy's desk in front of him. "Would you like to hear some of the things I've sketched out?"

"Definitely."

"My objective is to create a homeless awareness network that will work with area churches to solicit their support," he began. "I think a simple way to get homeless people off the streets is to open up God's doors to give them a place to live. I know from personal experience that most churches prosecute the homeless for trespassing on their property or for sleeping in their parking lots or in the doorways. So…"

"Well, there have been many horror stories of churches that were severely hurt over their embracing the homeless," Randy interrupted. "So, naturally, they would be wary and cautious."

"Agreed," Marty replied. "Yes, the homeless may destroy property, cause problems for the congregations, and create uneasy feelings. Some don't comply with the rules and some even vandalize the churches." He became emotionally charged and added, "But God does not care about the buildings because He'll make the necessary adjustments for any problems that may arise as long as we're helping the poor. You see, I'm not talking about actually 'bringing' the homeless into the sanctuary. I'm talking about the churches *adopting* the homeless. By adopting the homeless, the churches will help finance the homeless shelters so we could get the problem under control."

"Oh."

"You see, Pastor, there are roughly 10,000 homeless individuals and families on any given day here in Broward County alone. So what we could do is ask the 5,000 churches in South Florida to adopt two homeless people each, and the bulk of the problems would be solved. The community will benefit by this program because their property values will not decline since no homeless will be living on the streets but will have a safe place to live and work toward successfully making the transition back into society."

"Makes sense," Randy agreed.

Marty slowly shook his head as he glossed over his notes. "Over the course of a year, as many as 3.5 million people become homeless. This is nearly 11 percent of the poor population. A 25-city survey published by the U. S. Conference of Mayors documented a 19 percent increase in homelessness in 2002-2003, the steepest rise in a decade. Each year 5,000 runaway and homeless youth die from assault, illness, and suicide. There are medical evaluation and maintenance problems with these people. Then there's the healthcare surrogate situations, and the recidivism and preventing homelessness among people leaving prisons." He shufflef the papers and lamented, "It just goes on and on."

Randy's breath caught in his throat. "And your list doesn't even include public support and community advocacy to help with the problems with law enforcement where the homeless are arrested and incarcerated and not assisted with problems such as mental illness which caused the problem, or education for youth about the problem of homelessness so they do not romanticize being on the streets."

"Really a colossal project. When you stop to thing about it, it's a life-long project," Marty said optimistically.

"It's a worthy ministry, a worthy mission."

"That reminds me, Pastor," Marty said. "Can you help me prepare a mission statement?"

Randy's eyes lit up, then he asked Yvonne to bring in two cups of coffee. Over the next hour they carved out a mission statement that would act as Marty's platform for ministry. "So here it is," Randy said as he held the document up in the air. "We begin this ministry by making it an offering up to God." He lowered the document and read it aloud:

"To honor God in all our endeavors to meet the needs of the homeless. To offer adequate and affordable housing to the homeless. To offer shelter to abused persons including domestic violence, and homeless individuals and families. To offer employment for formerly homeless individuals through vocational rehabilitation. To provide job training for the homeless that will qualify them for the outside workforce. To give every homeless person a chance to achieve self-sufficiency to enable them to give something back to society."

Marty smiled, reveling in the sound of it. "It's a masterpiece!"

But would it fly? That was the problem. Getting the churches to see the homeless as a mission field within their own community instead of a mission field half a continent away was a vexing dilemma. "What we will do," Randy explained, "is to have you present when we convene the pastor's coalition we're forming to meet the homeless challenge here in South Florida. Together we should be able to craft a concrete plan to move the agenda along."

Gratitude swept over Marty's face. He stood to embrace Randy. "Thanks Pastor."

Randy grinned. "Go and be a blessing."

104

As Marty exited the office, Yvonne handed Randy a written telephone message. "Laurie telephoned while you were in with Marty. She asked for you to return her call."

Randy closed the door behind him, then walked to his desk. He sat at his chair and lowered his head to pray. "Lord Jesus, as sovereign Lord, you're in control of all things," he whispered. "And I know that all things work together for good for those who love you, so cause my Laurie to yield to your will in the matters of our church, our family, and our marriage." He picked up his phone and punched in her cell phone number.

"Hello, darling," Laurie answered after reading his number on her caller-ID.

Resolved in his heart not to bring up their last conflict, he was determined to allow her the benefit of the doubt. Hopefully her communing with nature at Butterfly World allowed her an opportunity to see things more clearly, namely her connection with God. She had to think things through and settle them with God so change could occur. "Hi, Babe. Is everything all right?"

"Yes, darling. Everything is fine," she replied warmly. A momentary pause, then, "I guess you're thinking that I have a shelf-life problem, right?"

Throwing those "darling's" around always made him nervous. *Is she protecting herself by denial?* "Never," he replied. He quickly recalled his last words with her and paraphrased them. "You'll always be my girl."

"Can we have a special evening tonight?" she asked coquettishly. "Sort of like a pre-anniversary celebration?"

Randy was puzzled. "Is there something special we should be celebrating?"

"In a way, yes. I had a very peaceful time with God at Butterfly World, and I've made up my mind not to let your decisions about church policy come between us anymore."

Wow, Randy thought. *Now we're getting someplace. Praise the Lord!* "I will look forward to tonight with baited breath," he teased.

"Love ya, mean it, bye," she replied. *Click.* Looking at the phone brought a pang of guilt. Apparently there was conflict in her soul that troubled her and she knew she couldn't bring it to her husband, nor to God for that matter, for neither would have approved of her reasoning. So, things would just have to play themselves out.

* * *

Randy had to move the day's agenda along so he headed down the hallway to his worship minister's office and stood in the doorway. He wanted to make sure that he kept Mike in the loop of the ministry's strategy, despite his busyness with the homeless project. In conscience, he felt he may have unwittingly overlooked that responsibility to him.

Michael Rice and his wife, Suzy, had come to Plantation Gate slightly over three years ago after serving six years as worship leader at a Baptist church in Atlanta with over 5,000 members. His reason for the lateral move was indicative of a problem becoming increasingly troublesome in the nation's churches. The philosophy of ministry had changed since he had been hired on after seminary in that his pastor believed that gospel drama and a heavy music ministry appealed to the congregation's physical and emotional senses, but he came to realize the so-called contemporary look when coupled with a feel-good message left a spiritual vacuum that severely hampered true worship in his family. Further, he began to see a shift in the congregation's appetite for the sensual instead of the spiritual. People were unwittingly coming to the church to be entertained, not to be spiritually challenged or to hear a victory-in-Christ message that was so vitally needed in today's compromising world. So Mike sought out a senior pastor who had the same vision as he did. A vision to raise the standard in the church by the example of living a holy life and a "heavy" concentration on learning the Word of God, despite public craving for sensationalism.

Once on-board at Plantation Gate, Randy made it a priority to bond with Mike to develop a relationship that would lead to a complementary union as pastor and assistant pastor. One that would be obvious to the congregation that they shared the same theology, philosophy of ministry, vision, and purpose. The end game being that when Randy got up to preach on Sunday, his congregation had been prepped to hear the Scriptures expounded by truly experiencing the real meaning of worship because Mike brought to the platform the spirit, energy, and enthusiasm to transport the person in the pew directly into the throne room of God.

"Good morning, Mike," Randy said, breaking Mike's concentration. Mike sat at his computer, downloading graphics for the Sunday worship *Power-Point* presentation that supplemented the bulletin outline supplied by Randy the day before.

"Busy morning, right?" Mike spun around on his swivel chair, referring to Randy's meeting with Yvonne and Marty.

Randy gave him a soft laugh. "Goes with the territory."

"Right."

"Mike, I need you to be a part of a meeting tomorrow with Avi Bekker from Beth Yeshua. We're forming a coalition of pastors in this area to develop a program to meet the growing needs of the homeless."

"A worthy mission field," Mike replied with a nod.

Randy could always count on Mike for support, even if he were not fully informed as to the nature or purpose of the project, trusting Randy for the good of the kingdom and the ministry at Plantation Gate. "One that I hope the congregation will stay behind." Changing the subject: "How are you coming along with the messianic music for the Moishe Rosen, *Jews for Jesus*, seminar?"

Mike rotated on his chair and pulled out a file folder labeled *Messianic Seminar* and opened it up on top of his desk. "Looking good," he announced. "I've been on their website and downloaded several of their songs. We've been practicing them on and off for several weeks now to prepare for the big event."

"Marvelous!" Randy replied. "And the praise group? Are they excited about the messianic music?"

"Very. In fact, Ronnie Edelson, being Jewish, has really taken up the banner and spread the enthusiasm among the other members of the praise group. So, we will be in good shape come the seminar."

"Having Jewish believers in the church really pays off, doesn't it," Randy said with a chuckle.

"Amen."

"Busy morning, Pastor," Yvonne said as she walked up behind Randy. She pointed her pinky finger toward the lobby. "Stephanie dropped in to see you."

Randy turned on his heel in the direction of the lobby. Uninvited people coming to the church was standard operating procedure. "Oh, that's fine. Tell her I'll be right there." Yvonne walked away as Randy gave Mike a salute. "See you later."

* * *

"Whoa, look at you!" Randy gave Stephanie a visual sweep. Her hair was cut into a pixie with blond highlights, and she sported a colorful short-sleeve blouse and new jeans. She was becoming increasingly attractive as the wear and tear of homelessness faded, augmented by good hygiene and decent clothes. Obviously she was feeling better about herself. It seemed that the homeless organization allowed their residents to keep a small percentage of their street collections for personal use.

Modestly she replied, "Thank you."

Randy escorted her to a seat in his office, then pulled up a chair and sat across from her. "So, what brings you here this morning?"

She crossed her legs demurely, then nervously rubbed her palms on her jeans. "Well, you can tell me it's not my business to make any assessments on what I see here at your church, and I can respect that position. But if you want to know what a casual observer, one that does not belong to your church or fully believe what you preach, sees when they come here, then you should let me speak my piece."

Randy exhaled deeply and mentally braced himself for an emotional flailing. *Lord, do I have to take it all in one slug?* "Hmm," he said after a moment of contemplation, "will this build up or tear down the kingdom of God?" He had to qualify the upcoming discussion with some kind of disclaimer.

"Hopefully, it will build up your ministry, but there may be some tearing down first."

Randy smiled wryly. "I was afraid of that." He walked over to his bookshelves in a conscious effort to collect his thoughts. *The pioneers and trailblazers take all the arrows, right? Yes, as the trail blazing pastor, I want to be open to constructive criticism, but criticism coming from a relative stranger and not a staff or congregation member might not be in the Spirit. But then again,* he realized, *there was one instance where God gave a prophetic dream to a non-believer to get his message across to Israel and the world.* One such case that came to his mind was out of Daniel 2 where the heathen Babylonian king Nebuchadnezzar saw the great statue that was later interpreted by Daniel to mean the four coming empires to rule the world. "Okay," he allowed, "tell me what's on your heart."

She inhaled deeply. "When you first saw me three months ago, I was at the lowest point in my life. But somehow my life has changed, and now that I feel better about myself, I am able to see more clearly, and if there's anything I've come to realize, it's that I know how I got to that low level in the first place."

"Interesting," Randy commented.

"What's *really* interesting, Pastor Randy, is that I see a similar series of events taking place in *your* family."

"Whoa, now hold on!" Randy said in controlled alarm. "What do you mean *my* family?"

Fidgeting: "If you will allow me, I will explain."

Randy walked closer and pulled up a chair. "Go on."

"I'm sure you remember my last talk with you and how I wandered the streets of Fort Lauderdale."

Randy would never forget her descriptive narration of one slice of her life as she considered her reflection in the storefront window. "Almost word for word," he replied.

She nodded in appreciation that someone had listened to her. "I think it may be the right time to tell you something of how it all began." She paused as if waiting for a go-ahead signal from him.

He swallowed hard and nodded. "Yes, I really want to know."

She ran her fingers through her hair. "I'm originally from Queens, New York, actually, Howard Beach. It was there that I grew up and met my husband when I was at Queens College. His name was Keith, and he was very smart and very handsome. Our dating gave way to a live-in relationship during our senior year, and we married after graduation. Keith went on to work for a defense plant in Suffolk county on Long Island, while I began to have children and raise a family. After our second child was four years old, I began to get restless and felt that my education was wasted on being a mother and housekeeper, so I badgered Keith to let me go to work outside the home.

"By this time Keith had moved up the corporate ladder and was a purchaser, making over $100,000 a year with a great future ahead of him. While Keith was a family man and spent all his free time with me and the children, I wanted more. I wanted the best of both worlds—a domestic life and a career. Keith relented and let me go to work on one condition: that if the family began to suffer, I would quit. Well, at first I was able to juggle both the home and the career, but after the first year, things began to deteriorate. I would drop the children off in the morning at a daycare center and, invariably, be late in picking them up, and when I did, it was like they didn't really know me. By the time I got home, my day was so full that I really didn't have the patience for the children's needs. Before long, I didn't have time for Keith's, either.

"We began to drift apart, and in order to keep the children content, we would inundate them with new toys to keep them occupied while we pursued our own agendas. Sure, we would take family vacations to Disney, but that wasn't what our family needed. Another year passed, and Keith and I were living separate lives, yet living in the same house. He had his career, and I had mine. Before long, we began to have problems with the children. We would be called down to daycare because they were unmanageable. They were fighting with other children and constantly talking back to adults. They became rebellious so we sought out medical care to give them drugs to subdue them so they wouldn't get into trouble…"

She began to sob. "I know now that I became an administrative mother to our children. I was *officially* their mother, but the attention, the love, and the kissing of their boo-boos after they scratched their knees, was surrendered over to another; the woman at the daycare center. In a way, she became their mother. I was too busy getting my career up and running. Then things worsened. We decided to sell our modest home and buy a bigger home out further on Long Island—bigger and better. We thought a change of scenery would patch up the wrongs in our family, but it didn't. We simply transported our problems to another location. The real problem was with us: Keith and me. Mostly me. It was me who wanted bigger and better. It was me who wanted to get away from the house and the kids and make a difference in the world. Keith was content with his family and station in life, but I wasn't."

Now Stephanie held her head high. "This is why I wanted to come to you, to tell you what I see. I see a similar, if not uncanny pattern taking place in *your* family. Yes, you're a pastor, and your wife is still working on her education and your children are older and many of the other details are different, but I have observed your wife and I am familiar with the mindset. It scares me because I see a lot of myself in her. I'm not judging her; I'm only trying to keep from happening in your family what happened in mine."

A pause. Randy was upset, because the rapid-fire outpouring put him on overload. He could feel a headache coming on. Then there was the hurt. The accusation hurt, but the parallel hurt more. *Is this the lifestyle that brought her to the streets? Was this the path her family took to calamity? There had to be more, if not a devastating blow that exploded the family. There's a lesson here,* he reminded himself. *A lesson for my family?*

In reflection, Randy recalled reading about a family research poll that indicated the one factor that has done more damage to families than any other was the two-career family. Many parents suffering from fatigue and time pressure come home exhausted and harried, having nothing left to invest in their marriage or in the nurturing of children. Boys and girls come home to empty houses every afternoon, during which anything can happen. During the childrearing years, the two-career family creates a level of stress that tears people apart, often depriving children of something that they'll search the rest of their lives for. Often this stress ends in divorce, compounding the problem. A footnote in the poll added that a scale-back from a materialistic, two-career lifestyle could bring about national harmony in the home once again.

"I appreciate your taking the time to explain this to me," Randy said after his moment of meditation. "I was wondering what event triggered this?"

She waved him off wearily and stood. "I've said enough for now." She added somberly as she walked toward the door, "Sometimes my big mouth gets me in trouble."

Randy joined her at the door. "Stephanie, everything that happens in life has a purpose in the counsel of God, and you can be sure that His purpose will not be thwarted. So take heart, and trust the Lord for your life."

Stephanie nodded as she regained control of her emotions. "Trusting the Lord is going to be a big step for me, Pastor Randy. Keep praying for me."

"I promise," he said as she walked out of his office.

Randy paced back and forth in front of his bookshelves to process Stephanie's testimony, which didn't seem to have a happy ending. *Not yet, anyway*, he thought, *but God is in the business to change lives, and this is one life I know He is going to use mightily to win souls.*

He stopped short and looked at his watch. *Time to go.*

He threw his Bible into his attaché case and walked to Yvonne's office. "I'm taking off to go buy an anniversary present for Laurie, then I'm going home. See you tomorrow."

"Melt some plastic!" Yvonne said with a grin.

"Ha, ha."

10

The Florida hurricane season was quickly yielding to the cooler October weather that signaled greater opportunities to dine outside in comfort. Dinner outdoors with Laurie in their screened-in patio was on Randy's agenda for tonight. His goal was to spend a quality evening with her after the children went to bed, talking and reaching out to one another, the patio ensuring relative privacy from the rest of the house. He wanted it to be a special night.

Nature was cooperating. A cool breeze flowed through the screens, yet not enough to extinguish the row of scented candles that flickered in the half-moon light. The cicadas and crickets that frequented their backyard must have burrowed into the lawn or sought refuge in the shrubbery for the night for they were very subdued. The neighborhood, too, was quiet. The alchemy for a wonderful evening had come together.

"The kids are asleep," Laurie announced gleefully as she walked out onto the patio in her bathrobe.

Randy sat at their patio table munching on salted almonds. "How do you know?" he asked with a smile.

"There's no light coming from under their bedroom doors."

"Cool beans," he replied, his smile growing luminously.

Laurie meandered around the patio, looking at her flowering plants for several moments. Then she said quietly, "Randy, I want you to know that I need peace in my life. I want to stop fighting."

Randy unconsciously went into counseling mode as he nodded in assent. "Oh? That's fine with me, but what can we do to contribute to the peace process?" He wanted to be sure that this was real this time around.

"When I was at Butterfly World, I realized that God's creation longs for peace and that when there is peace, there is tranquility and stability in many places in the world. I know that's what I want for our family."

"Go on."

She fiddled with the dead petals of the potted impatiens. "So I'm prepared to do whatever it takes to bring that peace about." She turned toward him. "That means that for one, I'm going to support you in ministry and adjust my schoolwork hours to accommodate the needs of the family."

"Man, you really did experience a peaceful time at Butterfly World," Randy quipped.

She grinned. "That means I'm going to carefully manage my time so that I'm not consumed with school. This way I can spend more time with you and the children."

It sounded too good to be true. *Lord, You are beautiful!* As she walked toward him, he pulled her into his arms. "That's my girl," he said as he looked into her eyes. "I love you." A thought shot through his mind. A thought that, if acted upon, would show his appreciation for her. *Am I rewarding her for her good behavior?* he asked himself. *No, I don't think so.* "Wait here for a minute. I want to get something for you."

"What?" she asked curiously.

"Just wait here."

He bolted out from the patio to his bedroom dresser and pulled out her anniversary gift hidden beneath his T-shirts, beautifully wrapped in her favorite color paper, accented with a small bow and a small card. Dashing back to the patio, where Laurie waited expectantly, he said with a childish grin that resembled a smile button, "Your anniversary present, three days early. I couldn't hold out any longer."

She read the card aloud. *"To my helpmate. Happy anniversary darling. All my love, Randy."* She backed up to sit in a patio chair as she began to cautiously unwrap the gift. Under the wrapping was a felt-covered, flat type jewelry box. "Whoa," she said in surprise as she flipped up the cover. "This is magnificent!" It was a 14-carat gold braided chain with a white pearl mounted on a gold slide. She held it up and stared at it for a moment. Flabbergasted: "Okay, who helped you pick this out? Tiffy?"

With a proud look: "Nobody. I had it made special for you."

"Randy, this is beautiful!" she added with absolute delight.

"Just for you, baby, just for you."

Their hearts filled with surrender from their trials for the rest of the night, where reminiscing and talk of love and the goodness of God dominated their conversation.

* * *

"Time to go to lunch, gents," Randy announced to Lester and Ronnie. Welcoming their input and insight, he had decided to invite his deacons to the luncheon with Mike and Avi Bekker. It would be a ministry expense at the modest seafood restaurant, the Sea Shack, by the Sawgrass Mills mall. Randy always tried to steer luncheons away from the places that offered mostly beef and sweets on their menu that invariably brought on the sluggish fallout after the meal.

To Randy's delight, Avi was waiting for them in front of the restaurant.

All but Randy were surprised at Avi Bekker's appearance, being somewhat conservative in his own comportment. Avi was tall, lean, and bald-headed, except for exceptionally long hair on the sides that he pulled tightly into a ponytail that dangled nearly six inches in the air. He sported a Vandyke beard that accented his chiseled facial features. Lester's first impression was that Avi was a radical rabbi or a hippy seminary professor, or the like. His calling to lead a messianic congregation seemed to be ironic and out of character, but then, Lester thought, Christ was called a radical and a misfit as well. Ronnie thought he looked cool, while Mike simply studied him and reserved any judgments pending their discussions.

Randy ordered his traditional potato soup and chicken Caesar salad, while the others indulged in the daily special. Once the orders were placed, Avi asked, "Randy, how is your approach to the homeless going?"

"In one word—interesting."

"How so?"

"Well, I'm convinced the Lord is going to bless our efforts, citing one interesting incident that occurred recently. Not long ago I had a visit from a 'graduate' from the HO homeless shelter by the name of Marty, who wanted my advice on his plan to minister to the homeless. His plan is to recruit area churches to financially adopt the homeless at the rate of two families per church. His idea would solicit the cooperation of participating churches in Broward county to help finance shelters. Based on the number of churches in Broward, he predicted that the homeless challenge would be met."

"A noble gesture," Avi commented.

Lester exchanged looks with Ronnie and Mike. "Sounds good," he added.

Randy squinted at Avi. "While I commend Marty's passion, I don't think he has the political clout to really make a difference here in South Florida. I believe we need an organization that has 'teeth' to fulfill Sam Knowles' dream."

"Sam Knowles?" Avi said.

"Oh, you'll meet him in time," Randy explained. "He's the director of Homeless Outreach. The man with which I've had the pleasure of working with, who, along with the Holy Spirit, first ignited a flame in my heart for the homeless. You see, his vision for the homeless is broad. It includes Operation Rescue, which works with law-enforcement agencies to locate and place vagrants and the homeless in his shelter, as well as enlisting area churches to form a coalition to fight politicians seeking to rid the towns of the homeless. His goal is to rebuild his people to prepare them to reenter society as productive members."

"Sounds a bit like the Salvation Army, only for the homeless," Mike inserted.

"That's a good point, Mike," Randy said. "You see, I believe the Salvation Army, along with Alcoholics Anonymous, have sound spiritual principles in place to guide them—the so-called 'step method' of surrendering your weakness over to a 'Higher Power.' That's why I'd like to see the coalition that we form have a spiritual or faith-base that would operate in a similar fashion."

"Well," Ronnie put in, "there already is a Broward Coalition for the homeless organization in place."

"Yes, I'm aware of their organization, and they are doing a commendable job of helping the homeless. But our coalition would be different. Their foundation is based on secular and societal reasons to help others, and if that works for them, great. But our coalition would be based on Biblical reasons to help others—namely, Christ's instructions to help the needy in His Sermon on the Mount. With a Biblical mandate and the right approach to this problem, I believe we can have a significant impact on the homeless community."

"We'll call it the 'Open Arms Coalition for the Homeless,'" Mike suggested.

Randy smiled. "Sounds like a winner."

"We'd need some kind of day training program in a central location to meet the growing problem of employment among the homeless, along with a transitional program to prepare the candidates to return to society in a productive way," Avi advised.

"Agreed," Randy said. "The coalition will have to raise up teachers from area churches to teach GED classes and work on the recruiting of businesses who will take a chance on a graduate and hire them."

"Establishing emergency funds to help people avoid eviction when their life hits a crisis and to pay the funds necessary to again get housing if an eviction has occurred should be a priority," Ronnie suggested.

"See, this is what we need," Randy proffered. "A brainstorming session to get things out on the table."

"I've been writing things down as we go along," Mike announced perkily.

Avi pulled a folded piece of paper from his shirt pocket and handed it to Randy. "I went Online and downloaded a 'toolkit' from the National Alliance to End Homelessness. It should help us in the formation of the coalition."

Randy read the list aloud: "Create a plan. Create a data system. Institute prevention programs. Make systems changes. Outreach on the streets. Shorten time un-housed. Rapid re-housing. Treatment and services. Create affordable housing. Increasing incomes." He handed the list over to Lester, who read it, then passed it around.

"Seems like a huge task," Lester finally said after several shakes of the head.

"It is," Randy agreed. "But with the help of the Lord, nothing is impossible."

Several amens sounded.

"Should we conduct a comprehensive survey of the area churches? Form focus groups, or perhaps host an annual planning day? Then there's a demographic study we could...?" Ronnie asked before Randy waved him off.

"Too soon," Randy replied. "We don't want to make this effort so complicated that we scare volunteers off, or get so busy in the organization of it, we lose sight of the spirit of the project. Let's get the coalition formed and take it one step at a time. That's how they built the pyramids, right?"

Smiles.

* * *

Randy pulled out of the Sawgrass Mills mall parking lot with a broad smile. *Something great has been accomplished today for the kingdom of God. I just know it.* But his smile faded when he thought on Stephanie's visit. *Blast! Why can't things go right for a while? There's always something going on that spoils a person's joy. Just for once I'd like to experience a season where I didn't have to fight off some enemy attacking the church, or some enemy attacking my family.*

He glanced at his reflection in the rearview mirror. Seconds later a thought shot through his mind. "Okay, Lord, I get the message," he said to himself. *Right, no personal attacks. Yes, I'm grateful..* There were no lawsuits against him. There were no traffic violations against him. There were no moral or ethical attacks against him. His family had no medical or financial problems. He was walking with the Lord, and the Lord saw fit to entrust His sacred Word to him to share with his congregation. He had the power of Pentecost in the pulpit. There were no personal temptations that he had yielded to. He had spiritual discernment to counsel. He had a beautiful, healthy family. And most of all, he had Jesus.

So what's your problem, Randy? the Spirit asked him.

"None, Lord," he answered.

But Stephanie's observations about Laurie that amounted to an attack on his family had to be dealt with. If not now, then sometime in the near future, for he knew the day would come when the Lord would require him to permanently settle the issue of her relationship with God.

Soon he was back at the church.

* * *

Within an hour he cleared his schedule, then leaned back in his desk chair and interlocked his hands behind his head. *Hmm*, he thought, *I have an idea.* "Mike!" he yelled toward his door, "if you're not doing anything real important now, how about taking a ride with me?"

"Sure!" he heard echoing through the hallway. "Just give me a few minutes to shut down my computer." He was downloading music for the Sunday worship service. Moments later he appeared at Randy's doorway. "What's up?"

"Let's do some 'visitation.'" He grabbed his car keys off the bookshelf and his attaché case off the floor, then turned off his office light. "Yvonne, Mike and I are going to drop in on Sam Knowles down at Homeless Outreach. If you need me, get me on my cell phone."

"Will do," Yvonne answered while never breaking her stride on the computer keyboard.

The ride down to the Homeless Outreach headquarters building in Hollywood was another opportunity for Randy to bond with Mike. Ministry matters that included goals, strategy, and problems, were addressed at their scheduled weekly meeting. But personal time to catch up on family and fun seemed to be relegated to unscheduled encounters. "Suzie and Eric okay?" Randy asked. Eric was their adopted 14-year old.

Mike smiled and shot his eyes upward. "Yes, praise God."

"Sweet," Randy gave him a thumbs'-up. "So you're still having a 'good time' here?"

Mike knew that was Randy's way of asking if he was happy to be at Plantation Gate church, and was he experiencing the joy of the Lord as he served in God's ministry. "It keeps getting better!" he said convincingly.

"Sweet," Randy repeated as wave of exhilaration swept over him. It felt good to have a partner in ministry that supported him and remained on the same page of purpose.

* * *

The Homeless Outreach building was uniquely different than Randy envisioned. His notion of what a shelter should look like resembled a large colonial farmhouse that served adequately as an administration, dining, and recreation facility. In his mind, the sleeping residence should be connected to the farmhouse to resemble a motel with fine accommodations to house the homeless. Instead, the Homeless Outreach shelter was a two-story concrete building, formerly used as a nursing home for the elderly, that, despite every attempt to improve on its appearance, remained an eyesore.

"Not what you expected, was it?" Mike observed as they pulled into the parking lot that ran under half the building.

"No," Randy replied as he scanned the premises, noting several dismal areas that reminded him of squalor and heartbreak surrounding the indigent. "I had a different image in my mind."

"Oh, well, hopefully our ministry to help them will change things around here," Mike said optimistically.

"May it be so."

* * *

"Pastor Randy and his assistant Pastor from Plantation Gate church to see Sam Knowles," Randy announced into the intercom speaker at the front door of the Homeless Outreach building. The receptionist gave them a strange look through the wire reinforced glass door, then pressed the button that energized the electromagnetic latch.

"Is he expecting you?" the working homeless lady of about 42 years old asked.

"No," Randy replied, "but he knows who we are."

The receptionist by the name of Michelle picked up her phone, informing the party on the other end of their presence, then said, "You can go up." She pointed down the hallway. "Just take the elevator to the second floor and make a sharp right to his office." Seconds later Randy was knocking on the director's door.

A loud, "Come in," was heard through the door. As they walked in, Sam was on his wireless phone, waving them to sit down in his office. Talk about the homeless committing suicide dominated the phone conversation as Randy and Mike exchanged several glances of surprise before Sam ended the call.

"Randy, how good of you to stop in for a visit!" Sam boomed.

Randy nodded toward Mike and made the introduction. "This is Mike, my worship leader."

Sam stood to give Mike a vigorous handshake. "Great to meet you." He sat down and pointed to the phone. "That was Nick Darcy down in Key West. He runs a homeless shelter called the Sanctuary and I like to keep in touch with him every now and then to get a feel for the way others run their operation." He paused and shook his head several times. "Nick was telling me that the stats of suicides among the homeless has risen sharply, an area of highest concern for him. It seems that an extraordinary number of homeless gravitate to Key West during the winter months, hoping to panhandle the vast volume of tourists that come there. Of course city officials don't want their city to have a bad impression when travelers tour the mangrove trees along the beaches and see barefoot vagrants sleeping on cardboard surrounded by empty beer cans. Balanced in the trees are plastic crates with food, toilet paper, and various other sundries necessary for the squatters' survival. The officials complain that the transients are violating endangered wetlands by their presence, but it's their impact on the tourist dollar that they are really worried about. So the police evict them to enforce an ordinance that prohibits trespassing, leaving them with no place to go. So, they wind up dead on a slab in the coroner's office of apparent suicides.

"Extremely vulnerable people are left homeless, which wreaks havoc with their emotional and physical well-being. Add to that living in unsuitable living conditions, lack of a home environment and appropriate levels of care and nurture, and you have alarming statistics of suicide among the homeless. Being left homeless isolates people from friends, family, and social services, all of which many fail to realize can be vital lifelines to those in crisis. Then lay on top of that pile the stress, anxiety, and depression that often puts them over the edge where they take their own lives." He read off his scratch pad. "A recent study reported that 19 of the 48 suicides were those of homeless." He steepled his fingers on his desk as he pondered his own commentary.

Randy nibbled on his lower lip. "A very grim picture."

"They need to set up a 'safe zone' with shelters where the homeless can go and thus avoid the tourist areas," Mike suggested. "Maybe even provide bus service for them to places of employment. I mean, after all, if the city invests the necessary money to meet the needs of the homeless that continue to migrate there, in the long run, they'll make more money from the tourist trade to make up for it."

"Good suggestion," Sam replied. "Unfortunately, they tried something like that and it failed because nobody wants the homeless in their back yard.

Bottom line, the environmentalists and city officials feel the mangrove trees and tourist trade is more important than helping a human life."

A deafening silence fell upon them.

Moments later Sam lamented, "I believe it was in Dante's Inferno where it was said, 'The hottest places in Hell are reserved for those who, in times of moral crisis, maintain their neutrality.'" Looking at Randy and Mike collectively: "It's just a shame how we humans treat each other, isn't it?"

They nodded slowly in unison.

Randy searching for relief from the oppressive pall that hung in the air, slapped his knee to initiate a new episode. "Let me give you some good news, Sam."

"I'm up for it," he replied.

"Well, Mike and I, along with Avi Bekker, the head of Beth Yeshua, and two of my deacons met at lunch today to discuss our plan to develop a homeless ministry that we hope will help fulfill your dream," Randy began. "It's called 'Open Arms.'"

Sam's eyes locked on Randy's as he took a deep breath that marked a positive turn of events in his outreach organization. "Tell me more, please."

Randy continued: "Today I received a visit from one of your guests, Marty Fitzgerald, and he told me of his plan to recruit area churches to financially adopt the homeless at the rate of 2 families per church. His plan has merit, and I hope to incorporate his plan in with ours."

"Glad to see Marty is finding his place in the community," Sam noted.

Randy pointed to Mike. "We pastors have the inside track and connections with other pastors, so it follows that we would spearhead the solicitation of area churches."

"It's not going to be so easy," Sam allowed cautiously.

Randy and Mike nodded, then Randy waved him off. "We know, we know. We've already had a taste of the rejections. But if we can convince area churches to join our coalition to work to advance a homeless network and community, then we believe it has a good chance at success because of its spiritual underpinnings, in sharp contrast to other organizations that simply have societal or secular motivations."

"They may have the financial clout, but we have the Spirit to help us," Mike said solemnly.

Sam nodded as he cracked a tight smile, signaling his tension was wilting. "I'm feeling better already, men. Keep it going."

"You could say that the Spirit would be our operating guide," Mike asserted.

Randy grinned at Mike. "One of my fellow pastors, Avi, downloaded a checklist from the National Alliance to End Homelessness that I believe can be modified and adopted for our use."

Mike pulled from his pocket his notepaper from lunch, and waved it in the air. "I have the essential toolkit from National Alliance here."

Sam nodded and reached into an accordion file in his desk drawer, pulled out a folder, and tapped it with his finger. "I have the more elaborate version from National Alliance that details that toolkit."

Randy smiled at Mike and took the list. "Their ten essentials to end homelessness just need to be touched with God's Spirit. Instead of 'what your community needs to do to end homelessness,' we adjust it to read 'what your *church* needs to do to end homelessness.' If the church leads the way with a faith-based program, we can believe that the communities will follow in time.

"Then we add some practical measures such as establishing a day training program to prepare the homeless to return to society. Include the raising up of teachers from these churches to teach GED classes as well as enlisting church business owners to take a chance on graduates from the program and give them a job. Finally, add to the toolkit the need for a emergency fund to help people avoid eviction."

Sam gazed out his window and ruminated for several seconds. "If we can get the churches involved, we have a good chance at licking the problem."

Ideas and methods started to come together in Randy's head. "Suppose we set an ultimate goal of 100 faith-based units or churches here in South Florida to host two families in their facility." He nodded at Mike and added, "Then *Open Arms*, together with *Homeless Outreach*, provides the process that will enable them to begin the road to recovery."

"You mean *Open Arms* will be the religious arm and the *Homeless Outreach* will be the secular arm?" Sam asked for clarification.

"Well, not exactly. We will both be working together, but *Homeless Outreach* will provide the intake and evaluation with appropriate referrals, the transportation to and from the churches sponsored by *Open Arms*, the cots and linens, and all the supplies and the facility for necessary hygiene. The churches in the coalition will provide supervised overnight shelter, dinner, fellowship, breakfast, and a bag lunch for the day. From there, we just have to work out the training and transitional programs using the teacher and business resources from the member churches."

A gleam appeared in Sam's eye. "Ah, a turn of events!" he exclaimed optimistically. "Maybe we would be able to make a difference to end homelessness in this region if that plan were to work." He shuffled some papers on his desk and pulled one out. "If we can make this fly, maybe we could partner with the workers at the Salvation Army."

Randy wanted to keep the program within the jurisdiction of the church until there was a measurable success before bringing in outside support. His inclination was like Sam's regarding the rejection of public or city subsidy that could in turn dictate policy matters. "We'll see how it goes."

"Agreed," Sam conceded.

"Your *Operation Rescue* would also be an important part of this," Randy explained. "By providing law enforcement a place for them to deliver vagrants and the homeless—in a sense, take them off their hands—we will win their support, then use that support to fight the politicians who seek to rid towns of the homeless."

Sam clapped his hands and exulted, "Sweet!"

Randy and Mike exchanged glances and smiled. "You like what you hear, then, right?"

Sam sighed. "Now all we have to do is make this vision a reality."

"That's God's job," Randy declared emphatically.

"Amen," Mike concurred.

Sam stood and announced, "Let me show you what a difference we can make in the life of the homeless. Let me take you on a tour of our facility."

"Let's go," they agreed and headed out of Sam's office and into the main corridor.

Some 20 feet from his office was a metal door with a window in the center. He opened the door and said, "Here are our dormitories, and our first stop will be to one of your friends." After knocking on the resident's door, he opened it and said, "Here is Stephanie's room. She shares it with another woman, Viola."

Viola's face flashed in Randy's mind. Then he remembered her tilting her head down at the Wednesday night Bible study and showing off her medal to the class, the long scar on her skull her boyfriend gave her for not sharing her drugs with him. The story about her trying to sell her kid for drugs was still emblazoned in his mind. But the best part was when she received the Lord that night. "Yes, I know this Viola," Randy said. "She came to our church with Stephanie, and it was there she got saved."

"Interesting." Sam slowly closed the door and ushered Randy to the side. "You know, I'm still thinking about our conversation that we had a while ago in your office. Someday I plan to talk to you further about it."

"I'll look forward to that." Randy shot a praise up to God. Every time one of his witnesses or testimonies came back to him, he thanked the Lord for the opportunity to share the gospel with someone once more.

They rounded a corner and stopped at another metal door with a window. "This is the men's side," Randy explained. They walked through the doorway into the hallway to a room where a man in shorts and a T-shirt stood outside with his arm outstretched in the doorway. "Hello, Jake," he said and nodded to Randy and Mike. "These are pastors Randy and Mike who are working with us here at Homeless Outreach to make the churches aware of who we are."

"Gentlemen," Jake said politely, "it is a pleasure to meet you." He made a sweeping invitation motion with his hand toward the inside of his room and added, "my home is your home."

"Good to meet you, Jake," Randy replied. He turned and waved as they moved down the corridor.

"Likewise." Jake saluted.

"Four weeks ago," Sam explained with a look of accomplishment, "Jake was wrapped in an old fatigue-green army blanket that was dirty and moth-eaten. No shirt or underwear, just the old blanket and a pair of grungy cut-offs. Operation Rescue found him sleeping behind a Walmart store in a cardboard carton. For the first two weeks, his silence was the only conversation we could muster out of him. But, with a little TLC, he's beginning to come around."

"I'll say!" Mike commented. "Wonderful."

He stopped halfway down the hallway. "This is Marty's room. I saw him leave this morning with a handful of religious tracts."

Randy could only imagine where he got them from. "May God bless him," he said with a grin.

"Sam," Mike asked, "what is your opinion on the major cause of homelessness?"

Sam didn't have to dig too deeply to reply. He was constantly surrounded by living statistics. "A breakdown of the family unit."

"Ah, yes, the God-instituted vehicle for stabilizing humanity," Mike said, turning on his soothing voice. His didactic voice. He knew the other two God-instituted regulators for society were the government and the church. They too were under relentless attack by liberals and self-seeking politicians.

Sam ticked off on his fingers several examples. "There's the ever-present divorce problem with its severe impact on children. One landmark study revealed 90 percent of children from divorced homes suffer from an acute sense of shock when the separation occurs, including profound grieving from a sense of abandonment and irrational fears that contribute to homelessness later on in life. Then there's the feminist movement, which has destylized homemaking. Add to the mix a hostile-to-family media that is busy opposing moral principles at every turn. And don't forget the homosexual movement decimating the one-man, one-woman marriage that is so essential to proper societal growth. Throw on top the tax imbalance where married couples are taxed at a higher rate than those living together without benefit of marriage, abortion zealots, and haters of the Judeo-Christian ethic, and it is no wonder that our world is full of misfits, the homeless being just one of many."

"I hear ya," Mike replied with a shake of the head.

Grim thoughts of mothers gone wild shot into Randy's mind. Deanna Laney from Tyler, Texas, who killed her two boys by bashing in their heads with a rock, and Andrea Yates, mother of five from Houston, who drowned all five of them in a bathtub were sobering examples of the mounting crisis in the family. He reminded himself of the great need to keep his priorities right. After God came his family, then the needs of the church.

He remembered hearing from a fellow minister, a youth pastor, who told him that a child from a broken home is in greater jeopardy of rejecting Christ than those from normal homes, underscoring the indisputable fact that the family is critical to the propagation of the faith.

They arrived at the kitchen that had an adjoining dining room.

The kitchen was cafeteria-style with a long stainless-steel counter with a tray slide and food display shelves. The dining room was adequate to serve between 40-55 persons with its metal picnic tables and connecting benches.

As they moved inside the dining room, a group of two men and a woman were seated on a bench having coffee. As Sam guided Mike over toward the kitchen area to continue the tour, Randy zigzagged over toward the group. He was slightly repulsed when he saw the woman had several patches of red, oozing pus on her scalp that looked like the hair had been pulled out by the handful. She wore a torn shirt with ill-fitting pants that hung midway down her hips and black scaly blotches on her bare feet. Randy's mind refused to allow his eyes to wander and inspect the men, whose condition was far worse.

As he neared them, they dropped their heads and exchanged glances between themselves. "Hello," he said, "hope you have a nice day." They looked up but said nothing. Seconds later he joined Sam and Mike.

"They're our new, raw recruits straight off the streets," Sam commented. "You can see that the streets have had their way with them."

Randy said gruffly, "Yes, I can see it has." *Lord, help them,* he prayed. Seconds later he amended his prayer. *Lord, help me so I can help them.*

11

The moment Randy stepped inside his house, his eye caught the decorative banner hanging across the living room wall. "What's this all about?" he asked his family as they met him with a Happy Anniversary greeting card. Sean, Tiffany, and Laurie were standing in ascending order at the front door, waiting for him to arrive.

Sean acted as spokesperson: "Mom said you were going out to dinner tonight to celebrate your anniversary since it falls on a Saturday and that's not a good night for you because you need to prepare your sermon."

Randy grinned expansively, then gave them all a peck on the cheek. "Good thinking!"

"They chipped in and bought us a gift certificate to Leonard's in Boca," Laurie said, her eyes blurred with tears.

"Oh, that was really nice." Randy scooped Tiffany and Sean into his arms and gave them a big hug. Seconds later he opened their card and carefully read it. He rejoiced at their personal notes, then held up the gift certificate.

"Many lawns had to be mowed for that, Dad," Sean joked.

"Many babysitting jobs for that, Dad," Tiffany chimed in with a grin. Then she clapped her hands. "We'll take care of everything here. All you have to do is go out and have a good time."

Randy reached down and picked up his attaché case, then extended his arm toward Sean. "My son, I leave this in your charge."

"I am worthy to act as the custodian of thy documents," Sean said mockingly.

Laurie turned to them as she took Randy's arm and headed for the door. "Be good."

They both curtsied.

* * *

Randy thought the half-hour drive to Leonard's should be part of their special evening, so he reduced his speed and lowered the front windows of the car, allowing the cool October air to blow softly into the cabin. It offered a refreshing change from the air-conditioning and brought with it the wafting aroma of many tropical flowers . "Ah, what a glorious night," he remarked as he put his arm around Laurie. She pulled out a CD from the console and popped it into the CD player, adjusting the volume so it wouldn't overpower their conversation.

"All right," Randy said smiling, pleased with her selection. The voice of Richard Tucker singing Puccini arias eclipsing the roadway noise.

"So how was your day?" Laurie asked, her tone conveying interest.

"In one word, terrific! Mike and I had a great time down at Homeless Outreach," Randy answered.

She wiggled out from under his arm. "Tell me about it."

Sensing the change in her demeanor he swallowed hard and said, almost apologetically, "First, the deacons, Mike, and I had a meeting with Avi Bekker where we framed out what we coined our 'Open Arms' ministry. That included a serious discussion about forming the coalition to act as an advocate for the homeless. Next, Mike and I stopped in on Sam Knowles down at Homeless Outreach who gave us a tour of the facility." He glanced at her. "And it was quite an experience. Really."

Cooly: "So what's the next move?"

"We agreed to bring the concept of Open Arms to the church on Wednesday for their vote of approval. Once the church approves, we propose to link up with Homeless Outreach and run with it. I just know God is in this."

"If God is in this, who can argue with God?" Laurie replied.

* * *

"So, how was your evening?" Tiffany asked her mother as the family assembled around the kitchen table for breakfast the next day.

Laurie forced a smile at Randy, who was pouring himself a cup of coffee. After several seconds of contemplation, she managed, "We had a nice time."

"It was a delight," Randy added swiftly. "And thanks again for your card and gift."

Sean nodded acceptance, then asked, "Mom, would you be able to help me with *my* schoolwork today?"

"I don't think so, honey. Today wouldn't be a good day because I'm cramming for a test myself." She inserted her English muffins into the toaster.

"But today is Saturday," Sean, replied, his eyes begging for attention.

Randy's eyebrows shot up. *Didn't we already talk about this?* He rose from the table and joined her at the toaster. "Laurie," he whispered, "I thought we agreed that he needed help with his homework, and that you would be there for him."

"Yes, we agreed on that, Randy!" She strummed her fingers on the countertop, her tone rising exponentially with her anger.

"Well, then, can't you find time to work with him? Can't you *sandwich* your son into your *busy, demanding schedule?"* His own voice modulated to the challenge.

Tiffany and Sean exchanged troubled glances, then slowly and mechanically placed their utensils down on the table and braced themselves for the next blowout.

Laurie forcibly ejected the English muffins prematurely from the toaster and threw them down on the counter. "I will work with him according to *my* schedule!" she snarled.

Despite his pledge not to stoop to her combative level, he yielded to his anger. He turned and pointed to Sean, saying fiercely, "But you agreed to help him and that he was going to be a priority in your life!"

She gave him a lethal glance. "No! *You* agreed! *I* will pick and choose *what* is a priority in my life, and *when* I will spend time on that priority, clear?"

Randy clenched his teeth and resisted the urge to pound the counter with his fist, wincing at the vitriol in her voice. A deluge of prior skirmishes over family priorities, ministry goals, and her career path gushed out in his mind's eye. He suddenly realized that her trip to Butterfly World was nothing more than an excursion into nature. As far as her "very peaceful time" with God was concerned, he now saw the adventure as nothing more than spiritual gymnastics, a flexing of her spiritual muscles, but no change in her heart.

Then Stephanie's observations of Laurie instantly replayed in his mind. *Lord,* he prayed, *show me if Stephanie was right. Tell me what to do.*

He backed off. He looked at his hands balled into fists and immediately recognized who was in control. It was his emotions. *You will win the battle but not the war,* a voice from within cried out. "Yes, we're clear," he conceded. He turned and stared at his children, hands now in his pockets.

Tiffany blinked rapidly and looked away. Sean's eyes were teary, but he caught his father's eye. He stood and bolted out of the kitchen. Tiffany simply sat there, immobilized.

"Are you happy now? Do you see what you started?" Laurie stepped back and lifted her hand in a see-you-sometime gesture and stalked off.

In the frenetic environment, Randy lost his presence of mind. The mantle of regret weighed heavy on his soul. *"Only the dead have seen the end of war." Do you have to quote Plato now?* he scolded himself.

The front door slammed.

Happy anniversary to you too, he didn't say in the direction of the door.

Tiffany shook her head. "Mom is changing, isn't she, Dad?"

Randy sat at the table and clutched her hand. "Go easy on her; she's under a lot of pressure."

"Dad, why are you making excuses for her?" Tiffany asked. "If I put in my two cents, I'd say Mom has a problem with being selfish."

"Don't talk that way about your mother, Tiffy," Randy warned.

"Dad, I'm not being disrespectful, I'm only saying the truth, and you know it. Mom could only be pursuing her education to gratify some unsatisfied longing inside her. After all, it can't be about the money. I mean, let's face it: even after Mom gets her degree and then lands her job, is the money she earns really needed? Has she thought about the cost for our family?

"I remember reading the stats on working mothers, and once you deduct taxes, commuting expenses, lunches, and clothing, the net amount of income for a working mother was something like 17,000 thousand dollars a year. For all the aggravation, it hardly seems worth it. Not to mention the conflict in the family that goes with it." She breathed deeply. "Why doesn't she want to be a stay-at-home mom, anyway?"

Randy had always believed his daughter thought well beyond her years. This discussion seemed to be another confirmation of it. *That's a good question. And when you boil it all down, the question was really the right question: why doesn't she want to be a stay-at-home mom?* "Maybe there's something missing in her life and she's trying to find it. Until then, she's filling it with school and career. We need to pray the Lord fills that void."

"Don't you see: the home and church ministry just doesn't do it for Mom. Her schooling seems to be all she cares about. And when it comes to being present at church functions, it's like Mom isn't really there. She's always looking for—" She searched for a word.

"...diversions," Randy said to complete her sentence. *Sure, that would also explain her lack of interest in anything to do with the homeless. Not to mention the tenuous nature of her interest in the church.* "There's a term for it," Randy noted dryly when the truth, once again, was presented to him.

"I know what it is," Tiffany said bluntly. "It's called an 'administrative mother.' I've been going online to the *Focus on the Family* ministry hotline and reading all their articles. And Mom fits the profile to a T."

Randy sat down, grappling with the enormity of the problem. Laurie's cyclical behavior, he believed, was an attempt to camouflage her expanding interest in her education and career over her duties of a wife and mother. Performing domestic duties only when necessary, and then without any sense of fulfillment or joy; interaction with the children only when convenient; no concern for the ministry or the congregation. Looking at the journey of life as if it were an official mission without taking the time to mingle with the lives of others. Standoffish, selfish, inconsistent with the character of a Christian.

There was Stephanie's critical, yet right-on observations, and now, Tiffany's unprofessional, youthful, yet discerning counsel. A huge sigh. C.S. Lewis' quote flashed in his mind: *"A wise man can't always be defending the truth, there must be time to feed on it."* He waved a hand in the air in an attempt to stop the flow of information. "Pray for me today, Tiffy. Ask the Lord to give me the wisdom to speak to your mother."

Several tears rolled down her cheeks before she sniffled and reached for a napkin. She held her father's han. "Dad, I've been praying for you every day since Stephanie came to the church because I had a leading of the Spirit that she's going to be the one God uses to change things in our church and family."

He gazed into his daughter's eyes with wonder. This was the second time in four months that he heard what he believed was a divine oracle. He patted her hand. "I've got to see how your brother is doing."

* * *

On her way to the mall, Laurie made up her mind that it was time to put her plan into action.

* * *

Once again, communication between members in the Bradshaw family was suspended. From Saturday morning to Wednesday afternoon, eyes would lock and body gestures would transmit information, but only official dialog or necessary conversation was heard. The backwash from the Saturday morning argument hung over the household like a dismal black cloud.

But on Wednesday afternoon the ice-breaker arrived when his cell phone rang. "Dad, Mom wants to talk," Tiffany said in a tone conveying apologies.

"Now you're in the business of mediating?" Randy replied jokingly, both suspicious and relieved that the end of the crisis appeared to be in view.

"Weak link, maybe, but not mediator," she said. "Mom met me at school and drove me home. I think she wanted to feel me out and talk to someone who might agree with her."

"And did you agree with her?" The thought that their relationship was now deteriorating to the level that they would communicate through their children was not very appealing. *Ask your father if he's coming home for dinner. Tell your father that the trash has to be brought out. Remind your father that the lawn has to be mowed.* And on and on it goes when husband and wife stop talking.

"On some things, not all," she astutely replied. "I agreed with Mom that we need peace in the family, and that you both need to watch how you talk to one another. But I disagreed with Mom over Sean."

"Oh?"

"Mom thinks he is old enough to learn the material himself and that if she helps him, he'll become dependent on her. I thought Mom was a little off base so I said that he does need the attention, not only for his schoolwork but also as his mom."

"You're kidding me, right? You really said that?"

Tiffany nodded. "Yup."

Out of the mouths of babes... "Tiffy, you didn't let on about our talk after Mom walked out on Saturday, did you?"

"Nope."

"What else did she say?"

"I was surprised when she brought up your homeless people project. It sounded to me like Mom is beginning to see the light."

Skeptically: "How so?"

"I guess it was when I didn't really agree with her about Sean that Mom asked me about my thoughts regarding the homeless people, and after I said that I believed you were doing the right thing to help them, Mom went quiet for a while. Then Mom shook her head and said something about being the 'odd-man out,' 'needing to get with it,' and that maybe it was really time to support the whole project." A pause, then: "Sounds like God is answering our prayers, Dad."

Randy's heart was softened by his daughter's report, but unrelenting doubts gnawed at his soul. *Seeing is believing, right? Is it real this time?*

Silence.

"Dad?"

"May our prayers go from our lips to God's ears, Tiffy," he said tonelessly. "May it be so."

"See you at the Bible study, Daddy."

Click.

* * *

Three hours later Laurie appeared at the church with coffee and donuts in hand. She walked into the office lobby then paused inside the doorway, giving the room a quick visual audit. *Good, no one here.* Then her eye caught him walking out of Yvonne's office. "Randy, I thought we could spend some time alone before people start to arrive for the Bible study."

Yvonne saw her and discreetly closed her door.

Spotting the cardboard tray in Laurie's hand, he paused momentarily. *Another peace offering?* "Okay with me," he replied, almost deadpan, while curiosity trickled in to his heart. *Her taking the initiative is a good sign.* He looked behind her. "Where are the kids?"

Walking into his office and setting the goodies on his desk, she said, "I asked Lester to bring them tonight." After closing the door, she got her coffee and sat in one of the stuffed chairs. "You're thinking I'm a nut, right?"

Strategic planning, he thought. *When this woman wants to get her way, she can move heaven and earth. Sleek dress, high heels, hair in a twist, nice. Arrangements for the kids. Schedule maneuvering to ensure privacy. Good work.* He picked up his coffee and sat in the chair across from her. "A nut? No. A woman needing to yield to God's Spirit so He can guide and give her peace? Yes."

She crossed her legs and ignored the critique. "I came early to explain to you that I know I've been wrong about Sean, and the homeless."

Randy steepled his fingers on his desk. "Really?"

"You don't believe me?"

His eyes flicked to her face, then away. She looked penitent, or was it that she appeared to be unjustly accused, and slightly offended? He wasn't sure which. "I want to. But I guess we've reached the place where it would be more convincing if your apology had some teeth in it." He took a slug of coffee and peered over the rim at her.

She nodded. "You're right. When you're right, you're right. And to demonstrate my good faith and commitment to our family, I met with Sean before coming here and promised him that I would help him with his homework." She smiled. *"He's* very forgiving.

"Then I thought that, since I haven't had the chance to get to know a lot of the people in the church and from the Homeless Outreach, we invite select members of the congregation and some of your friends over to our home for a day of fellowship. You know, use the pool, have a barbecue, enjoy the backyard, and just share life for the day with our church family, friends, and

131

each other." She tapped the side of her coffee cup with her fingernail. Then an afterthought: "You could even invite what's-his-name…you know, the head man from that shelter, too. That would be a good mix."

"Sam Knowles is his name," Randy muttered. He gazed out the window as he pondered her deal. He took particular notice of her use of the terms *forgiving, friends,* and the catchy *what's-his-name. I should take the cue from my son and forgive, right? And, darling, am I hearing you right? Are you saying they are my friends, not yours or ours? Just mine?* He scratched his head in bewilderment and fired a prayer up the God. *Lord, help!*

Seconds later: "Sure, why not? We haven't had church folk over the house in quite a while. And it would be a good opportunity for you to get to know some of the people from the Homeless Outreach." He reassured himself that this time the deal was genuine. "I think it's a good idea; let's go for it."

"Good. I think this Sunday after the worship service would be ideal, so suppose we agree on the list and I'll start making the invites tonight at the Bible study. You can call Mr. Knowles and make the arrangements with the Homeless Outreach people."

"Amazing grace," Randy whispered to himself in wonder. *Is this for real?*
"What did you say?"
A muscle jerked in his left cheek. "Oh, nothing. Just praising the Lord."

Once they agreed on the list, they went out for dinner, Randy reveling in the renewed possibility of having his wife really committed to the Lord and their church.

Laurie viewed the agreement as a sign from God that she should move forward with her plan to protect her husband's ministry.

* * *

Mike asked Suzy to assist him during the praise and prayer time that preceded the Bible study. Suzy had a knack for remembering and playing all the pastor's favorite hymns on the piano; it was her way of showing her appreciation for him as a godly leader. "Redeemed," being the number one selection, followed by "My Jesus, I Love Thee." After that, she took hymn requests from the congregation, intermingled with their praise and prayer reports. Twenty-five minutes later, it was time for Randy to make his important announcement and take the vote.

"Nice crowd tonight, Pastor." Lester scanned the overflowing group finding their way to their chairs. "Guess the congregation got the word on the Homeless Outreach and Open Arms thing. Looks like they're excited about it."

Randy replied with one of his favorite expressions, "From your lips to God's ears." He shot a look over at Laurie talking to Judy Edelson. They both looked perky and highly animated. *A noticeable change in Laurie's demeanor,* Randy thought. *Huh.* Tiffany and Sean sat toward the rear of the room with the homeless contingent who encompassed Stephanie and Marty.

All the angst and strain from their squabbling faded as Randy took the lectern to make his announcements. "Just a reminder that Moishe Rosen from Jews for Jesus will be here November 15, so get the word out and invite your Jewish friends to hear his important message." He nodded at Judy Edelson and added, "Much planning and advertising has gone into this, so let's be responsible and see Judy for the tickets ASAP."

"Pastor," Judy said as she raised her hand, "we have put up posters advertising the event in the supermarkets, theaters, and bagel joints near the Jewish communities, and we've received a very positive response."

Hand clapping.

"Outstanding!" Randy exclaimed. "Keep up the good work."

Judy beamed as several people tapped her on the shoulder to place their orders.

"The next item we need to discuss is our homeless project," Randy said with a twinkle in his eye. He motioned to Ronnie and Mike. "Brothers Ronnie and Mike are handing out a detail sheet for you to review before we take a vote tonight. It contains all the highlights and pertinent information relative to the Homeless Outreach and our Open Arms ministry." He took a sip of water. "Take your time and read this now." He left the lectern and wandered around the room answering individual questions. Twenty minutes later he returned to the front of the room.

"Now that you've had a chance to review the highlights of our proposal, I would like to explain a few things," Randy instructed. "Let's address the focus of this program first. That is, what is the goal of this outreach? We've thought about it for many hours and believe the design is simply an extension of our ministry statement: to reach the lost for Christ. That's our number-one priority. You'll remember our church philosophy of ministry is to 'uphold the Word of God to reach the souls of men.' Well, we aim to fulfill that mandate by making a turn in our ministry to embrace the homeless. That's not to say that our other ministry outreaches, such as foreign missions and supporting Israel, is to be put on hold. No. We are going to *add* this to our evangelism program just the same as if we were voting to take on another missionary family serving some place in Africa." He tapped the lectern several times and added for emphasis, "Although this is not our objective, let it be said that we as a church will be blessed beyond measure when we leave our comfort zone and minister to the homeless." He signaled Mike, who walked to the lectern. "I've asked Brother Mike to explain the 'How-to' of this ministry since he visited the Homeless Outreach shelter and saw firsthand what that organization is all about and how it relates to our ministry."

"Thanks, Pastor," Mike replied with a smile. "On the outset, let me say that, although I'm called to be the worship leader here at Plantation Gate, I have no problem joining with Pastor's heart and invest myself in this important need." Several cheers erupted from the group. Embarrassed, yet in humor, he waved off the cheers: "No heckling, no heckling, please.

"You'll note on the handout that in the introductory remarks we want this project to be a faith-based program. We believe that differs widely from the secular model. In time the public may get involved with this, but for now, we're going to keep it within the confines of the South Florida area churches. Next, you'll see there is a diagram that shows how Plantation Gate along with other committed area churches will form a coalition and work with the Homeless Outreach facility. We will call the church end of it *Open Arms*. The goal of Open Arms would be to enlist 100 faith-based churches to host two families in the Homeless Outreach facility. Homeless Outreach would provide the intake, evaluation, transportation, and sleeping equipment. Open Arms would provide the supervised shelter, breakfast, lunch, and dinner, along with a strong spiritual message. Together we will form a formidable pair that will make a profound difference here in South Florida's homeless community." He stopped and turned to Randy. "Our pastor will finish up on the 'How to,' then discuss the church's participation."

There was a noticeable glow about Randy as he returned to the podium—the kind of glow that accompanies a man who has found God's purpose in his life and is confident he's exactly where God wants him to be. "What we also need to know that will help us in our vote is that the Homeless Outreach facility has implemented what is known as *Operation Rescue* that works with law enforcement officials to locate and place vagrants in their shelters. They also solicit churches to fight politicians seeking to rid towns of whom they consider undesirable." He paused to check his watch, then signaled Lester to distribute another info sheet. "We're running out of time, so for future reference, you can read the 'ten essentials' or what we call the 'toolkit' that brother Lester is handing out now. This describes our 'how-to' in fine detail. It includes a step-by-step process to ensure a successful recovery system for the homeless. From the plan through systems prevention, outreach, rapid re-housing to income, this toolkit will be our pattern once we get going."

He stopped and randomly pointed his finger at several members. "What's equally important is where you fit in. We won't be able to effectively minister to the homeless without your participation. Whether you're a senior or a young believer, every person in this church can be involved. And let me remind you that with your investment, time, labor, or otherwise, you will be blessed."

Mike stepped up to the podium. "Some may be able to help with contacting area churches, others with devoting time at night when the homeless would be coming in for the day to sleep, others with the meals, while still others can help by being the spiritual mothers and fathers these people need after being on the streets for so long. And let us not forget the mighty stay-at-home prayer warriors who are unable to physically leave their homes but can certainly keep the project before God's throne of grace."

"Here, here!" several older folks cried out. "We're ready!"

Randy nodded to Ronnie and Lester. "As a congregation-rule church, we can only act on any measure or proposal when we have a majority vote. Accordingly, I've asked the deacons to conduct the balloting process."

Randy's expectations were surpassed. The vote was almost consonant, with only one abstention. God was moving His mighty hand; the Open Arms ministry would soon be a reality.

After the vote, Randy realized he was out of time. *Oh, well,* he thought, *tonight was better than a Bible study. This vote was the application of faith, a giant leap of faith. Let everything that has breath praise the Lord!* He closed the meeting with a prayer of thanksgiving.

As the congregation broke up into groups, Laurie made it a point to approach Stephanie, Marty, and their companions to invite them to Sunday's barbecue at her home. Then she selected members of the church body to join them as well.

Tiffany walked up to her father and nodded toward her mother and noted with a chuckle, "Dad, can you believe it? Mom's really making the rounds tonight."

Really atoning for her sins, he thought. "The Lord moves in mysterious ways, doesn't He?"

They both stood and watched in awe as Laurie worked the crowd.

12

Laurie walked out onto her screened-in patio to check the barbecue grill, then continued on to the swimming pool and dipped her fingers in the water. *Just right.* Casting her eyes upward she saw resplendent sunshine radiating through scattered clouds. *No threat of rain. Excellent for swimming. It's going to be a nice day.* Outside the screened-in patio, the St. Augustine grass provided a lush carpet for eight lounge chairs, two picnic tables with umbrellas and benches, and the volleyball net set off in the corner of the property. The prospect for the Sunday afternoon gathering looked promising.

Fifteen minutes later, the guests began arriving.

Lester raised his hands in the air as he walked up to the Bradshaws' front door where Randy met him. "Nice weather for late October, wouldn't you say, Pastor?"

Judy Edeleson walked gingerly behind him carrying a tuna casserole and reaffirmed the pleasant weather report. Ronnie followed in step carrying a tray of home-baked cookies.

"God is good!" Randy replied with a smile as he held the door open for them.

Sam Knowles came shortly afterward in a minivan, transporting Stephanie, Marty, Viola, and Alexis, each exiting with a small carry bag and a towel. Within thirty minutes, all the invited guests from Homeless Outreach and Plantation Gate church had arrived.

"Wow, look at you!" Suzi Rice exclaimed as she caught sight of Laurie in her black pantsuit. She paused in her walk and scanned her from head to toe, then strolled up to her and gazed at her gold chain with the pearl slide. "We're talking some serious jewelry, here!"

Laurie beamed and rotated in place. "Thank you," she said modestly. "Randy gave it to me for our anniversary." She brushed her sleeve and added, "I'll just keep this outfit on until we all go in the pool." Suzi smiled and moved away. Seconds later a woman tapped her on the shoulder. It was Stephanie.

"Thank you for having us," Stephanie said in a lowly way. Laurie nodded to her and the other guests from Homeless Outreach as they paraded past her to their target table in the far corner of the patio. She realized by their attire they were all planning to use the pool.

"I'm Sam Knowles," a voice announced to Laurie as he stepped into the patio room. "And you must be Laurie Bradshaw." He extended his hand and added, "I've looked forward to meeting you."

"Why, yes," she answered courteously. "Randy speaks of you often." Turning toward the refreshment table where Randy stood preparing the soft drinks, she pointed and added, "Randy will be happy to serve you."

"Thank you, kindly," he replied and slowly brushed past her toward the table where his people sat talking together.

Sam stood in the corner next to the table for several moments with his shoulders slumped, observing Laurie and the influx of guests. Something bothered him about the introduction, but he couldn't put his finger on it. *Was it the way I was greeted? Mrs. Bradshaw didn't seem too friendly. Maybe it's me, and I'm just overreacting?*

He scanned the table where his people sat, then over to Laurie and the church group, processing the scene unfolding before him. *What's the message I'm receiving here? Isn't there something in the Bible about Jesus breaking down walls?* Standing in one area next to the refreshment table were all the church folk with their back-patting conversations and head-nodding laughter, while his people sat isolated in the corner. To cover the niggling discomfort in the pit of his stomach, he whistled a Broadway show tune to himself.

"That's 'O, What a Beautiful Morning' from Oklahoma, isn't it?" Randy asked as he approached him from an angle.

"You bet," Sam answered, snapping out of his preoccupation.

Randy extended his hand. "Welcome! We're so glad you could make it."

Sam dismissed his feelings for the moment after thinking, *I wonder if your wife agrees?* "We're happy to be a part of this."

"Wonderful," Randy rejoined while tugging Sam's arm and pulling him toward the group near the refreshment table. "Now let me introduce you to some of the congregation who so eagerly said 'yes' to our proposal to form Open Arms." Sam graciously succumbed to the invitation and cordially made the rounds with Randy.

Tiffany, dressed in cut-off jeans and a halter, as well as sporting a MP-3 player on her belt and headset in her ears, circulated in and among the crowd with trays of hors d'oeuvres while Laurie played the ideal hostess, flitting from guest to guest, making it a point to stop at Stephanie's table to dispense several amenities before moving on. Sean patrolled the perimeter, maintaining surveillance over the litter and discards.

"Who are you listening to?" Stephanie asked Tiffany as she paused at her table with the snack tray.

Definitely embarrassed, yet startled into truth: "Oh, it's Madonna. It's her new album." She quickly removed the earphones.

"You listen to Madonna?" Viola and Alexis asked simultaneously, apparently surprised that a pastor's daughter would mimic a rock star with questionable standards.

"Well, I..." She swiftly turned toward another table.

Marty leaned forward conspiratorially and whispered to Stephanie, "You need to talk to that girl about role models."

Stephanie knew exactly what Marty meant and how important role models are in life, especially those who represent spiritual and ethical values. *Where is her mother and father in this?* she wondered. "You're right. Someday I will."

"Everybody listen up!" Randy shouted. "The pool is now open, so let's get changed into our bathing suits, if you haven't already, while I prepare the main course on the barbecue grill." He pointed to the bathrooms and added, "We have two bathrooms—one next to the kids' rooms and one next to the master bedroom. Both are open." As expected in south Florida at outdoor home events, most of the guests wore their bathing suits under a beach robe or pool outfit.

Laurie took the cue and casually waved to her guests before walking to her bedroom to change. Randy had opted out of the pool for the day, arguing his need to operate the grill.

"I need to use the bathroom to change," Stephanie whispered to Marty.

Marty pointed to the long line next to the kids' rooms and said, "Use the express lane next to the master bedroom." Stephanie nodded in agreement and walked off.

"No pool for you?" Randy shouted to Sam while flipping the hamburgers and hot dogs on the grill.

Sam walked over to Randy and said, almost apologetically, "I'm not a pool person. I enjoy the Florida weather, but I guess you could say I'm a land-lover."

"I hear that." Randy grinned expansively and ran his fingers through his hair.

Focusing on Randy's full head of hair, then rubbing his bald head, Sam replied, "Well, the hair isn't my problem; it's just that I don't like to get my parts wet."

"Ha, ha!" Randy laughed and patted him on the back. There was something about Sam that he really liked. He thought it might be that he respected him as one who rose above the terrible fate of homelessness to face the challenge of running a shelter for the homeless. A feat few were able to pull off with any degree of success. He suddenly halted in his actions. *Could this be a God-ordained moment?* "Say, have you had any time to think about our discussions?"

Sam shifted his weight to one leg and leaned against the patio wall. "Um, yes, sometimes. In particular, when I observe the positive changes that have come over Marty, Viola, and Alexis, I have to take a second look at how that happened."

"It's the Lord in their lives," Randy said, full of conviction. "It's the promise from God about changing a new believer through the operation of the Holy Spirit. It's all part of the salvation experience in Christ I spoke to you about."

"Something to think about," Sam replied with a nod.

"Well, don't think too long," Randy quipped. "Remember, today is the day of salvation."

Sam turned his head to watch Stephanie emerge through the patio door in her bathing suit. "Have you noticed the change in Stephanie?"

Randy scanned Stephanie as she walked to the pool. He wasn't sure what kind of a change Sam was referring to. "A significant change on the outside, but I don't believe there's much of a change on the inside."

"What do you mean?" Sam replied.

"One can see she has cleaned up her act, taken on responsibilities down at HO, put on some new clothes and cut her hair, but there hasn't been any internal change"—he circled his heart with his finger—"in her heart. That's something only God can perform once she has made a decision to receive Christ as her personal Savior."

"Yeah, but you know," Sam argued with a wave of his hand, "we all have our own way of bringing God into our hearts. And for whatever it's worth, I think Stephanie has become a good person and that she's going to heaven along with the rest of us."

Randy simply nodded out of politeness. *It wasn't worth much since his secular theology was light-years from the truth.* His discerning spirit and experience in witnessing for Christ alerted him that Sam's heart was still not ready to hear the truth of the gospel. "Sam, you've lost your bearings on the path to salvation, but suffice to say that I look forward to the day when we can really get into the Bible and search out God's truth for you to see with your own eyes."

"Something to think about," he repeated and walked over to Viola and Alexis's table to join in their conversation.

Stephanie climbed out of the pool, toweled herself off, then walked over to the grill with her beach robe over her shoulder. "How's the food coming?" she asked.

"Should be ready shortly," Randy replied. He turned several pieces of chicken, then asked, "Are you enjoying yourself?"

Stephanie temporized. "Um, sure." She looked over to the table where her friends were sitting and noticed blank looks on their faces, silently scanning the crowd. She nodded toward the table and added, "Although I'm not too sure they are."

"What's wrong with them?"

"They're probably experiencing a social gap. I guess that's a problem the homeless people have to contend with when mixing with mainstream America."

"Well, we hope to remedy that in the future," Randy replied. "It's the wall of partition between the two that we aim to remove."

She moved closer to the grill and put her hand on his free arm. "I just want to thank you for all you're doing to help the homeless. I think it's wonderful that you and your church are willing to stick your necks out to fight the public who seem to want to hide us from view."

Randy looked at her hand, then followed it up to her neck and focused on her face. She was really an attractive woman whose hard exterior was quickly softening with each passing encounter, revealing an inner beauty that beckoned for exploration. He set the barbecue tongs down and gave her a hug. "You watch and see what the Lord is going to do in your life, Stephanie."

She held him for a few seconds, then intently gazed into his eyes and whispered, "You'll be there to help me along, right?" She gave him a peck on the cheek.

"Of course," Randy replied.

A woman clearing her throat was heard from behind. They both turned to see Laurie with her hands on her hips. "Mr. Bradshaw, are we ready to begin serving?" she asked with a tinge of sarcasm.

Stephanie abruptly walked away as Laurie approached him. "Coming right up, babe," he answered.

"Don't you 'babe' me," she replied with eyebrows raised and pointing to his pants. "You're all wet, Wilson Randolph Bradshaw!" With that she rotated in place, then stalked off into the kitchen. Randy looked down and saw that his clothes were dampened from Stephanie's wet bathing suit.

Randy swallowed hard. "Ugh," he muttered.

Sam stood in a corner and observed the rest of the evening's atmosphere deteriorate exponentially. The schism between the two groups noticeably widened with Laurie keeping her distance from the homeless group while stimulating members into a swarming beehive-like event that seemed to buzz and hum with the mundane. Obviously also, he discerned, she was fighting with Randy over something because they apparently were ministering in different arenas of operation—her with members, him with his deacons. *Hmm. Polarization? Why?* It was time to leave. He moseyed over to Stephanie's table and gave them all a hand signal and a nod. They eagerly stood and paraded out of the patio into the house and waited for him by the front door. Ten minutes passed before Sam appeared with both Randy and Laurie at his side. Stephanie would remark later that the departure resembled an exiting crowd at a movie theater.

Within an hour all the guests departed. Then came the clean-up.

Randy quickly stacked the folding chairs and disposed of the paper plates and plastic utensils scattered about the patio and yard while Laurie fastidiously restored the kitchen to its prebarbecue state. Tiffany and Sean were conspicuously absent, huddled in their rooms. *It's better this way*, Randy thought, *I have a bridge to mend.*

He walked up to Laurie. She turned and remained taciturn. Then the cold shoulder. He moved in front of her and asked, "Are you sore about Stephanie giving me a peck on the cheek?"

"Randy, it was the way you looked at her that bummed me," she replied with penetrating eyes.

"You're exaggerating it, Laurie. It was nothing," he explained.

"A woman can tell these things, Mr. Bradshaw. There was a message in the way you exchanged looks." She made quotations marks in the air with her fingers. "It went beyond the 'pastor thing.'"

Randy broke out in an everything-will-be-fine smile.

"Don't give me that look, Randy," she fired back. "I'm very upset with you." With that, she walked out of the kitchen into their bedroom. Moments later he heard her rustling through her dresser drawers. Then she stormed out into the kitchen. "We've got a problem," she announced in a hoarse whisper. "My necklace and slide is missing."

"What?" Randy said. "You're kidding, right?"

She slowly shook her head and began to cry. "No, I'm not. I've searched everywhere in our room. It's gone."

"But you were wearing it just before you changed into your bathing suit," he reasoned. "So it must be in there somewhere," he added with a nod in the direction of their room.

"Randy," she demanded, "I told you I looked everywhere, especially where I keep my jewelry. I know exactly where I left this because it's my best piece!" She ticked off her moves with her fingers. "I walked into the bedroom, then took off the necklace and slide, then walked to the jewelry box, opened the cover, and placed it in the first drawer where I always keep it." Her eyes filled with tears. "Now it's gone."

"Let's go back into the bedroom and have another look. A second pair of eyes can do wonders." Randy soothed.

She sniffled and nodded, then followed him back into their bedroom. Once inside, Randy surveyed the entire room but saw nothing, so he escalated the search. He turned over the articles on her dresser, flipped the pillows, spilled out her ring cases on the counter, all to no avail. Then he concentrated on the jewelry box. He pulled out the three drawers, carefully examining the contents, then looked behind and under them. Nothing. The upper compartment had hooks on the cover and one large cell for a necklace along with three smaller cells designed for earrings and broaches. The necklace holder under the top cover contained a pearl necklace given to her by her mother, but no sign of the gold necklace with the pearl slide. He then rummaged through the two remaining drawers. No sign of her new piece of jewelry.

"Hmm," he said, pulling back to look at her, "you probably put it in the wrong place." He started pulling out her clothing from the dresser drawers. When a pile of clothes had accumulated on the floor, he backed up and stood staring at the jewelry box. "This can't be happening," he said in disgust.

She scanned his face. "Could somebody have stolen it?"

Randy blinked as he processed her question. "Of course not!"

"Well, where could it have gone?" She meandered around the bedroom and pointed in several directions. "You can see that it's not here."

Randy snapped his fingers. "Tiffany. I'll bet she knows where it is." He hustled to the hallway and yelled for her to join them in the master bedroom.

The volume of his voice carried with it a great degree of urgency. Within one minute she was standing in front of him. "Tiffany, your mother can't find her necklace and slide. Have you seen it? Did you move it or put it someplace?"

She shook her head as Sean, walked in. He repeated the question to him. Sean just shrugged and shook his head.

"Okay, thanks," Randy said as he motioned for them to leave the bedroom. He closed the door. "I can't imagine somebody taking your jewelry…especially from the church."

"Could it be somebody who's not in the church?" she asked curiously.

"What do you mean?"

"Well, what about the folks from Homeless Outreach?" she suggested. "They were roaming around the house when it came to changing into their bathing suits. Some of them, I'm sure, used the bathroom by our bedroom."

Randy concentrated on her claim. From his vantage point, where he was tending the barbecue grill on the patio, he had no clear view of the hallway leading to the bathroom and certainly had no way of knowing who used it. *This is preposterous*, he reasoned. *Nobody from either the church or HO would have the nerve to steal from our home. And besides, why would they? Our church and family have been nothing but grand toward them both.* A sobering thought flew into his mind. *Could one of the guests from HO be a recovering drug addict perhaps? Needing to pawn the necklace for cash? Maybe. But then again, the only guests from HO were either saved or, to the best of his knowledge, did not have a drug problem. Nuts! Why now, when things were moving along so well?*

"Did you see any of the folks from HO by our bedroom?" he asked.

"Several people from the church moved in and out of that area," she replied while dwelling on the question. "But as far as your people from HO is concerned, I only remember seeing Stephanie using the bathroom."

He nodded when he remembered seeing her walk past him in her clothes and return in her bathing suit. "Hmm. Yes, I remember that as well." A sudden dread swept over him when the realization of the implication came into view. If this were true and there was a theft by somebody from HO, then this could destroy everything he was planning to accomplish. Another thought raised its ugly head. *Was that friendly gesture from Stephanie some kind of phony front or diversionary tactic?*

He scratched his head nervously. "I'll stop down at the HO center tomorrow and make some inquiries. Let's not jump to conclusions, okay?" They nodded together as another thought flew into his mind. "What do you think, should we call the police?"

"Not yet. Let's wait until you make your inquiries."

Keeping a low profile suited him just right, for now. To embroil the police and insurance authorities at this juncture when the dilemma could be remedied locally without them seemed to be a better choice. If his inquiries proved fruitless, then the incident would have to be reported and the consequences for both the church and Homeless Outreach would be unavoidable. "Smart idea. We'll wait."

A sudden cloudburst accompanied Randy as he arrived at the Homeless Outreach center. He looked up into the dark cumulus clouds. *I guess it's time to collect my thoughts. What am I going to say to Sam? To Stephanie?* Fifteen minutes of car-pelting rain caused him to make up his mind. He looked up at the clouds once more. *I guess the shower is not going to ease up.* He would chance the rain on his freshly pressed shirt and pants to move his day along. The anxiety of his dilemma brought pressure to bear that needed to be relieved.

Ah, a friendly face, he thought as he saw Marty at the welcome center waving him into the center. Seconds later he heard the electromagnetic door latch open.

"What are you doing here so early in the morning?" Marty's gaze narrowed on Randy's face.

"Nothing serious. I came to see Sam. Is he in?" Randy replied cautiously so as not to alarm him.

"He's always here by 8 o'clock sharp. A real punctual guy," Marty said reverently.

Randy suddenly realized Marty's new task. "Say, what are you doing at the welcome center, anyway?"

"Oh, I'm just filling in for one of the girls who took sick during the night, that's all."

"Jack of all trades, right?" Randy quipped.

Marty gave him a thumbs'-up. "Whatever I can do for God's kingdom, whether it be large or small is okay with me."

Randy would have liked to converse with Marty further, but the dilemma pressed heavy on his heart. It wouldn't wait. "Stop by the church this week so I can catch up on what's going on in your life."

Marty nodded as he picked up the telephone. "Sam should be at his desk, so let me see if you can go up now." He punched in the extension number, then announced Randy's unexpected arrival. Randy heard Sam's voice giving Marty the go-ahead to admit him.

"See you soon, Marty," Randy said as he walked to the elevator.

As the elevator doors opened on the second floor, Randy was surprised to see Sam waiting. "Well, hello there, Pastor Randy! Early call for you, no?"

"I guess you could say I am beleaguered by the tyranny of the urgent."

Sam grinned as he escorted him to his office. "Now that sounds serious," he joked.

Once inside Sam's office, Randy paced several times before Sam walked up to him and halted his procession. "What's troubling you?"

"Sam, I hate to say this, but a problem developed after our barbecue yesterday that I must talk to you about."

"Okay. What is it?" Sam asked, his face beginning to reflect Randy's deep concern.

Randy organized his thoughts. "Well, after everybody left, my wife discovered her necklace and slider was missing from our bedroom. We searched everywhere, questioned our children, and thought this out carefully. Unfortunately, there is a finger of suspicion pointing to the folks from Homeless Outreach who used the bathroom next to our bedroom to change their clothes."

"That can't be," Sam said incredulously. "Our residents are way beyond that."

Randy patted the air in front of him several times. "I believe that. I believe that with all my heart and soul. But then what other explanation could there be?"

"Well, what about *your* people from the church?" he countered defensively. "Are they all above suspicion?"

"Of course not!" Randy said hotly, his emotions flaring. "But Laurie did distinctly see some residents from here use our bathroom to change into their bathing suits, and in particular, Stephanie."

"Is Laurie accusing Stephanie?" Sam snapped.

"Sam, please, let's not let this escalate into a big thing, okay?" he pleaded. "I'd just like to ask Stephanie if she happened to notice anything unusual while she was in that area of our house, or if she might have seen someone step into our bedroom, that's all."

"Randy, those questions are highly speculative and very incriminating, especially for our residents, since the homeless are often mistakenly accused of thievery while the real culprits in their fancy cars and three-piece suits go free."

Randy's fears that this incident could explode his vision for Plantation Gate's outreach program was quickly coming into view. If he couldn't embrace and convince Sam that his inquiries were nothing more than a probe and not a full-blown investigation, then where would that leave his questioning Stephanie and the others if need be? They would undoubtedly react adversely and his plan to minister to the homeless through *Open Arms* would be over before it really took off. "Sam, can I just speak to her for a moment? I promise not to accuse her."

145

It would not be that easy for Randy today.

Sam slowly and silently circled around Randy for what seemed like an interminable period, then stopped cold. "I don't mind telling you, Randy, that I believe my people were mistreated at your home yesterday. And to add this accusation is simply the crowning glory that will set my people against your church."

Randy was floored. "What on earth are you talking about? We did not mistreat your people, but in fact embraced them as our own," he argued.

"Not so, Randy," he protested. "I personally felt a coldness toward my people coming from your congregation and, in fact, the coldness amounted to alienation. Your congregation stayed on one side of your patio, while my people were isolated to a corner table. There was no solicitude from any member of your church whatsoever." He took a deep breath. "What's more, your wife was the greatest offender. I observed her carefully and noticed that she simply made a cursory acknowledgment that we were present at the function, but it was obvious we were not really wanted. The invite seemed to be only a salving of conscience."

Randy was not prepared for the onslaught. "This is crazy," he said, feeling a cluster headache forming. Today was going to be a brute of a day; he just knew it by the way it was shaping up. "Sam," he begged, "I'm really in a quandary. I need your help to resolve this, so please try to understand where I'm coming from."

Sam threw his hands up in the air in mock surrender. "Fine. Let's see where this goes." He walked to his desk and picked up the phone. "Marty, please ask Stephanie to come to my office," he said into the mouthpiece. "This is going to be rich," he said with a shake of his head.

Randy said nothing while praying silently that his work with Homeless Outreach would not be disrupted, if not lost altogether.

Moments later, there was a knock at the door.

Sam glanced at Randy, then opened the door.

Stephanie walked in with a broad smile for Sam. Then her eyes fell on Randy. "Well, Pastor Randy," she said brightly, "to what act of God do we owe this visit so early in the morning?"

Randy's pulse hammered in his neck. There was so much at stake. Every word spoken at this meeting would be critical to the future of his ministry, yet he needed to question her if there was to be any resolution. "Stephanie," he began as his eyes darted between her and Sam, "Sam and I have been discussing a problem that has come up and we were hoping you could help us with it. It has to do with the get-together at my home last night."

"Oh?" She gave Sam a bewildered look. "Did we eat too much?"

Sam cracked a smile at the quip while Randy waved her off. "Oh, no. Nothing like that. It's just that after everybody left, we discovered...." He sucked in a deep breath of air. "...something missing."

"His wife, Laurie's necklace," Sam blurted.

"Ouch!" Stephanie said. "That's terrible." She turned toward Sam, who was pacing, and her eyes flashed with discovery and the insult. "Pastor Randy, you don't think for one moment that it was one of us, do you?"

Randy sat mute for several seconds, then stared at Sam in helpless frustration. "Sam, I'm not sure how to put this."

"Yes, suspicion has fallen upon us," Sam replied abruptly to fill in the gap. "In point-of-fact, Stephanie, you were the one seen in the area of Mrs. Bradshaw's bedroom, and Pastor Randy wanted to hear your explanation, if any."

She bolted upright, eyes widened in shock. She kneaded her temples, then turned to Randy and said apologetically, "My heart is really saddened that I would be accused of stealing your wife's jewelry, especially since I have demonstrated my gratefulness in your ministering to the homeless here at HO, and, in particular, your interest in my life."

The mantle of regret was heavy on Randy's heart now that the complaint was out in the open. "I don't want to hurt you in any way, Stephanie," he pleaded. "I'm not accusing you, only searching for clues. Could it be someone else?"

"The issue is the same, Randy," Sam inserted. "If you're pointing the finger at Stephanie, you're also pointing it at Marty, Viola, and Alexis, and everybody else here at HO."

With his shoulders now hunched, Randy silently nibbled at his index finger as he waited for the right words. His Biblical education and ability to counsel failed him at this crucial time in his ministry. He was speechless. *Lord, how long will You look on? Help.*

"Let me help you, Pastor Randy," Stephanie said gracefully, recognizing his emotional fatigue. "First, let me say on record that I did not take your wife's jewelry. Second, I'll gingerly quiz the others who were at your home so that neither you nor Sam will be involved, at least for now." She nodded toward Sam. "I'll give Sam a report in the morning."

"There's your answer, Pastor Randy," Sam said with a slight acerbic tone.

Randy's eyes misted. "I just want to say, thank you for..."

"Keep it, Pastor Randy," Sam said, his hand in a halting gesture. "But let me speak my piece before you go, okay?"

Randy winced at the vitriol in Sam's voice and wiped his eyes dry. "Sure, go on."

"My people may not be all Christians in your sense of the word," Sam explained, "but I stand behind them and believe in them to be *good* people. Unfortunate and often abused, but good people, who would not do such a thing to bring down the reputation of our home here. So you go and perform your little investigation while I wait for the day when my people will be vindicated."

Randy knew the meeting was over, and in his heart, he hoped his association with Sam and Homeless Outreach did not follow the same path. He turned to Stephanie and said approvingly, "Kindly call me when you learn something."

A frosty silence. Then sharply: "If not me, then Sam will call you."

Suppressing any further dialogue Randy simply nodded and walked out of Sam's office, leaving both Sam and Stephanie behind.

Fortunately for Randy, Marty had been relieved, so he didn't have to face him as he left the building. Unfortunately, it was still raining, and his headache was worsening.

* * *

Randy's prediction came true: the rest of his day deteriorated exponentially, culminating with Laurie's interrogation-like questioning of his meeting with Sam and Stephanie. "I'm tired and need to go to bed," he said wearily after reviewing the details several times to her satisfaction.

"Me too," Laurie replied. "This whole thing has me exhausted." She glanced at her wristwatch. It was 10:30 p.m. "This will be interesting to see how this all turns out," she added through a long sigh.

The phone rang as they walked into the bedroom.

Randy checked the caller-ID. "It's Homeless Outreach."

"Oh," Laurie said and proceeded to prepare for bed.

"Pastor Randy," Sam said in an official tone, "I hope you're ready for the consequences of your accusation."

Randy bobbed his head gloomily with the phone to his ear. "Sam, let it never be," he said solemnly.

"I'll give it to you all in one shot, Randy," Sam said fiercely. "Stephanie discreetly went on a mission after she left my office to exculpate herself and her companions here at HO. She went and talked with the others for several hours, then came to me and told me they were all innocent, and I believe her totally. But here's the rub and the price tag for this caper, Randy. Stephanie left a note saying she couldn't bear to bring further shame upon Homeless Outreach, so she left for parts unknown." With that came a thunderous *click!*

"Oh, no!" Randy muttered into the phone and set it on its cradle.

"Who was that?" Laurie asked with a snort.

"Sam Knowles."

"What did he want at this hour?"

"He wanted to tell me that the investigation down at HO revealed nothing and that he believes they are innocent on any charges."

"Oh, really?" she replied. "Interesting."

"What's really interesting is that I believe him," Randy said resolutely.

Laurie looked at him. "We'll see what happens."

Randy shook his head in disgust, then silently slipped into bed and turned on his side, convinced that he needn't share all of Sam's news about Stephanie with Laurie. But it would be more than an hour before his tossing and turning would bring him sleep.

* * *

For Laurie, sleep came easily.

"My, my, but you are a pretty one," the man in the red sweatshirt said.

Laurie looked up at him fiercely. "If you touch me, I'll scream."

"Scream all you want, sweet one; there's nobody here," he replied with a voice full of menace. He put his hand on her neck. "Such tenderness."

She screamed.

"Laurie, are you all right?" Randy asked, feverishly shaking her shoulder.

She rubbed her eyes. "I had a nightmare."

"That must have been a rough one; you're all sweaty." He rested his arm on her shoulder. "Do you want to talk about it?"

She wasn't ready to share the recurrent dream with anyone. "Not really. It was just about a difficult time I had when attending a youth group in my home church some years ago, that's all."

Randy hugged her. "Can I get you anything? Water? Anything?"

"No. It's over for now, I'm going to take a quick shower. You go back to sleep. I'll be all right," she promised.

Randy fell back into his pillow. Within minutes he was fast asleep.

As she reflected on the nightmare, a sense of satisfaction swept over her that she was winning the battle with the man in the red sweatshirt.

13

Randy opened his kitchen cabinet to get a coffee cup and his eyes fell upon the colorful Scripture calendar fastened to the back of the door. Circled in red was *November 15* with the words *Moishe Rosen/Jews For Jesus Presentation. Just a few days away, but who cares?* He shook his head several times, retrieved a cup, and closed the door.

"What's the matter?" Laurie asked as she watched his face. "Why the shake of the head and why do you look so down?"

"Oh, nothing," he replied dispassionately. Then he poured the coffee and sat at the kitchen table. He felt a nuzzling of Sonny's nose on his leg. *Good boy, Sonny, good boy. Thanks for the good morning kiss.* He reached down and rubbed Sonny's chin and forehead before taking a sip of his coffee.

Laurie frowned. "How long are you going to grieve over this thing with that woman Stephanie and the Homeless Outreach? It's been two weeks now since you came back from the meeting with Sam what's-his-name, and you're still not yourself."

Randy sighed, then walked to the bread basket on the kitchen counter, pulled an English muffin out of a plastic bag, divided it, and stuffed it into the toaster. He hovered over the toaster, watching the heat convection waves ascend. After the muffin popped up, he retrieved it and headed back to the table to sit down.

"Randy," Laurie persisted, "I asked you a question. Will you answer me, please?"

Randy simply gazed at her. "I just don't know what to do," he said numbly. Then he slowly spread marmalade jelly over the muffin and mechanically ate it.

Laurie didn't like that response. In a way it frightened her. For the first time in their marriage, Randy seemed to be immobilized—even paralyzed—to the point where it was beginning to affect his demeanor and, in her mind, possibly his decision-making process. Weakness was something Randy had never exhibited before. It was unnerving.

She stepped behind him and massaged his shoulders for a couple minutes. Then, peering at the clock on the wall, she said, "The kids are at school. What do you say we go back to bed?"

He placed the coffee cup on the table as his lips curved sardonically. *Is this your way of helping me? Making love? Yes, my heart is heavy and my emotions are unstable, but the remedy is not in our bedroom. It's my spirit that needs uplifting, not my sexual appetite.* He put himself in check. *Okay, she's only trying to help,* he reasoned, *but doggone it, my heartache is only going to return afterward.* "Tonight would be better."

Laurie slowly removed her hands and returned to her seat. "You know, Randy, now would be a good time to concentrate on the congregation God gave you. Maybe you should put this Homeless Outreach thing completely out of your mind and focus on Plantation Gate's vision."

He narrowed his gaze on her face but said nothing. Then he slowly and methodically walked to the bread basket again, took out another English muffin, divided it as with the first, placed it in the toaster, and lowered the lever. Then he turned to her and said with a degree of resignation, "Something to think about."

"Randy, how long are you going to seek sanctuary in short, three-to-four-word sentences?" she flared. "Can't I get a reasonable conversation out of you?"

"I'm tired," he replied as he spread jelly on his second muffin. "I think I'll eat this and go back to bed for a while."

This is so unlike him, Laurie thought. *This is getting serious.* "What about going into the office today? Don't you have work to do?" she said gruffly. "Isn't Yvonne expecting you? What about Moishe Rosen? Shouldn't you be preparing for his seminar this Sunday?"

The barrage of questions didn't work. They didn't stimulate or provoke him, nor did he respond to any degree of militancy. He simply yawned and said, "That will all keep."

Moments later he shuffled off to their bedroom and within several minutes was fast asleep.

Standing at the bedroom door, Laurie shook her head as sounds of Randy's snoring reverberated off the walls. *Maybe some cold reality will snap him out of this,* she thought. She returned to the kitchen and picked up the phone to call the church office.

* * *

Laurie looked at the kitchen clock. It was nearly lunchtime. Randy had been sleeping for over two hours. *Time for reveille, Mr. Bradshaw.* She walked into the bedroom and proceeded to wake him by tugging on his pillow. He simply turned over. "Time to get up, Randy," she coaxed. "I put on a fresh pot of coffee."

He raised one eyelid, then two. He glanced at the clock on the dresser and sighed with resignation. "Okay, I guess I'll get up."

"Good man," Laurie replied. "We can have lunch; then I have to go to class."

Yes, your class. You don't want to be late for your class. Everything else can be going in the toilet, but you don't want to be late for class. "I'll be right in," he replied tersely. He wasn't really hungry, but he could smell the tuna melt from the bedroom and it smelled good. *I'll indulge before I leave for the church so I won't have to stop later. Yeah, let's get lunch out of the way.*

"I called Yvonne while you were sleeping," Laurie said, "to ask her some questions about the attendance and financial records. And as I suspected, they tell an interesting tale."

"Like what for instance," Randy said with a shrug.

She poured herself a cup of coffee and elaborated. "Well, for one thing, the attendance from our regular congregation along with new visitors has dropped off considerably since you've been working on the homeless project. Then there's the issue of the tithes and offerings. It seems that we've taken a heavy hit in the pocketbook as well. But by sharp contrast, for the past two weeks, things are looking better. There have been more visitors and the support is up. It's almost as if the word is now out that we no longer cater to the homeless." She paused to look at him and, with her member-of-the-jury voice, added, "Haven't you been watching these figures?"

Randy lowered his sandwich onto his plate. He drummed his fingers on the table. "So, what you're saying is that God will only bless our ministry numerically and financially when we abandon the homeless? Is that what I'm hearing?" He stood and threw the napkin down on the table. Raising his voice an octave: "Is that what you're saying, Laurie?"

"Look at the facts, Randy," she answered in a civil tone. "They speak for themselves. It's apparent that many of the people in our congregation don't support your ministry outlook to reach the homeless."

He slowly sat down while massaging the back of his neck. "We took a vote, remember? The church voted to begin an outreach to the homeless."

"Yes, but obviously they have changed their minds."

He nodded several times as her words sank in. They were hurtful words that caused him to doubt his ability to make spiritual decisions for the welfare of the church. Words that challenged his ability to lead. "I have to go."

Within fifteen minutes he was dressed and out the door.

* * *

"Yvonne, bring me all the financials for the past six months and call Lester, Ronnie, and Mike to come in right away for an impromptu meeting," Randy instructed as soon as he was within Yvonne's range of hearing.

"Yes, Pastor," Yvonne replied in a muted tone. Seconds later she heard his office door close. *Troubling.*

Randy opened one of his desk drawers, pulled out a granola bar, and nibbled on it as he scrolled through his iPhone, stopping on Sam Knowles' private phone number. He swallowed his last bite then punched in Sam's number on the phone. "Hello from Homeless Outreach. This is Sam," he heard in melodic tones.

"Sam, this is Randy Bradshaw."

"Hello, Randy," Sam replied in a civil voice that bordered on rudeness.

Upset and somewhat unorganized in thought: "Sam," Randy spluttered, "any word on Stephanie? I mean, have you heard from her? Heard about her? Anything?"

"No. Nothing," Sam replied pungently.

"No idea as to where she may have gone?"

Sam must have detected Randy's genuine concern. "I'm sure she's all right. Probably visiting her old haunts while reeling from the 'bloody nose.'"

"Thanks for the word of encouragement," Randy said with a sigh of relief.

"Any word on the missing jewelry?" Sam probed without intimidation.

"No. Still missing."

"You watch and see how it will reappear quite mysteriously, Randy," Sam assured, "vindicating my people completely."

Randy meditated on Sam's assertion. "That would be a real blessing."

"But until then, I'll keep watch and let you know when we hear from or about Stephanie."

"That would be great, Sam," Randy said solemnly.

Click. Sam ended the call.

Twenty minutes later, his worship leader and deacons arrived for his unscheduled meeting.

* * *

Randy's leadership marched into his office and assumed a puzzled stance as they awaited his directions. "Sit down, men," he advised. "Now, I want you to

153

tell me straight. Do you men believe I'm doing the right job here at Plantation Gate?"

They exchanged glances, then said collectively. "Absolutely."

"Strange question," Ronnie said. "Why do you ask?"

Randy mentally organized his reply. "I guess you could say I'm going though a period where I'm questioning my ability to lead this ministry. The questions coming on the heels of the fiasco with Stephanie and the Homeless Outreach. She's still missing, you know."

Mike nodded several times as he pondered his pastor's dilemma. To him, Randy represented a tower of strength, spiritually, morally, and ethically. And for him to exhibit a weak, lethargic spirit was extremely disconcerting. "Pastor, I think I can speak for the rest of the leadership gathered here," he said, scanning the faces of the other men, "and we believe that you were and are called by the Lord to lead this congregation to a higher standard for Christ, and that you have not deviated from that goal."

Several "amens" were uttered.

He nodded in appreciation, then walked to them and handed them each a copy of the offering statement for the past three months. "Take a careful look at these figures, gentlemen, and tell me what you see." He added no commentary but simply returned to his seat and focused his gaze out the window. The sky was bright blue, with not a cloud in sight. *Nice touch, Lord.*

After what seemed like an interminable period, he rotated in his swivel chair and looked at Lester. "Let me start with you, Lester. What do you see?"

Lester scratched his head several times as he deliberated his answer, then flicked the side of his copy of the offering statement. "There has been a jump in the offerings in the past two weeks, if that's what you mean."

"Apparently the congregation is responding to our financial needs," Michael offered.

"Mike, we haven't had any requests for special financial needs," Randy advised coolly.

Mike shrugged and looked at Ronnie.

Ronnie took a deep breath. "Seems to me that you're looking for a reason for the increase in offerings, but let me remind you that the size of the offerings or the amount of a person's tithe has never been an indicator as to how the church or individual is doing spiritually. Many churches exceed their budget each week, but unfortunately fall into the category of the church in Ephesus or Laodicea—either they have left their first love, Jesus, or they're lukewarm and about to be spit out of His mouth."

"Here, here," Lester and Michael added.

"Let me connect some of the dots for you," Randy began. "It's been suggested to me that the reason for the sharp increase in the collections is because we are no longer pandering to the homeless. Furthermore, it has been implied that God is blessing our church financially since the incident at my home that led to Stephanie disappearing and my subsequent falling out with Homeless Outreach."

"That's not who our God is!" Ronnie protested vigorously. He stood and paced the floor. "If you're going to tell me that our God is no longer in the business of meeting the needs of the unfortunate, especially the homeless, and that He has forsaken them in favor of the well-to-do in our community, then I'm sorry, but I have a problem with that form of theology." He pointed out the window. "Frankly, I think that reasoning is coming from the other side, and Satan is working us over."

Lester nodded and said gruffly, "By *my* reasoning, he's having a field day right here in this office!"

Ronnie pulled out of his pocket one of the church's pamphlet and read from the reverse side: "Pastor, our mission statement states 'proclaiming the Word of God to reach the souls of men.'" Turning to the others in the room, he nodded to garner their collective support. "And that's what we've been doing here at Plantation Gate, especially in our effort to reach the homeless for Christ. So if someone has a problem with that, they need to take it up with God. It's really God they're fighting against."

"Hmm, yes, that's true," Randy agreed as the dawn of discovery reminded him as to what God's purpose in their church was originally intended to be. *I wonder how these men would react if I told them the voice of discouragement was coming from my wife? No, never mind.* "So the consensus is that we should go forward, despite whatever the financials reveal?"

A silence permeated the room for several moments before Ronnie walked behind Randy and put his hand on his shoulder, then waved the other men over to his side. "Pastor, we need to pray for you. A prayer of deliverance that Satan doesn't get a foothold in your heart, rob you of the joy of the Lord, and thereby diminish your strength and ability to lead this congregation." Ronnie signaled to the others that they should each in turn pray for their pastor.

A wave of guilt washed over Randy's soul. *Why did I doubt you, Lord? Why have I allowed my doubts as to who God is and what He is able to do to control me? To open up the door of lethargy? To pull me down into the spiritual quagmire that weakens my resolve to serve the Lord?* He began to weep as the men surrounded him and laid their hands on him. "Lord, help my unbelief!" he cried out.

"Lord," Ronnie prayed, "through the power of the Cross we pray that Satan would be bound by the blood of the Lamb and that our pastor would be released from the bondage of discouragement that has arrested his soul. Enable him to keep his eyes on you, Lord, not on the circumstances that have bogged him down. This we pray in the mighty name of Jesus." Randy's body shook as the Holy Spirit refreshed his spirit and renewed his heart.

"Father God," Mike prayed as his shoulders rose and fell, "I confess that I have not been praying for my pastor as I should. I confess that I have not entreated you for his protection from the wiles of the devil, from the constant barrage of negativity that abounds in the Christian life and, I confess, I have not prayed for him to be free from the attacks of discouragement that assail us all as we strive to serve You. I pledge now, before You, Lord, to place my pastor before Your throne of grace each day and pray for him."

Tears streamed down Randy's face as God's Spirit ministered to him in the inner recesses of his heart. *Lord, uphold me*, he prayed. *Strengthen me in my inner man to fight off discouragement.*

"Heavenly Father, in the name of Jesus," Lester added in a whisper. "Remember Your servant, Randy, and bring to his remembrance each and every time he begins to slip, that You saved him for a purpose, and that purpose was to lead this flock to a higher standard of righteousness as we seek to serve You. Remind him, O Lord, that he is needed as our shepherd, and that his working out of the vision for this ministry must go on. We cannot give the enemy even an inch."

A minute later, Randy wiped his eyes. "In the multitude of counselors, there is safety."

"Amen," they agreed, nodding as they paraded out of the room.

Randy walked to his briefcase, pulled out his Bible, and turned to Psalm 34, reading and meditating on if for nearly half an hour. Then he picked up the phone to call Laurie and tell her the good news that he was back.

14

Stephanie walked slowly through the Blue Dolphin entrance of the Sawgrass Mills mall, then scurried to the nearest ladies' room. Once inside, she lingered near the door until the last patron left, then she briskly walked to the first washbasin where she proceeded to wash her face. Then she looked up and saw her reflection in the mirror. *How you have aged,* she thought. The wrinkles on her brow appeared to have deepened and, for the first time, two scowl lines emerged to accentuate her mouth in an unfavorable way. The vicissitudes of a hard life were taking their toll.

"Getting old, girl," she muttered to herself. She backed up two paces to inspect herself in the mirror, only to spot several food stains on her sweater and one dark blotch from an unknown origin that found its resting place on her left pant leg. She reached over and pulled off a yard of paper towels from the dispenser, soaked one end in soap and water, then hastily brushed the stains until they were saturated. Then she walked to the hand dryer attached to the wall and turned the vent on herself and pressed the *start* button. The warm air dried the soiled areas, leaving only a faint residue. Once again she thanked God for the public restrooms where the homeless could refresh themselves.

She glanced up to the ceiling to spot the PA speaker as the sound of Christmas music played. *I might not have a home or family, but I love this holiday season.* It was only November 5, but most of the 85 vendor outlets, restaurants, and other stores were in full holiday array, hoping for another bountiful season. A perfect time for her to amble around and fantasize without being overly conspicuous. She started for the door, then thought she would use the toilet before embarking on her tour. Walking into a stall, she locked the door and stepped on a soft object. Looking down, she saw a woman's wallet. She blinked several times to gather her thoughts, then picked it up. She held it in her hand as she used the toilet, then opened it up.

There were numerous credit cards and what appeared to be family photos, a Florida driver's license, and several business cards listing the owner's address and phone numbers. When Stephanie opened the zippered part of the wallet, she bolted upright and gulped. She pulled out a wad of bills and gave it a quick count. There were ten 100-dollar bills and six 50-dollar bills, along with three 20-dollar bills. "I'm rich!" she whispered to herself. She quickly replaced the cash in the wallet, then stuffed the wallet into her pants pocket before leaving the wash room.

Outside the wash room in the middle of the promenade were two new automobiles from a local dealership on display. Stephanie circled the exhibit twice, imagining how it would be to buy one of the new cars and drive down to Homeless Outreach and show it off to her fellow residents. Pausing in front of the display, she tapped her pocket to remind herself that she had money now. *But not enough for a new car*, she thought. She moved on.

Moments later she came upon Utopia Jewelers. As she gazed though the glass at one of the diamond pendant earrings, she said to herself, "Now that's more like it!" She turned her head several different ways to get a good look at them, then felt her earlobes as she looked into the glass as if it were a mirror. *Oh, they would look so good on me.* She pushed her hair back and turned to the right. *Yes, I have the look.*

When she turned to the left, she glimpsed two women shoppers staring at her, giving her a dirty expression as they scanned her up and down. *Sure, I know what you're thinking. I don't belong here, right?* She patted her pocket that contained the wallet and moved on.

"I'm hungry," she said to herself as she rubbed her tummy. Moments later she was at the food court, sitting at one of the tables next to a concession, staring at the menu with the flashing lights. *So many choices. What shall I have?* She sighed. *Okay, I'll have a large hamburger with everything and a side of fries, and a large vanilla shake. For dessert, a cinnamon bun laden with pecans. Yes!* Suddenly a niggling of her conscience interrupted her thinking process. She patted her pocket once again and moved on.

Soon she found herself at a storefront looking up at a mannequin wearing a three-piece suit. She took a double-take of the sign. It was the ladies' apparel store, The Charlotte Shop. *One of my favorite places from another time zone!* The price tag on the suit she admired was $339.00. She pulled out the wallet and counted the money again. *Plenty left over. Okay.* Suddenly a torrent of memories flooded her mind. Shadows of her past life, where she frequented the finer clothing stores and dined at the best restaurants moved in and out of her consciousness. She looked around, embarrassed. There was only one other shopper next to her, writing numbers down on a pad, totally uninterested in her surroundings. *Good.* She wiped the single tear from her eye on her shirt sleeve, shook her head twice, and moved on.

She came upon a rest area that featured several benches and a water fountain. *Time to sit down.* She sat down, gazed at the preholiday shoppers as they quickly paraded by, and suddenly found herself wondering where everybody was going in such a frenzy. *Buying presents I guess*, she mused. *Ah, yes, presents.* Memories of how expensive presents were so important to her in her past life drifted into her mind. Gifts that really had no significant meaning but simply filled a void in both her and her husband's life. A void that she still didn't understand but had the presence of mind to realize that material things only temporarily relieved the problem. Passing those values on to their children seemed to be the only heritage she could account for.

Images of her children and ex-husband flashed in her mind's eye. *I wonder how my Emily is doing? Forgive me, Emily. Forgive me, Warren.* She even thought on her ex-husband with regret that her value system violated his very essence, bringing about the ruination of their marriage. *Sorry, Keith.*

Strangely enough, the bulge in her pocket seemed to be warming up and beginning to burn her leg. She reached in her pocket and clutched the wallet, then gazed up to the ceiling of the mall. Her conscience bothered her. *This is not mine. What am I doing? God, is this some kind of divine examination? A test of sorts?*

"Maybe it's a gift from God to help me in my time of distress," she whispered aloud. *Okay, so I'll turn in some of the money*, she reasoned. *I'm sure the owner will be grateful to get some of it back along with all of her ID.* She closed her eyes for several moments. *What should I do?*

She felt a pat on her shoulder. She opened her eyes and looked around, then to her lap where she spotted a 20-dollar bill. *Ha!* she thought, *some passerby gave me a donation!* No, it was more than that, she realized. *This is a divine sign.* Rising off the bench, she swiftly walked to the mall directory and made up her mind what she would do. The security office was only a short distance away.

"I found this wallet in the ladies' room by the Dolphin entrance," she said to the mall security officer, whose nametag read Shelia Smith.

Sheila regarded Stephanie curiously. She nodded as Stephanie handed her the wallet. "I'll need some information from you," she replied as she gave her a Lost and Found form.

"Everything is in there," Stephanie announced as the security guard began to open the wallet.

Stephanie watched the guard's eyes as she fingered the zippered compartment. "Whoa, there's a lot of cash here," the guard said in surprise. She had been a security guard for over 10 years and, in all that time, only one person had turned in a lost wallet, and then it only had fifteen dollars in it. As to how much was in there originally remained an unknown.

"There's 1,360 dollars there, friend," Stephanie said. "And that's the exact amount that was there when I found it."

"Really?" the guard said in dismay. "Now that's a first."

Stephanie nodded. "Would you be so kind as to give me a receipt for it, please?"

"Sure, honey," the guard replied. She reached under the counter and pulled out a form. "This will constitute the receipt, and I'll note the amount of cash turned in." She wrote the amount in the specified space then handed Stephanie the form. "Please fill in the information where you can be reached if necessary."

Stephanie noticed she didn't ask her for her home address or phone number. She paused, then filled in the information and handed the form back to her.

"You list two addresses here, Stephanie," the guard said. "One is the Homeless Outreach, the other is the Plantation Gate Church. Is that right?"

Stephanie nodded. "Yes."

"Okay," Sheila said as she handed her a copy. "Thanks for being so honest."

Stephanie stuffed the receipt in her pocket next to the 20-dollar bill and walked out of the security office. She noticed that her pocket was cool to the touch. *Thanks for the lesson, God,* she thought. *I'm beginning to believe You will provide for me.*

Fifteen minutes later Sheila picked up the phone and called the *Florida Sentinel* newspaper to report the unusual episode of her experience of the reawakening of the human conscience.

* * *

"Is everything in order for Dr. Rosen's presentation tomorrow?" Laurie asked Randy.

Randy simply nodded as he sat down to the dinner table. Then, after a few seconds, he added, "Yes, we're all set." He had resolved in his heart that he would set their dispute aside until after Moishe Rosen's visit, and for the time being, concentrate on the favorable vote of confidence from his deacons and assistant pastor. At the proper time he would confront Laurie on their defense of his posturing of the church.

"Dad, you're not going to believe this," Tiffany exclaimed as she hurried into the kitchen holding the *Florida Sentinel* newspaper, "but there's an article here in the Florida Living section about that lady, Stephanie, from the

Homeless Outreach. It says she found a woman's wallet at the Sawgrass Mills mall and turned it in, with all the money in it! Something like 1,300 dollars, and they're...ah...making her a hero!"

"Let me see that!" Randy gulped and stood to grab the newspaper. He reflexively sat down as his eyes scanned the article.

Laurie stood poised with her hands on her hips, ready to hear Randy's report as he hurriedly read the news piece. "Well? What happened? Is it that Stephanie you know from Homeless Outreach?"

Randy laid the newspaper down on the table. "There's a picture of her here," he said as he studied the photo and reread the article.

Laurie joined him at the table. "She doesn't look too good," she observed sourly. "The streets have really taken their toll on her."

Randy looked at her and snapped, "She would look a whole lot better if she were treated like a person instead of some kind of rejected chattel."

Laurie slowly lifted the newspaper from the table. "May I?"

"Help yourself."

"This is interesting," Laurie said as she read a follow-up article. "Here's a piece about the homeless, I guess in response to this piece on Stephanie, that attempts to answer the debate as to whether money should be given to those beggars at the street corners who carry those signs, *Will work for food* or say, *Spare change?*

"One side says that you only enable the destructive lifestyle that put the homeless on the street in the first place, adding that they often spend the money for alcohol or drugs, and may well keep a person from getting the real help they need—a real change, not spare change. This side wants to buy the homeless person a decent meal and point them in the direction of the nearest rescue mission. Once there, they get meals, clothes, boarding, and if it's a faith-based organization, they get a scheduled dose of the Good Word and in many cases a new life and a new relationship with God.

"The other side argues that some people wind up homeless through a series of misfortunes, adding that many homeless people have legitimate needs and that acts of kindness, such as giving them money, can be the catalyst to change. This proponent contends that, 'surveys have shown that nearly one-third of the requests to stay in a shelter were unmet and that food banks have turned people away hungry, adding that there isn't enough emergency food and shelter for everyone who is homeless or hungry.' This side maintains that when basic family needs are not met, this is a reflection of the massive failure of public policy and that society has unjustly labeled all panhandlers as addicts and con artists, thus stereotyping the poor."

Randy methodically lifted the newspaper out of Laurie's hands and laid it on the table next to his plate and glossed over the article she just read as he sipped his coffee. After several moments, he looked up at her. "I would be very interested to hear what your position is on the subject and what implication this piece on Stephanie has in relationship to the matter at hand."

Tiffany shot a look at Sean. They both nodded to each other and removed themselves from the table.

"Well," Laurie began, "I don't think it's a good idea to give them money on the street. If one really has a burden for the homeless, they can find out where the nearest shelter or rescue mission is and support them through that organization. As far as Stephanie goes, I guess you mean this is some form of vindication or exoneration, right? That this clears her of any wrongdoing?"

"You might say that, yes," Randy replied gruffly.

A distorted expression came over Laurie's face. "On the other hand, one could say that this was her way of salving her conscience and making things right with God and society. You know, like making a anonymous offering to a church to atone for one's sins."

Randy snorted. "That's just the kind of thing I'd expect you to say, Laurie. The voice of unbelief dripping with judgment without giving the person a fair trial. How would you like it if you were in her shoes and you were looking for someone to listen to your side of the story or reach out to support you and all you got was a shoe in the face and a kick in the butt? How would you like it?"

Laurie stiffened and silently turned to pour herself another cup of coffee.

"Well? What do you say to that?"

"What would I say?" She fumbled for words. "For one thing, I'd never find myself in that kind of position. But if I were, through some unfortunate set of bizarre circumstances, I would do everything possible to prove myself innocent of any charges."

"And if you were living in a shelter after being on the streets for a few years with no job, no family, and no friends except those companions back in the shelter, I ask you, Laurie, who would believe you?" he argued.

"Good point," she reluctantly assented.

"Thank you," Randy said as he exited the kitchen in mock triumph.

* * *

Two hours later Randy sat at his office desk rereading the newspaper articles on Stephanie, musing and questioning the purpose of God in his dealings with Stephanie and the Homeless Outreach.

Redeemed, how I love to proclaim it..., his cell phone chimed out.

He reached for his cell phone and glanced at the caller-ID then quickly hit the *Talk* button. "Sam, it's really good to hear from you," he began. "I'm sure you've read the news about Stephanie. Any word from her?"

"As a matter of fact, Randy, that's why I'm calling," Sam replied cordially. "I thought it ironic that, after the melee at your home involving Stephanie in that honesty dispute, that she would appear in a the newspaper after turning in a lost wallet. I hate to say it, but it feels good to say, 'I told you so.'"

"It certainly helps her case, that's for sure," Randy affirmed. "How is she doing?"

"Can't say. I haven't heard from her since she left last month. That's why it was so good to read about her in the newspaper. Now we know she's okay."

"Right," Randy said. "Well, if you should hear from her, would you please call me? I'm very concerned."

"I'll be sure to let you know, Randy."

Click.

The call was short but sweet, Randy thought. At last he knew she was in the neighborhood and not lying dead in some remote canal near the Everglades. He prayed for Providence to shield her and that their paths would cross again in the future.

* * *

"The pastor's wife appears to be having a good time," Ronnie said to Lester with a nudge of the arm as they both stood in the church lobby watching Laurie hand out programs at the front door. Alongside her were Tiffany and Sean, on call to escort visitors to their seats in the sanctuary.

The parking lot is filling up fast, Laurie thought as she glanced out the door. *I hope we have enough spaces.* Visitors and congregants alike were flocking to hear Dr. Moishe Rosen from Jews for Jesus speak about his ministry, a ministry Laurie gave little thought to, but the excitement of the outpouring from the community to hear the celebrated guest speaker ignited a good spirit within her. Being in the flux of things appealed to her nature.

Tiffany pointed her finger at a woman approaching the front door and said impulsively, "Hey, Mom, isn't that Stephanie from the Homeless Outreach?"

Laurie peered into the parking lot and locked her eyes on the woman Tiffany was pointing to. She was accompanied by another man who seemed vaguely familiar. "Yes, that's her." She turned and tapped Sean on the shoulder and said with an irritated edge, "Go tell your father that Stephanie is here. He should be delighted." Sean scurried off to make the report to his father.

Sean strolled through the crowds until he located his father standing on the stage directing the special event. He was reviewing the program with both his deacons and music minister. "Dad, guess who's here?"

"Sean, I haven't got time for games right now, okay?" his father replied sharply while continuing to discuss the operation at hand.

"But, Dad, it's that girl from Homeless Outreach who was in the newspaper. You know, Stephanie," Sean insisted.

Randy stopped in his tracks and turned to his son. "Did I hear you right? Stephanie's here?"

"Right, Dad," Sean replied, then jerked his thumb over his shoulder. "In the lobby."

"Pastor Randy," Randy heard from behind. "Dr. Rosen just arrived," Judy Edelson announced. "And your friend Avi Bekker and his wife have been seated in the first row of seats," she added as she moved about.

Randy shot a look at both Rosen and Bekker, then turned to see Stephanie walking into the auditorium with a man he quickly recognized as Marty. "Hmm," he muttered, then waved to Rosen and Bekker and walked over to Lester and pointed toward the front door. "Dr. Rosen and Avi Bekker just arrived, but I need to say 'Hi' to a lost soul and her friend that just turned up. Do me a favor and go over there and welcome them. I'll be there in a few minutes."

Lester nodded and walked over to greet the two guests. Randy then marched up to both Stephanie and Marty. "I can't believe my eyes," he exulted effusively. "It's so good to see you both!"

Marty approached Randy and gave him a big bear hug. "You're looking well, Pastor. It's good to see you too."

"We heard about your special speaker on the Christian radio station," Stephanie said with a tight smile. She scanned the crowd building in the church and added, "I hope it's all right that we..."

Randy waved her off. "Of course it's all right," he said, cutting short her apology. "You're always welcome."

Stephanie took a deep breath. Somewhat reserved: "That's nice."

"I read in the newspaper all about that incident over at the Sawgrass Mills," Randy said with a luminous smile. "You wait and see how the Lord will honor you."

Stephanie mediated on Randy's words momentarily, pondering in her heart if, once again, her integrity was in the balance as she came into the presence of those at Plantation Gate. "Pastor Randy, I don't have to wait. I believe God has honored me already."

Randy blinked. He didn't have time to engage in a conversation now, but he was taken aback by her retort. *She's been hurt, and I need to talk to her without a crowd around.* "Can you stay after the service so we can talk?" he asked, hoping for a favorable response.

She glanced over at Marty who nodded. "Okay."

"Great." He then pointed over to his guests and said, "I have to rush off to meet with our featured speaker. I'll get with you later." He checked his wristwatch, then quickly walked away.

Stephanie and Marty drifted into the sanctuary. Moments later Lester and Ronnie approached them, greeting them with open arms and showing them to a pew in the middle of the room. "Wonderful to see you back," Judy Edelson called out from the aisle as she walked past them. Several people went up to them and greeted them warmly.

Stephanie looked around the sanctuary and into the lobby until her eyes stopped on Laurie. *Hello, Mrs. Bradshaw. Hello, Tiffany and Sean. How are you? I'm fine, thank you.*

Marty must have sensed her feeling of rejection, for he reached over and clasped her hand. "Doing okay?"

She smiled at him. "So-so."

"You'll be fine."

Marty was distracted by a woman beckoning him to the welcome center to receive a nametag. He walked over.

"Hello, Stephanie," she heard from behind. It was a young girl's voice she remembered well. "It's good to see you again." When Stephanie turned, Tiffany and Sean were standing behind her. "Welcome again to our worship service," they said in unison. Tiffany threw her arms around Stephanie. "We've been worried about you," she whispered. "It's good to see you're safe."

"My dad read us the newspaper article on you," Sean said gleefully, "and it really made him feel good." With that he sauntered off into the sanctuary.

"Thank you..." Stephanie tracked Laurie, who remained at a safe distance, directing the hostess's preparation at the refreshment table.

Piano music began to play the hymn, "My Jesus, I Love Thee."

"It's time to sit down," Tiffany said and escorted her to a front seat just three rows from the stage and pulpit.

Michael greeted the congregation with a vibrant spirit of worship as he called them to stand to sing the hymn. Four hymns later, Michael called Pastor Randy to the pulpit.

"Today, my friends, we have a special speaker," Randy began. "Dr. Moishe Rosen from Jews for Jesus will share with us God's message and insight on Jewish evangelism from a passage often overlooked in the church today." He motioned to Rosen to come forward. "Having been in Jewish evangelism for over 30 years, we welcome Dr. Rosen to hear his interpretation of the famed text, Romans 1:16." He nodded. "Dr. Rosen." Applause broke out as Rosen ascended the stage platform.

Rosen walked to the pulpit with great dignity of that becoming a man exposed to great ridicule from his own Jewish brethren, yet pioneering in the domain of radical Jewish evangelism under the inspiration of the mighty hand of God. He was a paunchy elderly man with deep penetrating eyes and several stray hairs emerging from his bald head. Once in the pulpit, though, he became a different man. A man of passion for the salvation of his people, Israel. "Thank you, Pastor, for the opportunity to address your congregation and guests with a subject that I believe God wants his people, both Israel and the Church, to hear." He paused and opened his Bible and read Romans 1:16, then set his Bible down.

"It is with great sorrow that I speak to you this morning," Rosen began, his voice calm, yet a sense of foreboding emerged from his tone, as if he were going to explode with fury as his message deepened. "You see, I am a firm believer in God's Word, having been saved by the blood of Christ and the power of His divine word early in my life. And it is with deep sorrow that I recite a verse out of Genesis to augment my text: 'I will bless them that bless thee, and curse them that curse thee.' You see, what's happening in our world today can be directly linked to our treatment of God's chosen people, Israel. And may I say at the outset that the church is equally responsible as the secular world is. This is one of the reasons why the Lord is withholding his blessing from many churches. They do not have the heart for Jews, nor are they the slightest bit interested in their salvation. As a result, many churches seem to be going around in circles, attempting to draw Gentiles in while neglecting God's Chosen, a strategy that He simply cannot bless. Accordingly, many churches miss out on receiving God's best for them.

"Paul made it clear in our Romans text that the church has a responsibility to present the gospel to the Jewish person *first*, and then to the Gentile. But that is just not happening, and if the truth be known, the opposite is occurring in many churches." He paused to open his attaché case and retrieve several newspaper articles. "I have here an article that explains how a mainline Protestant church has proposed financial recriminations targeting Israel and siding with a Palestinian terrorist group along with the radical

166

Islamic gang, the Hezbollah, in Lebanon. The piece goes on to say that this church's general assembly has adopted a resolution calling on the denomination to dump its holdings in selective companies doing business with Israel. This move, the article points out, is designed to push Israel into negotiations with the very terrorist groups that have been killing their people for decades. Can you imagine that? Is this not anti-Semitism of the highest order? Right in the confines of the church?" He pulled out several other articles and held them up in the air.

"Other churches of the Protestant persuasion have joined in the campaign to alienate themselves from Israel in favor of the Arab countries as well. Here is ample documentation of widespread condemnation of Israel among member churches to economically divest themselves from the Jewish state until Israel implements U. N. resolutions to withdraw from areas they consider Israel captured illegally." He pounded the pulpit twice and shouted, "Don't these churches get God's message about His people, Israel? Don't they get Paul's message about the need to support Israel? Or are they all going to be sucked into Satan's lie, 'We need oil, not Jews,' that infamous notion that became popular right after the '73 oil embargo brought on by the Arabs as retaliation for the humiliation suffered at the hands of Israel in the Yom Kippur War? When are we going to see things God's way?"

"Amen!" Avi Bekker shouted out from the audience.

"'Jews Killed the Lord Jesus' the church marquee reads," he quoted from another article. "Yes, this is the sentiment of many churches that do not know the Bible. What the Bible states is very clear, and we need to repeat it once again to settle the matter." He opened his Bible and read, *"No one takes my life from me, but I lay it down of my own accord. I have authority to lay it down and authority to take it up again. This command I received from my Father.'* These were Jesus' words, stating that no one nation or group was responsible for his death, but in order for God to fulfill the prophecies and divine requirements for the atonement, Jesus had to die for sin. If he were not offered up as a sacrifice for sin, we would all be in our sin to this very day."

"Amen!" Avi Bekker repeated, an octave higher than his previous accolade.

"What's more," Rosen continued as he scanned the congregation, "Luke explains in the book of Acts that Jesus was handed over to the world's leaders by God's set purpose and foreknowledge, and with the help of wicked men, put to death by nailing him to the cross. Further, Luke explains, *'Indeed Herod and Pontius Pilate met together with the Gentiles and the people of Israel in this city to conspire against your holy servant Jesus, who you anointed. They did what your power and will had decided beforehand should happen.'"*

"You see, we are all responsible!" he shouted as he pointed to the cross suspended from the ceiling over the baptistry, then to himself, and then to the audience. "You, me, everybody! Israel or the Jews were not responsible, but our sin was responsible for nailing him to that cross." He walked in front of the pulpit and then down the steps of the platform to where he stood in front of the first pew. "Now, I would like to share with each and every one of you how your church can be blessed.

"Firstly, my friends, you need to pray that you receive a burden for the Jew. That's a must. Pray that God will put a genuine, unbiased concern in your heart for His people. Secondly, study to show yourself approved unto God by learning how to present the gospel to Jewish folks from an nonoffensive perspective. Review Old Testament passages and evangelism techniques that teach how to navigate through Scriptures that Jewish folks should be familiar with. Study notable passages such as Isaiah 53, Psalm 22, Zechariah 9, etc., until you have a handle on these prophetic texts. This way when you have the opportunity to open up your Bible with a Jewish person, you can show them these passages and then show them the fulfillment in the New Testament.

"Next, learn their language, holidays, and their culture just as you would if you were going to be a missionary to some African nation. Seize every opportunity to show interest in their Jewish feast days like Yom Kippur and Passover so that you can lead into a witness for Christ as he is the completion of them. Finally, take the time to ask the Lord to direct you to a Jewish person to whom you can share these truths. Believe me, when you do things God's way, you and your church will be blessed." He stopped and wiped his brow with his handkerchief. "Any questions?"

Laurie turned to Randy and whispered, "He really gets in your face, doesn't he?"

Randy could see that Rosen was not connecting with his wife. He slowly put his finger up to his lips to hush her up. He wanted to hear anything and everything that would yield a blessing for his church.

Stephanie's hand shot up in the air.

"Yes," Rosen called out as he nodded in her direction, "how can I help you?"

Every eye turned to see who was asking the question. Several faces went ashen when they saw it was Stephanie. One of them was Laurie. "Is she kidding?" she murmured in Randy's ear. He ignored her.

Stephanie stood from her pew and said, "Dr. Rosen, I've been wrestling for many years with the issue of Jesus being the true Messiah, and from what my parents told me and from what I was taught in Hebrew school, I always believed that when the Messiah came, there would be peace on the earth. Supposedly, he's the Prince of Peace, right? Well, if Jesus is really the Messiah, why isn't there peace on the earth?"

Laurie gulped twice and pulled on Randy's jacket. "She's Jewish?" she asked sharply.

"She never told me, so I don't know," Randy replied. "Her married name is Malone, but her parents could be Jewish for all I know."

"This just keeps getting better and better," Laurie snorted.

Rosen stepped away from the pulpit and walked toward the audience, stopping at the end of the stage area. "Now that's a very interesting question," he replied after a moment of contemplation. "In fact, Jesus addressed that very issue in John chapter 14 when he distinguished between the kind of peace the world offers, that is, a temporary peace based on circumstances, while the peace that he offers through salvation is independent of circumstances, but based on our relationship with God. The apostle Paul added in Colossians and Philippians that peace *with* God comes at the point of salvation when the sin issue is settled, but the peace *of* God comes only after we totally surrender to Christ. This is an oversimplification, but nevertheless, a truth that even many Christians miss."

Laurie, mystified at Rosen's answer, told Randy, "I never heard that before."

Randy just rolled his eyes, remembering when he personally gave a sermon on the two kinds of peace God offers, but obviously it was not Laurie's time to hear it. Then he turned and visually scanned the auditorium until his eyes settled on Stephanie. She was slowly returning to her seat. He took notice that she appeared to be very restless.

Several other congregants and visitors asked questions regarding their Jewish neighbors and relatives and the best way to approach them about Christ. Rosen drew upon his vast experiences to answer each one with loving tenderness. After 15 minutes, he turned to Pastor Randy, who took the cue and walked to the pulpit to join him. "My ministry finds its fulfillment when the Lord grants me the privilege of praying for others." He looked at Randy and said, "Pastor, can I pray for your people?"

"We would be honored if you would pray for us, Dr. Rosen."

"My prayer to You, heavenly Father," Rosen began, "is that You open hearts to Jesus. Allow the Ruach Hakodesh, Your Holy Spirit, to penetrate the scales of blindness that keep people from hearing the truth. Raise up from among Your people those with a heart toward Israel who will learn how to share the gospel with them. Bring those seeking salvation to their Messiah, Yeshua." He raised his hands as the pianist began to play "I Surrender All."

"With every eye closed and every head bowed, let those led by God's Spirit raise their hand to signify their calling upon the name of the Lord to be saved. Let them pour out their hearts to You, O Lord, and forgive their sin and heal their hurts. Encourage them to go on and take a stand for You." He stopped and looked at the audience. There were six hands in the air. "Yes, the Lord has seen your hand and read your hearts. And let me add that He will meet your every need according to his riches in glory in Christ Jesus." He turned to Randy. "Thank you for allowing me to share these important things with your people." He walked off the platform to a front pew and sat down.

"My friends,: Randy said, "this brother has charged us before God to reach out to His people, Israel. Let us be faithful. And to those who raised their hands before God, please come to my study after the service so I can pray with you." He motioned to Michael to close the service with a hymn.

Tiffany rushed up to her father as he neared the sanctuary exit. "Dad, Stephanie raised her hand to receive the Lord!"

Randy stopped short. "How did you know that?"

Tiffany shrugged and giggled. "I peeked."

"You're so bad," he said with a grin.

Numerous well-wishers surrounded Rosen with follow-up questions as Randy, Lester, and Ronnie escorted the respondents into his study. Once inside his office, Randy had Lester and Ronnie open up six folding chairs to accommodate the decision-makers, then walked over to Stephanie. "Welcome, Sister, to the family of God." She beamed as he moved down the line to congratulate and welcome each of them on their decision for Christ.

"Today you've made the singular most important decision in your life," he announced to the group. "By agreeing with God that you need Christ in your life, you can expect to receive God's richest blessings, including forgiveness of sin and the ever-present Holy Spirit to guide you and give you understanding to discern God's will for your life. As you study his Word, the Bible, you'll strengthen your relationship with the Lord and be better equipped to handle trials and difficulties that arise. They will draw you closer to your Savior as you depend on God's grace instead of your own natural resources. This is God's way of affirming your salvation experience. Finally, endeavor to get involved in our Bible studies so you may grow in grace and knowledge and discover where the Lord wants to use you in ministry."

After Lester closed in prayer, everyone except for Stephanie left Randy's office.

15

R andy began to close his office door, then reflected on ministry policy that no man meet privately with a woman except his wife. "Excuse me, Stephanie," he apologized, then stuck his head out the doorway as the group proceeded to exit the building. "Lester, join us for a few moments."

Lester nodded and walked back into Randy's office.

"It's so wonderful to see you again!" Randy said effusively. "And to think God's Spirit prompted you to make a decision for Christ today is truly wonderful. All the angels of heaven rejoiced at your salvation. Welcome into the kingdom of God!"

Lester urged her to sit down. "Mrs. Malone," he said with a broad smile.

Stephanie responded with a beaming grin as she settled into a chair. "It's hard to believe that a Jewish girl would come to believe on the God of the Christians, but I just couldn't hold out any longer."

Ah, Randy thought, *how great God is to use Brother Rosen, a Jewish-Christian, to speak a message that would provoke Stephanie to reach out to Christ for salvation. How marvelous!* "I had no idea you were Jewish."

"Both my parents were Jewish. My maiden name was Silverberg." She blushed and added, "Fell in love with a nice Irishman. Mom and Dad weren't crazy about the idea of me marrying a 'goy,' but they learned to live with it."

"Interesting," Randy noted. Sometime in the future he'd like to develop a ministry outreach to Jewish folks, one that offered many rewards both here on earth and in heaven. His face sobered. "I want you to know, Stephanie, that I hold you in the highest regard. I was heartbroken over the whole thing about the necklace." Later he'd fill Lester in on the details.

She held up her right hand. "I had nothing to do with that strange disappearance of your wife's jewelry. But once the accusation was made, I couldn't be around people anymore. I needed a break."

Althanasius contra mundum, Randy thought on the Latin for "against the world." *Yes, I can see how she would take a moral stand when she felt the world and the circumstances of life were piling up against her.* "God has a way of working things out."

"We're believing God, right?" Lester joined in. "'All things work together for good,'" he quoted with another broad smile.

Stephanie's eyes brightened. "As they say, 'one day at a time.'"

There was a knock at the door, and all eyes turned. Laurie was gazing at Stephanie. "Randy, it's time to go. The children are waiting in the parking lot. I'll meet you out there." Pivoting on one foot, she briskly walked away.

"The word from high command ," Lester said with a tinge of sarcasm.

Randy ignored Lester's remark. "Well, Stephanie," he said as he stood, "I pray that God's Spirit will guide and direct you in the days ahead. And, of course, we hope you will join us for our new Christian's class that will help you to learn more about the Bible and what you have come to believe."

Stephanie nodded toward the doorway. "Please give my regards to Mrs. Bradshaw," she said warmly. "I hope to see her at Wednesday's Bible study."

Humiliation swept over him as the embarrassment for his wife's rudeness suddenly struck him. He noted that there was not a single word of retaliation from Stephanie. "She must be very tired," he replied apologetically. "Yes, I will tell her you were asking for her."

* * *

Tense silence permeated the car for the first several minutes as they pulled out of the church parking lot. Then Tiffany said hesitantly, "Dad, I think it's great that Stephanie came forward to receive the Lord."

Randy turned to Laurie sitting in the passenger seat. "Stephanie asked for you. She extended her regards."

Laurie said through her teeth, "How nice."

Sean glanced at Tiffany as if to get approval and said sheepishly, "Mom, how come you don't like Stephanie?"

"A worthy question," Randy muttered to himself.

Laurie gave Randy a dirty look, then swiveled toward the back seat. "It's not that I don't like her personally; it's that I don't like what she stands for." She cleared her throat in what sounded like a stall to embolden and clarify her thinking. "You know, not rising above and getting out of that kind of life."

"But, Mom," Tiffany argued, "how can she help it? If she went through a series of unfortunate events and landed up homeless, shouldn't those who are able help her out until she gets back on her feet?"

"Here, here," Randy said as he winked to Tiffany in the rearview mirror.

Laurie retreated into her own private thoughts. Flashes of the man with the red sweatshirt jolted her. She saw him putting his hand on her waist and then on her breast.... *NO! FIGHT BACK!* she demanded of herself. The flashes obliterated themselves.

After several more minutes, she blurted out, "What do you think Dr. Rosen meant when he was talking about the two different kinds of peace?"

Ah, a divine moment, Randy thought. *God's Spirit is moving in her heart. The issue of peace keeps coming up, yet she doesn't seem to hear the answer from me.* "He meant that God offers two kinds of peace. One comes when we receive Christ, peace *with* God; the other comes when we surrender to Him, the peace *of* God. Otherwise, we experience only the world's peace, a false peace. It's a 'happiness' based simply on favorable circumstances in our life."

Laurie pondered Randy's explanation, then replied, "Very interesting."

Randy prayed that her repetitive question came from a soul-searching experience brought on by the Holy Spirit, not merely a curious mind. *Maybe things are going to change. With God, all things are possible.*

* * *

Sean grabbed one half of his peanut-butter-and-jelly sandwich off his plate while stuffing the remainder of the other half in his mouth. He washed the mouthfuls down with several gulps of milk before announcing, "Dad, I'm meeting the guys in the street to play ball. See ya." He darted to his room to get his lacrosse stick and face guard, then bolted out the front door.

"I'm coming out to watch you play," Tiffany said in support. Seconds later she jumped up and scooted out the door after her brother.

Laurie said with a shake of the head, "If only our lives could remain that simple."

Randy finished his coffee. "I think we make our lives complicated. I don't believe God intended our lives to be so complicated that we would overlook the good times and fun parts of life. *'I've come to give you life, and that more abundantly.'*"

Here we go with the Bible quotes again. Laurie sighed.

The front door flew open, and feet ran toward them. "Dad!" Tiffany shouted, "Sean's been hit in the eye with the lacrosse ball! He's bleeding like crazy—" Nearly paralyzed with fear, she dropped into a seat at the table and started crying hysterically.

Randy dropped his cup on the table and ran out the door. Laurie sat dazed for several seconds, then followed Randy into the street, where Sean lay on the pavement, moaning and squirming uncontrollably as he held his right eye. His friends stood over him in horror, crying. Their dog, Sonny, started barking wildly as if to signal the falling of his master.

Randy shoved the onlookers out of the way and raised Sean's hand from off his eye. The color drained from his face. Above Sean's eye was a wide gash down to the bone, at least four inches long, cutting through his eyebrow. The eye socket was filled with blood, making it impossible to see the eyeball itself.

"Do something!" Laurie yelled out.

Randy reached in vain for his cell phone, only to remember leaving it on his dresser. He quickly turned toward the front door of the house to see Tiffany sobbing on the step. "Call 9-1-1 and get an ambulance immediately!" he yelled.

She ran inside the house.

"Mom, it hurts!" Sean groaned, trying to lift his head off the pavement.

"Don't move," Randy spluttered, "you'll only make it worse..."

Guilt panged in Laurie's heart. Numb with shock, she spoke out of the side of her mouth to Randy. "It's because of me this happened; I just know it."

Somehow Randy had the presence of mind not to react to her claim. "Now is not the time to assess blame. Let's just get him to the hospital."

Laurie bent down and stroked her son's face, then burst into tears and cried out, "Lord, don't let him lose his eye, please!"

"Dad, the ambulance is on the way!" Tiffany shouted from the doorway.

Randy dropped to his knees at Sean's side. Reaching for Laurie's hand, he prayed silently, then shouted heavenward, "Lord, we're believing you! You promise not to give us more than we can bear. Don't let him lose his eye! Cover his wound with Your blood and heal him. This we pray in the mighty name of Jesus." When he released Laurie's hand, half the neighborhood was coming out of their homes to gather on the curb. Many approached within 10 feet of his son while most of the crowd kept their distance.

The ambulance siren blared. It would arrive in a matter of seconds.

Randy stood and gazed at his fallen son. His eyes fell on his son's blood beginning to dry on the pavement and his stomach spasmed. Suddenly the horror of the event gripped him, and he began to weep. "Lord," he murmured, "don't take our arguing out on him."

The ambulance pulled up and, within seconds, two paramedics had pulled a gurney from the back of the ambulance and rushed to Sean's side. One took his vitals while the other readied him to travel. "Give us some room, sir!" one said to Randy.

Randy pulled Laurie away from their son and walked her a short distance away as the paramedics placed Sean on to the gurney. Then one of the paramedics waved Randy over to get the necessary information as the other wheeled the gurney to the rear of the ambulance and slid it into the holding tracks. "We're taking him to Westside Regional Hospital, Mr. Bradshaw,"

174

Randy heard. "If you want to follow along, you can."

"Yes, we will." Randy turned toward his front door to see Tiffany crying with her head in her lap. "Tiffy," he yelled, "get my car keys. We're going to the hospital!" She signaled she understood and bolted back into the house.

Three minutes later Randy and Laurie were in the car behind the ambulance. Randy glanced in his rearview mirror. His neighbors converged in the street where his son's drying blood marked the spot of the accident. His stomach wrenched once more.

* * *

Randy stared at the clock on the ER waiting room wall, knowing now how one's life could totally change in a matter of minutes. *One minute I was sitting at the kitchen table having lunch, and in the next, I was kneeling in the middle of the street over my son.* His gaze raked the other persons in the room; they, too, waited for a good word from the duty nurse or doctor. He watched Laurie, her eyes closed in anguish, sighly deeping as if making secret pacts with God to extend his hand of mercy.

Perhaps the Lord is bringing this on to develop graces in my life. Randy turned his gaze toward the blue sky out the window. *Certain graces that would never be discovered if it were not for trials. Ah, yes, trials to strengthen my faith can be like hope itself that can be likened unto a star, not to be seen in the sunshine of well-being or prosperity, but only to be discovered in the night of adversity. Yes, affliction can often be the black folds in which God does set the jewels of his children's graces to make them shine even better.*

His thoughts quickly gave way to a prayer: *Lord, You often send trials that my graces may be discovered and I may be certified of their existence, so that I may grow in grace and knowledge of Your divine will. Is that why I am undergoing this trial, O, Lord? Is this the reason You are contending with me?*

"Mr. and Mrs. Bradshaw." Both broke out of their preoccupations and stood as a doctor in green scrubs approached. "I'm Doctor Cutler, a pediatric ophthalmologist. The ER duty doctor called me in to look at your son's eye."

"And?" Laurie said, taking a deep breath.

Dr. Cutler addressed Randy. "I may as well give it to you all in one slug. His condition is serious."

Laurie bit her fingernail. "How serious?"

"For one thing, he has a large hematoma behind the eye—a collection of blood that is trapped after escaping from the vessels, no doubt from the impact of the object that hit him. This blood is clotting, and we need to operate to tie off the bleeding vessels."

Laurie vainly attempted to stifle a gasp. Scanning the doctor's eyes, she sensed there were complications. "Please tell me there's no more, Doctor."

He shook his head. "I wish it weren't so, but there is more."

Laurie's knees began to wobble and she grabbed Randy's arm.

"I'm afraid we may be dealing with a retinal detachment as well," he explained as he held up an X-ray to the overhead light. "There appears to be a division of the retina of the eye from the choroid covering in the back of the eye. There could be a small hole."

Laurie grabbed Cutler's arm. "Is he in any pain?"

"From the retinal detachment, no. But there is considerable pain from the hematoma. This is why we must go in and relieve the pressure from the escaping blood and also determine what needs to be done about his retina. Surgery will repair the hole and prevent any further leakage of the vitreous humor that divides the retina from its source of food, the choroid. Once we repair this damage, he should be fine in about three months."

Randy drew from a hidden strength that he would later attribute only to God's grace and said, "Do what you can to save his eye, Doctor Cutler. We will be in prayer that God's hand will guide you."

Dr. Cutler nodded in approval of the prayer for divine assistance, then looked deeply into Randy's eyes, seeming to feel his pain. Then he turned to Laurie and said calmly, "We'll do everything we can. I'll treat him like my own son. Keep praying." Both Randy and Laurie followed Dr. Cutler with their eyes as he walked through the double swinging doors into the ER.

Without another word, Laurie sat down again. Lowering her head into her hand, she groaned. *Tired, so tired. This life is hard. God, why is this life so hard? Answer me, please.* A string of thoughts assailed her. *God, it's one thing to bring pain on me, but it's quite another to bring pain on one of my children. Why, God, why?*

She glanced at her husband, who sat reading Psalms out of his pocket Bible. *Is it him, God, or am I to blame? Am I the obstacle to Your blessing this family? Are we to look at ourselves or should we look to other causes? God, answer me, please. I'm pleading with You!*

"We came as soon as we could," she heard, waking from her meditation.

Her eyes focused on Lester, Ronnie, and Mike, talking with Randy, motioning with their arms and hands as if to express their horror and consternation over the tragedy. Seconds later they were encircling him, laying hands on their pastor, praying aloud for God's miraculous intervention. Laurie broke into the circle and joined them in prayer.

After what seemed like several minutes, Lester prayed audibly. "Lord, don't let your servants, Pastor and his wife, blame themselves for this accident because *'we know that in all things God works for the good of those who love him and who have been called according to his purpose.'* Grant them an extra measure of grace to get through this crisis and give the doctors the wisdom and ability to save little Sean's eye. This we pray in the mighty name of Jesus." Everybody added their own "amen" to Lester's prayer.

"I want to see him now," Laurie said to Randy, eyes pleading for help.

"Of course," Randy replied softly. He nodded to the others, then held Laurie's arm and walked into the emergency room.

"I want to see my son," Laurie said to the duty nurse who simply looked at her with understanding eyes, then signaled them both to follow her. On the way they noticed that all but one of the cubical curtains were open with several child occupants accompanied by one or two adults with nurses busily attending to their needs. Two were groaning from minor accidents while the others appeared to be simply suffering from upset stomachs or sprained muscles. When they stopped in front of the closed curtain, Laurie swallowed hard, then held her breath as her eyes searched Randy's. Randy nodded to the nurse, who in turn pulled back the curtain.

Laurie could not have braced herself for what her eyes saw that first moment when the curtain was drawn back. The color drained from her face. "Oh, God!" she said and mechanically held her hand up to her mouth.

"He's sedated," the nurse said. "We gave him a shot of morphine and Motrin to quiet him down."

Both Randy and Laurie surveyed their fallen son's face in horror. His face was severely bloated, with dried blood caked in his hair and eyebrows. His uninjured eye socket had red stains from blood pooling that had been partly wiped away. His nose was swollen with bruising, leaching out into his cheeks. The injured eye had a large white piece of gauze taped over it.

Randy walked to his son's side and raked his sleeping body with a deep gaze, then began fingering the dried blood on his shirt. Sean must have sensed his father's presence, since he writhed his body several times before fluttered his good eye. His father touched his hand. "Lie still, son. Don't move. We'll be right here."

"We have to get him ready for surgery now," the nurse said while holding an aspirator tube in her hand. "You can wait for him in the surgery waiting room on the fourth floor."

Randy traded looks with Laurie and nodded. "We would like to pray over him before he goes up. Okay?"

"Of course," the nurse said and withdrew from the cubicle.

Randy reached over and clutched Laurie's hand, then closed his eyes. Thoughts of King David praying for God to intercede and spare his son born to Bathsheba out of his adulterous act flashed into his mind. Of course the illness was not of the same magnitude, nor was the cause, but somehow Randy could identify with David's grief and petition to restore his son. "Lord," he prayed aloud, "we come before you as husband and wife asking for your mercy on our son's behalf. We pray that you would guide the doctors and that our boy's sight would be restored. This we pray in the mighty name of Jesus. Amen."

Both of them leaned over and kissed their son. Moments later the nurse returned and wheeled Sean out of the ER and into the elevator that would bring him up to surgery.

* * *

A hospital waiting room—especially surgery—can be a lonely place, Randy thought as he scanned the faces of those anxiously biding their time, waiting for their respective doctors to report the results of their surgery. *How can they make it without a relationship with Jesus? How much better things are when we can bring our petitions and our agonizing thoughts to Christ to help us through a crisis!* He studied several faces, attempting to enter into their pain and thought process at this critical juncture in their journey of life and wondered if they were praying or questioning God as to why this emergency came upon them. But then again, he realized that he too had to stop himself from asking the proverbial question of God: *Why?*

Then the thought came to mind: *Why not him?* The *why* questions can be a question that can lead one either into a theodicy that has no answer or down a spiraling path that ends in a pit of despair. God is under no obligation to explain his ways to his creation.

He squeezed his eyes shut to allow a distant memory of a devotion he had read the year before. *What was it all about?* he asked himself. *Hmm. Ah, yes, I remember now.* He opened his eyes and turned toward Laurie. She had curled herself up in the cushioned chair next to him. Her eyes were closed, but he knew she was only resting. There were few who could really sleep in the surgery waiting room.

He closed his eyes again and returned to his thoughts. *Yes,* he remembered, *God has hidden secrets that he keeps from the wise and prudent. I shouldn't fear what may come upon me, but be content to accept things that I cannot understand, God's ways are above my ways as the heavens are above the earth, right. I must wait patiently for His hand. When I cannot see His hand, I must trust His heart. Right. I know that presently He will reveal to me the treasures of darkness, the riches of the glory of the mystery. But I must wait upon the mystery that is only the veil of God's face. No, I cannot be afraid to enter the cloud that is settling down on our lives right now, because God is in it. The other side is radiant with His glory. Yes, He is in the dark cloud that has embraced us. I must plunge into the blackness of its darkness without flinching, through the shrouding curtain of His pavilion because that is where God is waiting for me.*

"Mr. Bradshaw," they heard. Doctor Cutler was standing by them, pulling off his rubber gloves.

Startled, Randy realized an hour had passed. "Yes, Dr. Cutler!" he said as his heart did a flip.

Randy and Laurie stood promptly and held hands. "How is he?" they asked in unison.

Dr. Cutler placed his hand on Randy's shoulder. "He'll recover full sight of his eye."

Randy and Laurie simultaneously sighed in relief. "How bad was it?" he asked.

"Well," Dr. Cutler explained, "his retina was detached and had to be sutured. We drained the hematoma, and as we suspected from the MRI, there was that small hole. We sewed that up as well." He looked at Laurie and added, "He's a real trooper. Brave lad."

Laurie burst into tears. "Thank you, God," she whispered. "Thank you!"

Dr. Cutler continued, "He'll have to be watched for several months to avoid any strain on that eye from any kind of impact, so no sports and no pool. He will have to wear a patch for two weeks followed by dark sunglasses for another four weeks. But that's a small price to pay to regain his sight from such a severe wound." He smiled. "I'll need to see him in my office every 10 days until that eye heals."

Randy raised his eyes to heaven to give praise. "God is good."

Dr. Cutler nodded as Laurie dried her eyes. "He's in recovery. Give him another half hour and then you can see him." He shook hands with them both before exiting the waiting room.

Randy put his arm around Laurie's waist. "Let's go share the good news with the men from the church down in the lobby."

Inside the elevator, Laurie couldn't help but notice the mixed emotions on the passengers' faces. Some were happy and talkative, and these she mentally assigned to the group visiting recovering patients, while those silent passengers with worried looks were probably, according to her reasoning, visiting those who were in serious or critical condition. She smiled with those who were smiling.

* * *

Randy stood on his tiptoes to locate the Dolphins helmet he fastened to his car radio antenna to spot his car easily in the crowded parking lot. Marking car antennae with various paraphanellia from colorful streamers to golf balls was a favorite pastime in South Florida, especially among the retired folk.

"That was really nice of Lester and the others to come to the hospital," Laurie said as they drove out of the lot.

"What's wrong with your voice?" Randy said, pulling back to look at her. He scanned her face. "What's wrong?"

She pulled a string of tissues from the box on the console and patted the tears forming in her eyes. "Just overwhelmed by it all, I guess."

"You've had a tough day, baby. When we get home, I'll draw you a hot bath so you can relax." She smiled at him and said through stifled tears, "That will be nice." *Yes, overwhelmed by it all*, she thought as she dropped her head back into the headrest. The image of Sean lying in the street after being hit by the lacrosse ball drifted into her mind, followed by a close-up of him in the ER with gauze over his eye, writhing in pain. She squirmed in the seat as the droning vibration of the roadway began to take its medicinal effect.

Where are you going, and what are you trying to accomplish? What are you trying to prove? Why do you want this college degree so badly and what price are you willing to pay to get it? Randy is the pastor of a large church and makes an excellent salary; we really don't need the money. When does the merry-go-round stop? The mounting conflict with Randy? The ill feelings I have toward the church people? My apathetic attitude toward the children? Then the words of a Christian titan sprang up in her mind: *"It is doubtful that God can use a man greatly unless He has hurt him deeply." Does that apply to women as well? It must.* She fluttered her eyes and looked out her window at the passing cars. *God, what is the message here? What do you want from me?*

As they drove into the driveway, Tiffany ran out to greet them.

Laurie sniffled several times, then dried her eyes as they focused on her daughter. "Thank you, God." she whispered. "Thank you!" Suddenly a strange feeling came over her as she walked into the house. An experience that in the future would be attributed to the prompting of the Holy Spirit. "I need to be alone for a while," she said, then set her handbag down on the kitchen table and walked into her bedroom.

Randy and Tiffany exchanged curious glances as they heard the bedroom door close slowly. "I need a hug," Randy said.

Teary-eyed, they both hugged. "Is Mom all right?" Tiffany asked, wiping her eyes.

"She's taking this pretty hard," Randy said. "I'll look in on her in a little while. She needs some time to unwind."

"Let me make you a cup of coffee while you tell me about Sean," Tiffany said, her voice calm but filled with apprehension.

"You're the best," he said with a look of approval.

For the next 20 minutes Randy recounted the tragic events at the hospital as he sipped his coffee and nibbled on some Oreo cookies.

In the bedroom, Laurie gazed into her dresser mirror. She touched the side of her face, then mussed up her hair, then stared at her reflection. She squeezed her eyes shut. She could no longer look at the person she had become. Her soul was troubled and her conscience tormented. *I can no longer live this way. I need relief. Oh, how I need relief,* she lamented.

She opened her eyes only to see dark images from the past float into her mind. Painful collages that reminded her once again of a part of her life she locked away in a vault that no one was allowed to enter. She rubbed her temples as the discomfort intensified, then slammed her fist down on the dresser. *No more!* she cried out in her heart, *no more!*

Spotted Randy's Bible on his night table, she picked it up and returned to the mirror. Holding up the Bible in one hand, she used the other to point to images that had been assailing her and whispered, "I don't know where it says it, but I know that God is greater than my past, and you will no longer control me with these nightmares!"

She squeezed her eyes shut for several minutes, then slowly opened them. When she looked again in the mirror, all the images were gone.

16

Randy peered at the kitchen clock, realizing Laurie had been alone for more than 30 minutes. "Time to check on your mother," he told Tiffany.

She nodded. "Good idea."

Seconds later Laurie called from the hallway, "Randy, can I see you for a minute?"

Randy registered the peculiar sound in Laurie's voice. She was sobbing. "Be right there!" He hurried into their bedroom.

She met him at the doorway. "Randy, something terrible has happened," she said solemnly, tears streaming down her face. Her eyes were swollen, her face flushed with redness.

Randy put his arm around her. "What is it? Are you sick?"

"I'm sick all right," she answered through sniffles. "Sick when I look in the mirror." She closed the door, then walked him over to her dresser and pulled out the lower left-hand drawer and placed it on the floor. Then she reached her hand into the dresser, where the drawer was to the space along side the drawer slide mechanism. As she pulled out a small black felt bag with a drawstring, she said through several gulps, "I have a confession to make."

Randy's heart pumped wildly as his eyes focused on the bag. It looked familiar. "What's this?" he managed to say, despite his disorientation.

"It's my necklace and slide," she said while opening the bag. She turned it upside down and emptied its contents on the top of the dresser.

"But I thought...?"

She was sobbing so hard, she could barely get the words out. "I lied. I lied."

Randy was dazed. He found it difficult to comprehend what was happening, yet felt his hands tightly balled at his side. "You what?" he finally choked out. "You lied?"

She nodded, then in the next instant sat on the edge of the bed. "That's why I didn't want to report it to the insurance company."

He sat next to her and said gravely, "But why, Laurie? Why would you do such a thing?"

She took a deep breath to rally more courage before answering. "I was sick and tired of all the attention given to *those* homeless people, especially that Stephanie."

"So you thought, by staging this act of thievery, we would blame *those* homeless people as you call them, and this would send them packing, right?"

"Something like that," she said through several more sniffles.

A light knock at the door and Tiffany asked, "Dad, is Mom all right?"

"Mom's upset, Tiffy," he replied tersely.

"Can I help?" she asked.

"She'll be fine," he said, turning on his soothing voice. "Don't worry." Seconds later he heard footsteps walking away.

Stunned as he grappled with the enormity of the problem, Randy had the presence of mind not to react in anger, but the feeling of despair in his heart was almost palpable. He stood and walked to the window, then opened the vertical blinds to allow more light into the room. His breath caught in his throat. "This is unreal. A terrible nightmare."

"Yes, a nightmare is right," she replied. "I never told you this, but now I must." She paced in front of him for a few seconds, then stopped abruptly. "Before we were married, I was assaulted by a homeless man. While attending my youth fellowship class in my home church, a homeless man tried to molest me. I was sent to get a volleyball in the equipment storage room when one of the homeless men that our pastor was trying to help followed me and started fondling me from behind. I was only sixteen at the time, leading a very sheltered life. And when this happened, something in me just shut down.

"He held his hand over my mouth and continued to fondle me until I bit his hand and screamed at the top of my lungs. Within seconds, our youth pastor, a big burly quarterback in his college days, was pulling him off me. The homeless man was arrested and that was the last I ever saw of him. I can't remember his face...I guess I blocked it out...because I only remember seeing the food stains on his red sweatshirt."

Randy sat on the bed, shocked. "Why haven't you ever told me this?"

"It must have been suppressed in the inner recesses of my subconscious mind, screaming for release. Then when this whole thing with the homeless started, especially that Stephanie woman who was wearing that red shirt when I first saw her, it must have triggered that inner nightmare to come forward and rear its ugly head." She gazed at him for some sign of understanding and potential absolution. "Can you ever forgive me?"

Randy turned once more toward the window. *Does this justify how a woman who has the Holy Spirit dwelling inside her can be a party to such an atrocity as this? How can she perpetrate a colossal lie that impugns the name* and character of another and not have her conscience bother her? Where is the operation of the Holy Spirit to bring on conviction and...unless...?

He dare not entertain the notion, but it had to be asked. *How can this be, Lord? Unless...is it possible this woman is not really regernerated in the Spirit...not really born-again?*

He rotated in place and his eyes probed deeply into hers. "Laurie, I can forgive you. That is not the problem. What *is* the problem is forgiveness from God *and* explaining how you could have gone this long and not be troubled internally or have your conscience bother you, if nothing else, in the name of common decency? And what about your relationship with God? Can you tell me that wasn't affected? And didn't you realize the damage you'd inflict? On Stephanie. Our church? Our family?"

"There were times when I was grieved, yes," she explained, "but I always planned to make things right. Whenever the nightmare would come or when I thought about the man who molested me, I felt justified in getting back at the homeless for the hurt inflicted on me. As far as Homeless Outreach and Stephanie are concerned, after a while, things just went out of control. So I let it go, thinking it would work itself out."

"Or until God intervened, right?"

The mantle of regret was heavy on her heart, but for the wrong reasons. Finally she threw up her hands in self-defense. "Okay. Okay. Guilty!" She buried her face in her hands

More melding of dark, troubling thoughts tumbled into Randy's mind. A niggling in his spirit signaled an uneasiness with her reaction. There didn't seem to be any regret that she had grieved the heart of the most important person, God. Sure, Sean's accident brought on anguish that led to soul searching that ended in confession, but what about godly contrition? He pondered the equation, knowing that if he had a solution for this problem, he'd rival the ancient sages in Solomon's court.

A glimpse of Sean lying in the hospital crossed his mind. "Sean's accident has put things in perspective for me, and after hearing you, I'm sure you feel the same way. There's nothing worse than having a sick or injured kid in your family, and right now, we can't allow the tyranny of your nightmare and this whole thing of Homeless Outreach from robbing us of the joy of God protecting Sean so he didn't lose his eye."

"I know you're right," she said, lifting her head with lingering sniffles.

"I can't imagine the heartache you've endured all these years in dealing with that incident in your past, but I can only say at this point that you need to experience some relief from God." He held up his hand in a halting manner.

"No, not relief," he corrected himself. "But that peace with *and* of God you asked about in the car on the way back from Dr. Rosen's message to our church. That's what you need to carry you through."

"I do, I do," she said numbly.

He gazed intently into her eyes. "Well, if you really desire it, not the kind of peace the world offers, you must search for it in Christ. He is the Prince of Peace, the only One who can grant it to you. It's the one gift from God that enables us to put harmful memories in their proper place in our hearts."

She had heard this thing about peace with God before, but it never really made sense until now. Or, it didn't have as much significance until this moment. "I want it, really, Randy," she said wearily.

"Let me ask you something. I know you've probably heard this before in a sermon, but have you ever forgiven this man who molested you? I mean he seems to have reached over the years and exerted control over you where you're still in bondage to the ugly memories. This is oppressive control."

"No, it's still too raw in my heart right now."

Randy nodded in understanding. The peace with God and the peace of God, along with forgiveness, is not something that can be learned or forced upon someone. It only comes from God through the operation of the Holy Spirit. So we'll have to wait for God to bring it about, that's all."

Laurie's shoulders rose and fell. "I've really made a mess of things. What are we going to do about Stephanie and the Homeless Outreach dilemma?"

Randy sucked in a deep breath. "I'm not sure where this leaves us just yet," he observed bleakly. "One thing I know for sure is that we're going to have to draw upon God's extra grace for this one."

"Can you square things with the people down at Homeless Outreach?" Laurie queried, sighing in hopeful expectation.

"I'm sure Sam will be delighted to hear his people have been exonerated, but I'm not so sure how Stephanie will take this," Randy ventured.

Laurie's eyes were drying, and her normal demeanor was slowly returning. "I hate to put this on you. Would you want me to go with you?"

"Hmm. To tell you the truth, I don't think that would work right now," Randy advised. "You might polarize things." He pursed his lips and scratched his head. "Let me think on it. My first reaction is to go by myself in the morning and try to mend some fences. But we'll see in the morning."

Laurie raised her eyebrows and nodded. "Whatever you say."

"All right, let's leave it there for now." He extended his hand to her and they walked out of the bedroom together into the kitchen, where Tiffany stood by the sink with her hand on her waist.

"What's going on?" she asked, inquiring eyes darting back and forth between her mother and father.

"We found out what happened to your mother's necklace," Randy said, remaining utterly still, a statue. Only his eyes moved.

Laurie sheepishly raised her hand, dangling the necklace in the air. "I made the whole story up," she admitted as her eyes flicked toward Tiffany's face, then away. She looked guilty.

A frosty silence. Then, "I can't believe it!" Tiffany said, eyes widening in shock. "You mean you deliberately lied so as to blame the homeless people?"

Laurie looked into her daughter's eyes and saw a fire blazing that seemed to match her flaming red hair. "Tiffy, what I did was wrong. I know that now. I hope you will try to understand that I'm not an evil person."

Tiffany picked up a cup off the kitchen counter and threw it to the floor. "Wrong?! Wrong?!" she yelled. "What you did was not only wrong, but inexcusable!" She jerked her head back and forth, then cried out, "Now I know why Sean is in the hospital! It's because of you! God is punishing us for your vicious lie!"

"Now wait a minute, young lady!" Randy interjected. "That's your mother you're talking to. And Sean's accident was not caused by your mother. That's *not* who our God is. Thankfully, He doesn't punish us according to our mistakes or sins."

Tiffany burst into tears as she glared at her mother. "How could you do this thing?" She stalked off to find sanctuary in her bedroom.

Laurie clapped her hand over her mouth and shook her head in disbelief. Her family was disintegrating before her very eyes. She stumbled into a nearby chair, then buried her head in her arms and began to sob once more. "She's right," she said, barely coherent. "I did cause Sean's accident."

Randy placed his hand on her shoulder. *We'll get through this*, he thought, *we'll get through this.* "Let me help you,"

Tiffany's bedroom door flew open!

Randy turned. "Tiffany," he said. "Come in so we can talk this out."

"I'm done talking!" she yelled while running to the front door. Seconds later, they heard the front door slam.

* * *

Laurie turned in bed to see Randy lying next to her with his eyes wide open. "What time did you finally get to bed?" she asked as she wiped the sleep from her eyes. It was 6:15 a.m.

Randy sighed deeply. "It was after 2:30 and still no sign of her."

"Should we call the police?"

Randy climbed out of bed and glanced in the mirror to pat down what Tiffany called "bedhead." "Not just yet. She probably went to sleep at one of her friends' houses. I'm hoping she'll come home before today is out." He slipped into his gym shorts. "I'd like to visit Sam Knowles today to discuss some 'damage control,' so suppose you go to see Sean this morning, and I'll catch up with you before lunch at the hospital."

After a moment of contemplation, Laurie realized her classes were being shoved aside with her family matters taking priority, and accordingly realigned her thinking to meet the crisis. "Of course," she replied.

Randy started for the bathroom when Laurie began patting the bedspread and said, "Randy, this might sound out of character for me, but let's pray for God to help us."

There were critical times in their married life when an emergency necessitated immediate or intercessory prayer, but normally Randy initiated it. This was a welcome change. "Yes, by all means," he said and kneeled down at the bedside next to her.

* * *

Randy stopped at the traffic light on University Drive and Broward Boulevard and fixed his eyes on the two Homeless Outreach vendors soliciting funds from the motorists as they waited for the light to change. *A strange breed,* Randy thought. *Perilously risking their lives dodging oncoming traffic to pander the HO newspaper and to beg from people who care little about their plight. A busy community considered to be a bunch of nobodies, working feverishly to overcome the shame of homelessness and the loss of dignity. Individuals determined to recover some degree of usefulness amidst a world that labels them discards. Persons whose lives mean something to God and who have feelings like the rest of us. Souls who are looking for their fellow man to reach out and help them in their journey of life.*

Randy arrived at the Homeless Outreach shelter to see an ambulance outside the entrance with two paramedics loading a gurney into the holding tracks. He quickly noticed the white sheet fully extended over the person's entire body. A number of onlookers from the street and the shelter crowded the area, apparently discussing the cause of death. Randy grimaced, then walked through the open door to the receptionist's counter. "What happened?" he asked the attendant whom he did not recognize.

"He overdosed last night," the woman said.

Randy's heart jumped. He looked at the woman's name tag and said, "Shelly, was he a resident or a newcomer?" Marty's face flashed before him, heightening his anxiety.

"Why do you ask?" Shelly, a middle-aged woman with a short-cropped haircut and flowery blouse replied. Giving out information to strangers was a violation of the HO policy.

Randy nodded in understanding and changed his question. "Well, I know some of the residents here." He waved her off and said, "It's okay. Is Sam Knowles here?"

Shelly assumed he knew Sam and replied, "He's upstairs with the doctor filling out the paperwork on the OD. He'll probably be down soon."

"Oh, I see." Randy backed up a few steps. "I'll wait here in the lobby for him."

It was 15 minutes until the elevator door opened. Then Sam emerged at a brisk pace with an uniformed paramedic and a man in a blue suit trailing behind them. Randy surmised it was the doctor. Sam spotted Randy and said, "Nice to see you, Pastor Randy." He stopped short in front of him. "How much time do you have? Can you wait until we finish?"

Randy waved a hand in the air. "I have total time to wait." Sam smiled at him, then continued to walk out the door.

Twenty minutes later the ambulance pulled away and the crowd dispersed.

Sam approached Randy as he reentered the building. "Come on upstairs for a while." Once inside the elevator he asked warmly, "How's your boy doing?"

"You heard about the accident?"

"Yes, Stephanie told me all about it. She likes to keep up with what's going on in your church," Sam added.

Randy was surprised until he remembered that bad news travels fast. "Well, he'll make a full recovery, thank God, but he'll really have to be careful for at least six months for the eye to completely heal."

"That's good news," Sam replied. Moments later they were in Sam's office. "Have a seat, Randy," Sam said cordially as he motioned toward a chair in front of his desk.

Randy pulled the chair two feet forward so as to be right next to the desk. "Sam, there's been a development in that situation at my home regarding Laurie's missing necklace."

The tragedy of the morning still dominated Sam's thoughts. "Crazy way to start a day around here, Randy, real crazy. Everyone around here feels terrible whenever we lose somebody. Every person is important to us, even the walk-ins we don't know anything about."

Randy blinked. "I can't imagine the heartbreak..."

"Oh, I'm sorry, Randy, you were saying something," Sam said, touching the side of his head to jog his memory.

"Well, yes," Randy began. "I came to talk to you about my wife's missing necklace."

"You found it, right?" Sam replied with a snort of confidence.

"Well, um, yes." His eyes probed deeply into Sam's. "How did you know?"

"I told you when this thing first happened that my people had nothing to do with it," he answered with an I-told-you-so look. "I knew it would be just a matter of time before it turned up, that's all."

Randy kneaded his temples. The mantle of guilt was heavy. The decision whether to tell Sam about Laurie's conspiracy or not made him increasing edgy as he thought on the consequences. He bit his lip, scratched his head, avoided Sam's eyes. Then, in a reasonable, controlled voice, "Yes, it turned up. Laurie found it in her dresser."

"Great," Sam said. Then he bent in closer to Randy and whispered, almost conspiratorially, "Now all you have to do is to square this thing with Stephanie, and we'll be back on track again."

Randy nodded as a wave of relief washed over him. *Some people can be so forgiving.* Of course the thought of telling Stephanie about Laurie's conspiracy seemed as much fun as nailing his tongue to the wall and setting his church on fire. But the decision to divulge all the details still was up in the air at this point. *Does she need to know about Laurie? Will it build up her relationship with God or break it down?* "Yes, I'd like to see her if she's here."

"She's here, all right. I saw her early this morning. But this newcomer who died last night of an overdose has had a dramatic impact on our residents. You see, they realize where they have come from and believe it could be any one of them on that gurney being loaded into an ambulance, so most of them hide out in their rooms or in the cafeteria until the body is removed."

Another dimension of life that he never gave thought to, Randy realized, nodding slowly as he processed the information.

Sam turned and picked up the phone then gave his secretary instructions to send Stephanie to his office. Moments later a knock on the door was heard.

"Nice to see you, Stephanie," Sam said, greeting her with a soft handshake.

Stephanie's eyes darted back and forth between Sam and Randy as she stood in front of Sam's desk. "Strange morning," she said, gesturing to acknowledge the death of the transient. "It saddens me to learn of a human life dying from an overdose of drugs."

"We all feel your pain, Stephanie," Sam said. "Whenever a 'family' member leaves us under those circumstances, we all suffer."

*Redeemed, how I love to proclaim it...*sang out from Randy's cell phone. He read the caller ID and said to Sam apologetically, "My wife. I have to get this." Sam and Stephanie both nodded as Randy flipped up the phone's cover.

"Randy, Tiffany hasn't come home yet, and I'm about to leave for the hospital to see Sean. What should I do? I'm getting worried about her."

Randy eyed Sam and Stephanie. "I should be finished here in 15 minutes. Wait at home, and I'll call you from my car." He ended the call.

"Trouble?" Sam asked intuitively.

"We had a disagreement at home, and my daughter became upset. That's all," Randy explained half-heartedly.

Stephanie gave him a curious look as if she knew there was more to the call. "Tiffany is a special girl, Pastor Randy," she said. "Her and I seem to get along well. Please let me know if I can ever help."

Randy was touched by the offer and unwittingly filed it in the back of his mind. "Thank you. I will," he replied with gratitude.

"Pastor Randy has something to tell you, Stephanie," Sam announced. "A *development*, if you will."

"Oh?"

Randy looked into her probing eyes, them averted his eyes momentarily, believing he had to keep the truth from her in order to maintain the integrity of his household and the image of the church. Whether that belief was right or wrong, only God would tell. "Yes, the development is that my wife found the necklace and slide that was missing," he choked out. "The whole thing was a horrible mistake, and we are praying for your consideration and forgiveness for this misunderstanding."

Stephanie shot a look of triumph at Sam, then turned to Randy and said, "This may come as a shock to you, but I've already forgiven you and your church. It seems that shortly after I made a decision to receive Christ as my personal Savior, God flooded my heart with a different kind of love for people. A kind of love that sees beyond the physical—you know, the things that separate us from one another, to see the spiritual, the good in people that God wants me to see. If God can forgive me, so too can I forgive others. So as far as I'm concerned, it's already a done deal."

Randy glanced at Sam and marveled. "Wow. Unbelievable."

"And I might add," Stephanie continued, "that any feelings I might have had toward your wife, Laurie, have also been filtered through God's love."

Sam simply shook his head slowly, being mystified by what he was hearing. "Where I come from that's called a whopper."

"Pastor, Randy," Stephanie asked, "what did the congregation have to say about this whole thing?"

"Well," Randy replied sheepishly, "we never even mentioned it to our church folk. We believed it should remain a family matter."

"I see," Stephanie replied, her eyes suddenly brightening. "Interesting."

Randy sensed Stephanie had more to say but exercised restraint. "With this behind us, Sam, do you feel comfortable resuming our development of Open Arms?"

Sam pursed his lips as he thought on the question. "I don't see any reason why we shouldn't, Randy. Let's allow things to cool down a bit, you know with the OD and then this thing with Stephanie. Let's give it a few days."

"I'll call you," Randy said as he rose from the chair. He walked to the door. "Stephanie, I hope to see you at church real soon."

She smiled and nodded. "Marty and I plan to be at your Bible study."

Randy beamed. "That's great. I'll look forward to seeing you both." He walked out of Sam's office and within minutes was inside his car. As he pulled out of the parking lot he pressed Laurie's speed dial number on his cell phone. "I thought it over," he advised her. "I'll meet you at the hospital and we'll plan from there."

* * *

Laurie stood at the nurse's station waiting for the duty nurse when Randy walked up behind her. "Hi, doll," he said and put his arm around her waist as he pecked her on the cheek. "How's our boy doing?"

"He's doing well," she said with a smile. "I'm just waiting for his nurse to ask her some questions."

"Like when he's going to go home, right?"

She nodded. "Among other things." She stepped back and, with probing eyes, asked, "Any word on Tiffany?"

"Nothing yet. But she'll be all right. She's probably on her way home as we speak."

Laurie's shoulders drooped. Suddenly her cell phone flashed bright yellow indicating a message. She flipped up the cover to see Judy Edelson's number on the "calls missed" list, then pressed the *return call* button as the head nurse turned her head and silently pointed to a sign that read: *As a Courtesy to Our Patients, Please Turn Off Your Cell Phone.*

Laurie squeaked out an apology and quickly walked to the nearest window for a stronger signal, leaving Randy to entertain and divert the nurse's attention. "Hi, Laurie," Judy said cheerfully, "how's Sean doing?"

"We're waiting for the latest update, but he looks as good as can be expected."

"Laurie," she entreated, "both Ronnie and I want you to know that our hearts really go out to you and that we're praying all will be well with Sean."

"I appreciate that," Laurie replied. She felt a prompting in her heart to be more friendly.

"Well, if there's anything we can do for you or Randy, just let us know," Judy proffered.

Laurie surprised herself by adding, "There is one thing."

"Name it."

"Would it be all right if I called you once in a while and prayed with you over the phone?"

"That would be fine. I will look forward to it."

"Thanks, Judy,"

"Blessings to you and Randy," Judy said.

When Judy ended the call, she turned to Ronnie sitting nearby and said, somewhat mystified, "You're not going to believe this, but Laurie as much as asked me to be her prayer partner just now."

"Will wonders ever cease?" he replied.

"This accident with Sean is really getting hold of her," Judy observed. "It will be interesting to watch how the Lord will use this in their family."

"The position of a pastor's wife can be a lonely place. She doesn't have too many friends, so maybe you can use this as a platform to minister to her," Ronnie ventured.

"I'll be here if she needs me."

* * *

Randy and Laurie walked into Sean's room to see him watching the Ranger game with the volume several decibels above the normal hearing range. Randy smiled at him, then focused on the padded patch over his eye that was held in place with clear adhesive. Sean hit the mute button. "Hi, Dad!" His face brightened as he held out his hand.

Randy shook his hand as he leaned over and kissed him on the forehead. "Things are not the same at home without you, Sean,"

Sean nodded. "I'll be going home soon, right, Mom?"

Laurie nodded. "Very soon, darling."

Sean glanced toward the door. "Where's Tiffy?"

Laurie's eyes flicked to Randy's, then she looked away. "She's staying with a friend."

Sean nodded and then said, almost smiling, "The doctor came in to see me early this morning and said I'm doing fine."

Laurie patted his shoulder. "You know more than I do, young man. Now that *is* good news."

"Then he said I might be able to go home in a few days," he added gleefully. After a moment he wrinkled his nose and said ruefully, "He warned me that I can't play lacrosse or any other sports until he says so." Then he looked at Randy. "But that's all right as long as I can go home."

"That's the spirit!" Randy said with a luminous smile.

The next 45 minutes included catch-up time and future plans, then Randy looked at his watch and gave Laurie the nod. "I have to go, son, but I'll be back later tonight."

Laurie took the cue. "I'll walk your father to the elevator and be right back."

Out of Sean's hearing, Randy grasped Laurie's hand as he walked. "Things went well down at Homeless Outreach, but now I'm troubled about Tiffany. We should have heard from her by now. Keep your cell phone on in case she should call you. I'm going to ride around; do some investigating."

Laurie wrapped her arms around herself. "When I get home, I'll call some of her friends to see if they know anything."

Randy expelled a sigh as they resumed their walk to the elevator. "I need to remember that God is still on the throne and that He's in control of all things, including this thing with Tiffany, even when we can't see what's going on."

Laurie admired his faith and trusted his judgment. "I need you," she said warmly and clutched his arm as the elevator door opened. Two nurses walked out, acknowledged their presence, then moved on. "I'll talk to you later," Laurie said and gave him a kiss.

The elevator door closed.

17

There were no benches, only two acres of grass and several trees to block the ubiquitous Florida sunlight. Holiday Park on Sunrise Boulevard in Fort Lauderdale was not a place for families to enjoy a walk or for couples to stroll on Sunday afternoons, but a refuge for the homeless. It was a park of cardboard beds and empty beer cans. Plastic shopping bags blowing like tumbleweeds conspicuously replaced ornamental shrubs and park niceties that attracted the genteel section of society. It was a neglected site in a sordid part of town that city officials avoided on their way to work. Yet, a safe place for the unwanted element of the community to hang around.

I wonder if Stephanie ever came here, Tiffany wondered as she meandered around the park, looking for a secluded location to rest from her long walk.

"Need help, girlfriend?" a voice from behind a tree yelled out. She turned to see what looked like a dirty old man leering at her while holding a beer bottle wrapped in a brown paper bag. He stared at her and her red hair as if drilling her image into his mind.

"No thanks, mister!" She yelled back and accelerated her pace toward the back of the park where there appeared to be unpopulated open spaces.

"Welcome to the armpit of Florida!" a man sitting on a tree stump bellowed out.

One of the official greeters to the obvious newcomer, she reasoned, then simply waved to him and continued to walk until she reached the chain link fence on the south side of the park. The fence served as the line of demarcation between the industrial condominiums on the outside of the park and the beginning of what was once a bright, shiny place for the gentry to frolic and discuss their recreational plans.

She pulled a towel out of her backpack and sat on it just in time to see a woman approaching her from the west side of the park where several large appliance cartons were strategically stationed as if they were miniature trailers. "Ugh," she muttered.

Minutes later the woman, apparently in her early 60s with long, stringy gray hair and facial wrinkles resembling spider webs, was upon her. "Have any food, dearie?" she said in a gravelly tone. "I'll trade you for some toilet paper."

Tiffany stared at the strange woman who now stood in front of her. "I have some granola bars that I can share with you." There was no way she was ready to use any outside toilet facility. "But no thanks to the toilet paper."

"Suit ya self. The granola bars will do, dearie." The woman smiled.

Tiffany focused on the woman's rotten teeth and wondered how long she was living on candy bars. "How long have you been here?"

The woman plopped down in front of Tiffany and ticked off three fingers as she stuffed the two granola bars into her shirt pocket. "Nearly three months, I guess. When the weather gets chilly next month, I'll head down toward the Keys to keep warm. My summer place, so to speak." She jerked her thumb over her shoulder back toward the appliance carton area and added, "I'll rent you my apartment for a small fee if you want."

Tiffany cracked a smile. "No thanks. I'll probably only stay here for today and then I'll mosey on somewhere."

After many years on the streets, the woman could spot a newcomer. "If you don't mind my asking," the woman said, scanning Tiffany's body, "what are you running away from? I mean, you're pretty dolled up for this neighborhood."

Tiffany took a gulp of air to gather her senses. "Say, what's your name anyway? If I'm going to get personal, I want to know whom I'm speaking to."

"Ha," the woman said with a devilish guffaw, "my name is Alice." Then she made a sweeping motion with her hand. "But everybody here calls me 'Mom.'"

"Oooo-kay, nice, Mom. But how did you know I was running away?"

Alice then reached over and touched Tiffany's hair. "Nobody here has clean hair, dearie. And what beautiful red hair you have, too." Then she pointed to her clothes and shoes. "And nobody here dresses like that."

"Well, let's just say that I'm here because of a family matter, that's all."

Alice held up her hand in a halting matter. "That's good enough for me. It's refreshing to know that you're not running from the law."

"No, just some family problems."

Alice started to walk away, then stopped and said as an afterthought, "Say, dearie, if you want a good place to hang, stop off at the Homeless Outreach. The food and lodging is good if you can handle the rules."

Tiffany took a double-take. "Is that why you're not living there? Because of the rules?"

"That's it, dearie. The place is one of the best in South Florida, but they make you get up early each morning and ride their van to a designated place to peddle their newspaper and beg for money."

"So what's so terrible about that if you get a decent place to live?" Tiffany asked in wonder.

"To each his or her own," Alice replied tersely as she threw her hands up and walked away.

Weird, Tiffany thought, *real weird.* But then again this wasn't the kind of place for normal people to frequently congregate. *My hair,* she thought, *she mentioned my hair.* She raked her hand through her hair, then pulled out her compact from her handbag and studied her face and hair in the mirror. She took out a brush and stroked her several times, then peered closely in the mirror. Her eyes widened in shock when an image flashed back at her. It was the face of her mother. She blinked several times, bewildered by the discovery, then looked again. This time it was her face.

"I'm becoming more like my mother," she said to herself. The thought unsettled her. She quickly closed her compact and stuffed it into her handbag, then abruptly stood. In one fell swoop she picked up the towel, shook it off, and walked out of the park.

* * *

Randy pulled his car over to the curb and took out his cell phone from his shirt pocket as it chirped out his favorite hymn. "Hi, babe."

"Anything yet?" Laurie asked with a degree of anxiety.

"No, nothing. I've just finished a sweep of Sunrise Heights High, and no sign of her." He sighed. "From here I'm going over to the Fashion Mall, and then to the Sawgrass Mills Mall. That's probably where she is, so don't worry. We'll find her."

"I made some calls to her friends, Randy, but nothing."

"I'll keep looking until I find her, so let's just trust the Lord."

Click.

* * *

Tiffany patted her jeans pocket to confirm the presence of her cash holdings, then walked into the Broadway diner. Once inside she sat in a booth and looked over at the pay telephone on the wall by the doorway. There would be no phone call to home today.

"Can I start you off with a soft drink?" the peppy waitress asked as she handed her a menu.

"Yes, I'll have a cola with lemon, and hold the ice," Tiffany replied.

The waitress nodded and walked off. Tiffany unwittingly stuck her fingers in her mouth and began to bite her fingernails as she surveyed the décor on the walls. The portraits and photographs of Broadway and Hollywood movie starlets and stars of times past formed an interesting photomontage. It reminded her of the artificial nature of those stars who act out on the silver screen parts of persons totally different from themselves in order to entertain the public. An art form that many people do in reality. *Am I one of them?* she asked herself. *I find myself going down a path after my mother, yet there's a part of me that rejects that life. On one hand I want to honor the Lord with my life, but on the other, I want to get as much out of life as I can. I guess that sounds selfish, but I think I'm young enough to accomplish both.*

Sometimes I feel I'm acting when I'm in church or with my friends or with my dad, to show them how spiritual I am, but when I'm alone, I don't think that way. In my own mind, I often see myself as being a famous actress or pop singer with my name on the cover of magazines or performing on stage to entertain my fans.

At times I want expensive clothes and look forward to shiny new cars and glittery homes that will bring me happiness, while at other times, I realize that stuff cannot bring fulfillment. No sooner do you get what you thought would make you really happy, when the novelty wears off and you want something else to fill the empty space. A vicious cycle. I know what the problem is. It's the same problem my mom has. My dad often preached on it. We're not satisfied with Jesus.

"Are you ready to order, miss?" the waitress asked, shattering Tiffany's reverie.

* * *

Randy walked out of the Sawgrass Mills Mall Dolphin exit into the searing heat of the day. As he opened up his car, a blast of scalding air that had built up inside the automobile momentarily took his breath away. The steering wheel was so hot he had to wait until the air conditioner lowered the cabin temperature before he could touch it. "Laurie," he said into his cell phone, "I've spent the last two hours scouring both the Sawgrass Mills Mall and the Fashion Mall. Nothing. No sign of her."

"What do we do now? Should we call the police?"

"Not just yet. I have one more place that I need to check, and if nothing turns up, then we'll notify the police," Randy assured.

The sound of a deep sigh came through the phone. Adverse circumstances were taking their toll on her. "I'll be at home waiting for you. After dinner we can both go back to see Sean."

"Okay. Keep your spirits up."

Click.

* * *

It was nearly three o'clock in the afternoon by the time Randy pulled into the Homeless Outreach's parking lot. Once he turned off the car's ignition he shot a short prayer up to the Lord asking for help, then quickly walked to the building. He peered though the thick glass door and gave the woman behind the desk a wave. Seconds later the electromagnetic door latch unlocked.

"Hi, Pastor Randy," the receptionist said.

Randy gave her a hard look. "Hi again." He tapped the side of his head with his finger then gave her a quizzical glance.

The woman understood his gesture and said, "Shelly. My name is Shelly."

"Oh, right," he countered. "Say, could you ask Stephanie Malone to come down so I could speak to her?" He pointed to the small sofa in the lobby and added, "I'll wait for her over there."

"No problem, doll," Shelly replied with a New York accent he hadn't recognized before this time.

Randy smiled and walked to the sofa.

Ten minutes later he heard the elevator doors open. Stephanie stepped out and walked briskly to him. "Well, hello, Pastor Randy. Long time no see."

Randy nodded as he stood. "I have an important favor to ask of you," he said, then nervously sat down again. He patted the cushion next to him. "It's about Tiffany."

Her smile faded, and she abruptly sat next to him. "Is she all right? Nothing has happened to her, has it?"

Randy shook his head several times to signal his increasing anxiety level. "Well, I didn't want to mention it this morning when I visited with you and Sam, thinking she would have come home by now, but the truth is, she has run away."

Stephanie clenched her teeth and fidgeted. "Oh, no. But why? I would have thought everything was fine with her."

His conscience wouldn't allow him to divulge the true nature of the conflict in order to preserve the family's confidentiality. "We had a family quarrel, and she took off."

Stephanie's lips pursed in a soundless whistle. "This is not good, Pastor Randy."

"If you mean not good for the church, I agree, but at this point, I'm only concerned with her safety and getting her back."

"I can see you're upset over this. Have you explored other avenues? Friends, school, hangouts?"

Randy waved her off. "We've done all of that. I've been looking for hours. Nothing."

"Police?"

He took a deep breath and exhaled slowly. "Not yet. It's too soon. I thought I would exhaust my search first, but if by tomorrow I haven't heard from her, then I'll go to the police."

Stephanie nodded her understanding. "So how can I help?"

"Because you know the streets, I thought you would go out with me and show me the places where you think she might go."

She stood immediately. "I'll go get my purse and be right with you."

A wave of relief swept over him. "Thanks, Stephanie. You're a lifesaver, and I really appreciate it."

Moments later they were driving north on Federal Highway heading toward Fort Lauderdale.

* * *

Unwittingly, Laurie set the dinner table for three before realizing that Tiffany was still missing. Then all at once the microwave timer started beeping, signaling the corn and sweet peas packets were cooked as the pot with the red potatoes boiled over and the phone rang. She mechanically turned off the items in their order of urgency, then picked up the phone. Quickly returning to the oven, she pulled out the baked filet of sole and set it to cool on the counter as she pressed the *Talk* button.

"Laurie, this is Judy. I just called to see how you're doing. How is everything going with Sean? Is he okay?"

Laurie recognized the call as a reaching out to her. "Um, yeah, sure. He's doing a lot better, thanks."

"That's a blessing. We've been praying for your family."

Solicitously: "We really appreciate your prayers, too. Thanks."

"Ronnie and I were wondering if you and Pastor Randy wanted to come over tonight for some fellowship. You know, get out of the house. I baked a loaf of banana-nut bread and thought we might have an evening together."

Laurie rolled her eyes. *What lousy timing! Go out visiting when Tiffany is missing?* Suddenly thoughts of Randy urging her to embrace the congregation and make friends with the ladies along with Judy's call at the hospital shot into her mind. She couldn't say no. "Yes, I guess it will be okay. Randy should be home any moment now, so I'll check with him, but it should be okay," she said as her shoulders rose and fell.

"Oh, and bring Tiffany along," Judy added. "She's such a darling, and we would love having her over, too."

Laurie's eyes suddenly blurred with tears. "Um, she's visiting one of her friends, so Randy and I will come by ourselves."

"Fine," Judy replied, "We'll see you later; about 8 o'clock."

"Right."

Several seconds passed before she burst out crying, almost uncontrollably. She staggered over to the kitchen table, pulled out a chair, and dropped into it. A nightmarish glimpse of Tiffany walking the streets at night, being accosted by a dirty old man, like the kind that molested her years ago, raced through her consciousness. "God, please protect her," she cried out. She looked over at the third place setting, next to the fourth where Sean normally sat, and took a deep breath before breaking out into a sob. She suddenly felt all alone. Folding her arms, she placed her head in them on top of her plate and just closed her eyes.

* * *

The front door opened and closed. Laurie raised her head off the table then quickly looked at the clock on the stove. Twenty-five minutes had passed.

"Tiffany?!" she called.

"No, babe, it's me," Randy said as he peeked into the kitchen.

Laurie ran to him and wrapped her arms around him. She desperately needed his strength and stable presence of mind. "Please tell me everything is all right! Tell me you know where she is and that she's safe," she pleaded.

Randy returned the embrace, then took a deep breath as his eyes met hers. "I wish I could, Laurie, but I can't. I spent the last three hours riding around with Stephanie looking for Tiffy, but nothing."

Laurie began crying again. "I can't take any more, Randy. I just can't." She swallowed hard, then reached for a napkin to wipe away her tears.

Randy reached for the napkin and patted her eyes softly. Within seconds, his own eyes began to tear, and his chest began to heave. "We need each other," he said in hopeless frustration. "We need each other."

They fell silent. For nearly five minutes they simply embraced each other, drawing strength from God for a united purpose.

* * *

Daylight was quickly fading as the sun set over the Everglades in the west. The big red and yellow ball on the horizon shimmered from its radiant light and gave off an eerie glow over I-595 that caused the series of exit signs to cast long shadows over the heavily traveled roadway. The darkened underpasses looked like subterranean caves with lofty ledges that provided secure sleeping quarters for those on the move. The underpasses were one of the several favorite hideouts for the homeless and the first place on Stephanie's list to look for Tiffany. The kind of place she wouldn't dare bring Pastor Randy.

When she drove up to the underpass on Flamingo Road at the intersection of I-595 in Sam's car, the evening traffic was extremely heavy. She would not be able to drive by and scan the underpass from her car without disrupting the flow of traffic. No, she would have to park Sam's car in a secure location and venture out on foot.

Ah, she thought as she visually searched the area, *the turn-off on Flamingo Road to I-595 heading south was a double lane with a wide shoulder. Perfect.* She parked the car, then quickly maneuvered herself through the oncoming traffic until she stood at the foot of the underpass. The concrete blocks that formed the apron leading to the underpinning and stanchions of the bridge were slippery from an earlier sun shower, but nevertheless, navigable, especially since she remembered to wear sneakers.

From where she stood there appeared to be two new tenants at the Flamingo Road underpass—both of them, men. They were drinking from beer cans and munching on potato chips while smoking what appeared to be normal cigarettes. "Hello, guys!" she shouted to announce her arrival. She had to scream at the top of her lungs to overpower the pounding of the overhead traffic as it passed over the bridge.

They both squinted at her, then gave her a wave to come up to where they were seated. Stephanie surmised the wave signaled ownership. They were acting like this was their private residence.

She sat next to them as they exchanged curious glances and said with her I've-been-here-before voice, "Listen, guys, I know the drill and don't want any baloney from you. So give it to me straight." She pulled out a wallet-sized picture of Tiffany that Randy gave her and flashed it in front of them. "I'm looking for this young lady. Have you seen her or heard anything about her?"

The younger looking man with a long, dirty, red-and-brown beard took the photo from Stephanie's hand and examined it carefully. He shook his head, then handed it to his older companion, who gave a devilish grin. "Yeah, I think I saw her this morning."

Stephanie's spirits soared. "Where? Where did you see her?"

The man, who later identified himself as Walter, scratched his head several times. "I can't remember right off."

Stephanie patted him on the shoulder and said patiently, "Take your time. This is important." Then she slowly looked around and saw at least eight or ten empty beer cans stacked up on the ledge of the concrete abutment like dead soldiers who had faithfully served their cause. She sighed, remembering where she was three years ago and said to herself, *I can't imagine you could remember anything after downing all that beer.*

"I know I was in Fort Lauderdale this morning for breakfast with my buddies," he said after several minutes of contemplation. "Then I went walking..." He shook his head several times to jog his memory. "Then I think I went to see some of my pals for lunch...you know how things are. I have to mooch a little for lunch from my friends, seeing as my finances are a little low." He giggled.

"Yeah, yeah, come on, man," Stephanie said with a tough look. "Let's have it."

He shot his face up in the air as if divine inspiration had taken place and said, "I remember seeing her walking in Holiday Park when I was standing by a tree." He flicked the side of the photograph. "Her red hair stuck in my head. She was a real looker!"

"That's her!" Stephanie exulted. "Now think carefully, pal, where did she go?"

He shrugged. "I saw her talking to that old hag Alice, ya know, the one who grubs food off everybody that visits the park. Then—"

"And?!" Stephanie demanded. "And then what happened?"

He giggled again. The beer was in control. "And then, and then," he laughed with a twinkle in his eye, "and then 'they tied her to the railroad tracks,' and then, 'they lit the fuse to the dynamite,' and then, 'along came Jones; tall handsome Jones...'"

Stephanie waved him off. It was enough of the old Coaster's song for today. "Okay, bub, so, where is she?"

A moment of sobriety followed. "I saw her talking with Alice, then I saw her venture to the back of the park, then turn around and walk out. That's the last I saw of her."

Stephanie blinked and thought how lucky she was to hit on this guy right off. Then again, she thought, luck had nothing to do with it. "You're the man," she said and gave him a hug. Then she looked them both in the eyes and said, "If you're tired of this kind of life and you really want your life to count for something, try Jesus." They looked at each other and sneered.

Stephanie stood. "Three years ago, I was where you guys are now. Then I found Homeless Outreach and they really helped me." She pulled out two business cards from her pocket and pressed them into their hands. "If you really want to leave this life, come down to the shelter." They reached over and shook her hand.

Moments later she was back on the road heading toward Holiday Park.

* * *

The street lights lining AIA on Fort Lauderdale's strip lit up the community like a side show at a circus. The neon lights flashing their advertisements on the various storefronts added to the carnival-like atmosphere that charms thousands of sightseers to the ocean paradise everyday. Just over 1,000 feet from AIA, the main road that services the huge tourist attraction, one can see and smell the Atlantic ocean as it sweeps along the coastline. At night, the beach is a hangout for the homeless who enjoy the fresh air while they party; remaining just far enough away to be hidden from the crowds yet still able to frolic under the cover of darkness.

But tonight things were different. There was a full moon that hung suspended above the horizon and cast a beam of bright light over the water, illuminating the beach so as to discourage the homeless from picnicking and nesting. Lovers, however, found it romantic and strolled along the seaside walking hand in hand.

The strip was a favorite place for the Bradshaw family to visit, have lunch, and amble along the avenue observing the sunbathers, surfers, and shoppers who popped in and out of the shops while diligently dodging the sidewalk maniacs on their roller-blade skates. It was a fun place to visit but not a good location to look for a place to sleep.

Ah, Tiffany thought as she sat in the sand, *the smell of the ocean is refreshing.* She removed her tennis shoes and pushed her feet into the sand. It felt cool as it sifted through her toes. *I need to walk along the ocean and let the water wash over my feet.* The idea of being cleansed by the eternal sea appealed to her sense of hygiene and even her spiritual well-being. She picked her way to the water, carefully avoiding the debris and clutter that littered the beach, until the early morning crews on their ATV's patrolled the shoreline to clean and rake the resort strip for the next assault by the daily sunbathers.

Wading in and out in a zigzag pattern up to her knees exhilarated her. At one point she paused and looked in a westerly direction to watch the commotion on the strip. The crowds were bustling and laughing. There was much bravado and back-slapping by hordes of men that walked by. Groups of American sailors from the U.S. Navy piers in Fort Lauderdale added a degree of patriotism and security to the parade as they strolled along the avenue. Surprisingly, emerging in the diminishing evening light were numerous older women in bikinis who appeared to possess a magical quality to retain their youth. Or so they thought. There didn't appear to be many families frequenting the strip at this hour. Overall, the activity captivated her. *Where are they going, Lord?* she asked herself. *Busy, busy, but going nowhere. Going around in circles with no purpose. Or so it appears.*

An unexpected surge in the surf brought a wave that washed over her. *Oh, Lord, that felt good.* She took a deep breath and walked out of the water to the sidewalk. *Now, what do I do? How do I dry off?*

Passerby after passerby ignored her and simply walked on, enjoying themselves as the seawater dripped off her body on to the sidewalk. A chill ran through her body. *I need to get somewhere to dry off before I catch pneumonia,* she realized. She looked off into the distance and saw a cross atop a long steeple that stood towering above the storefronts. It was on the block behind the strip. *I'll go there for help.*

* * *

Several of the higher class tenants of Holiday Park carried flashlights, while the others just relied on whatever moonlight might be available or the streetlights if they wanted to bed down near the road. Many preferred the shroud of darkness to light because it hid their lifestyle that would be repulsive to onlookers. These few seemed to thrive at night.

"Hey, buddy," Stephanie said to her first prospect, who occupied the only bus stop bench at the park. "Have you seen a young girl with red hair today?" The black man was lying prostrate on the bench with a brown paper bag over his head. No movement.

Stephanie lifted her leg and kicked his shoe that hung over the arm of the bench. The man stirred slowly then lifted the bag off his face. "Yo!" he said angrily, "what's the big idea? Can't you leave a man in peace when he's sleeping?"

This was a matter of life or death to Stephanie. A crisis that warranted dispensing with amenities. "Look, man, I have to find this girl before it's too late. Help me out, will ya!" She pulled Tiffany's photograph out of her pocket and dangled it in front of the man's face.

The man shook his head and slowly pulled the bag over his face and dropped back into the bench.

"Thanks a lot." She pulled out her flashlight and glanced around fiercely. *Somebody must have seen her.* A woman pushing a shopping cart appeared before her. She ran to her and stood in front of her advancing cart and focused the flashlight on the woman's face. The woman came to a sudden halt. "You wanna get out of my way, lady!" the middle-aged woman demanded.

"I need your help," Stephanie said with pleading eyes. "Is your name Alice?"

The woman reached into the shopping cart and pulled out a foot-long piece of rebar and held it up to Stephanie. "Maybe I didn't make myself clear, girlie," she said with a churlish growl. "I said, get out of my way!"

Stephanie held up her hands in mock surrender. "Fine, fine, you old crab. Go your way." The lady sneered at her, then slid the rebar back under her belongings in the cart and pushed on.

"Model citizen," Stephanie muttered as the woman walked out of hearing range. *Obviously that's not Alice. Where are you, Alice?*

She gazed deep into the back of the park and saw a series of moving lights and shadows coming from an area that looked like a suitable place where several clusters of people might congregate. She walked slowly toward the lights. Moments later she came upon what looked like a cardboard apartment complex made from appliance cartons, complete with a makeshift barbecue, port-a-potty, and several stolen shopping carts piled up with canned goods and boxes of what appeared to be macaroni and powdered milk. The shopping carts reminded her of her former life when she would ask for food from the neighborhood churches and then bring the offerings to one central collecting place where her companions would pick out their selections from the communal grocery store. It was commonly known as the homeless person's supermarket.

"Is there an Alice here?" she called out as she stood in front of the complex while selectively shining her flashlight into the appliance cartons.

"Over here, dearie," she heard emerging from the end carton.

Stephanie walked to the end carton and squatted down in front of it. She peered into the makeshift home that was illuminated by a candle and said to the woman lying on a air mattress, "Are you Alice?"

The woman nodded. "What of it, dearie?"

Stephanie held up the photograph of Tiffany, then cast her flashlight on it. "There's a man who comes here often who told me that he saw this girl talking to you this morning. Do you know where she is?"

Alice closed her eyes momentarily to collect her thoughts. She had been around the block a few times and knew a good thing when she saw it. The nice red-headed girl looked like she came from money, the commodity that opens up mouths. She sat up and took the flashlight from Stephanie's hand, then shone the light on the photograph. She looked closely at it. "Hmm, yeah, well maybe," she said.

"It's really important to me, Alice," Stephanie said, conveying urgency. "Take a good look. Please." She lifted the photograph closer to Alice's face.

Alice deliberately hesitated, then after a moment of gazing off into the distance said, "How important?"

Stephanie suddenly realized what was happening. She read the scene. In a way it was déjà vu. Reaching into her pocket, she pulled out a 10-dollar bill and placed it on Alice's lap. "Very important."

"Um, yes, I did talk to her this morning," Alice said with a nod. "Real pretty girl. Nice clothes. Striking red hair."

"Can you tell me where she is? Is she here in the park somewhere?" Stephanie asked with heightening anxiety.

"Could be," Alice said as her head teetered back and forth with a shake of the shoulders.

Stephanie quickly pulled out another 10-dollar bill and dropped it on top of the first 10-dollar bill. "Listen, girl, I need to know!"

Alice sighed deeply, realizing there would be no more cash forthcoming. "She took off toward the beach. I watched her walk to the back of the park, rest a few minutes, then take off in the direction of the ocean."

"Now you're talking, Alice," Stephanie said with a snap of her fingers.

"Glad to help, dearie." Alice tucked the two 10s into her bra.

Stephanie stood and started to leave. "May God bless you, Alice."

"Oh, one more thing, dearie," Alice added after blinking in torpid agreement.

"Sure," Stephanie said.

"Leave the flashlight."

Stephanie grinned and tossed it into Alice's lap. "You drive a hard bargain, Alice."

Stephanie walked out of the park in triumph.

18

The cross on the top of the Congregational Church steeple seemed very distant from Tiffany's perspective. A floodlight mounted on the roof that illuminated the cross in the night sky, giving it a majestic radiance that overwhelmed her. *Lord, why do I feel like you're so far away?* Looking up at it from the sidewalk adjacent to the church, she recalled how she would stare at the illuminated cross above the pulpit at Plantation Gate Christian Church when her father would be preaching, imagining Jesus looking down at him, smiling. Now she looked upon the cross, imagining Jesus frowning. *Is it because of me, Lord? My mother?*

She walked around to the side of the church into a vestibule. The vestibule resembled a covered antechamber, enclosed on two sides with walls of fieldstone leading to a large wooden door that apparently opened up into the nave of the church. The entranceway appeared to be heavily trafficked with worn floor tiles and excessive nicks by the door handle. There were some cobwebs and litter scattered about, but overall, the makeshift bedroom seemed relatively clean. She inspected the area for vermin and insects, then brushed off a section of the inside quadrant with her backpack. She felt her clothes and realized they were almost dry from the warm air. *Great. This way I don't have to change. I only have one more set of clothes anyway.*

She pulled the towel out of her backpack and set it on the floor before turning around and squatting on it. The ground was cold and damp, and eerie shadows moved in and out of the antechamber like uninvited demons, hastened by the darkened light.

Sudden waves of loneliness washed over her as she prepared to settle in for the night. She sighed deeply, then shook her head to defy the feelings of despair. Reaching into her backpack, she pulled out a granola bar. *I'm alone, yet I just discovered that my thinking has been wrong. God has been in my thoughts. I wonder what it all means? I guess when I'm down and out, I unwittingly reach for God, but when things are going good, God is just an afterthought. Hmm...*

She studied her surroundings then brought her eyes to rest on the large wooden door. *I'm in a corner of a passageway to a church, separated from God's house by a wooden door. Close, but yet so far away. Yeah, it sounds like my life. A PK who has access to God's house all the time, yet separated by the wooden door of my hardened heart. Enough reflection, Tiff,* she commanded herself. *Enough!*

But lingering thoughts would not let her rest tonight. There was Mom. What to do about her? She zipped up her windbreaker, then placed the backpack behind her and dropped back onto it. It was not the kind of bed she was used to.

Screeching tires then headlights from an approaching car in the street caught her attention. *More screeching tires.* As it rapidly approached, she turned her head into the fieldstone wall.

Glass crashing against a stone wall!

The car sped away. More screeching tires.

She bolted upright. *What in blazes was that?*

She stood and headed out of the vestibule and in the direction of the crashing sound. There, on the wall of the church, was a large wet spot and on the sidewalk lay the fragments of a beer bottle. The liquid on the ground was still fizzing.

She shook her head. *Phew! Don't people have any respect for a church building anymore? God, what is going on?*

She returned to her cleft in the vestibule and shot a prayer up to God for a peaceful night's rest, then closed her eyes. *I'm so very tired.*

When she opened her eyes, she was on a painted bench under a heavy plastic canopy that shielded playground equipment from the scorching sun. Dozens of children were yelling and frolicking as they climbed the slide, pushing each other on the swings, and balancing their friends on the seesaws. In the distance she saw several attentive mothers hovering over their children in a sandbox, smiling expansively at their little bundles of joy. Tiffany immediately recognized the playground. It was Welleby Park, a place she often went to roller blade since it boasted of long, winding, and hilly bicycle paths.

"I hear you're planning to go back to work," the young woman standing next to the bench and holding an infant said.

"I really don't have a choice, you know," Tiffany said defensively. "On Jim's salary, we could never afford to get the swimming pool in the back yard at this time."

"Watch your little sister, Adam!" the woman next to Tiffany who sat pushing and pulling a stroller yelled out. Then she turned to Tiffany and said, "Do you really think you need a swimming pool right now? I mean, can't you use the community pool until Jim gets on his feet? After all, he just started this new job as a Christian counselor, and you have two small children. Who's going to watch them while you work?"

Tiffany felt violated. *Nervy!* Defensively: "Well, I'm going to place them in day care."

"You'll be giving up an important part of their lives, Tiffany," the woman pushing the stroller advised. "They really need you at this age. Remember, Randy, Jr., is only four, and Jill is just three. For them to be under the care of a 'surrogate' mother while you work is quite a price to pay for a swimming pool. Don't you think?"

"Well, it's easy for you to say, Jo," Tiffany replied with her brow raised in challenge to the woman rocking the stroller, "when your husband is a lawyer and you can afford all the niceties of life and still stay home and raise your family. But for Jim and I, we can't afford any luxuries unless I go back to work."

"Tiffany," Jo replied readily, "remember, you have exactly what God wants you to have at this very moment. I really don't think it is in the mind of God for you to forfeit your mothering at this critical stage of your family's life for a swimming pool or any other major purchase that will put you in debt for that matter."

"Does the word *sacrifice* mean anything to you?" the woman holding the infant interjected.

Tiffany drilled her eyes into the woman. "And who made you my judge and jury, Rachel? Of course I know what the word *sacrifice* means. I sacrificed all the years when Jim was in college and graduate school. Now it's time I live a little; catch some of the world as it goes by. Besides, it's only a pool, for God's sake. It's not as if I want to sell the house and go out and buy a mansion."

"Listen, Tiffany," Jo said passionately, "we love you and only want the best for you. But the direction you're heading in will bring you heartache down the line. I've seen it happen in my sister's marriage. After they were married two years, she wanted a better car, then it was a better dining room set. Then it was better carpeting. Then after the house was furnished the way she wanted it, her and her husband started arguing. It seemed as long as they were occupied building and decorating their little empire, busy picking out new things, they were happy. But they never really got to know one another. Their entire married life revolved around having a better home, not a better marriage. The children were loved, but they could sense that their parents' quest for material things was more important than them."

"Not to mention that you'll build resentment toward your husband," Rachel added. "You start to blame him for not being able to mother your children as God intended. You begin to think that he deprived you of your natural right to raise your children because he didn't provide enough money from his job to support you in the style you felt entitled."

Tiffany looked away from them to her children in the playground and shot a praise up to God for their good health. She eyed Jo, then Rachel, and shook her head in frustration. *What are you saying, and who do you represent? Why are you pressing me so?* she asked herself. *Is this counsel from them or from God?* She couldn't decide. Her heart was in turmoil and a spirit of confusion seemed to be in control. She squeezed her eyes shut. *I have to discover the answer.*

A violent shaking of her shoulders.

"Tiffany, wake up!" she heard in a voice that seemed so distant.

Her eyelids opened, then shut quickly. They were so heavy. *Leave me alone, please!*

"Tiffany, it's Stephanie. Wake up!"

Her eyelids fluttered several times, then fully opened. "What are you doing here?" she asked in utter amazement.

Stephanie gently stroked Tiffany's face. "I came to rescue you!"

"But how did you find me?" she asked incredulously.

"It wasn't easy, I can tell you that. But I do remember all my old haunts, and this was an area I used to cruise in. I just drove around for miles and prayed to God to direct me to you." She smiled and winked. "So, here I am."

Tiffany hugged her tightly. "I'm so happy to see you!"

"Get your things together. I'll treat you to a cup of coffee and a donut while we talk."

"Deal."

* * *

The smell of sugar as they entered Stanley's Donut Shop overpowered the aroma of the deep-roasted coffee. "Ah, the smell of caffeine and sugar in the evening; it's the smell of victory!" Stephanie said as sat down at the counter. She had paraphrased a similar line from a move about the Vietnam war.

Tiffany looked at the clock on the wall. "Wow! Is it really 9:15 already?"

"Well, they say time flies when you're having fun," Stephanie quipped. She pointed over to the racks of donuts stacked up behind the counter and said to the waitress, "Pick me a winner, will ya? And I'll have a cup of the French roast coffee, with half-and-half."

"Likewise," Tiffany said.

Stephanie signaled Tiffany to follow her to a nearby table, then sat down and said, "So, tell me, Tiffany, what's this all about?"

Tiffany tapped her fingers sequentially on the tabletop for nearly 15 seconds. "Family matter."

"Please don't try to find sanctuary in one- or two-word sentences, Tiffany. Tell me what the trouble is," Stephanie pleaded. "It's obvious it was serious enough for you to run away. This can't be because of a simple 'family matter.'"

Tiffany shook her head a few times, then resumed her finger tapping. "I don't know if I can talk about it."

"It's that painful?"

Tiffany nodded. "Shattered images of your parents. The fall of a role model. Betrayal. Deception. Envy," she replied as tears appeared in her eyes. "Just to name a few of the words that describe my pain."

Stephanie grasped her hand over the table top. "Tell me about it. I'm your friend, and I want to help you."

"It's family stuff," Tiffany protested.

A child screeched from behind them. They both turned to see a three-year-old-boy throwing a donut at his mother in protest. Another shriek bellowed forth. Stephanie shot a look of disgust at Tiffany and whispered, "An example of our permissive society. Guess who's in control of that family?"

Stephanie sighed. "I recognize your need for loyalty and duty to protect family privacy, Tiffany, but the dilemma is that your family is part of the problem and you need to step out of the family in order to arrive at a solution. Besides, I feel like a part of your family anyway." She grinned. "Especially the family of God."

Tiffany recalled Stephanie's decision to receive Christ as her Savior, bringing her into the family of God. "Praise God! In a way, you're my sister, is that what you mean?"

"Precisely."

Their coffee and donuts arrived.

Tiffany groaned deeply before taking a slug of her coffee. Her physical exhaustion and mental fatigue was not satiated in the brief period of sleep in the church vestibule. "I guess the whole thing started when my brother got hit in the eye and was taken to the hospital in an ambulance. The shock seemed to set me off. From there everything seem to go downhill in our family."

"And then what?"

Tiffany took a huge bite out of her donut, then another slug of her coffee. She squirmed in her seat, then stared directly at Stephanie. "My mom is a liar."

Her eyes brimmed with tears. "A big fat liar! That's the real problem."

"Whoa, now," Stephanie soothed. "Hold on, honey."

"No, she really is, and I don't know what to do about it."

"Did she lie to you?" Stephanie asked. "I mean, personally? Is that it?"

"She lied to everybody, even you!"

"What do you mean, even me? How did I get into the picture?"

"Believe me, Stephanie, you're in it!" Tiffany breathed.

"How so?"

"She made up that whole story about her necklace and slide being stolen. She deliberately lied to put the blame on you and those of Homeless Outreach."

Stephanie was not prepared for the onslaught of truth. In her mind, a pastor's wife was some kind of saint, a person who would sacrifice anything to make her husband's ministry work. A helpmate dedicated to spiritual, moral, and ethical excellence. So, to hatch a colossal lie, albeit a conspiracy, would be unthinkable.

Stephanie moved next to Tiffany and held her. After reflection, Stephanie asked, "But why would she do that? Does she hate us that much?"

"I know my mom and in her mind she thought she was protecting my dad's church from the homeless people. She thinks they drag the church down...that 'upper-class' people won't stay if there are a lot of homeless people in the church. So, she probably figured that if the people at Homeless Outreach got a bad rap, they wouldn't come back. That would solve the problem."

Stephanie dropped her hands to her side as she processed Tiffany's explanation. "I can see what you mean. It makes sense." She cracked a smile. "It's a brilliant plan—to rid the earth of undesirables by blaming them for something they didn't do. This way public opinion would be swayed to pass measures to enforce that belief so the church or the State can carry out the decree and have the taxpayers foot the bill. If I remember, emperor Nero did the same thing in Rome to rid the land of the Christians; in Europe, Hitler and his Nazi regime did it to the undesirable Jews; and here in American abortion proponents have been doing it for the past 30-plus years to eliminate undesirable children. It's brilliant. And yet Satanic at the same time."

"I'm afraid for my mom, I really am," Tiffany said, pulling back and scanning Stephanie's face for assistance.

"You mean God punishing her?"

Tiffany nodded slowly as her face contorted with anguish. "I'm afraid what God will do. He will not be mocked, and we've already seen His hand in dealing with my mom through my brother; he nearly lost his eye. Who knows what will happen next?" She started to shake.

Stephanie embraced her. "Hey, hey," she soothed. "I recently discovered an altogether different opinion of God, Sweetpea, and it's not one of anger and retaliation. It's one of love, goodness, and mercy. In fact, I remember reading a Bible verse just a few days ago that went something like *the goodness of God brings men to repentance.'* So why are we going the other way with this?"

"I know, I know, I always start out thinking negative." She stopped as the flood of discovery washed over her. "Oh, no! That's the way my mom is! She always thinks negative. Whenever my dad has an idea or a plan to expand the ministry, my mom always brings up the drawbacks. When I asked if I could go out for cheerleading at school, mom carried on with all sorts of objections to talk me out of it. I guess you could say my mom's a pessimist." She turned away from Stephanie. "I'm becoming just like my mother."

Stephanie simply held her hand firmly to show her support as the realization developed.

"Now I know what that dream was all about," Tiffany whispered in wonder.

"What dream?"

"I had a strange dream back at the church before you came to get me." She reached for a napkin from the dispenser and wiped her nose. "I guess the dream was about the future. I was married with two small children. We were at a playground, and my girlfriends were trying to convince me not to take a job to pay for a swimming pool in our backyard. I was arguing that we couldn't afford it on my husband's salary, so I needed to go to work." She scratched her head. "It all makes sense now. Wow!"

Stephanie possessed the wisdom to let Tiffany vent her feelings and, hopefully, her shortcomings to avoid any heartache in the future. "What do you mean?"

"If I were to try to interpret it, I would say that in the dream my girlfriends were counseling me to concentrate on raising my family and not to focus on my own agenda, the things that I think are important, while my children are dependent on me. The desire for the swimming pool was in their minds, just the beginning of the trip that would lead me away from my family responsibilities, I guess."

Stephanie tried to help her sort it out. "So what's the connection?"

"In many ways my mom is like that. It seems her agenda is to get through school so she can do her own thing. There isn't much of a concern for the church or for ministry for that matter; it's like it gets in her way. And when I think about it, when it comes to family matters, my mom seems very indifferent. What do you think?"

"Since you asked me, I'd say that your mom sounds like an administrative mother. This seems to be a phenomenon sweeping our nation where moms aren't satisfied with being moms. They need family *plus.* Moms today want to have their children, then turn them over during infancy to be raised by daycare centers. Others hold out until the children reach toddler age. This gives them the freedom they believe marriage deprived them of. Often the excuse is they have to go back to work to help pay the bills or for a major purchase. But in reality, they're not satisfied with staying home and being a homemaker and mother, so they seek satisfaction and fulfillment outside of the home." Stephanie fell silent.

"How do you know so much about this?"

The pall of regret was heavy on Stephanie's heart. "Because your mother is walking down the path I have already traveled, and it leads to a dead end. In the unforgiving calculus of life, it cost me my marriage, children, and home. The price was very great. Very great."

"I'm sorry for you."

Stephanie patted Tiffany's hand. "Don't be. If it weren't for that tragedy in my life, I don't think I would have been open to receive the truth about Christ and His forgiveness; it was all in God's plan. Because He forgave me, I was able to forgive myself and those who hurt me over the years."

Tiffany marveled. "Man, God is awesome."

"Yes, He is awesome," Stephanie echoed. "Now the question is, do *you* want to honor Him?"

"What do you mean?"

"What I mean, Tiffany, is, do you want to honor Him by forgiving your mom?"

Tiffany swallowed hard. "When you put it that way, I really don't have much of a choice."

Stephanie was really enjoying her new life in Christ and thanked God in her spirit for allowing her to minister to Tiffany. "Then let's get out of here."

* * *

Laurie fidgeted in her chair as she gazed at Ronnie's bar mitzvah portrait on the wall above his dining room sideboard and made a mental note to ask him about his testimony of how he became a Christian some time. But for now, the images in her mind of Tiffany walking the streets overpowered her very thought. She wanted to go home. They had a nice time talking about the impact of current world events in relationship to Bible prophecy, church business in relationship to the expanding community, and church family matters. But now as she sat at their dining room table, having coffee and cake, she wanted to go home. She gingerly kicked Randy's foot under the table and said, "It's getting late, Randy."

Randy took the cue. "Hey, it's been a great night. But I'm not leaving without another slice of that banana-nut loaf."

Judy smiled at the compliment.

Redeemed, how I love to proclaim it, his cell phone sang out.

Laurie looked at her wristwatch as a wave of fear hit her. *This is going to be bad. I just know it.*

Randy shot Laurie a concerned look as he read the number on his caller-ID. Homeless Outreach. "Excuse me folks," he said. "I have to take this call." He stood from the table, walked into another room, and closed the door behind him. "This is Pastor Randy."

"Pastor Randy, this is Stephanie," the voice said. "I wanted to call you as soon as we learned about Tiffany."

Adrenaline swept through his body like a flash flood. He grabbed for the nearby wall to brace himself for bad news. "Yes, yes, what is it?"

"I have her! She's sitting here right beside me." In the next instant Randy heard her hand off the phone.

"Daddy, can I come home?" he heard through muffled sobs.

His heart raced as the sound of his daughter's voice registered in his ear. "Of course, darling, of course!" His chest started to heave. "We love you and are lost without you. Of course you can come home."

More crying on the phone.

"You stay there with Stephanie, and I'll be right over to get you," Randy choked out.

"Please bring Mom with you."

19

Tiffany hung up the phone and said happily to Stephanie, "Dad and Mom are on their way."

Stephanie smiled. "We need to talk before they get here." She held Tiffany by the hand and escorted her over to the reception area in the lobby where they both sat down on a small sofa. "There's something about myself that I feel compelled to tell your mother when she gets here."

Tiffany read the expression of concern on Stephanie's face. "Oh? This sounds serious."

"It is serious, but my only motive is to help your family recognize some danger signs before it's too late." She gave her a hug. "So please do me a favor. When they get here, take your father out into the parking lot or somewhere for a while so I can talk to your mother privately. Agreed?"

Tiffany nodded. "I'll be praying."

Fifteen minutes later, Randy and Laurie arrived.

The moment Laurie saw Tiffany, she burst into tears. With a great rush of emotions, she ran to her and exclaimed, "Thank God you're all right!" She embraced her tightly as Randy wrapped his arms around them both. He mouthed out a "Thank you" to Stephanie.

Tiffany broke from the huddle and pointed to Stephanie standing behind them and said, "Mom, Stephanie needs to talk to you."

Laurie looked quizzically at Stephanie. "Okay. Right now?"

Tiffany nodded and said, "It's important." With that she clutched her father by the arm. "Let's take a walk outside."

Seconds later, Stephanie was alone with Laurie.

Later in life Stephanie would recall this conversation and attribute the following discussion to the working of the Holy Spirit, but for the present moment, she had to connect her own history to that of Randy's family. She motioned to Laurie to follow her back to the sofa and sat down. "You know, Mrs. Bradshaw," she began softly, "I never really told anybody what I'm about to tell you, and I believe you need to know because it should lend clarity to your family life and meaning to the events you've been through recently."

Uncertain about the content, and slightly defensive of the approach, Laurie smiled wryly. "Um, okay."

"To begin with, when I first met Pastor Randy, I told him part of my story but never felt obliged nor felt ready to finish. But now, things are different. It seems that your family and my life are inseparably linked by some divine decree, and I feel in my spirit the great need to tell you something about my past that will help you."

Laurie sat back in the sofa, bracing herself for what she believed would be nothing short of a "telling-off" session. "Go on."

Stephanie turned to Laurie and hugged her for what seemed like an interminable period. "I am very fond of you and you family."

It was a expression of love that Laurie never expected. She whimpered, escalating into a series of sobs. A floodgate of emotions opened, exposing her inner spirit. Her defenses came down. God was preparing her heart.

"There is an important part of my story that I haven't shared with anybody," Stephanie said. "It's the part that led to my losing my family and ultimately becoming homeless."

Laurie sniffled. "I want to hear about it. The whole thing."

"I believe you're ready. To begin with, there was a pivotal event that triggered my losing my family that parallels yours. I was *unfaithful.*"

Laurie nodded. "Oh? You cheated on your husband with another man?"

"Not at all. I became unfaithful by estrangement. One night something in me snapped and I determined that I was done! Done with all the domestic stuff that breeds the classic dowdy housewife with the dishrag around her hair as she stands at the ironing board watching soap operas, wishing her life turned out differently. Done with the domestic stuff of growing orchids on the patio to fill my 'down time' while really wishing I could express myself in the business world and truly make something of my life. *No, I was done with the wifely and motherly life.*

"So, I became unfaithful to my family. I alienated myself from them, so to speak. I made the choice to move *my* agenda along and force it upon my husband and family. You see, I wasn't satisfied with my so-called 'lot in life,' so I set out to change it to suit *my* needs. I wanted more out of life than just being a homemaker. I thought the great void in my life could be filled with the alluring trinkets of the world. I thought a promising career would yield independence and a chance at doing something great, while all along I was gambling on losing something that was already great, a family that loved me and needed me at home. At the time, I believed that I could have the best of both worlds, but in reality, a choice must be made. You cannot have both.

"In time my career blossomed, but my family wilted. The world and *self* blinded me to their suffering due to the compromises I'd made to maintain my profession. My grip on religious principles, along with my social ethics, slipped. I started to enjoy the 'fast lane' of the business world, dabbled in illegal drugs from time to time, and made wine one of my soul-mates. My value system rapidly deteriorated and I continued to make selfish decisions my mantra. Yes, I loved my family in my own way, but it was really all about *me.*

"Then one day my husband asked me out to lunch and implored me to leave the business world and return to our home, claiming I'd become *unfaithful* to him, not to the extent of adultery, but that I'd fallen into *infidelity.* I looked at him as if he had two heads! Imagine him calling me an infidel! I was outraged that he'd accuse me of such a thing, and on and on it went until there was no remedy. The defense mechanism I used became my undoing. I refused to hear truth and lived in the playground of denial. In the end, our divorce was granted on the grounds of what has become the badge of the American divorce spree—*irreconcilable differences.*"

The hairs on the back of Laurie's neck nose. She put a palm to her forehead as she retreated into her own mind. A mind besotted with the social and ethical standards of the world that had seized control of her. A mind that needed the overpowering influence of the Spirit of God to assuage the modern septic teachings of self-indulgence and autonomy. "That's quite a story, Stephanie."

"It's not *a* story, Mrs. Bradshaw. It's *my* story. *My* life. And I'm reaching out to you so that you can learn, not from your mistakes, but from mine."

Laurie raised her brow in challenge. "I can see you're trying to help, but your situation is not the same as mine and I fail to see all the parallels you do."

"I believe you're protecting yourself by denial and serving self," Stephanie said. "That's why you, along with everybody else, must serve a higher law, one written in blood on a cross 2,000 years ago. Unless we are willing to surrender our life to Christ, we serve our own law, not the law of Christ. When I turned my life over to Christ, I began to see things differently. I saw for the first time what happens when a person really yields their life to Christ. They become *renewed* or *regenerated* in the Spirit and then things change. I fell in love with Jesus and His Word. I now crave the Scriptures and long to understand more of the counsel of God. I now have a burden for the lost. I want to pull them from the fires of hell that threatened to engulf me for years. Now I really care about others, wanting them to be saved as I am. Then there's the change. My value system has changed. I no longer have the same desires I had before I met Christ. Those areas of my life that brought me pleasure now come under the scrutiny of the Holy Spirit, and because many of them dishonored the Lord, by God's grace I've turned away from them."

218

Laurie turned to Stephanie as the light of discovery dawned. "I want *that!* I want that passion for God that you have!"

"Laurie, let me be brutally honest," Stephanie ventured.

"Please."

"I haven't seen any evidence of salvation in your life. What's more, with Sean's accident and now with Tiffany running away, nothing you've done convinces me that you have a relationship with Christ."

Laurie studied Stephanie, as if to measure her sincerity and motive. She waved her hand from side to side. "I know, I know, you're right. All my life I've been secretly asking myself, why doesn't God speak to me in my spirit like he does to Randy? How come I don't have the desire to read my Bible like other Christians do? Why doesn't God answer my prayers, and why don't I have the desire to have discussions with Randy or others about spiritual things? I don't mean things about the church—anybody can do that. I mean godly things that I've heard so much about from the pulpit over the years, like sitting down by myself and having a Bible study with God or just having some peace in my life, so that when emergencies comes upon me, I don't fall to pieces. But as a pastor's wife, I couldn't ask those questions for fear that it would be misunderstood. People would judge me." She lowered her head once more. "I'm really confused."

Stephanie clutched Laurie's hand. "You mean people might think that you're not a believer. That's what you're really saying, right?"

"I guess so," she said in a muffled tone. "And that would bring shame on Randy and the ministry."

"Would you rather your life brought shame on the One who came to save you? If you continue in your unregenerate state and pretend to be a Christian,-a 'pseudo-Believer' if you will, then your life is a lie and you will die in your sins."

Stephanie's words bit Laurie's heart like the fangs of an asp, with the venom quickly arresting her spirit. *No, I can't hide behind Randy's spirituality any longer. No, I can't hide under the umbrella of the church. No, I don't want to die in my sins. Help me, Lord. Help, me.* "Would you pray with me?"

Stephanie's heart filled with the joy of the Lord. All her failure would be wiped away in one fell swoop in the next few moments as she prayed with Laurie to receive Christ as her personal Savior. If for no other reason that she was to be the vessel used of God to lead her to Christ, then her life had been fulfilled, her life had purpose and meaning. "Hold my hand while we pray."

Moments later, Laurie's sins were forgiven as she laid them at the foot of the Cross.

* * *

"Are we ready to go?" Randy said aloud to Stephanie as he walked in the door with Tiffany trailing behind.

Tiffany approached her mother and saw her crying. "Mom, what's the matter?"

"Tears of joy," Stephanie said as she patted Laurie's hand.

Randy lived with Laurie long enough to quickly recognize her change of countenance. "Something happened. What is it?"

Laurie simply shook her head several times, unable to speak.

"Laurie made a decision for Christ. She just prayed with me to ask Jesus into her heart," Stephanie said, her eyes blurred with tears.

"But I thought?" Tiffany blurted out before her father clutched her hand.

"Never mind all that, Tiff," Randy interjected, warding off any questions. "The important thing is that your mother made her peace with God."

All the pain and anguish, even the tears from trying to please God, and the pressure of pretending to be a Christian for the sake of appearances, was suddenly washed away with the prayer of repentance. God in his benevolence and mercy had seen fit to grant Laurie salvation. "I feel like a giant weight has been lifted off my soul," Laurie breathed.

Randy walked to the sofa and extended his hand to Laurie and pulled her to her feet, hugging her for several minutes in silence. Then: "Let's go home and celebrate your new life."

* * *

As Laurie opened her eyes, they were immediately drawn to the resplendent sunshine coming through her bedroom window. Radiant rays of light reflected off every glass object in the room from her perfume bottles to the mirrors above her dresser. It reminded her of a rainbow after a summer thunderstorm. *Yes, the storm is over, Lord.* She rolled on her side and watched Randy sleep. As he began to wake, she once again realized: *He really is a handsome man. But more importantly, he's a spiritual man. Not condemning me. Not ostracizing me or interrogating me about my past. Not finding fault with me.* She stroked the side of his face and his eyes fluttered, then opened. He smiled. "Good morning, babe," she said.

He put his arm around her and pulled her into his chest, running his fingers through her hair. "Sleep well?"

"I had a wonderful night's sleep." She broke from his embrace. "Remember the night I told you about the necklace and you in turn tried to tell me about the peace with God and all that?"

"Precisely."

"Well, now I know what you meant. Last night was the first night in so many years that I didn't think about the man that molested me. The haunting memories no longer have a hold on me. I think I finally came to the place where I forgave him for assaulting me."

Randy nodded. "I've been praying for you to get that release, and it's my guess that God granted it to you for making the decision for him last night."

With sudden realization: "God forgave me, so I forgave the man. Is that it?"

"That's it. That's God's way."

Laurie bounced out of bed and put on her robe. "Go wake up Tiffany so we can have breakfast."

"I'm buying," Randy said with a grin.

Within the hour Randy lifted three cinnamon-blueberry pancakes off the hot griddle and placed them on the stack, then walked to the table. "Dad's finest," he boasted to his two girls.

"You're the breakfast man, Dad," Tiffany agreed as she reached for the maple syrup. She pulled off two pancakes from the platter and doused them with syrup and butter.

"Don't forget that he makes a fine waffle and unbeatable cheese omelet," Laurie added in defense.

"No contest," Randy quipped.

"I'd like all of us to go see Sean after breakfast," Laurie said out of the blue. "As a *family*."

Randy and Tiffany exchanged looks, taking notice of her emphasis on *family*. Somehow they perceived this signal a change of sorts. Now there seemed to be more meaning and cohesiveness in the term. Now there would be unity, not just on the weekends when Mom wasn't in school, but always. "I guess I better bulk up," Randy joked, pulling two more pancakes from the platter and adding them to the three half-eaten ones on his plate.

* * *

Tiffany observed a renewed gentleness in her mother as she tended to Sean. A tenderness that she hadn't noticed in a long time. *In just one day, I see a difference*, she thought. A word she hadn't used but heard her father mention several times seemed to fit: *altruism,* an unselfish concern for the welfare of others, *I think that's the word*, she thought. *Yes, that works.*

"When you come home, there's so many things we need to catch up on," Laurie began as she sat on the end of Sean's bed. "For one, I'm going to help you with the homework you'll have to make up from being in the hospital."

Sean lay in the hospital bed examining his mother's face with a wistful expression. "Great, Mom," he said, not sure how to evaluate his mother's serious tone. "But don't forget that I have to get to bed early, doctor's orders."

Laurie could count on Sean's nature, one of forgiveness and mirth to bring out a good spirit in her. She patted his head. "Don't you worry, my son, don't you worry about that!"

It was apparent to Randy that Laurie had turned a corner and that she would make amends for her indifference to family matters. He turned to Sean. "The doctor said you're good to go in two more days. Can you hold out?"

Sean held up a get-well card from his grandmother and then dangled the 20-dollar bill from inside it in the air. "Dad, if the mail keeps coming in like this, I won't have to mow the lawn any more to collect my allowance. I'll be a rich man."

"He's got a point, Dad," Tiffany said with a nod. Then she reached into her purse and pulled out a five dollar bill and laid it on Sean's end table. She smiled and added, "Just a little more to ease the pain."

The family laughed together.

* * *

Lester walked into the church lobby to see his fellow deacon, Ronnie, and the worship leader, Mike, sitting side by side waiting for the signal from Yvonne to move into Pastor Randy's office. Moments later Yvonne stuck her head out of her office and said, "Now that you're all here, Pastor will see you now." They exchanged looks as they stood, wondering what necessitated the meeting in the first place.

Randy stood erect by one of his bookshelves with a cryptic smile. The impromptu meeting was unusual, but his demeanor was even more unusual. Both Ronnie and Mike raised an eyebrow as they found their seats.

"Gentlemen," Randy began as he closed his office door, "I have some important news to share with you. News that may shock you, but news that is very good news." The news would not include Tiffany's experience, since Randy and Laurie agreed that it would impugn the integrity of the ministry.

More exchanges of looks, but with sighs of relief. "We're ready for some good news, Pastor," Mike quipped as he slapped his knee.

Randy simply nodded as he contemplated his next sentence carefully. "What I'm about to tell you men comes on the heels of my family experiencing a string of crises, that only now I believe had to happen in order for the Lord to carry out his plan." As he paused, the men seemed to move toward the edge of their seats. "Last night, the Lord used Stephanie Malone to bring my Laurie to Christ. She prayed with her to receive the Lord as her personal Savior."

"Your Laurie?!" Mike asked, eyes wide with shock.

"Yes, my Laurie," Randy replied, his gaze narrowing on Mike's face. "She has given me permission to share this with you, knowing that she may suffer some humiliation and embarrassment in the days ahead, but yes, my Laurie."

"And it was Stephanie, the homeless lady?" Lester asked, astonished. "She prayed with her?"

"Yes, Stephanie, *the homeless lady.*" Randy started to tear. "God's ways are above our ways, and we cannot begin to understand *who* or *what* he will use to fulfill his divine will."

Stunned into silence, Ronnie could only stare at Randy.

"I'm not defending, merely explaining what has happened," Randy instructed, shooting a look at Ronnie to solicit his comments. "God's amazing grace opened her eyes and saved her."

They all walked to Randy, circling him, resting their hands on his neck and shoulders. "We love you, Pastor Randy," Lester said, "and we're with you. We rejoice with you in the good news about Laurie."

"I guess God is saying once again, never take anybody's salvation for granted," Ronnie said as he retreated back to his chair.

"A sobering reminder that there is no universal or inherited Christianity," Mike added, almost apologetically and without malice. "We all need to come to Christ on an individual basis."

Several amens resounded.

"Laurie plans to make a public announcement as soon as God's Spirit opens up an opportunity," Randy continued, "so until then, I would ask that you keep this information confidential to honor her wishes. Naturally, we hope and pray that this will have a positive effect on the congregation."

Lester nodded. "I believe this is going to be Plantation Gate's finest hour."

"It may even spark a revival," Mike affirmed.

"May it go from your lips to God's ears," Ronnie whispered in wonder.

Randy sighed deeply in relief, then said, "May it be so."

20

Randy began asking God several questions as he studied a large painting from Israel's Holocaust Center that hung on his office wall. While he couldn't rationally ask God questions about the slaughter of six million Jews by the Nazi war machine, he hoped God would help him to answer questions about his own life. Questions that he knew could potentially lead him down a path that would injure his faith and ultimately his Christian testimony. They were questions that started with "*why.*" He knew in his spirit that those type of questions only come during or after a crisis of great magnitude. But he had to get them out. He had to ask. To him it would be a catharsis of sorts. *Why, Lord, have you brought these trials upon our family and our church? Why hurt my tender little Sean? Why this thing with Tiffany? Why the pain with Laurie?*

It had to be a theodicy, he reasoned. Calamitous events that God allowed to come upon his ministry and family to ultimately demonstrate His holiness and justice. *I guess I could say the same thing about the Holocaust that birthed Israel as a nation. Such a price, Lord.*

Luther's solution came to his mind as he attempted to reason things out: *A true believer will crucify the question why. He will obey without question.* He turned to look out the window and fixed his gaze on a distant cloud that hung suspended in the blue sky. *Yes, I will commit to obey, Lord, but oftentimes I forget that what You take in fire is the only way to the resurrected life and the ascension mount is the way of the Garden; the Cross, the way of the grave.*

He sighed deeply, denoting his desire to change his mindset, then walked to his desk and picked up the phone to tell Sam Knowles that he would like to meet with him. *It's time to move things along.*

* * *

Sam looked relaxed and confident in his role as director of the Homeless Outreach this morning, Randy observed. He imagined his demeanor to be a sign their meeting would yield favorable results.

"Stephanie tells me your ministry had a few setbacks, but now you're ready to move forward," Sam began. "That's good news."

With renewed vigor Randy replied: "Yes, we're ready to launch our Homeless Outreach/Open Arms program if that works for you."

"I'm in agreement, Pastor Randy. The sooner the better. Do you have all the wrinkles ironed out of the plan at this point?"

Randy believed he was really asking if the church was in full support of the project. "Yes, we're good to go. Of course, we may encounter some roadblocks as we proceed, but once again, yes, we're ready to roll."

"Good, then I'll move on implementing Operation Rescue to get law enforcement involved in bringing any homeless and vagrants they pick up on the streets and bring them to the churches you designate," Sam advised with a clap of his hands. "Let's agree on the start date. Say two weeks?"

Randy gave him the nod. "By then I'll have the coalition of churches prepped and ready so we can process them into pre-employment training sessions. Those church pastors will also be looking within their congregations for business owners who can employ them after they've been in the program for at least six months."

"I love it when a plan comes together," Sam lauded with a snap of his fingers. He rotated in place and paused before saying, "And we agreed that we'll keep the jurisdiction within the churches to avoid public or government entanglements, right?"

Randy was 1,000 percent in favor of church jurisdiction until enough financial support could be generated from private philanthropic sources. "There's no way we want the state involved in this. We want to keep it in the *family*," Randy asserted.

"Then all we need is God's blessing," Sam said with a grin.

Sam beat Randy to the punch on that one. "Yeah, we just need God's blessing." Randy hesitated, then bit his upper lip while changing gears. "Sam, speaking about God and His blessings, do you remember our conversation a while back? When you were over our home at the barbecue? You know, we were talking about God's blessing of salvation?"

"Vaguely," Sam replied half-heartedly.

"Well, maybe now is a good time for us to pick up our little talk."

Sam scratched the side of his head and looked like he was not in the mood for a debate of any kind. Gesturing with this hand over his desk he replied, "Pastor, as you can see, I do have a pile of work here that needs tending to."

Today is the day of salvation flashed into Randy's mind. Seconds later came the reminder that God prepares hearts to hear the Word. *Maybe now's not a good time*, he thought. But he had to test the waters further. "Some things can't wait, Sam," he insisted. "I know you're a man of faith, because no one could build an organization that helps people like you do without faith in God. But believing *in* God is not the same as *believing* God. When you have an intimate relationship with Christ and believe He has died for your sins, you go way beyond just belief *in* God. You enter a different spiritual dimension that can only come about through the direct intervention of the Holy Spirit." Randy's passion for the lost poured out of him. "This dimension is a unique spiritual relationship that Jesus calls being 'born-again.'"

Sam waved him off. "Pastor Randy, please don't start preaching to the choir, okay? I've heard all about that movement, and as far as I'm concerned, I believe I am," he paused to make quotation marks in the air, "'born-again.' Maybe not according to your guide book, but nevertheless, 'born-again' through my church." Then with finality, he added, "And that's where we want to leave it for today. So let's get back to the business of Homeless Outreach, okay?"

Slam dunk! Randy took a deep breath with the realization that Sam's heart was not ready to hear truth. His heart ached for him, but perhaps there would be another time. He comforted himself with the consolation that he planted some seeds of salvation, leaving the cultivating and harvesting to God. "Fine, Sam."

"Good. Suppose you call me next week to check the progress of things as we move our agenda along."

Randy nodded and extended his hand. "We're going to make a difference in the community for God, I just know it."

They shook hands, but Randy made up his mind that he would be stopping by next week to sample the waters once again. He would continue to share Christ's gift of salvation as long as Sam kept the door open to listen.

* * *

As Sean stepped out of the car his eye caught the banner hanging over the front door: *Welcome Home, Sean!*

He closed the car door and stood looking up at the sign. "Slick," he exclaimed. Then he turned and looked back at the place in the street where he was laying when the ambulance picked him up weeks earlier.

Watching his eyes, Laurie hugged him and said, "Don't you think about that now, Sean; you're home now. Think only good things."

He smiled at his mother. "I really missed being home, Mom."

"And we really missed you," Randy said, coming up from behind, carrying Sean's belongings.

"Tiffy?" Sean asked.

"She's inside, waiting for you," Laurie said with a cryptic grin.

Sean reached for the door and pulled it open to hear a loud, "Surprise!"

Whistles and applause ascended in the room from his friends who greeted him as he walked in. He scanned the faces and stopped on Tiffany's. His heart told him she put it all together. "Thanks, Sis," he said while hugging her.

"You're the man!" his friend Alex shouted out. "Welcome home, Sean!"

Laurie clutched Randy's hand and smiled at him. "We're a family again."

* * *

Supernatural of sorts, Randy thought, as he looked at the crowds filing into the Bible study room. *Maybe the word got out about Sean? Who knows? Unusually large turn out tonight*, he soon realized.

Moments later a van from Homeless Outreach pulled into the parking lot with Marty and Stephanie in the front seat. They stepped out unto the parking lot, then several residents from HO exited the van and accompanied them to the Bible study room.

"Pleasant surprise, Stephanie," Randy said as he greeted them at the door. He blinked several times as he took notice of the lovely red dress she had on. *Hmm,* he thought. *Something's up.*

"Special night, Pastor Randy," Stephanie said. "And we want to celebrate it."

Randy scratched his head. *Something's up.*

Several hymns, prayer requests, and praises later, Laurie raised her hand above the seated crowd. "I would like to praise the Lord about something." Randy waved her forward to the head of the room. On her way up to the front of the room, Laurie stopped where Stephanie was seated and said in a whisper, "We're on." Stephanie smiled and followed her as Marty clasped his hands in a cheering motion.

Something is going on here, Randy realized.

Laurie stepped up to the lectern, then turned to her husband and said, "I know the pastor will be surprised at what I'm going to say, but I have the confidence of God to say it." She glanced at Stephanie, then faced the class as several tears glimmered in her eyes. "Dear friends, I would like to take this time to share something very personal with you." Laurie smiled in her heart when she realized the irony of God's sense of humor. The red dress Stephanie had on was a bright reminder of the red sweater she had on when she first caught sight of her, and the very color of the man's sweatshirt who haunted her all these years. But now, Jesus had freed her from those nightmares.

Marty turned to one of the HO residents and whispered, "Here comes the good part."

"What I'm about to say may come as a shock to some, but I must confess what's on my heart." She turned to Stephanie and blurted out, "This woman led me to Christ a few days ago."

"What did she say?" a woman next to Pastor Randy asked. "Did I hear right? She said she was just led to Christ? Does that mean she just got saved? How can that be?"

Randy smiled at the woman, patted her arm, and said with a grin, "It gets better."

"It was not until Stephanie prayed with me to receive Christ," Laurie continued, "that I began to recognize how far away from God I really was. What made me turn the corner was that I really believed her. I didn't necessarily believe in *what* she was saying, but I had to believe her!

"In many ways I've been living a double life. Yes, you heard me. A double life. I would put on a bright smiling face as the pastor's wife, doing what is expected of a pastor's wife, while all along, having no interest nor the heart to serve anybody but myself. This attitude emerged from a heart that fooled itself into thinking that I belonged to God when in fact I did not. Let me say to you that you must check your own salvation, never taking your salvation for granted. Be sure to set aside your own agenda and uphold godly priorities, putting God first, and avoid ungodly influences so that you may set a good example to your children and others who constantly watch your life."

She smiled at Stephanie. "In God's providence, He chose a person who I would never even have wasted my breath on"—she paused to wipe her tears— "a person I first saw on my way home from school one day, walking along the road, homeless and broken, and to me disgusting and not worthy to look upon, to be the very vessel to bring me to Christ."

"Unbelievable!" Randy whispered aloud. "Unbelievable."

"While I want to take this time to praise the Lord for my son, Sean, coming home from the hospital," Laurie said as she put her arm around Stephanie, "I must also praise the Lord for what God is going to do here at Plantation Gate. You see, Stephanie and I, along with Tiffany, are going to be working together in our homeless ministry!" She turned and looked at Marty and added, "Brother Marty is going to be our liaison between our outreach and the churches."

Thunderous applause broke out!

Stephanie raised her hand in the air then waved Tiffany forward. "A three-fold cord is not easily broken," she quoted, then added as they all held hands forming a circle, "the four of us will be working with Pastor Randy and Homeless Outreach to launch and maintain Operation Rescue, the new ministry to the homeless here in Broward County." Several members rushed to their side, breaking into their circle, forming a chain.

Randy merged into the chain and raised one hand. "Let's go before the Lord and thank Him for what he *is* doing and *will do* here at Plantation Gate."

Deacons Lester and Ronnie walked up to widen the chain as Michael began singing *Redeemed.*

Within minutes, a spirit of thanksgiving overwhelmed everyone.

Randy knew in his heart that this Christmas was going to a special one because God had pronounced his blessing on Plantation Gate Church.

About the Author

DR. RALPH D. CURTIN, also the author of the End Times *Tribulation* series (OakTara), is a family man, pastor, and counselor in a large Christian denomination and a college professor at Trinity College, where he teaches Biblical Studies. When he's not preaching or teaching, he's either writing a book or riding his big Harley.

Other interests include a passion for nature photography, of which he has had many of his images published by a stock agent in national magazines. Photographing his grandchildren and making DVDs for the family gives him great pleasure as well.

The Family Matter is the outworking of Dr. Curtin's witnessing the hardships of the homeless that frequent South Florida, a haven for the vagrant, and the unawareness of society's responsibility to minister to them. As a pastor of a church with a food pantry for the homeless, Dr. Curtin has had numerous experiences that gave birth to the story line presented in this novel.

"Through many years of Bible research and being a bit of a news junkie," says Dr. Curtin about his *Tribulation* series, "I arrived at the place where I earnestly desired to transform Bible prophecy into reality so that it would be believable. Many people don't read the Bible, but will read Biblical fiction. This is my way of educating the public in a non-preaching manner, while giving them a taste of my interpretation of what we may expect in the future. I don't like fluff, so my writing is designed to intrigue the reader, give them facts that interest them, as well as raise their level of understanding on a particular subject. Readers are fascinated with science fiction, so prophetic fiction—which has a great degree of the supernatural—will only excite the reader who craves suspense, yet knows that our Good God will win in the end."

You may write Dr. Curtin at: **drrcurtin@bellsouth.net**
www.oaktara.com